FLIGHT OF THE BONE CROW

THE NOWHERE CHRONICLES
BOOK 2

REBECCA L. FEARNLEY

LIGHTNING HYENA PRESS

First published by Lightning Hyena Press in 2024

This novel is entirely a work of fiction. Names, characters and incidents portrayed in the book are the work of the author's imagination and any resemblance to actual persons, living or dead, or actual events or places, is purely coincidental.

Cover image © by Getcovers

Map images © Rebecca L. Fearnley, created using Inkarnate.com

Chapter image © Popovartem.com, licensed via Shutterstock.com (advanced license.)

Final image © bogaveda1983, licensed via Shutterstock (advanced license.)

ISBN: 978-1-915124-13-5

PORTAL TREE
NIGH
Darkeye foxes
roam here
Lizard shar
nest here
SOOTHER TREE
NOSTA B
SNATCHING SAN
Beware the
Cherish screamers

ARE TREE
Seer toads migrate here every spring
SEER TOAD SWAMPS
Got bitten by a bone ghoul here
NESTS
HOWLER HORSE PLAINS
We rode the howler horses here, once
RE MISTS
SHEB'S MAP OF NOWHERE

Sorrow's Lake
Wood's Fang
Vane
Misty Harbour
North Claw
Rivertooth
Jormund Territory
S
The Dee
The portal at
Giant's Reach
Eel's Rock
The black ash
Marsh Wilds
The graveyard
Fogburn
de Callis Territory

RIVERFELL
RITORY
HELLSMOUTH
IDE
BEAST'S DROP
LAST SOLACE
VAMP
HORROR'S KEEP
MAIDEN'S CREEK
HEART
E SWAMP
SAND'S MOUTH
GRAYLING TERRITORY
FOGSBANE
HOWL TERRITORTY
WILD EDGE
DARKHOLD

TRIGGER WARNING

This story contains references to domestic abuse from the beginning. If you find this causes you undue stress or disturbance, please stop reading and seek help.

You matter, and your recovery matters.

CONTENTS

Chapter One

THE LIGHTNING SNAKE AND THE ICEFIRE BEAR

THE AIR SPARKLES WITH monstrous energy. Me and Maeve stand opposite each other, ten meters apart. The rainbow river gurgles beside us. I glare at her, fists clenched. It's like I'm looking at an echo of myself, five years ago. The bunched muscles, the fury in her eyes. I meet her with equal ferocity. Mainly because she's doing my head in. Girl's got a mouth that could make a howler horse blush. We've been trading insults all morning.

Our shouting's attracted a flock of nosta birds. They natter in the trees above, green eyes peeking between the multi-colored leaves of the canopy. The red and yellow of their feathers flash in the sunlight. Their black, dagger beaks gleam. I eye them warily, but it ain't singing season for them yet. Our memories should be safe for now.

The forest's alive this morning. Cracklemice scurry beneath leaf litter. Birdsong, loud and violent as war drums, batters the air. The sun's reached its peak and the red-and-indigo sky glows bright and fierce. This is home. This strange not-quite-world we call Nowhere. A place between universes. A haven.

Or at least, it *was,* until we brought Maeve into it two weeks ago. Girl's a firestorm. Temper like a tornado, fists like battering rams. And if that wasn't enough, she's got a giant, horned bear-monster with burning eyes and icefire powers that feeds off her rage. It stands before her, now, about the height of a horse, head lowered, ready to charge.

Nightmare.

"Well?" Maeve barks. "You ready?"

I clench my jaw. Damn cheek! Who's calling the shots here? "'Course I'm bloody ready!" I yell back. "Can't you tell?"

Because Maeve's not the only one with a monster. I've got one of my own. A great, green-scaled serpent with a crown of ferocious spikes adorning his head, eyes gleaming scarlet, scales that sparkle with lightning and a pair of vast, blood-red wings. Normally, I manage to keep him small enough to drape round my neck, but today, I've let him grow. He's matched Maeve's monster for size and sways tauntingly.

Don't tell! He hisses, straight into my brain. His voice tingles, but I'm used to it. *Let's take 'em by surprise!*

Easy, Wriggler, I think back. *It's not an* actual *fight, remember.*

I keep a tight hold on him. Won't let him grow any bigger. He wants to, I can tell. But it ain't happening. When I let Wriggler loose, bad things happen. When I let him loose, he becomes the part of me I'm most terrified of. The monster I barely managed to wrestle under my control five years ago. The Oraqua.

Wriggler glares. *It was an actual fight last time,* he grumbles. *Bear tore my wing.*

I roll my eyes but don't bother answering. That was three days ago and it's not as bad as Wriggler makes out. Bear—Maeve's monster—caught the tip of Wriggler's left wing and left a slash. It's already healing. Wriggler's just sore he lost. If I'm honest, I'm sore, too. Maeve let Bear get too big. Out of control. That's what I'm trying to teach her today. Control.

Oak knows, she bloody needs it.

"I'm gonna send Wriggler in," I say, ignoring my lightning-snake's stroppy protests. "Remember, you got to—"

"Keep Bear small," Maeve drawls. "Yeah, yeah. You told me a million times."

I clamp my mouth shut on a dozen retorts. I'm supposed to be helping Maeve manage her anger, not unleash it. I scowl at her. At the sheen of sweat shining on her dark skin, the curls of black hair piled on her head, the muscles rippling in her arms. She's wearing a loose, sleeveless shirt and the flax pants Sheb finished making for her two days ago. Fur boots, just like mine, cover her feet.

I wonder what she sees when she looks at me. My death-pale skin, my ash-grey eyes with wild curls of scorch-black hair. Wriggler flicks me with the tip of one wing.

Who cares? He sneers. *Let's fight!*

No, Wriggler, wait a minute—

But that bloody snake's never done a thing I've told him. With a crackle of lightning, he lunges for Bear. Maeve yells as the two beasts clash. The ground shakes. Nosta birds take wing, screaming their heads off. Scarlet feathers rain down as me and Maeve clamp our hands over our ears. Might not be singing season, but nosta bird cries can still steal a few memories if we ain't careful.

It doesn't affect the monsters, though. Wriggler even snaps one out of the air, gulping it down in a flurry of feathers before he wraps Bear in his massive coils, squeezing.

"Hey!" Maeve yells, clutching her chest as Bear's pain travels down their bond, affecting her, too. "Let go!"

"Wriggler!" I yell. "Not so tight!"

He glares, grumbles, but relents. His coils loosen and Bear thrashes free, leaving great gouges through Wriggler's scales. They circle each other. Wriggler sends lightning shooting in all directions. Maeve dives, narrowly avoiding a bolt of scarlet electricity. Bear rears, opens his jaws.

And *screams*.

I throw my arms over my head as the noise rattles through my bones. My brain fizzes with remembered pain. The scar across my back—the one my daddy gave me before I killed him—burns.

Monsters are funny like that. They're not regular creatures like nosta birds and howler horses. Or like Bartok, the grumpy owl-squirrel that lives with us. Monsters are made of something darker. An energy that feeds off anger and despair. I don't know what gives them shape, or how they decide whose anger to attach themselves to. I don't know if Maeve or me will ever break free of our monsters. All I know is they're here with us, now. They feed off our pain. Wriggler was drawn to me when I killed my daddy, escaped his clutches, and ran from the town that tried to kill me. Maeve? Maybe she had it worse. Her mother murdered by the priests who were supposed to protect her town, while she was forced to watch. Bear was bonded to her for ages, killed three people before she realized he was hers. He's out of control.

And the *whole point* in these training sessions is that she's supposed to learn to contain him.

Sod that for a laugh, Wriggler hisses. *Annie, give me more anger!*

I shake my head, squeezing tight on the thread of energy that ties me to him. *Not happening, Wriggler!* I say. *Control!*

Bear charges, barreling into Wriggler before my snake has a chance to react. White fire bursts from his paws and shoots across the leaf litter. It's not even hot but cracklemice and butcher beetles flee from it all the same. That fire might not burn skin, but it burns other things. Power. Hope. The will to fight. I shrink back as it surrounds me, the ghostly flames dancing higher.

"Maeve!" I yell. "Calm him down!"

Maeve doesn't answer. Her eyes glow green. Bear's white fire dances round her feet, up her pant-leg, along her arms. She's awash with it. My gut drops.

"Maeve!" I yell. "Stop it! Let go!"

Bear's huge. Like Wriggler, he grows in both size and power the more anger Maeve feels. She's losing her grip. Bear's black fur ruffles in some otherworldly wind. He swipes at Wriggler, claws narrowly missing my snake's throat.

Annie! Wriggler roars. *Stop holding back!*

But I can't, can I? It's the thing I must never do—release my fury so it shoots down the invisible vein that ties me to my monster. If I do that, he'll become the thing I fear. Chaos incarnate.

Get over yourself, Annie! Wriggler bellows. *We had a deal, remember?*

We did. He listens to me and I listen to him. But it's hard to batter down a fortress I've spent five years building. I keep my rage locked tight in the darkest corners of my mind.

But Maeve clearly ain't learned to do the same. Wriggler might still be the size he was when this fight started, but Bear's grown. He's taller than the trees, horns slicing the leaves at the top of the canopy. He beats his chest and howls, his cry tearing the skies. His white fire catches the trees, bleaching their bark. Maeve's not in control. I see it in her face. The wild, feral ecstasy of knowing this monster is hers to command.

If I don't stop her, she'll kill Wriggler.

Which might kill me, too.

Damn this painful girl! I unclench my fists, open my mouth wide. I shriek like a banshee at full moon. I let my anger loose. Feel it race down my bond with Wriggler, igniting our nerve endings.

Yes, Annie! Wriggler laughs. My anger floods him with power. He grows until his wings cast shadows so black it's almost impossible to see. He towers over Bear, glaring down at his rival. His eyes burn with bloody fire.

Now we'll see who needs three days to recover before the next fight, he snarls.

Wriggler! I yell, warning in my voice. *Don't—*

But he's not listening. He lunges at Maeve's monster. His huge maw clamps Bear's head. Bear bellows, slashing Wriggler's belly. Wriggler hisses but doesn't let go. He shakes his head until Bear goes limp, then throws him against the ground. His vast coils wrap Bear in a crushing grip. Tightening.

Maeve gasps for breath, clutching her chest. The green fire goes out of her eyes as they bulge. She drops to one knee, then all fours.

"Wriggler!" I scream. "Let *go!*"

I run for him, reaching down our bond to pull him back. He's not listening. Bastard snake's going to kill them! Maeve's eyelids flutter. She topples to her side, mouth frothing. I reach Wriggler in a whirlwind of limbs, beat his side. "Let go, you evil creature. Let *go!*"

Wriggler looks down at me, eyes flashing scarlet. I punch and kick. Tears pour down my face. I don't bother to wipe them away. "Stop!" I scream.

And this time, he does. With a sigh, he lets his coils fall loose. Bear flops to the leaf litter, spluttering.

"Shrink down!" I snap.

Wriggler grumbles but does as he's told. His scales dull to black. He reduces until he's no longer than my forearm, a harmless serpent with vestigial wings and a flickering green tongue. He concertinas his body with embarrassment.

Sorry, Annie, he mutters.

I kick leaf litter at him. "Too bloody right, you're sorry!" I growl. "Now piss off! I don't wanna see you 'til dark. Go on! Go!"

Wriggler knows he's in disgrace. Without another word, he slithers into the gurgling rainbow river. I don't bother to watch him go. I rush to Maeve's side, cradling her against my chest until she comes to. I push her hair out of her face, hush her as she panics.

Her fear shrinks Bear, too. He scampers over to us, no more than a mewling bear cub with stubby horns and brown fur. He paws Maeve's pant leg. Maeve tries to speak, but her voice is hoarse.

"What?" I say, leaning closer. Maeve grabs my shirt in her fist, her breath hot against my ear.

"Piss off, Annie," she croaks, then faints.

I sit there, staring at her prone form for a good ten minutes. I suppose I deserved that, really.

Chapter Two

DOMESTIC CHAOS

Maeve comes round after a bit. She's still sore about the fight. I can't blame her, really. Bear, now small, whimpers as I help Maeve to her feet, shunt my shoulder under her arm to steady her. She's got a nasty bruise, like a necklace, round her throat. Her left leg's bleeding.

"We should clean that up," I say.

Maeve lets loose a torrent of insults, which I take. She doesn't resist when I guide her down to the rushing rainbow waters of the river. She sits on the bank, her injured leg trailing in the water.

"I hate this," she growls. "I hate *you.*"

"Yeah, yeah," I mumble, pretending those words don't sting. I don't think Maeve hates me, really. We rescued her, see. Along with her monster, and her best friend—though I reckon they're more than friends, actually—a girl called Lin with a remarkable power to read souls. Their own world wasn't safe for them, so we brought them here, thinking we'd raise them. Help them heal.

Turns out, parenting two seventeen-year-olds with monstrous issues ain't easy when you're barely out of kidhood yourself, got monstrous issues of your own.

I told Sheb this was a terrible idea. Would he listen?

The rainbow waters stir and Maeve looks away, grimacing. I hold her leg steady as a blunt, grey head pushes above the surface, stares at me with round, black eyes, then ducks beneath the foam. Lizard-shark. They're harmless. Though they look terrifying. Usually about the length of my forearm, they're shark-like things with lizard legs that they use to clamp to the riverbed. They've got whopping, razor teeth, but I ain't ever been attacked by one. Instead, a few of them gather round Maeve's injured leg and, gentle as you like, begin cleaning it with their long tongues. When they're done, they melt back into the many-colored waters. I help Maeve up again.

"Bartok can help with the pain when we get home," I say.

"Piss off, Annie," Maeve replies. That, and *I hate you,* are pretty much all she's said to me since Wriggler almost squeezed the life from her. I clench my jaw against the buck of anger. Getting cross with Maeve won't do. Wriggler could be a mile away by now, but wherever he is, he'll feel my rage.

"Look, Maeve," I say. "I really am sorry. I never realized he was still so cross about Bear tearing his wing. If I'd known, I'd never—"

"Please shut up," Maeve says, wincing. Her voice is raw from the suffocation. "Just ... you already apologized, yeah? Let me swear at you for a bit."

I blink, hating the burn in my eyes. "Yeah," I grumble. "Okay. Fine."

We head home in silence, climbing the shallow incline away from the river. A few curious trees reach creeping tendrils towards us. I bat them away, and Bear swipes at them whenever they get too close to Maeve.

Finally, we reach the little clearing at the top of the incline. There's a break in the canopy here. I glance up to see wisps of green clouds scudding across the red-and-indigo sky. A few of the smaller, less obnoxious birds warble in the branches. In the middle of this clearing stands the Soother Tree. It's taller than the surrounding trees, with wide, splaying branches and bright leaves. It's festooned with vines, which shimmer and stir, even though the day is still. Its trunk is so wide, I reckon we'd struggle, the four of us, to wrap our arms round it. At its base, there's a hollow. The entrance to our home, which we built beneath the tree's sprawling roots. When me and Maeve approach, the wooden door stands wide. There's a modest fire burning in a pit outside, something delicious-smelling bubbling over it. A girl with short, shiny black hair, pale skin and hooded eyes sits on an upturned stump, nodding emphatically as the young man beside her chatters away. He's kneeling, one hand outstretched. An electric blue deer about the size of a large dog feeds from the dead cracklemouse in his palm.

"Blood fawns are nervous things," he's saying quietly. "But if you're patient, they'll come to you."

He grins, showing crooked teeth. His shoulder-length hair, so grubby I don't reckon I've ever seen its true color, falls over his face. A vicious-looking harpoon is strapped across his back, but nothing hides the sparkle in those grey eyes.

This is Sheb. My best friend in all the worlds. The man who rescued me five years ago, when I stumbled through the portal at the bottom of my daddy's garden and found myself in Nowhere. We were both still kids back them. Him, a lonely, terrified eighteen-year-old fresh from escaping his family. Me, a frightened, murderous seventeen-year-old girl with nowhere to turn and no-one to help her. No-one except Sheb. His smile always settles my heart. He's become my family. My brother. My shelter.

Although I can't help noticing the blood fawn's fangs are dangerously close to his palm.

"Sheb!" I snap, making everyone jump. The blood fawn springs away.

Sheb and the girl stand.

"Hey, Annie," Sheb says. His face falls as he takes in the state of Maeve. "What happened?"

The girl gasps, rushing to Maeve's side. She cups Maeve's face in her hands, checks her over, then makes frantic signs with her hands.

"I'm alright, Lin," Maeve says. "Don't fuss."

She wraps an arm round Lin's shoulders, kisses her on the mouth. I roll my eyes.

"Time for that later," I say. "First, you should eat. Rest."

Sheb scrambles about for a few more seats. He brings out some of the rickety chairs he's built, arranges another upturned stump by the fire. He ushers us to sit, plants a kiss on my forehead.

"Dear Annie," he says, in that ridiculous, posh accent of his. "What happened this time?"

He's so gentle. Not accusing me at all. But I see concern dancing in his eyes as he hurries to ladle thick, creamy stew into three wooden bowls. He serves Maeve first, watching as she spoons the stew into her mouth, then rushes to make sure me and Lin have some, too.

My hands tremble so much I can barely hold my bowl. My throat tightens.

"Annie," Sheb says gently. He takes the bowl from my hands, sets it on the floor, then he holds my shoulders.

"Something you see."

I blink away a blur of tears and fix my gaze on his face. "You," I whisper. "I see you. My best friend."

Sheb nods, smiling. "Something you hear."

We go through our ritual. Sheb does it every time he sees me slipping out of myself, every time my rage and fear threatens to crush me. Slowly, I come back to myself. My hands stop shaking. He sets the bowl back in my hands. I stare at the creamy contents, stomach twisting.

"Is it too hot?" Sheb asks. "Blow on it a bit, Annie."

I try my best to smile. "It's fine, Sheb," I say. "It's lovely."

And it is. Sheb's a good cook. A good parent to the orphans we brought home two weeks ago. A good *person*. I don't deserve him. I never have.

Sheb continues bustling. He brings out a blanket for Maeve and wraps it round her shoulders. She grumbles and throws it off, but Sheb's up again in seconds, insisting she keep it on for the shock. He rummages in the many pouches he's got strapped to his belt until he finds the vials of healing poultice he makes from various plants in Nowhere. He coaxes me into drinking something to calm my nerves, then starts tending Maeve's leg, nattering away to Lin as he does so.

"Grumbleshroom poultice to stop infection," he says, as Lin frowns and scribbles some notes in a book Sheb gave her. I notice she's also wearing the belt he made for her, stuffed with almost as many pouches and pockets as Sheb's own. Lin's a soft soul. I can see why she wants to learn everything Sheb knows about Nowhere, it's animals and plants, and their uses. The Soother Tree reaches its long vines towards us, sensing tension. It caresses my face, gently wipes a tear from my cheek, then drapes a comforting tendril round Maeve's shoulder. It's most concerned about Sheb, though. Its vines touch his face, searching for his hands. It even holds vials and tools for him while he works to sew Maeve's leg shut. I shake my head with a smile. Nowhere's always loved Sheb most. Its creatures let him pass unharmed. Its trees part for him. Its birds sing gently in his presence. For the rest of us, living in Nowhere is like tiptoeing along the edge of a dagger. But Sheb charms this place. It loves him.

He finishes tending Maeve's leg, then unstraps his harpoon, leans it carefully against his chair. He looks at us.

"What happened?"

Lin puts her notebook and pencil down, makes some more signs with her hands. Lin doesn't talk, at least not that I've heard. Maeve says she hasn't spoken since her mother disappeared over ten years ago—although it turns out her mother actually transformed into a powerful magical creature and now lives in the Wild Wood in their home world. She helped us solve the mystery of who Bear belonged to a few weeks ago. Still, Lin prefers to stay silent. She has an elaborate, beautiful language that she signs with her hands. Sheb, of course, made a massive effort to learn her signs in the first week after she and Maeve came to Nowhere. Ever the scholar, he's already picked up loads. I'm still struggling. I catch the sign I've learned means *event* or *happening,* (both hands making a circle), a sign that means a question, (one finger crooked against the opposite palm) and one Lin seems to have used a lot since she arrived here—the fingers of her left hand to her chin, the other palm swiping upwards over her face—which I'm pretty certain means *foolish.*

My cheeks heat as I explain what happened. Maeve, of course, keeps leaping in, making out like it's worse than it is. *Annie got so angry she couldn't control Wriggler. Disaster.*

"It weren't like that!" I snap. "*I* wasn't mad! Bear hurt Wriggler's wing, and—"

Maeve glares, a hand resting between Bear's stubby horns. "Oh, so, it's *Bear's* fault, now?"

I roll my eyes. "No, Maeve. I just—"

"Then whose, Annie?" she says, needling me. "You gonna blame the lizard-sharks this time? Or the angle of the sun? Seriously, when you gonna just—"

"You lost control!" I snap. I'm on my feet, my chair tipping backwards. Bear gives a questioning whine. From the branches of the Soother Tree, I hear a warning hoot. But I ain't listening. This *ain't* my fault! "I told you to keep Bear small, but you let him grow, and then you wonder why Wriggler goes for you like that? If you ain't even gonna *try* to keep control, Maeve, then why'm I bothering?"

I glare at her and she at me. Sheb touches my arm.

"Annie," he says gently. "Your eyes—"

I shove him off. I know my eyes are glowing. I don't care. I ain't backing down. "This ain't a game, Maeve!"

Sheb tries to weigh in again. "She knows that, Annie. You must give her time to learn. Your monsters are very different, you know. Serpentines like Wriggler may be linked more to emotions like rage and hate. But I think the Hot-Bloods like Bear are different. We have to—"

I turn my glare on him. He falls silent. I ain't in the mood to hear about his studies, his theories about the monsters. He's got these *categories* he came up with. He's called reptilian monsters like Wriggler *Serpentines,* and mammalian monsters like Bear *Hot-Bloods* and he keeps harping on about the difference. But I don't care! The issue ain't with our monsters, is it? It's with *us!* I round on Maeve.

"You can't control Bear," I growl.

Maeve leans back in her own chair, sighing. "I can control him, Annie," she says. "I let him grow 'cos I wanted him to. You're always trying to hold me back, like I'm some kid who doesn't—"

"You *are* a kid!" I burst out. "You're a kid who killed three people before she realized the monster was hers! You *almost* killed more! If I hadn't been there to stop you, you'd have ended up—"

"Ended up what, Annie?" Maeve says, her voice dangerously quiet. "Go on. Say it."

But I can't. All the fight goes out of me. The scar across my back aches. I feel Wriggler in my head. Wherever he is, he senses my distress. I push him away. I can't deal with him now. This is partly his fault.

"You can't say it, can you?" Maeve murmurs. "Fine. I'll say it for you. You don't want me to end up like you." She stands, leaning on Lin for support. "You don't gotta worry about that, you know," she says. "I don't wanna end up like you. I'll *never* end up like you."

Lin's eyes widen. She makes a frantic sign with both hands pressed together. Gratitude. Because we rescued them. And Maeve's being a stuck-up sod.

Maeve at least has the decency to look subdued by Lin's reminder. Her cheeks color, she falls quiet.

Still, her words cut through me. I flinch. Maeve sees, and triumph flickers in her eyes. She hobbles towards the Soother Tree, which reaches its vines towards her, wrapping her in a welcoming hug.

She and Lin duck inside the cave, wedge the door shut behind them.

I stare at the ground, hating the way my eyes burn. I feel a hand clasp mine, look up to find Sheb beside me. His grey eyes sparkle with concern.

"Dear Annie," he says. "It's okay, she's just—"

I snatch my hand away. I don't want to be comforted. I deserved what Maeve said. She's right. She should never end up like me. All I do is break and beat and destroy. Sheb grabs my shoulders, turns me to face him. He looks suddenly fierce.

"Don't do that," he says. "I know what's going on in your head. You're more than your past. More than the bad things that happened to you."

I shrink away. "Ain't more than my present though, am I?" I snap. "This was a stupid idea, Sheb! How can we keep two kids safe in a world like this? You and me, we're so broken—"

Sheb tries to gather me into a hug. "We're not broken, Annie," he says. "It's okay. We can do this—"

I push him away, harder than I meant to. He staggers back and I'm ashamed of myself. But the rage-grief-guilt churns in me like poison. Far away, I feel Wriggler sparkle with power.

"Stop trying to make it better, Sheb!" I yell. "You're just as broken as me. Don't pretend you ain't!"

Sheb's eyes shutter for a moment. I see his jaw tighten. "That's not fair, Annie," he says. "We both suffered at the hands of those who should have loved us. We don't use it against each other."

I kick sullenly at the ground. He's right. Obviously. "Sorry," I grumble. "I didn't mean it. I just—we dunno how to play families, do we? Last time either of us were in a family, it ended in murder."

Sheb flinches. I hate that all I'm doing right now is hurting him. His shoulders sag.

"Annie, what happened to us isn't normal. You know that, right?"

I nod automatically, even though I ain't got a clue what any kind of normal should look like. My normal was a mother who left me twice. A father who would've killed me, except I killed him first.

And Sheb's normal—well, he only ever talked about it with me once. Years ago, when I first came to Nowhere. I know he had brothers. I know one of them died. I know Sheb killed him.

I've never asked anything further. Though I've been tempted. I'm tempted now, as I watch a shadow cross his face. I'm not used to seeing his pain. He's dealt with it. Put it aside and learned to accept it. Unlike me and Maeve, he managed to detach himself from his monster, (Wriggler spent some time tormenting Sheb before he moved onto me.) Unlike Lin, he doesn't have any kind of power. He's just Sheb. Brilliant in his own way and completely together. Our safe place.

He tries to put his arm round me, but I can't take it. I'm angry. Mostly with myself, I guess. "You can't always make things better!" I snap. "Just ... let me be, okay?"

He blinks, color rising in his cheeks. Those grey eyes shine with hurt. "Okay, Annie," he whispers. Shame stabs me. He doesn't deserve this. I try to reach for him. "Sheb, I—"

But he pulls away. "No, you're right," he says. "I can't fix it. I'm sorry."

He grabs his harpoon, though I doubt any of the day creatures of Nowhere would hurt him. The night beasts are another matter. He trudges out of the clearing, ignoring me when I call him back. I'm left alone beside the fire, my bowl of stew unfinished. I kick it over, swearing. This is too much. I can't *do* this. How do I manage to drive everyone around me away?

Well, not quite everyone.

That warning hoot comes again from the trees. A purple shape swoops from the branches, landing on the ground beside me. It rouses its feathers, fixes me with a ferocious, tawny-eyed glare. I glare right back.

"What do *you* want?" I grumble.

The creature beside me growls in answer. He's about eight inches tall with a fluffy, furry body. He looks mostly like an owl, with feathery discs around his eyes, a hooked beak and little ear tufts at the top of his head. He tucks his mottled grey wings against his side, flicks his squirrel tail in agitation. Instead of talons, his back feet are long and furry, like those of a rabbit. This is Bartok. An owl-squirrel Sheb adopted before we met, who seems to think I'm a complete waste of space. He's probably right. He thumps once against the ground to get my attention, chirps angrily.

"I don't need you telling me off, too," I say. "I know I'm an idiot."

Bartok fixes me with an appraising stare. He can't talk, but we've got an unspoken understanding, me and him. He knows what I am. He sees right through me, through the anger to the churning fear beneath. And I try to see me the way he does. I try to show him I can be better.

Only, right now, I ain't convinced I can.

"Go after Sheb, then," I say. "He needs you more than I do right now."

Bartok doesn't move. He keeps staring at me. I imagine he's saying, *You are an idiot, Annie.* He's saying, *surprise, surprise.* He's saying, *So, what are you going to do about it now?*

And the truth is, I don't know.

CHAPTER THREE

WHAT COULD HAVE BEEN

I DOUSE THE FIRE with the bucket of water Sheb keeps handy but leave the pot and its contents. When Maeve finishes fuming, she'll be hungry.

I've lost my appetite, though. I need to get out of here. I usher Bartok onto my shoulder and head northeast, continuing up the incline, away from the river. Bartok nips my ear, growls. I bat him off. Not like I don't *know* I've been an idiot, is it? No-one needs me around right now.

The trees are wilder up this way. Their leaves glimmer gold, red, and yellow. Their creepers are excitable, snatching at my hair and arms. I smack them away, draw one of the throwing knives I keep sheathed on my belt.

"Let me alone," I tell them. "Or I'll get nasty."

The trees know I ain't messing around. With a groan of old bark, they drop their creepers, let me pass un-bothered. I trudge until the ground flattens and the trees thin into another clearing. This one's smaller. Quieter. There's a hush over this place, like the plants and creatures of Nowhere hold it in reverence. The howler horses never come through here. There are birds in the trees, but they're silent.

I head, like I have every day for the past two weeks, to the moss-covered rock at the edge of the clearing and settle on it, knees drawn up to my chest. I fix my gaze on the tree in the middle of the clearing. And wait. And hope.

Because this tree ain't like the other trees in Nowhere. It looks like the lightning-struck corpse of a years-old oak. It must once have reached dozens of feet into the sky, dominating the forests of Nowhere for miles around. It must've been a sight to behold. Now, though, it's no more than a blackened husk, hollow down the center, a few twisted branches clinging to its corpse.

You'd be forgiven for reckoning it was nothing more than a dead tree, if it weren't for the lights dancing from within. Greens, golds, pearly whites, threaded with blues. It's an ever-shifting, ever-living thing. It showed itself a few months after I first arrived, once Nowhere decided it was safe for me to leave. It's a portal. If I was to walk up to it, peer over the blackened lip into its hollow innards, I'd see world after world flicker into view. Dancing galaxies, sweeping deserts, worlds where the geometry and physics defy belief. And if I leaned in a little further, let myself tumble inside, I'd fall into one of those worlds. I'd feel the pull of light and dark, life and death, beyond and within, tugging at my heart. And then I wouldn't be in Nowhere anymore.

Nowhere ain't like other worlds, see. I ain't sure it's a world at all, really. It's a place between. A haven. This portal could take me to any world I choose. Universe upon universe upon universe, waiting inside that hollow tree. But as far as I know, the other worlds don't have portals to each other. Only to here.

Today, I ain't interested in visiting other worlds. I'm waiting for someone, though I reckon he ain't coming soon.

The hope hurts so much, I can't bear it, but I can't seem to stop. Tears trickle down my cheeks as I stare at the portal. No-one comes through. There's no bright flash. No thunderclap of worlds colliding. Nothing.

Bartok grumbles, glaring at the ground. Something nudges my ankle. I look down to find Wriggler. He's no more than a harmless, black snake, little wings pressed against his sinuous body.

Can we be friends again? He whines. I sigh, scooping him up. Bartok shrieks. He takes off into the trees, squawking his disdain from a nearby branch. He and Wriggler ain't the best of friends. Wriggler ignores him. My lightning-snake concertinas his coils in my lap. I stroke his scales. I'm trying to treat Wriggler with kindness, these days. I ain't good at it yet, but I've realized that he's a part of me. Pulled to my darkness and rage. No point fighting him, really. Treating him with kindness is about treating myself with kindness.

I ain't always good at that, either.

"You made life difficult for me today," I tell him. "Now everyone's mad at me."

Wriggler fixes me with a beady-eyed stare. *Because you were handling it so well before I slithered in,* he drawls. I roll my eyes, but, annoyingly, he has a point.

"I don't wanna talk about it," I say. Wriggler nudges my arm.

You never do.

We sit in silence for a bit. I stare at the portal tree.

He's not coming, Annie, Wriggler says. He says it gently, but the words are like a needle in my heart. I clench my jaw.

"I know," I snap. "I'm just—"

Just what? Wriggler says. *He said he'd find you when he's ready. Stop rushing him. Stop rushing yourself.*

"I'm not rushing anyone!" I retort, though I know that ain't true.

I can't explain it, this longing. I haven't known Sasha that long. I met him in Maeve's world, when me and Sheb went through the portal to rescue

Maeve and Lin from a monster. It turned out, that monster was Bear, who belonged to Maeve, and the whole situation was far messier than we'd first realized.

But in that world, I'd met this dark-eyed priest with a gentle smile, who could transform into a giant, grey maned cat. Skin-switching, Sheb's been calling it. I don't know what you'd call our connection, but it felt...*right*...straight from the start. Like I'd known him my whole life.

Obviously, things got complicated. He escaped his priesthood and they weren't pleased. Then he left, promised he'd find me when he was ready. When he'd discovered what he needed to about himself. Whatever that means.

But it's already been two weeks. How long does it take someone to find themselves? How lost *is* he?

And why the hell do I feel so adrift without him?

Wriggler nudges me again.

Forget it, Annie.

I scowl at him. I know he's trying to help, in his own thoroughly unhelpful way. We watch the portal tree for a while, lights flickering around the clearing. Gradually, the sun sets, the red-and-indigo sky darkens. The twin moons rise. One a bright, blue crescent, the other fat, white, and full.

Time to go, Wriggler says. He slithers off my lap and oozes through the leaf litter. I follow, head bowed. Bartok swoops onto my shoulder, watching through the darkness in case a howler horse or a cherish screamer decides to ambush us.

Not that any of them have been that stupid for some time. The predators of Nowhere are acquainted with Wriggler. They attack me once, and never make that mistake again.

•••••●••●•••

At home, the girls have emerged from beneath the Soother Tree and stoked the fire to life again. The Soother's more active now, its vines snapping at the butcher beetles—thumb-sized, mosquito-like blood suckers that come out this time of evening. It's good at keeping them away.

Lin, stirring the pot of stew, waves when she sees me approach. Maeve sits beside her, prodding the wound on her leg. She grunts as I sit next to her. From Maeve, that's pretty much as good as a hug. I grunt back. No-one says anything for a bit. Bartok gives an anxious hoot. I scan the trees.

"Where's Sheb?" I ask. Maeve shrugs.

"Dunno."

We fall silent again. The last of the daylight fades. Now the clearing is washed in the strange, silver-blue light of the twin moons. I jiggle my leg. Bartok flicks his tail. Maeve and Lin frown. I can't stand this anymore.

I bolt to my feet. "I'm gonna look for him."

Maeve stands. "I'll come with you," she offers. "It's my fault, too. We should—"

I shake my head. "It's too dangerous," I say. "Stay here with Lin. I can—"

"I have a monster, too, Annie," Maeve points out. "I can handle it."

I glare at her, about to retort that she has no idea what she's talking about. She's been in Nowhere for two weeks, that's all. She saw her first howler horse two days ago and it took her nearly twenty-four hours to recover. (Strangely, Lin was fine. No-one's *ever* fine after they see a howler horse for the first time.)

Maeve bristles before I've uttered a word. Lin holds up her hand before we can go for each other again. I pause mid-breath, staring at Lin, who points towards the edge of the clearing.

There's Sheb, emerging from the brush. His head's bowed, hair covering his eyes. But there are no cuts or bruises that I can see. He's not limping, and his harpoon's strapped across his back.

Bartok squeals with delight, makes a beeline for Sheb's shoulder. Sheb smiles as the owl-squirrel nuzzles his face.

"Hey, buddy," Sheb mutters, tickling Bartok's belly. Bartok chirps, glares at the rest of us like he can't believe we've been so mean. Bloody owl-squirrel.

"Sheb!" Maeve says. "We were worried. Me and Annie were gonna look for you—"

I turn my glare on her. "*We* weren't going *any-where,*" I growl. But a warning look from Lin shuts me up before I start another fight.

Sheb comes into the firelight, smiling faintly. His eyes look red, his cheeks puffy. I feel my ribs tighten at the sight. I did that. My best friend, the person who saved me from myself.

And this is how I repay him.

I take his hand, squeeze it. "I'm sorry," I say. "Really sorry, Sheb. I just ... come have some dinner, yeah?"

Sheb holds my hand tightly. "Dear Annie," he says, flopping into a rickety chair. "Smells good, Lin."

Lin blushes as she serves up the stew, signs something about how it was all Sheb's work, really, she just added a bit. Sheb chuckles, tells her she's a quick learner and he's proud of her. Lin smiles, signs some more. I spot the gestures for *good* and *teacher* and catch the drift.

I feel Maeve's eyes on me. Hopeful. I know what she wants me to say. She wants me to report to

Sheb and Lin that she's doing well, too. That she's learning fast.

And she *is*. Too fast. I wish she wouldn't be in such a hurry. It takes time to tame your monster. Rage is a fickle beast, and it summons fickle beasts. She's too quick to free hers. Too brave with her energy. She might be learning fast, but I want her to slow down. I avoid her gaze, say nothing. Maeve deflates. Lin ducks her head, stirs the stew. No-one speaks, except to make awkward comments about today's weather, or that we're running low on mushrooms.

A howler horse screeches. The thunder of hooves makes the ground tremble. They're out in force tonight.

Sheb stands, douses the fire. "Time for bed," he says.

No-one argues, though Wriggler huffs in my brain.

Cowards.

I shoot him a glare, then help Sheb carry our cooking things inside. Maeve puts her arm round Lin's shoulders.

And a crack like thunder rips through the clearing. I duck, grabbing Sheb's arm to steady him as a flash of white light blinds me. I pull Sheb to me, shielding him with my body. Wriggler's as tall as me in seconds, lightning sparkling along his scales. Bear's responded to Maeve's fear, too.

"What's happening?" Maeve cries.

I don't answer, though I already know. My heart swells with fear and hope.

"Get inside," I say.

Maeve starts to argue. I silence her with a glare.

It's the portal tree.

My pulse is a wild thing, roaring through me. Hope scratches my throat.

Someone's come through the portal.

Sasha.

Chapter Four

THE BOY IN THE DARK

It's not Sasha.

Before we've had a chance to move, a figure stumbles into the clearing, collapses face first in the dirt. Lin and Sheb rush to his side, turn him over. He's no more than a boy. I've never seen him before. He's dressed in a ragged shirt tucked into a pair of waxed overalls, heavy boots. Sweat shines on his dark-skinned face. He's so small. Can't be more than twelve, I reckon. He clenches his fists but he's trembling all over. I see fear in his eyes.

There's a bruise blooming on his temple.

"Who is he?" Maeve asks, peering over Lin's shoulder. "Oak, he looks *awful.*"

I don't answer. Can't. I'm struggling to temper my disappointment that this boy ain't Sasha. I flop against the Soother Tree, fighting the tightness in my throat.

The boy stirs. His eyes flutter open, widen as he takes in the four of us—six, if you count Wriggler and Bear, which I mostly don't. Sheb helps him up.

"Hello," he says, ever the gentleman. "I'm Sheb."

He smiles. The boy gapes. Sheb's smile falters and he looks at me.

"Why do they always insist on arriving at night-fall?" he asks.

I shrug, but Maeve shoots him a mean glare. "Who's *they?*" she demands, though it's obvious.

When Maeve came hurtling through that por-tal, yelling about a giant god-bear killing a priest, she arrived at nightfall, too. Night ain't a com-fortable time in Nowhere. It's when dark things come out to play. Howler horses, cherish scream-ers, and dawn wights. These ain't just creatures that eat flesh and sinew. They devour soul and shadow, memory and pain. A howler horse will eat everything you are if you let it. It'll eat your body, then it'll eat your footprints, your thoughts, your history, and your future. It'll erase the fact you ever existed. Not an end I relish. I flick a throwing knife into my hand.

"We need to get inside," I growl. As if to make my point, a piercing shriek cuts the night, joined by a second, then a third. It's a mournful, bloodthirsty sound that strikes the marrow in my bones. The howler horses are awake. "Now!" I say, grabbing Maeve's arm. She doesn't move. She's looking at the boy. I look at him, too.

"Do you live here?" he asks us. "Are you the ones that fight monsters?"

I blink. What? *The ones who fight monsters?* Far as I remember, we've fought exactly *one* monster, and that monster now sleeps at Maeve's feet in the form of a helpless, horned bear cub. So, I ain't sure we can call that a success.

And anyway, how would he know? We don't exactly advertise. I'm about to open my mouth to point this out, but Sheb gets there first. He puffs out his chest.

"We are," he says, which makes me stare at him. On his shoulder, Bartok fixes me with a tawny glare, challenging me to deny it.

Even Wriggler balks at that. He flicks his tongue. *Are we?* he says, sounding worried.

I shrug. *Apparently.*

This conversation ain't going the way I'd hoped. But if the others see the warning in my face, they ignore it. Sheb puts an arm round the kid.

"Do you have a monster?" he asks. "Can you describe it to us?" he points towards Wriggler. "If it's scaled like this one, it's likely a Serpentine. We think they have powers that control the weather." He smiles, then indicates Bear. "Or perhaps it's a more mammalian monster, like Bear? If it has fur it could be a Hot Blood. They have elemental powers, like fire and water."

The boy gapes at Wriggler and Bear in turn, then turns wide, awe-struck eyes on me and Maeve. His lips move, but no sound comes out. He shakes his head slowly. "No," he murmurs. "Nothing like that."

Sheb's face falls. "We need to understand the monster so we can help," he says.

Help? Holy Oak, this is getting out of control. I open my mouth again, ready to give them all a sharp word, but the boy buries his face in his hands. The protest dies in my throat. He looks so helpless. He's far younger than I was when I turned up here. But there's age in those eyes. He's lived a life far beyond his meagre years. I cast a sideways glance at Maeve and see the kid reflected in her eyes.

We've both been this kid before, not all that long ago.

Hell, sometimes, we both still *are* this kid.

"It took her," the boy says. "It took my sister. I tried to stop it, honestly. But it was so strong. So vicious. I couldn't—"

He lets out this sound, halfway between a roar and a keen, that slices my heart like butter. My scar pulses. It's the sound of torture. I've made sounds like that before.

Wriggler nudges my ankle. *Annie,* he says, a warning in his voice. *The horses.*

He's right. They come thundering through our clearing every night.

"Sheb," I say. "We need to move."

Bartok hoots in nervous agreement. Sheb nods without looking at me. "In a minute, Annie," he says. I feel my pulse buck. This is not an *in a minute* situation!

Maeve squares her shoulders. "What took your sister?" she asks.

I throw up my hands. For Oak's *sake!* Are they serious? It's like we've said yes to this crazy quest before the kid's even asked.

"Can we have this conversation *inside?*" I hiss. "I really don't want to get eaten by a howler horse!"

Maeve shoots me a glare, which I meet with equal ferocity. She turns back to the boy. "Kid?" she says gently. "What took your sister?"

The boy looks up. The twin moons reflect in his tear-filled eyes. "We call it the Corvos," he says. "The bone crow."

The bone crow.

I go very, very still. That name echoes round my skull, filling the clearing with its eerie presence.

I've never heard it before, can't picture the monster it belongs to, yet something about it tugs at me. Suddenly, the howler horses don't seem important.

"The what?" Sheb says quietly.

"The bone crow," the boy repeats. He whispers it, like he'll draw the terrible creature if he speaks too loudly.

I shake my head. Whatever this thing is, it's powerful. Only one creature's name has ever struck fear into me like that, and that creature is now a little black snake at my feet. But he wasn't always. Once, he was beyond control. Vast, brutal, infernal with rage. A beast whose name made my insides scream with fear. The Oraqua. I've never known what that word means, what language it comes from, but even the memory of what Wriggler used to be makes my gut curdle with dread.

And this thing—this *bone crow*—feels similar. I can't face a monster like this. I'm not ready. I back away.

"I'm sorry, kid," I say. "I really am, but we can't—"

"We *can.*"

The voice that speaks is so fierce, it takes me a moment to realize it's Sheb. I look at him and almost don't recognize him. He's bunched like a cat about to strike. His eyes are alight with a fire I've never seen before. He's drawn his harpoon and I blink several times to make sure my eyes aren't deceiving me. Is the weapon glowing faintly with a strange, green light? It's never done that before.

"Sheb?" I say. Lin touches his shoulder but he flinches away.

"We *can,*" he says again. "And we will."

He sounds crazed. I gape at him, wondering what the hell's going on. This ain't my gentle Sheb who'd always love rather than fight, who'd lay down his own life rather than take another's.

Except that one time. But we don't talk about that.

Sheb fixes me with that wildfire gaze. "I have to go," he says. "You don't have to come with me."

I narrow my eyes. Even Bartok looks at him like he's lost his mind. What the hell? I shake my head. But the others are on Sheb's side. Lin puts her hand on the boy's shoulder, gives me a pleading look. Maeve folds her arms, glares. Sheb doesn't take his eyes from me. The look on his face is terrifying.

I throw up my hands. "*Fine!*" I say. "Fine! We'll hunt this bloody bone crow. But can I *at least* finish my dinner, first?"

Wriggler flicks his tail. *Inside,* he says. *Where there aren't any howler horses.*

Good point. The night creatures shriek again, uncomfortably close. I growl-sigh, usher the others—the kid included—towards the Soother Tree. This time, no-one argues.

The Soother Tree reaches its vines to us, pulling us inside. We fix the door in place to keep out the predators, draw a curtain across it. Outside, the Soother will have draped its vines over the entrance, hiding it. If anything comes sniffing round, those vines will deal with it. I've seen our Soother Tree chase off a howler stallion before, sending it limping away with a bruised rump. We're safe here.

Still, the memory of the kid's words echoes round my brain.

Bone crow.

Why does that name fill me with such fear? And what the hell did it do to Sheb?

There's a strike-and-hiss as Lin lights some candles, places them around the room. Our little home is washed in warm light. It isn't a large space, though me and Sheb spent some time making it bigger after Maeve and Lin arrived. A round, earthen chamber, supported by the great pillars of the Soother Tree's roots. The ceiling's low, but I like it that way. At one end is the table and chairs Sheb built from dead wood, his handmade books strewn across it, the improvised ink from his latest drawings and observations still drying. Sheb's passion is for the creatures of Nowhere, and he sketches and studies them as if his life depends on it, but lately he's been more interested in Wriggler and Bear, trying to work out what they are, where they come from.

Bartok chirrups and flies to the perch Maeve made for him. It's tall enough that he can sit at eye level with the rest of us, glaring whenever we say anything he disapproves of. (Which is always.) He rouses his feathers, tucks his head under his wing and is snoring softly in seconds. I roll my eyes, but at least he won't add his opinion to this conversation.

At the other end, opposite the table, is a heap of blankets and makeshift sleeping bags, still crumpled where we tossed them aside this morning. Sheb's tried to make the place nice with a reed-woven rug across the floor, herbs hanging from the ceiling. There's a hearth dug into the wall beneath a makeshift chimney, which the Soother Tree grew for us. Sheb piles the pots and cooking equipment by the hearth, sets about lighting a fire. No-one speaks, but I watch the boy as he peers, open-mouthed, around our little home.

"It's ..." he says, clearly trying to find the right word. "Nice," he manages.

I bark a laugh, throw a blanket at him, and tell him to wrap up. Sheb gets the fire going. Maeve and Lin look shattered, so I tell them to set up their beds. Keep warm. Whatever we decide about this

... this *bone crow,* nothing's happening tonight. Wearily, the girls snuggle under their blankets. Bear mewls and curls up between them. His eyes reflect firelight.

I scoop Wriggler into my arms and pace. I need to think. Fire zips through my veins. I'm too alert to sleep. Sheb watches me, expressionless. I can't look at him. If I look at him, I'm scared I'll break. I've never seen him like this before.

"Right, kid," I growl. "Start talking."

Lin and Maeve shuffle closer. The fire spits sparks. The kid takes a breath.

"My name is Einan," he says. "And I come from a world called Riverfell. This is what I saw ..."

Chapter Five

EINAN'S TRUTH

As Einan speaks, I feel my body tighten. I sneak glances at Sheb. The more Einan speaks, the more lost my friend looks.

I listen to Einan's story, and it's like I'm watching it happening in front of me. This is what he says.

. . . .

His breath mists in the frigid, night air. The sky is clear and dark, studded with stars. But Einan doesn't have time to admire them. His skin prickles with gooseflesh, though he knows it's not from the cold.

There's something here. Something that shouldn't be.

The murky waters of the swamp lap at his little boat. There's an engine attached to the stern. It's an unreliable, rusted thing that runs off steam. He'd get there a lot quicker if he used it, but he dares not disturb the water at night. There are ... *things* ... lurking beneath the surface of this swamp. A few years ago, the swamp would never have dared upturn a boat in de Callis territory. But it's different, now. And Einan is no de Callis. He doesn't carry a harpoon. He's just a frightened boy on a secret mission. Carefully, he paddles the boat forward. First over the starboard gunwale, then switching to port to keep the vessel heading true. His lantern hangs from the boat's prow, lighting his way. Vast, twisted trees, clinging vines, and huge, swaying reeds loom from the dark. He thinks he sees eyes in the shadows and tries not to meet their gaze. Occasionally, a strange mist forms between the trees and a human-like shape floats past him, making him shudder. The remnants have been growing in number these few years. They're drifting out of the graveyard, too.

Entering the town itself. Gliding over the murky waters, howling their despair.

Einan shudders. He shouldn't be out here. His mother would kill him if she knew, but she didn't see him slip out of the house, hear him take the boat. She's too busy panicking about Zuma. Einan's sister.

Who didn't come home today.

Einan's heart kicks. His little sister. Eight-years-old and shining with a light so bright she could illuminate the whole world. Just being near her makes Einan feel like a better person. She's so full of gentleness, but there's a mischief in her, too. She gets Einan into trouble, sneaking out on adventures she's far too young for. Their father despairs, and it's always Einan who gets the blame. It's worth it, though, for the sparkle in her eyes. She's been different lately, though. She gets up earlier. Arrives home later, looking feral. Einan knows she's missed lessons at the town's school. Einan's seen her with Imberg, too. The old widow from the edge of town. Their father worries that

Zuma might be murk-touched, but Einan doesn't think it's that.

He hopes it isn't that.

Now, though, she's missing. Out alone. At night.

Marsh Wilds isn't safe at night. Not anymore.

A cry cuts the darkness. Sharp. Animal. Einan starts, pulls his paddle into his boat, and waits. Slowly, he reaches for the gutting knife kept at the bottom of the boat. There are weapons in the bottom of every boat in this town, and there's not a single one that hasn't been used. The swamp is vicious these days. Giant fanged eels burst from the depths, wrap themselves round unsuspecting vessels. Creeperscorps—aquatic, scorpion-like creatures as long as a man's arm—deliver a paralyzing sting before eating their victims alive. The de Callis brothers should be able to keep them at bay, but the beasts are growing too strong.

And there are the hellgators.

Einan shudders.

They're the swamp's oldest, most sacred monsters. No-one kills a hellgator. To kill a hellgator is to draw the swamp's wrath. As far as he knows, only one person has ever been killed by a hellgator in this town. But that's a small miracle. Especially these days. Hellgators are more than just violent creatures. They're spirits of the swamp itself, steeped in magic, deeply powerful and deadly. Spirits best avoided by *never going out alone at night.*

Einan scans the darkened waters for signs of movement, but there's none. He paddles until his boat bumps against a narrow jetty. His lantern illuminates tough, wild grasses, a narrow path winding into the dark, and the outlines of gravestones, tilted and sunken in the unstable ground. Trembling, he moors his boat, tucks his paddle under the seat. He takes his knife in one hand, his lantern in the other, and clambers ashore.

The ground squelches. He lifts his lantern ahead of him. He's lived in Marsh Wilds, the biggest town in de Callis territory, his whole life. He's past the age where he thinks being on land makes him safe. The swamp is a death trap, whether you're walking or floating on it.

Shapes skitter away from the lantern light. The back of Einan's neck prickles. The misty, human figure of a remnant flutters from a tree, moaning softly, before it evaporates a few feet above Einan's head. He hugs himself as that familiar cold washes over him. Mist oozes and shifts across the graveyard, making shapes that hover for a moment before vanishing. The graveyard is full of remnants. It's worse tonight than Einan's seen it before.

He clamps down on the urge to call Zuma's name. He's going to give her such a telling off when he gets her home. Much as he loves her, she needs a firm word. She can't keep running off like this.

Something shifts in the darkness. Something big. Einan freezes, fear clawing his throat. He strains to listen but can't hear anything over the roar of blood in his ears.

There comes a deep, throaty rumbling. Deeper than the roar of a hellgator. It makes the ground tremble. Rattles Einan's bones. He feels it grate the inside of his skull and winces.

The rumbling intensifies. He staggers back, drops his knife. It lands without a sound in the grass and he stoops to retrieve it, hands brushing soggy grass.

The rumbling changes, becomes more like a wheezing snarl that reminds Einan of ...

Of *laughter*.

His muscles bunch. His lungs have forgotten how to draw air. He freezes as the ground trembles with heavy footfalls. The creature—whatever it is—prowls into the light.

The flame of Einan's lantern falls across it and Einan thinks he might be staring at death itself. Slowly, he raises his gaze, taking in the nightmare a piece at a time.

It stalks towards him on two, column-like legs, talons gouging the wet earth. A reptilian tail lashes behind it, cracking a headstone in two. Its powerful body looms over Einan, muscle rippling beneath feathery down. It opens a pair of vast, feathered wings, ragged and torn, dripping black blood, but huge enough that the thing could easily get airborne. Those wings. So black they darken the inside of Einan's mind. His brain begins to buzz, horrors crawling inside it. Finally, Einan meets the thing's eyes.

Eyes swimming with violence. Blind to everything but fury. They're deep, unfathomable black, burning with dark fire. Set into a head so hellish, Einan looks at it and forgets who he is. Because this is a monster like none he's ever seen.

That sharp, mottled skull. That razor beak lined with fangs, that lashing red tongue, that frill of horns at its crown. The black feathers bent and broken, oozing blood.

Einan knows what it is. A murk-touched monster. Someone here, in Marsh Wilds, has summoned it. Cursed by the swamp.

He can't move. His legs are heavy, yet every part of him is screaming to run.

Only he can't do that. He's here for something. There's a nagging at the back of his mind. A distant cry in a voice he recognizes. Einan opens his mouth as the monster lumbers towards him, peering at him out of one, infernal eye. Finally, Einan manages to speak. Just one word.

"Z-Zuma..." he says.

The monster rumbles a laugh. Einan's mind falls dark. A fog chokes his mind. The beast lifts a wing, revealing a little, trembling figure at its side, black curls bunched behind her ears. Her usually glowing black skin is waxy and grey. Einan's heart thumps.

"Zuma?"

She doesn't answer. Her eyes are glassy, distant. It's like she's in a trance. The cry in Einan's mind becomes a scream, then a shriek of terrible pain. He can't see. Visions swirl before his eyes.

He sees his sister's body, torn and bloody, on the ground in front of him, only he can't reach her.

He sees his mother melting into mist.

He sees his father striding into the swamp, arms spread, waiting to be devoured.

And he sees a headstone with his own name on it.

The monster's laughter grows until it fills Einan's head. It delights in his terror. It closes its wing over Zuma and she disappears into its shadow. Ice forms in Einan's heart, creeping through his veins. He can't see. Can't breathe.

"What ... are you?" he gasps.

The monster stalks closer. It's inches from him, now. He feels its putrid breath on his face. Its razor beak touches the tip of his nose. It stares into his eyes.

"You know what I am," it rasps. Its voice is an echo of an echo of a dream. It beats in his blood. It laces his bones. *"I am a nightmare. I am the Corvos."*

"My sister ..." Einan whispers.

The bone crow laughs again. It opens its beak in a twisted grin. *"Is mine,"* it hisses. *"Run."*

And Einan does. He drops his lantern, doesn't bother to retrieve his knife. He turns and flees as the monster roars. The air thumps behind him as the vile thing takes flight. It's in the sky. All around him. He feels it bearing down on him, swears its talons scratch the back of his neck. He stumbles. Falls. Scrambles up and keeps running. He tumbles into his boat, fumbles with the mooring until it falls free. He has no idea which direction he's going. No idea if he'll live to see the dawn.

But he can't get the image of Zuma out of his head. Distant, hypnotized, disappearing into the Corvos' shadow. It's taken her. And he couldn't stop it.

Einan paddles until his arms ache, until his breath is ragged. He's so tired he leans over the gunwale and is thoroughly sick. When he finally sits back, glances up, his breath catches.

He's not home. He's miles from home. But the swamp, as it so often does, has taken him where he needed to go.

To the forbidden place only the de Callis brothers are allowed to enter. The circle of five sharp, spearhead rocks that stab out of the swamp like the fingers of a giant's reaching hand. The town calls this place the Giant's Reach. But Einan's heard it called something else, too.

It's something to do with the way the water within those rocks moves differently. Something to do with the strange light that pulses from inside. If Einan creeps close enough, he knows he'll feel sunlight on his face from another world.

A portal. To the place called Nowhere.

CHAPTER SIX

DON'T TURN YOUR BACK ON ME

AFTER EINAN FINISHES SPEAKING, no-one says a word. What is there to say? Einan stares at his lap, a tear rolling down his face. Maeve and Lin sit rigid, faces pale. In my arms, Wriggler stirs.

Corvos, he says. *The bone crow.*

In my head, his voice is a whisper. He speaks that name like I used to speak his. Not too loud in case the sound summons it.

I've seen Wriggler at his worst. A monumental serpent made of rage and lightning, shattering buildings. He's a monster. *My* monster.

And he's afraid.

Ice laces my insides. I sneak a sideways glance round our little home. At Maeve and Lin. Their ashen faces, the memories of their own fight fresh in their minds. They ain't had a chance to recover yet. Hell, neither have I! The cuts and bruises from that final, colossal fight haven't even faded.

And Sheb. He looks like a shadow of himself. I nudge his shoulder.

"What d'you think?" I ask, trying to smile. "Serpentine or Hot Blood?"

Sheb doesn't look at me. "Neither," he says. "Something new."

He doesn't add any more. I notice he hasn't let go of his harpoon. He clutches it to his chest. It glows with that strange, faint light.

I shake my head. We can't do this. Not so soon.

But as I open my mouth to say so, my gaze snags on Einan. He's just a kid. Like Maeve and Lin were. Like I was. Should I send him back to face the Corvos alone? And for what? The truth is, with a beast like that, his sister's likely dead.

Not true, Wriggler thinks into my head. *Depends what it wants. Depends whose it is.*

I frown at him, run my fingertips over the rough, black scales on his head. A memory swims into my mind. Wriggler. Back *before* he was Wriggler. When he was still the monstrous, uncontainable monster called from the darkness by my rage. Five years ago, I'd been so lost and frightened, I hadn't understood how to control him. He'd made a cave. A deep, dark cavern built from my hate and anger. In it, he'd kept my mother trapped. The mother I believed had left me to deal with my daddy alone. All that time, Wriggler had her imprisoned. He didn't kill her. It wasn't her he wanted, was it?

It was me. My mother had been bait.

Wriggler stirs. I reckon I feel something a little like shame pulse down our bond. *If I'd known she'd abandon you again, I'd have picked someone else*, he says.

I roll my eyes. *Comforting thought.*

Wriggler chuckles. He's quickly serious again. *The Corvos could be using Zuma the way I used your mother*, he says.

My gaze flicks to Einan. He looks distraught. Could the Corvos be using Zuma to get to him? Could it be *his* monster? I shudder. For a kid of twelve to have called a creature as brutal as the bone crow, he'd have to be very angry. Angrier than I was. I ain't sure I can help him through that.

Maybe we should try, Wriggler says. I look at him. Is he serious? I heard how he said the bone crow's name! I know exactly how that fight would go. This is ludicrous. I open my mouth to say so, but Einan lets out a sob.

"I'm scared for my sister," he says. "I'm scared she's been murk-touched."

He buries his face in his hands.

I meet Maeve's gaze. She quirks an eyebrow at me. "Murk-touched?" she asks. I wonder if she's thinking the same thing I am.

Einan wipes his eyes. "Sometimes," he says. "In Riverfell—the world I'm from—the swamp calls certain people. It sends them a beast. A ... a monster." He looks between me and Maeve. "Like you two. Murk-touched. It means the person is forever linked to the swamp. They're s'posed to be messengers, but ..." he bites his lip. "Well, the de Callis brothers don't trust murk-touched. Don't trust the swamp."

I don't say anything, but I hold Maeve's gaze. This sounds a lot like what the people in her home world called *dark children*. Back in Wilderness, the folk reckoned the dark children were linked to the Wild Wood. Now, I'm being told in Riverfell, it's the swamp. I ain't sure any of it's true. All I know is I was raging and Wriggler turned up.

Monsters don't really do boundaries. Not even the boundaries between worlds.

"You think the Corvos belongs to your sister?" I ask. "She summoned it?"

Einan shrugs, covers his face again.

I'm about to ask him more about these murk-touched, about these de Callis brothers he's mentioned that I don't like the sound of.

But Sheb makes a strange noise. He stands in one fluid movement, harpoon in his hand. I reckon I see a tear glittering on his cheek. "I'm going," he says. His voice is quiet but makes us jump. I try to meet his eye, but he won't look at me.

"I'm going," Sheb says again. "You don't have to come with me. I'll go alone."

"Sheb—" Maeve says, as Lin signs frantically.

"No," Sheb says, sharp this time. "You stay here. All of you. I'll go."

Bartok opens one tawny eye and narrows it in Sheb's direction. I couldn't agree more. Something's going on here that I don't understand. I let Wriggler slither to the floor and get to my feet, arms folded.

Einan looks between us, fear in his eyes. "I don't think it's something you can fight by yourself," he says. "If it's a murk-monster, like I think it is, it'll need to be fought by a murk-monster. It'll need your murk-touched to fight it."

He gestures at me and Maeve as he says it, then looks at us hopefully. Sheb shakes his head.

"No," he says. "My family stay here."

I bristle. "No chance," I snap before I can stop myself. "I'm coming with you."

Sheb shakes his head. "No, Annie—"

But Maeve and Lin are standing, too. Maeve's arms are folded, mirroring mine. Bear sparkles with white fire. Lin signs something and I catch the signs for *together* (hands sweeping in an arc), and *family* (hands over her heart). It's clear what she means.

"We're going, too," Maeve says. "All of us."

Me and Sheb start to protest at the same time but Bear pulses with energy, growing until he's the size of a small pony. "Stop it!" Maeve growls. "Oak's sake, the pair of you are so overprotective! You forgotten what me'n Lin already been through? You need us. You need Bear. You need Lin's Soul Reading. We're coming. That's that."

Finally, Sheb lifts his head, looks at us. When his eyes meet mine, they're so full of fear and pain it makes me feel hollow. But there's gratitude there, too. Maeve's right. Whatever's going on with Sheb, he needs us. All of us.

And, somehow, I'll have to keep us all safe.

But Maeve mentioning Lin's power has given me an idea. Maybe the Corvos is Zuma's, but maybe Zuma is only being used as bait to trap someone else. If Einan and the bone crow are one person, Lin's power could tell us.

"Lin," I say. "Check Einan."

Einan's head snaps up. He frowns at me. "What?"

Lin blinks, but she only looks shocked for a moment. Maybe a similar thought occurred to her, too. She kneels in front of Einan, smiles as she signs.

"This'll only take a moment," Maeve translates. "And it won't hurt."

Einan doesn't look convinced. He wriggles on his seat as Lin lifts her hands, closes her eyes. The fire flickers and falls dim, not quite going out. Einan's breathing gets faster, louder. Lin grimaces. At first, nothing happens, and then ...

A fine, blue mist forms around Einan. It sparkles with flashing stars. A green and grey thread weaves through it, stirring as if in a soft wind. There's orange in there, too. Like a sunset. But the overriding color is blue. I've learned from Lin, and from Sheb's studies of her over the last two weeks, that soul colors can mean all sorts of different things. Lin reckons Maeve's dominant green represents her determination. She reckons my dominant red represents my sense of justice. Interestingly, Sheb's soul doesn't seem to have a dominant color. It's a riot of rainbow hues, all swirling together like a dance.

But I know, immediately, looking at Einan's blue, that this is love. Love for his sister. Love for his family. Love that would mean he puts himself in danger to defend them. *Could* it be him the Corvos wants?

Lin lowers her hands. The soul colors dissipate. She turns to me and shakes her head, signing. Maeve translates again.

"She can't be sure," Maeve says. "But she doesn't think it's him."

Lin's staring at Einan strangely, like he's a puzzle she can't work out. I narrow my eyes. Lin's strong. Powerful. And that Soul Reading of hers was what revealed the truth to us two weeks ago, when we defeated Princeling Jax and his puppet priests, uncovered the terrible thing they'd done. I trust Lin.

I nod. "Fine," I say. Even though it ain't fine. It's obviously *not fine.* "Let's get some rest. We'll wake early, pack supplies—"

"No."

We all jump again. I gape at Sheb. *"No?"* I repeat. "Sheb, we can't just—"

"I'm going now," Sheb says, cutting me off. He never does that. He doesn't look at me as he flings the door open, revealing the dark, predator-filled night. "Come with me if you like," Sheb says, ducking outside. "Or stay here. But I'm going now."

Bartok gives a worried hoot, swoops after Sheb. The Soother Tree shivers with concern. I feel Maeve's and Lin's eyes on me, too. Questioning. Frightened.

I roll my eyes, try to look like this ain't a problem. Like it's just Sheb being Sheb—even though he's the most un-Sheblike he's ever been right now.

"Right," I grumble. "Grab your things. I guess we're going *now,* aren't we?"

Einan stands, dusts himself down. "Thanks," he says. He flashes me a grin as I pass. I reply with as mean a scowl as I can muster, tell myself not to feel guilty when the smile falls from Einan's face.

Maybe the kid is only here to save his sister. Maybe his soul is as clean as Lin seems to think it is.

But one thing's for sure. Ever since Einan told his story, Sheb's been different. Something's haunting him. Something to do with Einan, and Riverfell. Something to do with the bone crow.

CHAPTER SEVEN

REMNANTS IN THE TREES

THE PORTAL LOOKS DIFFERENT at night. Vivid. The sounds and smells of the worlds beyond intermingle. Around it, Nowhere is in the thrall of night-stalking predators. I hear the distant thunder of howler horses tearing through the forest, devouring everything in their path. A banshee shriek cuts the night. We flinch and cover our ears. Cherish screamers can burst blood vessels in sensitive places if you listen for too long.

"Can we get through the portal," I suggest in a half-growl, "before we get eaten?"

The others nod emphatically.

"There's a boat on the other side," Einan says. "The portal is in water. You'll have to swim up when you get through. I'll have the lantern ready. Just swim towards the light."

I scowl at him again. I'm about to fall through the portal into swampy water. Great.

"Fine," I snap. "Get on with it."

Without another word, Einan shimmies up the blackened stump and dives, headfirst, into its hollow center. There's a rumble, a flash of white light, and he's gone. I scoop Wriggler up.

"I'll go next," I say. I don't relish going through the portal. It's not a pleasant experience. But it lasts a split second, and I'd rather get it over with. "As soon as I'm through, Lin can follow. Then Maeve, then—"

Sheb doesn't wait for me to finish. Without a word, he clambers up the tree and disappears in a flash of light. I hear the echoes of Bartok's hoot as they both vanish. I stare at the place my best friend stood a second ago. Unease gnaws my gut. I turn to the girls, see the same concern in their faces. They're looking at me like baby animals might look at their parents. They want comfort.

And I can't give it to them.

"O-kay," I say slowly. "New plan. Lin goes next, then Maeve and Bear. Me'n Wriggler can bring up the rear."

I expect Maeve to argue. Something about how *she doesn't need me to watch her back, she's got a monster, have I forgotten what she did in Hollow Creek?*

But there's none of the usual arguments. Ashen-faced, the girls shuffle towards the portal. Lin, who's taken to carrying all the stuff Sheb normally does, climbs up first. A few small pots on her belt clang together, making us jump. She looks apologetic, then tucks her spare bandages around them to keep them quiet. After she disappears, Maeve follows. She looks back before she vanishes. There are questions in her eyes. Questions I can't answer.

"Go on, then," I say. "I'm right behind you, ain't I?"

Maeve nods, dives into the portal. Bear follows. Now, it's just me and Wriggler.

Something's not right, Wriggler says. I drape him round my neck.

"No kidding," I mutter.

I pause with my fingers curled around the lip of the hollow, peer into the world inside.

A faint, fetid smell of mud and stagnant water drifts through, making me wrinkle my nose. It's dark there. Like it's dark here. I don't know how the worlds that brush against Nowhere work. Whether their time is the same as our time, whether all their languages are the same as ours, if they are all human worlds where the air, the flora and fauna are safe for us, or there are worlds so alien that I couldn't walk in them. I know Sheb's trying to figure it out, but something tells me he'll be too distracted this time to take notes.

One thing we all agree on, though, is that moving through the portal is an ... *interesting* experience. It lasts a split second, and I know it'll be over before I have a chance to draw breath, but the memory of it still makes me hesitate. Wriggler fidgets, flexing his wings.

Come on, Annie, he grumbles. *Get it over with!*

I half-smile. *You hate it, too, eh?*

Wriggler mutters under his breath. Funny. I never thought about how the portal might affect him. We've only been through it together once before and Wriggler ain't exactly a great one for sharing his feelings.

I take a breath and pull myself inside.

For the first half a moment, I'm falling. Head-first into an unknown world. Gravity tips sideways. Above me, Nowhere evaporates into mist and the rough bark of the portal tree vanishes beneath my fingers. I tumble, holding Wriggler's coils so we don't get separated.

And then.

There's the *pause*. It's like the gravity of Nowhere pulls against the gravity of the new world, so I'm not falling, and I'm not rising. I'm suspended in nothingness. And there's this *tug*, just under my solar plexus. It's hard to explain. It doesn't feel like it's pulling at my body, more at my essence. It pulls at the light and the dark, teasing them away from each other so it feels like I'm unravelling. Everything I am divided into color and shadow. Riot and calm. Height and depth.

And the figure appears.

Freaked me out like nobody's business the first time this happened. The misty outline of another person suspended in front of me, slowly taking shape. My shape. In the moment between breaths, between heartbeats, it's as if I'm staring at myself in negative. A half-Annie, made of swirling fog. Dancing light and scuttling shadows.

Then I'm through. The figure disappears and icy cold bites my skin. I draw breath to cry out, but there's no air. Water rushes into my mouth. I splutter, flail. Wriggler slides from my neck as I struggle for air.

Hold onto me, Annie!

In my panic, he's grown. Large enough that I can grip the joints of his wing as he lances up towards a flickering, yellow light.

We burst through the surface in a halo-shower of moonlit water. I take a massive gasp of air. My vision swims into focus and I peer at the five, huge rocks spearheading out of the water, looming like giant fingers. I keep hold of Wriggler as he sidewinders through the water, carrying me towards the little boat bobbing a short way off.

Well, Wriggler drawls, his eyes flashing red. *That was awful.*

I couldn't agree more, but my lungs are starved of air. I can't get enough breath to speak. My black curls are plastered to my face. Gooseflesh prickles my skin. When we reach the boat, Maeve and Lin haul me up. I flop into the bilge and Wriggler, shrunken down, slithers in beside me. Lin strokes the hair off my face while Maeve helps me turn over so I can vomit the swamp water I swallowed.

"Urgh," I groan when I'm finally purged. Something tells me that's going to come back to haunt me later. I manage to sit up. Sheb's looking at me, eyes wide and sparkling, face deathly pale.

"Are you hurt?" he asks. I wipe my mouth, shake my head.

"No."

He doesn't say anything. Doesn't fuss over me like he normally would. Just grabs my hand and holds it.

Einan fumbles in the bilge until he finds a paddle.

"Keep your arms and legs inside the boat," he says. "The swamp isn't safe."

Sheb frowns, opens his mouth to retort but Einan shoots him a look. "It's angry," he says, an edge of accusation in his voice. "It's been angry since ..." he falls silent, glaring at Sheb. "It attacks boats. It sends ... *things* out of the deep."

My best friend's face crumples. He ducks his head. I frown.

What the hell is happening?

We shuffle away from the gunwales. I see Maeve cradle Bear close, casting nervous glances into the murk. Einan drives the paddle through the water and we're off, gliding through the moonlit dark with the silhouettes of twisted trees reaching across the star-studded sky. Once I've recovered my breath, I cover my nose against the boggy stench of soaked mud and algae. The night is silent. Too silent. There are no cries of night birds. No howl of hunting predators.

But shimmering, misty light dances between the trees. I peer at it, holding Wriggler close. A breeze stirs the branches and some of the mist brightens. I stare as a shape forms in it. A *human* shape. It's a boy, on the cusp of manhood, his fisherman's clothes in rags and half his face in shadow. As I watch, his eyes stretch wide, his mouth opens, and he lets out this noise. A keening that cuts through me. He reaches towards us, then lunges straight for the boat.

"What the—" I yell.

Wriggler expands to dog-sized, flaring his wings. I grab Maeve and Lin, throwing them flat in the boat.

"Cherish screamer!" I cry, but even as I say it, I know that ain't true. Cherish screamer males ain't aggressive. It's only the females that attack. This is something else.

Wriggler snaps at the air, sparks of red lightning shooting off his scales. But as the figure reaches him, it dissipates in a puff of mist. The keening cry cuts short, echoing across the swamp. I blink. Sheb's standing, harpoon raised, the tip glowing with green light. His face is fierce as he turns on Einan.

"What the hell was that?" he demands.

Einan doesn't look at us. He barely even reacted to the misty figure screaming from the trees.

"Remnant," he says. "I think that one was old Gideon's boy. He was killed by a creeperscorp last year. They've been rising for years, now. The swamp rejects their essence, sends them back to haunt us."

"Why didn't you tell me this was happening?" Sheb demands.

Einan fixes him with a cold stare. "You didn't ask, did you?"

I stare between them, struggling to work out what the hell is happening.

"A ghost?" Maeve says, cutting through my thoughts. "That was a bloody *ghost?*"

"A remnant," Einan corrects. "Yeah. When we die, the swamp takes our essence. Everything we were becomes the trees, the water, the creatures that live here. We live on in this place. But something happened years ago that angered the swamp.

It's been rejecting our essence ever since. Sending the broken pieces of what we once were back to us. They're everywhere. All over town. 'Specially at night."

I frown at Sheb, search his face for an explanation. He offers none. Quietly, he sits, clutching his harpoon. Bartok hoots softly on his shoulder.

Wriggler slithers onto my lap, still dog-sized. I hold him close, watching the misty shapes drift through the trees. Einan paddles us in silence.

What isn't Sheb telling us? I ask Wriggler, snatching suspicious looks at my friend.

Wriggler gives his weird, serpentine shrug. *More importantly,* he says. *Why does he know something we don't? What's his link to this place?*

I don't answer. I've got my suspicions, but I'm too scared to voice them. Too scared of what it'll mean.

Bear struggles out of Maeve's grip, wanders to the starboard gunwale. He pats the water experimentally. Einan makes a strangled noise, and Maeve pulls Bear back.

"Keep it *away* from the water," Einan growls. His voice is gruff, but it ain't lost on me that he immediately starts to paddle faster. His eyes dart, scanning the swamp.

Bartok chirps nervously. Everyone hushes him.

I thumb a throwing knife into my palm, feel my eyes glow red. My lightning snake responds, sparkling with energy.

Stay alert, I tell him.

Always, he thinks back.

Then all hell breaks loose.

CHAPTER EIGHT

INTO MARSH WILDS

THE BOAT PULLS UP short with a sharp tug. We lurch forward. Maeve grabs Bear to stop him tumbling over the side. Bartok screams and takes off. I hear him flapping in circles above us, yelling his head off. Sheb grips the gunwale, harpoon raised. Its glow is stronger. It hums with strange energy.

Einan's lantern flares. For a moment, its light blooms across Sheb's face. My stomach flops over as I look at him. He's unrecognizable. His face twists in a snarl, eyes alight with a fire I've never seen before. He looks wild. I don't know this man. I wonder if I've ever known him.

"Einan!" he barks. "The stern!"

Einan turns. We all see it at the same time. Thick, clinging weeds streaming from underwater, wrapping round the old engine. They hold it fast, creeping into the boat itself. Einan shrinks back. Something about the way he stares at those weeds makes me think it's a bad idea to let them touch us.

"Lin! Maeve!" I snap. "Behind me. Now!"

Lin scrambles across the boat as I send waves of rage down the bond to Wriggler, letting him expand. Maeve, though. Bloody Maeve! She's a different story, ain't she?

She turns to me, eyes burning green.

"I can help!" she says.

"No! Behind me, now!"

Maeve's jaw tenses. I feel waves of anger pouring off her. At her feet, Bear starts to grow. His fur blackens. His horns lengthen. The boat dips lower in the water. "You never let me do anything!"

"Maeve!" there's warning in my voice. "Calm down! This boat can only take so much. We—"

The boat lurches again, its planks creaking as the weeds tighten their hold, try to drag us under. Einan grips the port gunwale to avoid being thrown overboard. The boat rocks dangerously.

He cries out as the paddle slips from his hand. It's lost in the darkness.

Sheb leaps over Einan, jabbing his harpoon at the weeds. I rush to his side, kneeling, ready to slash the weeds away with my knife. Sheb grabs my arm. Vice-like. Fierce.

"Don't touch them!" he says, throwing me back. I'm so taken by surprise, I stumble, falling butt-first into the bilge.

I leap upright, about to yell at Sheb for shoving me, but the words die in my throat. I watch as the thick tangle of weeds responds to the jab of Sheb's harpoon, shrinking from it, then advancing again when the barbed tip withdraws. It's like they're scared of it. Scared of him. The weeds creep into the bilge, pushing between the wooden boards, trying to break the boat apart.

But I notice they don't touch Sheb.

Wriggler slithers onto my chest, nudging my face.

Annie! he says. *Rage! Now!*

I don't need telling twice. I'm angry enough to let Wriggler obliterate this whole bloody swamp.

But we're in a tiny boat, floating in the dark, and Einan clings to the vessel like his life depends on it.

I let my rage stream into Wriggler. But not too much. Never too much.

Wriggler grows. He's the size of a horse, then he's too big for the boat. He slithers into the churning waters, lightning crackling along his scales. His light illuminates things all around us. On the reedy banks. In the trees. Hungry eyes. Eyes above jaws that, I bet, contain a lot of sharp, eager teeth.

The mist in the trees flares, remnants forming. They wail piteously.

I'm on my feet again, trying to push past Sheb, to cut the weeds. He keeps throwing me back, jabbing at the tangles with his harpoon. His face is ashen.

"You know me!" he cries. "You know me! Calm down! Don't make me do this!"

But whoever or whatever he's talking to, it makes no difference. The weeds thicken, creeping over the gunwales, lassoing the prow of the boat.

Wriggler dives under the murk, still sparking lightning. I grab the starboard gunwale and peer down, watching as he fights the weeds below the surface. But as soon as he tears clumps away, more grows to replace it. Stronger, thicker. It takes more for him to rip it free.

The boat tips, groaning under the stress. Lin, Maeve and Einan slide towards me as the bow of the boat lifts. Bear growls as Maeve, frightened, floods him with power. The weeds tighten at stern and prow, pulling. The boards in the bilge groan, split.

"We have to get off the boat!" I yell.

"No!" Sheb and Einan shout together. I glare, about to point out that we either take our chances in the water, or die here, but Wriggler bursts from below, showering water over us.

I can't ... he says. I look at his face, my gut kicks painfully. His jaw is lacerated, gums oozing black blood. Despite the water, steam rises from the wounds around his head. *Gives off this acid,* he explains. *Corrosive. Can't get through. Need more rage.*

I could give him more. I could give him enough to blast the weeds all the way to hell, but in the light of Wriggler's sparks, I see the eyes in the darkness move. Slithering, prowling, crawling into the water. Coming for us. There's no time. We need to get to shore.

"Wriggler!" I yell. "Can you carry us?"

Wriggler fixes me with a hard stare. *I'm not a ferry,* he drawls. I smack him in the belly scales—not that it makes much difference to him when he's this size.

"If I die, you die, too!" I point out. "I ain't leaving *anyone* on this boat!"

Wriggler rolls his eyes. *Typical,* he says. Weeds thicken over the boat. Some brush my ankle and a searing pain shoots up my leg. I cry out, slash the weeds with my knife. A creeper brushes Lin's hand and she snatches it back with a yell. In the light of Einan's lamp, I see her wrist redden and blister. Maeve leaps to her defense, hacking at the grabbing weeds with her dagger. It makes no difference.

The only thing holding them back is Sheb and his harpoon. His *glowing, humming* harpoon.

"Get off the boat!" I yell. "Onto Wriggler's back! All of you!"

Einan clings to the gunwale, shaking his head. "No!" he whimpers. "Stay in here. It's safer in here!"

I growl-sigh and grab him round the middle, tossing him onto Wriggler. Maeve and Lin clamber aboard, too, but when Bear makes to follow, Wriggler strikes at him.

I'm not carrying that, he grumps. *That thing can swim!*

"Wriggler!" I yell. "Not *now!*"

But whatever strange energy exists between monsters means I reckon Bear heard. He ain't happy. His fur blackens. White and green fire bursts along his back. He opens his maw and *screams*, sending a pulse of pain through all our heads. He plunges into the water, swiping his massive paws at my lightning snake. Wriggler lunges back, the movement almost throwing Einan into the water.

"Will you two *stop it!*" I shout.

They desist, but Wriggler glares at me. *He started it.*

I *do not* have the time to argue, so I scowl at him until he does as he's told.

"Me and Lin can ride Bear," Maeve suggests. "Then Wriggler can—"

"*No!*" I yell again. "We stay together. All of us! Sheb! Come *on!*"

Bartok flutters down, landing on the crown of spiky scales on Wriggler's head. He spreads his wings, screams a warning. Sheb doesn't respond. Doesn't even look like he's heard me. He keeps stabbing at those vines. Even as the boat fills with water. Even as it breaks up around him. Tears pour down his face.

"I'm sorry," he sobs. "I'm sorry, I'm sorry!"

"*Sheb!*" I yell. I reach for him but he doesn't turn. Still battles the weeds alone. Einan screams.

Wriggler slithers closer to the boat. I grab Sheb by the collar, try to pull him off the sinking boat. Weeds shoot up around us, abandoning the boat, now, in favor of Wriggler's coils. He strikes at them, but the more he bites at them, the more his face bleeds. A tangle of reeds wraps round his wing, tugging it down. Wriggler snarls, lightning lancing along his body. It crackles around the reeds, withering them until they fall away. But more snake from the water, entangling him in a sticky net.

Hurry up, Annie! he yells.

I grit my teeth. What does he think I'm *doing?*

"Sheb!" I yell again. "Leave it! Come on! It—"

I freeze, watching as he jabs at the weeds. As the boat sinks, water gushing around his calves. He can barely stand, but he won't stop.

His face is streaked with tears, twisted with a terrible pain.

"I can't," he sobs. "It's my fault. My fault."

I blink, my belly churning. What's he talking about? Why has he chosen *now* to talk about it?

"Sheb!" I growl. "Not *now!* Come on, we've got to—"

There comes a shout from nearby. A hiss of air and a spear thuds into the sinking boat. For a split second, everyone stops, staring at the quivering shaft, wondering where in Oak's name it came from.

Then there's a pulse of white light. I throw my arm over my eyes to shield them. The wailing of the remnants falls silent. The weeds freeze, as if startled.

There's a boat alongside ours. Bigger. Sturdier. A strange engine, of a kind that looks like it runs off something older and more dangerous than oil, thunders at its stern. It bristles with weaponry. Spikes along both sides. There's a hefty lance at the prow, vicious hooks hanging off the stern.

"What the—" Maeve says. But I don't have time to answer.

Men appear at the starboard gunwale. They're dressed in black uniforms with leather breastplates and gauntlets. They carry wicked sabers and each has what looks like a glowing talisman hung on a chain around their necks. They clutch the talismans, muttering unintelligible words, then slash at the weeds attacking Wriggler. White light flashes where the sabers slice the weeds, and the weeds writhe, letting out this strange scream.

Three men appear among the warriors, shout-ing orders. Unlike the others, they don't wear pen-dants, but carry harpoons.

Harpoons that glow with a faint green light. Like Sheb's.

Their faces are ferocious. They bare their teeth, roaring. They look like they've done this before. And yet ...

They're dressed in black jackets trimmed with gold lace, boots polished to a mirror shine, hair coiffed and beards clipped. These three men look ... noble.

One, the tallest and bulkiest of them, leaps into our boat, landing beside Sheb. He grabs Sheb's arm and hurls him backwards just as a vine shoots from the water. The man bellows, slashes with his harpoon and hacks the vine in half. There's a pulse of energy as his weapon cuts the weeds. A strange kind of magic that holds the swamp back. The weeds shrink from him. He carries a pistol at his hip, too. I ain't seen a weapon like that since I left my own world. The man draws it, shoots at a clump of weeds until they withdraw, then sets about hacking the weeds from around Wriggler's wings. I notice how the weeds shrink as his harpoon gets near them.

I can't do anything except stare. There's something about the three men—their hair, their grey eyes—that feels horribly familiar.

Finally, the burly man chases off the last of the weeds, grabs Sheb round the middle and tosses him into the larger boat.

"Hey!" I bark, sending a pulse of rage to Wriggler. "You let him go!"

The man stares at Wriggler, the gigantic shape of my rage incarnate, and laughs.

"A murk-girl!" he roars. "Typical!"

He swings up from the wreckage of Einan's little boat, lands on the deck of the larger vessel with a thud. Einan's boat finally collapses, sinking. I feel my eyes glowing, rage sizzles along my scar. Wriggler rears, wings flaring.

And then something strange happens.

The burly man straps his harpoon to his back. Surrounded by his warriors and the other two harpoon-wielding men, he grabs Sheb and pulls him into a rough hug. I freeze, which means Wriggler freezes.

For the second time, Maeve says, "What the—?"

Nobody answers.

The burly man releases Sheb, holding him at arm's length. And suddenly, I know why these three men look so familiar. I glance between them, and then back to Sheb. My best friend. My family. At his kind grey eyes, and how they're the same shade of grey as the strangers' eyes.

Oh Oak. I know who they are. And we can't be here. I can't put Sheb through this.

The burly man smiles. It ain't a nice smile.

"Wondered when you'd slink home!" he says. "It's good to see you, little brother."

Chapter Nine

WELCOME HOME, SHEB

I GLARE AT THE man holding Sheb. I don't care if he's Sheb's brother, I see the way my best friend stands rigid in his arms, fists clenched so tight that they shake.

Finally, the man lets go, clapping him on the back. Sheb stumbles forward. The man turns to the rest of us.

"You going to ride on the murk-girl's eel all the way to Marsh Wilds, or are you coming up on this boat?"

Wriggler snarls. *Eel!* he protests. *Annie let me eat him. He's clearly evil. It'll make everything so much easier.*

No, Wriggler, I think quietly. Outwardly, I don't say anything. I can't help thinking how the powerful, intimidating man in front of me sounds like Sheb. That accent, like he's had elocution lessons his whole life.

Maeve mutters something under her breath. Something like, "Bloody dark children all over again."

I'm inclined to agree. Whatever Sheb's brothers think me and Maeve are, it's clear he doesn't like us.

Wriggler swims us to the boat and the burly man helps us aboard. Maeve and Lin go first. I stand, tensed for a fight, as they're lifted in his thick arms. Maeve scoops a cub-sized Bear out of the water as she goes.

As the man reaches down for me, Bartok flutters off my head and into the trees.

"Bartok!" Maeve calls. But he won't come down.

Sheb doesn't react. He looks numb, and my chest constricts at the sight.

Wriggler shrinks to normal size, wrapping himself round my wrist. The huge man lifts me like I'm no more than a doll. As I'm hauled over the side of the boat, I see a sturdy deck, ropes and various other important things neatly stowed by the gunwales. There's a covered cabin taking up space towards the stern, and a heavy, wooden helm is visible inside it. Lanterns hang on the outside of the cabin, casting a fluttering orange light across the deck. There are at least a dozen other men—besides Sheb and his brothers—scurrying about, securing ropes, yelling at each other. I notice they all have those strange, half-glowing talismans at their throats.

One of them—a reedy man with pale blond hair and a scar across his lip—pauses when he sees me and Maeve aboard. His gaze hardens.

"Sir, the murk-touched—" he says. "It's bad luck for them to be aboard. The swamp—"

"—Can boil in its own juices," the burly brother growls without looking away from me. I see Sheb flinch at the words, and frown. The brother sets me down, then folds his arms, chuckles.

"Trust you to find the scrawniest bunch of friends, brother," he says. "Two murk-touched and a rich-looking wench." His appraising gaze makes my skin prickle as if with spider's feet.

Sheb says nothing. When I sneak a glance at him, his gaze is lowered. Blood trickles from his temple to his jaw. He doesn't look at me. Or anyone. Pain scuttles along the scar on my back. Enough to make me think of my Daddy and how he put it there. Enough to make me think about how I ain't never going back to my own world. Sheb probably said the same, once. Yet here we are.

I turn a fierce glare on the burly brother, stood with a sneer on his lips. Look at him, squaring up to the world like it's his to dominate. We'll see about that.

"These *murk-touched* have survived just fine without idiots like you," I spit. Wriggler appears from my sleeve, snapping at the air to punctuate my point. The man laughs.

"Maybe," he says. "Maybe your luck is up." His grin is feral. "Maybe the swamp is hungry for you."

I glare at him, and Wriggler bares his fangs. "Funny," I drawl. "People in the last world we went to said that about me and their Wild Wood. Murk-Touched. Dark Child. Makes no difference to me. Ain't none of it true."

The man quirks an eyebrow. "We'll see," he says, folding his arms.

I fold my arms right back, position myself between this pretender and my family. Wriggler slithers to the deck. I give him just enough rage to let him grow. Nothing serious, just until he's the size of a large dog and his fangs could do some damage.

The two other well-dressed men stood behind—the younger brothers, I'm guessing—shrink back. I see one, slightly taller than the other, with scraped back blond hair and a wicked, zig-zag scar running down one bicep, reach for the harpoon over his back. It starts to glow.

"I wouldn't," I warn him. "Won't make no difference to Wriggler, anyway. Only one way I reckon you can kill a monster like him, and I ain't telling *you* what it is."

The other brother, shorter and more slender with dark brown hair, looks to his older brothers for reassurance. The burly brother laughs again.

"You've got some spirit, girl," he says. "I like that."

I imagine my fist connecting with his nose.

"I'm Ruben de Callis," he says.

De Callis.

I must be a little too slow to control my face because a cruel grin spreads across his. "Heard of us, eh?" he chuckles. "Good. Then you'll know this part of Riverfell is our territory. *My* territory. Here, the swamp does as we command it."

I don't answer. And I resist looking at Sheb. If these men are the de Callis brothers, then he was once one of them. Once shared in their power.

Ruben jerks a thumb over his shoulder at the blond brother reaching for his harpoon. "This is Locke." Then a thumb over his other shoulder, at the dark-haired brother. "And Cheran." Cheran shuffles his feet. He glances at Sheb, trying to catch his eye. I frown. It's like he's trying to warn him of something, but he catches Locke watching and lowers his gaze. Ruben sees none of this. The eldest brother points to the bow of the boat. "That's Nora," he says.

I whip round, knife in hand, as a fourth figure steps into the light. She's slender, diminutive really, with long, shining black hair and light brown skin. Her eyes are hooded, deep brown and watchful. She's barefoot, wrapped in a shawl, but I see the skirt of a grey dress. She looks older than me and Sheb, maybe in her early thirties, but younger than Ruben. She wears a pendant at her throat too, but it's nothing like the strange, talisman-like pendants the men wear. Hers looks like a curved tooth. Only it's bigger than any tooth I've ever seen. As long as my forefinger, serrated down one edge. I look away before I can imagine what kind of creature it came from. She carries blankets and gives one to each of us. She takes particular care to wrap one around Einan, who's huddled at the bow, shaking. She hesitates as she approaches me and Maeve. I see her gaze snap to Wriggler and Bear. Her jaw tightens.

Then, as quietly as she appeared, she glides back to the shadows, sits on an upended crate, her face turned towards the dark water.

I turn back to Ruben. I want to scream in his face. I want to take Sheb's hand, leap overboard and swim back to Nowhere. Something tells me that ain't an option though.

Ruben's grey eyes meet mine. He shows his teeth in a wicked smile, and his attention turns to Sheb. He claps his youngest brother on the shoulder, almost knocking him to the deck.

"Glad you're home, little brother!" he says again. The way he says it makes my skin prickle. "We've got lots to discuss, haven't we?"

Sheb shakes his head, his eyes lowered. "We have nothing to discuss."

Ruben's smile vanishes. "I hope," he growls, "you'll reconsider. I just saved your life, didn't I? Your power clearly isn't what it once was."

Sheb says nothing. Anger flashes in Ruben's face, but he shrugs. "We'll talk," he says. "And I'm sure you'll change your mind."

Before Sheb can answer, Ruben rounds on Locke and Cheran. I notice Cheran take a nervous step back.

"Back to Marsh Wilds, then," Ruben says. He raises his voice to be heard across deck. "Man the oars!"

Locke glances to the engine at the stern, starts to protest. "But Ruben—"

Ruben grabs him by the collar, shakes him roughly. "Oars," he growls in Locke's face. "Or you can swim."

He throws Locke away from him. Locke glares. He looks at Cheran for support, but the dark-haired brother glances the other way, pretending not to have seen. Locke growls under his breath, then turns to the dozen men paused on deck. "You heard him!" he yells. "Move!"

There's a general grumbling among the men, but none of them protest. Locke bullies them below and I hear oars splash into the water. The boat creaks forward. I pull my blanket tighter around me and scan the trees. The mist of half-formed remnants hangs in their branches, but they seem calm for now. A few drift across the water, then dissipate. But none comes for a screaming attack on us. The swamp is still.

I turn my gaze back on Ruben. He's watching me. Smiling.

"Where did you find this one, Shebbie?" he asks, eyes never leaving mine. "She's a right state. Powerful though. I can feel it. The swamp likes her. How long's she been murk-touched?"

He keeps saying that damn word. And his gaze never leaves mine. At my feet, Wriggler hisses.

Just one bite, Annie, he says. *I'll make it quick.*

I won't lie, I'm tempted. Something about Ruben's sneer, the way he talks to his brothers, makes me want to wipe him out of the world. But one look at Sheb tells me it wouldn't be a good idea. I reach for my friend's hand, but he snatches it away. He heads into the shadows at the port gunwale, leans on the railing and gazes at the dark. I clutch my belly. I ain't sure why his sullenness stings so much. Oak knows, I do it to him all the time. Somehow, though, it feels wrong.

"Girls," I say to Lin and Maeve, ushering them towards the bow. "Stay together, yeah? Maeve, keep a tight leash on Bear."

Maeve glowers at me. "I'm not a kid, Annie."

I want to snap that a kid's *exactly* what she is, that she needs to pipe down on her sass, but Nora rises from her crate and glides towards us. The words die on my lips. Nora regards us one at a time, her silent scrutiny makes me shrink inside myself. Wriggler reduces to regular size, coils up at my feet.

Who's she? He demands. I shrug.

Ruben said her name's Nora.

Wriggler flicks his tongue. *Something weird about her.*

You think all humans are weird, I point out. Wriggler huffs and doesn't answer, but I feel his curiosity pulsing down our bond. Nora kneels beside Maeve and Lin, who're both still clutching their blankets. Gently, she takes the blanket from Lin, drapes it round her shoulders.

"The waters are full of cruelty these days," she says. "Spend any time in them and they eat away at your mind. Wrap warmly. We have medicine in town."

I meet her gaze. "These days?" I ask. "Did something change?"

Nora stares at me distrustfully. "I'd expect a murk-touched to know," she says. "Yes, something changed. My husband became Heir."

I don't know what that means, but it sounds ominous. "Your hus—" my eyes widen. "Holy Oak, you mean *Ruben?*"

I can't help the taste of bile that floods my mouth.

"I do," Nora says, bitterly. "Trust me. It wasn't by choice. He's been trying to spread his control across the swamp since Sheb left. Since he inherited his father's power. And he's succeeded. But the swamp is furious, and even more dangerous because of it."

I open my mouth to ask more, but Maeve nudges me into silence. Nora's face is full of pain. She turns away, and I watch as she tucks Lin into the blanket, strokes a stray lock of hair from the girl's face. "You're a powerful one, aren't you?"

Lin blinks at her, nonplussed, but Nora doesn't seem to need a reply. She goes to Maeve.

"I can do it myself," Maeve snaps, but doesn't resist when Nora wraps the blanket round her. She even makes sure there's space for Bear to crawl onto Maeve's lap. Then, she turns to me.

What does she think she's doing? Wriggler squeaks as Nora takes my blanket from me. I want to protest, like Maeve did, that I'm perfectly capable of wrapping myself in my own damn blanket, but I can't find the words. And when Nora's arms encircle mine, I can't help but close her eyes, breathe in her warm scent of nightfall and waterlilies. She tucks the blanket round me. For a moment, if I keep my eyes closed, it's not Nora embracing me, but my mother. That hair, the same scorch-black as mine. Those eyes, soft as summer clouds. Her quiet gentleness. Her smile.

But when I open my eyes, it ain't my Mum standing there, is it? It's this woman I don't know. I stare at her dumbly.

"Sit," Nora murmurs. "The waters can make you dizzy."

"No, I'm—" *Fine,* I'm about to say, when the boat lurches. I lose my balance. The world bucks beneath me and I stagger. Wriggler hisses, striking at nothing. A sturdy hand grips my elbow.

"Easy," Nora says. She's surprisingly strong, taking both my arms and lowering me to the deck. Wriggler slithers onto my lap, glaring.

I don't like her, he says.

I roll my eyes. *You don't like anyone.*

Wriggler says nothing, only flicks his tongue against Nora's hand. To my surprise, she takes the hint and shuffles back, watching me until my vision swims back into focus. She smiles.

"My husband doesn't understand your creatures," she says, gesturing first to Wriggler and then to Maeve. "But I do. You should go back."

I bristle. "We ain't come all this way to turn back now," I snap.

Nora's eyes darken. "We will get you to Marsh Wilds, get you the medicine you need, and then you must *leave.* All of you. You aren't safe here. And here isn't safe with you."

I throw her a withering glare. "Trust me, lady," I say, "we ain't safe anywhere. We come from—"

"I know where you come from," Nora says, touching the tooth-pendant at her throat. "I know where Sheb has been. And he should go back. You should all go back."

Maeve and Lin stiffen, sitting up straight. Maeve scowls.

"We ain't leaving," she says. "We're here to fight the bone crow."

Nora looks at her. There's something like pity in her eyes. She turns her gaze from me, fixes it on Sheb. He turns slightly, like he can feel her watching, but doesn't want to meet her eye.

"No, murk-girl," Nora says, still watching Sheb. "If you stay, you die."

Chapter Ten

A Town at the Edge of Darkness

It takes ages before we reach civilization. The swamp is thick with trees and hanging vines, branches tangling in a wild canopy overhead. The water is mercifully still, though I keep an eye out for weeds.

Annie, Wriggler mutters at some point, slithering to the starboard gunwale. *The trees.*

What about them?

I join him, peering into the dark. At first, I don't know what he's on about. Then, moonlight crosses one of the gnarled trunks and I see it. A strange carving, like a circle with a diagonal slash through it, a crude eye carved in the middle.

I blink. A cloud drifts across the moon and the carving disappears, but I can't help the way the back of my neck prickles.

The pendants, Wriggler says. I wish he'd stop speaking in shadows and half-sentences and just say what the hell he means!

I heard that, he says, fixing me with a beady glare. *Look at the pendants, for Oak's sake!*

I throw him a filthy look, then snatch glances at Ruben's men as they trudge from below to take breaks from the oars. Wriggler's right. The damn pendants they're wearing carry the same symbols.

We should ask her about it, Wriggler says, looking in Nora's direction. She hasn't moved from her seat since she told us we were all going to die.

I ain't overly keen on talking with her.

Annie— Wriggler says.

Leave it, I snap, and return to Maeve and Lin. All I want is for the four of us to survive. Mysteries, monsters, and remnants be damned.

I pace at the bow, glaring at Nora, at Ruben and his brothers. No-one pays me the slightest attention. Sighing, I lean over the gunwale, stare at the water. Something brushes my fingers. I look down and realize there's some fabric caught in the boat's wooden planks. I reach over and pluck it free, frowning. It's a little black bow, like one you'd find on a pretty dress or a pair of shoes. What's it doing on Ruben's boat? Daft thing for anyone to wear in a place like this. I toss it overboard.

The town of Marsh Wilds is so camouflaged amongst the foliage that I don't realize we've drawn close until we're in it. Silent houses loom from the murk on stilts, wooden verandas jutting in front of their chipped and faded doors. Boats—mostly slender rowing boats—are moored outside, or drifting quietly across the water, their inhabitants peering at us with haunted eyes. Wooden walkways spiderweb between houses, creating arched bridges where they cross the swamp, so boats can pass beneath. The outskirts are quiet, and the people seem scared. They start and draw knives as we pass, staring with hard expressions until we're out of sight. I notice they're dressed for wading. Waxed overalls, thick boots, hair tucked into caps that cover their ears, scarves tied over their mouths and noses to keep the flies out. They carry nets and fishing poles over their shoulders, yell at each other in thick, gruff accents with rolling vowels. They walk hunched, eyes downcast. As we head further into town, the houses cluster closer and the townsfolk grow more animated. Still, they talk in hushed tones as they bustle across the walkways, carrying goods. There is a strong smell of fish.

As we glide under one bridge, I glance up to see the dawn-lit face of a woman staring at us. She's older, with a lined face and silver-grey hair tied in a braid over one shoulder. She's not dressed like the other townsfolk. No overalls or cap. Instead, she's draped in a grey shawl over a woolen dress and sturdy boots, but there's a rigidness to her spine, a tilt to her chin that makes me think she could handle herself in a fight. One hand is lifted to her throat, cradling a pendant that looks like a serrated tooth.

The same as Nora's.

Her green-eyed gaze locks with mine. Her jaw tightens. A jolt passes through me and I feel Wriggler sparkle. Maeve stirs beside me.

"Alright, Annie?" she asks groggily.

"Yeah," I lie. "Go back to sleep."

I glance at the bridge again. The woman is gone.

Dawn turns the town grey as children scurry across the walkways, getting in everyone's way. Parents grab them by their collars and yank them to heel, hissing warnings and pointing to the trees, where remnant-mist hangs between the branches.

"Don't wake them!" I hear a gaunt-looking woman scold a scrawny girl I assume is her daughter. I narrow my eyes as we pass.

This town is weird, Wriggler says as I scoop him up. *And I hate it here. No cracklemice to eat.*

I'll count that as a blessing, I tell him.

Fog hangs over the water. Doors open and men and women wander onto their verandas, watching with suspicious eyes as Ruben's soldiers emerge from below deck, fire the engine.

I glance towards Sheb, willing him to catch my eye. He doesn't. He hasn't moved since he pushed me away, just hunches over the gunwale, glaring into the mist-draped waters. I want to go to him.

Leave it, Annie, Wriggler says.

I scowl but do as he says. If anyone here knows Sheb even a tiny bit better than me, it's Wriggler.

Back before I came to Nowhere, Wriggler and Sheb had a bond of sorts. I don't know what it meant, why it happened, or how Sheb managed to break free without hurting himself or Wriggler. It's how he was able to see what was happening to me when Wriggler was still the Oraqua.

Only now, it looks like Sheb's got monsters of his own dancing through him. I bite my lip and taste blood.

I don't care if I have to get Wriggler to wrestle Sheb back to Nowhere. My mind's made up. We ain't staying. Not this time. Whatever's happening here, it's beyond us. And I'll be damned if I'm letting my family get eaten by some monster in this soulless place.

Wriggler nudges my hand. *Good luck with that,* he drawls. *You're here, now. And there's monsters to fight.*

I glare at him. *So?*

So, I know you, Wriggler boasts. *You'll stay.*

I'll leave, I argue. *Soon as we get the medicine. Just watch.*

Alright, Wriggler says, his laughter tinkling in my brain. *I'm watching.*

I shoot him a glare. *You're evil.*

I'm you, Wriggler retorts, then sticks his head under his wing to snooze. I roll my eyes and fall back to watching Sheb. He keeps his harpoon close. It's still glowing with that green light. Ruben keeps looking at it, his scowl deepening.

The boat stops and the engine cuts out. Cheran jumps onto a narrow, wooden jetty outside a huge old house. I stare at it, wonder why the hell Ruben brought us here. It must be easily the biggest house in the town, its long, wide veranda leading down to a boathouse, complete with two small vessels, on one side. It's three floors tall, boards painted a white that's faded to grey with neglect. Its windows are shuttered. The whole place stinks of age. And something else. I notice the mist around the house is thicker, paler, than in the rest of the town. Faces form in it. Smiling. Laughing. Sobbing. Then dissipate. The place hums with a strange energy that makes me feel nauseous.

Sheb stirs, looks up at the house. His face pales.

"No," he says. "Not here. I can't."

I reach for him, but he steps away. I let my hand fall to my side, don't know whether to feel furious or terrified.

Ruben claps Sheb on the back. "No-one here now, Shebbie," he says. "Ma died a year after you left. Pa, a few months after." He fixes Sheb with a cruel smirk. "You'd have known that if you hadn't run away. He might even have named you Heir. Too late now."

Sheb flinches from Ruben's touch. "He'd never have named me Heir," he murmurs. "Even if he had, I wouldn't have wanted it."

The smirk falls from Ruben's face. "We all wanted it, Sheb," he growls. "It's what we were born for. What we were promised. But now I have it and you don't. And you know what that means."

Sheb shakes his head. "You're wasting your time," he says. "I won't change my mind."

Ruben's jaw twitches. "You will," he says. "You'll see reason. We'll talk when you're rested. I've had Nora make up the rooms for you."

Beside me, Nora stiffens, her fist clench. I cast her a sideways glance. Something tells me this woman wasn't meant for domestic servitude, and Ruben putting her to it is insulting. Hell, I feel insulted on her behalf.

Sheb backs away from the gangplank. "I can't go back into the place," he whimpers.

Ruben gives him an impatient shove. "Sleep here," he growls, "or in the boat. Your choice."

Sheb gives his brother such a hateful glare that my breath catches. He trudges down the gang-plank. Me, Maeve, and Lin follow, tailed by Bear and Wriggler.

I stare at the old house with new understanding. This is where Sheb grew up. This *massive* house with its three floors and its boathouse. I think back to what he's told me about his life before Nowhere. His father, a frightening presence that terrorized his five sons. A mother who shrank herself to make room for her boys as they became men. Sheb was the youngest of five brothers. Sensitive and gentle in a world that punished him for it.

And the way it tried to fix him only shattered him further.

I reach for Sheb again. This time, he doesn't pull away, but I feel him tense as my fingers brush his arm. For a moment, the hardness in his face falls. I see the pain in his eyes and look away.

Nora ushers us inside as Sheb's brothers unmoor the boat, fire the engine. Cheran glances up, pushing his dark hair from his eyes.

"Sheb!" he calls. Sheb pauses, looks back. Cheran says nothing, but I see him shake his head slightly. Sheb's jaw tenses, but whatever Cheran's trying to say to him, he doesn't respond. He turns, marches into the house. I frown. Too many se-crets. I see Einan's face peering over the gunwale, eye wide and fixed on mine.

"Where are they going?" I grumble. Nora watches them leave.

"Einan must go home to his parents," she says. "And Ruben will have to talk to his warriors about the portal. It's been acting strangely for a while. Ruben and his brothers have been unable to pass through it. He put wards up to stop any-thing coming in, but you're here, which means they aren't working. He'll need to strengthen the wards."

I frown. *Is that what those symbols are?* I wonder into Wriggler's mind. *Wards?*

Wriggler flicks his tongue. *How should I know?*

"What's the portal to Ruben?" I demand, though I've got a horrible feeling I know.

"He's the guardian," Nora says. I nod, frown-ing.

Thought as much.

Why is it always the most terrible men who get to guard those precious portals? My daddy back in my world, Krogan in Maeve's, and now Ruben. I don't know much about the portal guardians, or how they're chosen, but it seems like they only pick the worst. I don't say as much, though. It's weird that the portal won't let him or his brothers through if he's the guardian.

Why does he want to get through, anyway? Wriggler points out. *It's only Nowhere on the other side.*

I frown, but don't answer, pushing that thought aside for later. Instead, I look up at the old house.

"Why doesn't Ruben live here if his parents are gone?" I ask. "It's easily the biggest house in town—"

"Ruben had his own manor built, closer to the Deep Swamp," Nora says. She doesn't sound happy about it. "Anyway, the remnants are drawn to this place. Too many memories. Too much pain."

I raise an eyebrow. "But you'll let us stay here?"

Nora looks at me, unsmiling. "Two murk-touched, a *very* powerful young woman and the youngest de Callis?" she says. "The remnants aren't what you should be scared of."

I open my mouth to ask her to explain, but my legs buckle. I almost fall, but someone catches me. I look up to find Sheb, his gentle grey eyes meeting mine.

"Easy, Annie," he says.

"Thanks," I reply. "Dunno what's wrong with me. Must be tiredness."

"It's the swamp water," Sheb says. "It's affecting you. We'll get you some medicine." I smile my thanks. He still looks distant, but he's there, arm wrapped around my waist as he guides me inside his childhood home.

My mouth falls open.

"It's—"

Magnificent.

I mean, it's draped in dust, a fog of spiderwebs coating the ceiling and walls. But still *magnificent*. We're in a grand hallway, the floorboards creaking beneath our feet. A stately staircase ascends to a grand-looking landing above us, a small staircase behind it leads down to what I reckon were the servants' quarters. On this floor, doors stand open to more rooms both left and right. Sheb leads into one such room with a ridiculously huge fire-place, vases so coated in dust I can't see what color they are, and furniture covered with white cloth. A huge chandelier hangs above us. I scowl at it. I can't square this opulence with the friend I've known for five years.

Sheb throws open a window to let out the damp smell, then helps me sit on a deep, wing-backed chair. I groan, my stomach threatening to empty itself.

Maeve turns in a full circle, frowning at the ceiling. "This place feels weird," she says. "Like it's—"

"Buzzing," I finish, voice thick with the effort of not throwing up. There's a faint hum at the back of my head, like a fly rattling around my skull. I try to shake it loose, but it only makes it worse. Wriggler curls up on my lap.

This place is broken, he says.

I'm concentrating too hard on not vomiting to ask what the hell he means.

Maeve and Lin don't look great, either. Maeve flops into a chair that matches mine, face ashen.

Lin slides down one wall and puts her head between her knees.

Sheb looks fine. Why does Sheb look fine?

Nora disappears into the hall. I hear her footfalls on the floorboards before she reappears, carrying several small, crystal vials. In each, a pale, green liquid glows gently. She hands one to me.

"Drink," she says. "All of it."

I'm too dizzy to argue, though when I un-stopper the bottle, the stench is almost enough to empty my stomach. I take a deep breath, tip the liquid down my throat.

"Urgh," I gasp, then claw my throat as it burns.

"Easy," Sheb says, grabbing my wrists before I leave welts across my collarbone. "Deep breaths."

But I can't. Can't breathe. My throat feels swollen, constricted. My eyes bulge, my tongue swells. I thrash against Sheb's hold.

And as quickly as it came, the sensation is gone. My throat tingles. I take deep, delicious gulps of air. I slump forward, moaning. Sheb rubs my back.

Well, Wriggler huffs. *I'm not drinking any of that.*

I ignore him and watch as Nora helps Maeve, then Lin, take their medicine. Their reaction is the same as mine. That momentary choking, followed by relief.

"You'll likely need more medicine," Nora says. "But that should hold off the effect of the waters for now. There's a supply of it in the old servants' kitchens. Despite Ruben's blustering, the beds haven't been made ready, but there are blankets and linen in all the rooms. Are you hungry?"

I realize I am. Ravenous. Maeve and Lin clearly agree because they nod emphatically. Nora inclines her head. "Stay here," she says. "Keep the door closed. I'll be back soon."

She leaves. I hear a vessel being unmoored from the boathouse, oars slicing through the water. We're alone, stuck in a house full of ghosts, in a town run by a bully, surrounded by water that will kill us if we touch it.

Great.

Lin and Maeve snuggle up on Maeve's chair, their faces death-pale. Bear clambers up alongside them, mewling. Sheb paces, moody and tense.

"You want to sit down?" I ask him.

"No," he says.

I chew my lip, wondering what else I can offer. But he looks lost again. He clutches his harpoon. It still glows faintly.

We stay like that for ages, me and the girls huddled in miserable silence while Sheb stalks back and forth. Nothing stirs. There's no sound of a returning boat.

We're so lost in ourselves that the sudden screech from outside makes us all jump. Sheb raises his harpoon. Wriggler leaps to the floor, three times his usual size. Maeve, Lin, and me are on our feet, reaching for our weapons.

"Oak's *sake!*" Maeve grumbles, when she realizes what it is. She flops back into the bed. "I can't cope with this!"

The rest of us lower our weapons, too. It's only Bartok. I'd forgotten he'd flown off. Now, he sits happily on the railings of the veranda, gulping down the remains of some poor swamp rodent. He flags his squirrel tail, chirps, then buries his beak under his wing to sleep.

'Least someone's happy, Wriggler drawls.

I don't say anything, just watch Sheb as he heads onto the porch, leans against the railings next to where Bartok sleeps. He's so quiet, so sad. I don't know what to do, and that makes me furious.

I get to my feet.

"Where you going?" Maeve demands.

"I can't just sit here," I tell her. "I'm looking around."

"Is that what Sheb would—" Maeve protests, then stops at the look on my face. "Fine. Yep. Go ahead. See you later."

I head out of the living room, glance down the hall, then decide I'll tackle the stairs. They're coated in a threadbare old carpet that muffles my footsteps.

The landing is dark, but even in the gloom, I see the paneled, painted walls, hung with the portraits of serious looking men in serious looking clothes. There are at least a dozen doors off this landing, leading to rooms upon rooms. I shove my way through one door on the right. It creaks closed behind me and I stop dead at the sight of the massive room. It's gloomy, heavy blue drapes blocking the light from the window. A square table dominates the center, cracked scrolls piled on one edge. Rows and rows and *rows* of bookshelves line the walls, stuffed to bursting with dusty tomes.

Sheb's old family house has a bloody *library*.

Chapter Eleven

THE DEATH-ROAR

For a moment, I just stand there, jaw open, looking at books upon books upon books. I ain't ever seen so many in one place! It's damp in here, and some of them look moldy. A few pages are scattered across the floor, their edges curled, ink fading. I stare as I wander between the shelves.

My daddy couldn't read, and didn't think Mum should be able to, either. She read to me whenever he wasn't around, but it was Sheb who taught me to read. I'm still not great at my letters, but I'm ten times as good as my daddy ever was. Good enough that, when I wander between the shelves, tracing the gold lettering on the spines, I can make out most of the titles.

A History of the Five Families

Swamp Beasts and Their Habits

The Murk-Touched and the Dangers They Pose

I bare my teeth at that last one, almost snatch it out to read, but Wriggler rumbles in my mind that it would be pointless. I move on before I'm tempted to tear the tome to pieces. I stumble a little, then catch myself on the shelves, waiting for a wave of dizziness to pass. Whatever that swamp water did to me ain't settled yet. I take a few deep breaths, trying to shake the buzzing at the back of my head.

On the next shelf, a huge, heavy book bound in blood-red leather catches my eye. Its gold lettering is elaborate and it takes me a while to read the title. When I do, my eyes widen.

The Complete de Callis Family Tree

My fingers grip the spine, tug out the book before I think what I'm doing. Would Sheb want this? Maybe not. Still …

I march the book to the table. There's mildew on the back cover and some of the pages are stuck together, but I manage to ease it open, spluttering as a cloud of dust and spores flies off the pages.

Wriggler bats the cloud away with his wings. I stare down at an illustration that covers a two-page spread.

It's a family. A huge man with cruel eyes and a clipped beard stands at the center, staring at me like he hates me. He's dressed in leather armor, vambraces strapped to his arms, and a black cape billowing behind him. He grasps a harpoon in one hand. Next to his head, in copperplate lettering, is the name, *Deimos. Heir of de Callis.*

Beside him, there's a woman. She's so small next to him, it looks like she might suffocate in his shadow. She, too, stares out from the page, un-smiling. She's wearing a simple shift-dress, but she has vambraces strapped to her arms, too, and her blond hair is thrown in a braid over one shoulder. There's a ring on one finger with what looks like a dark stone set into it. Next to her is the name, *Luana.*

I jolt when I see she's wearing a necklace that looks just like Nora's. That curved, serrated tooth …

Look at the children, Annie! Wriggler prompts. I do.

They're dressed like miniatures of their father; leather armor, with small harpoons clasped in their little hands. I recognize a boy-version of Ruben, puffed up like his father, though his eyes look scared. I see Locke smirking, Cheran with red cheeks. And two more boys. The youngest. In this drawing, they barely look eight years old.

My lips part. "Oh."

I stroke my fingers across the face I recognize. That floppy hair, gentle grey eyes, a smile that could calm a howler horse.

"Sheb."

I don't know why the sight of him as a boy makes my eyes burn, but it does. He's so sweet and carefree here. Whoever drew this picture must've loved him like I do. They've been tender with every curl of his hair, every shadow in his face.

And the other one? Wriggler asks.

My eyes shift to the remaining boy, standing next to Sheb. My heart constricts. He's just like Sheb, but ... not.

Same floppy hair. Same grey eyes.

But his face ...

It's like someone took my Sheb—my beautiful, gentle Sheb—tore him to pieces, and made him up again out of shadows and anger. This boy's smile is forced, full of malice. He's the only one not looking out from the page, but snatching a glance at his brother. There's something off about the look on his face.

"I didn't realize Sheb was ..." I start.

"A twin?"

The voice makes me jump. I knock the book off the table. It lands with a thump face down on the floor. My cheeks heat. I stare guiltily at the open door, where Sheb now stands.

"I ..." I say. "I'm ..."

"It's alright, Annie," Sheb sighs. He straps his harpoon across his back, goes to throw open the curtains. I blink against the sudden light as Sheb picks up the book, replaces it on the table. From his shoulder, Bartok glares. I make a rude gesture at him. He clicks his beak, affronted.

Sheb smooths the page, pointing at the brother who looks like him, but not him.

"Jeelie," he says.

Ice fills my gut. "The one you ...?" I start, then can't finish.

Sheb chews his lip, nodding. "He's buried in the family plot in the graveyard." He touches his brother's face, a faint, sad smile playing on his lips. "We didn't always fight, you know," he tells me. "He didn't always hate me. When we were very young, we were close. I used to distract Mama while Jeelie stole her cakes from the kitchen, and we'd sneak out on one of the boats to eat them." His smile disappears. "It's only when we got older that things started to go wrong."

I don't say anything. What is there to say? I watch Sheb's face as he scans the rest of his family portrait. He runs his fingers over the face of his mother. "It's my fault she's gone," he says.

I start to shake my head, then stop. How can I possibly comfort him about that, when I think the same about my own Mum? The one who left me twice, because I'm so hard to handle.

"She didn't deserve all the pain we put her through," Sheb say. "That's probably what killed her, in the end." He smiles. "She kept a lock of my hair in that ring," he says, pointing. "Just mine. She never told the others, but I reckon Jeelie knew. Maybe that's part of what made him hate me, in the end. It used to drive him to distraction. He always said I was her favorite."

I quirk a smile. "You probably were."

His smile fades. "Probably," he says. "But I was never my father's."

I watch him as he studies the picture. His fingers hover above the image of his father, ruthless and cruel.

"Deimos," he says. "Guardian of the Riverfell portal, the de Callis Heir, and the most powerful since our first. I wonder what killed him in the end?"

I say nothing. It ain't like my own father's death was simple, either. My gaze slides to the harpoon on his back. It glows faintly.

"Does everyone carry one of those harpoons?" I ask. "Are they ...?" I don't know why I can't bring myself to say the word *magic,* like it's some sort of dirty secret. Maeve and I wield magic through our monsters. Lin's power is magic.

I guess I always thought of Sheb as untouched by it. Pure, somehow. Seems silly, really.

Sheb shakes his head. "Only members of the five families carry harpoons," he says. "And each design is different."

He swallows. I see his throat bob. "It's hard," he admits. "To talk about."

I clench my fist against a wave of impatience. We don't have *time* for Sheb to find this hard. We need answers, or we need to go home. Sheb was determined to bring us here in the first place. The least he can do is admit what we're up against.

But I think about my family. My vicious daddy. My disappeared mother. The town that almost killed me. What if I was back there? What if it was my history being dragged into the light like this?

I stand quietly, say nothing. Just wait, which seem the safest thing to do.

Sheb turns the page, unstraps his harpoon, and holds it out to me. He points to the join where the barbed blade meets the shaft. I squint, then my eyes widen.

"It's the de Callis crest," Sheb says. "It channels the magic I have in my blood. That each of my brothers does, too. Our direct link with the swamp."

I stare at the silver circle inlaid into the shaft of the harpoon. I've seen it before. The circle with the diagonal slash through it, containing an eye. Just like the carving on the tree.

Like the talismans worn by Ruben's men.

"Years ago," Sheb says. "Pa used to say four hundred, and maybe that's true. I don't know. Anyway, however long it was, Riverfell was an impossible world to tame. The swamp is full of magic. It's a living thing, it has a temper. It was angry and vengeful, and humans could only survive as nomads, scraping by on flotillas, trying to avoid the swamp's notice. Some lucky individuals had some form of taming magic, but nothing that could protect more than a few dozen people.

"Then, the story goes that four brothers were born with immense power. Vane, Jormund,

Grayling, and Howl. Somehow, the brothers' magic was so strong that it fought back the swamp, binding the wild magic enough that humans could build towns. Kingdoms."

He shakes his head. "I don't know if this is true," he says. "It's just what I was taught. The four brothers had sons, and they had sons, and they became the four families. These families were able to establish territories, where their magic held sway over the swamp."

He holds up the book on a new page, showing a map of Riverfell. It's a labyrinth of waterways and tributaries, islands and lakes all tangled together. But I see dotted lines marking territories to the north, north-west, east and south. Sheb starts pointing.

"The Vane family control the north," he says. "They're the biggest. Most powerful. They're allied with Jormund in the north-west. Then Grayling is in the south, Howl in the east. Their magic holds the swamp at bay, taming the wild magic so towns can exist. Without the families, humans wouldn't survive here."

He places the book on the table. I frown at the map. "But you said there were five families," I point out. "What about ..." *Yours.* I can't say it. "What about the de Callis family?"

Sheb gives a mirthless smile. "We weren't meant to exist," he says. "We're an aberration." He points to a small territory I hadn't seen, right in the south-west corner of the map. It's barely a third of the size of the Vane territory, only big enough for three towns. "Perhaps a century ago, the Heir of the Vane family, I think his name was Astrus, took a mistress and had a bastard son. Everyn. He was a Vane, but he also kept his mother's name, too, after the Vane family imprisoned her to keep her silent. Everyn Vane de Callis. He inherited some of his father's power. A lot of it, actually. More than was expected. Families have to name Heirs. Whichever one of their children they choose will inherit the strongest, most potent share of magic. Once an Heir is named, and the rest of the family pledge fealty, the magic of any siblings is dimmed. It's still there, but not as strong.

"Astrus thought he could control Everyn's power by naming his oldest legitimate son as Heir. But Everyn refused to swear fealty, and his own power only grew. It was unheard of. Astrus thought Everyn was too much of a risk and tried to kill him. Everyn fled."

Sheb points to the spaces on the map between the marked territories. Places that seem darker, more drenched in shadow.

"There are parts of Riverfell the families don't control," he explains. "Where their magic doesn't reach. We call it the Deep Swamp. It's a wild place where the magic of the swamp has full reign. The creatures there are vicious, so is the plant life. The waters are full of power, even the rain holds a toxic magic." His fingers brush a small island right in the center of the map. "This is the heart of the swamp," he says. "The deepest, darkest, most dangerous part. Where the wild magic is at its most untamable. No Heir, even the strongest, has been able to control the beasts and plants in that place. Everyn fled there, knowing Astrus couldn't follow. He fled with a woman he loved. He was the first de Callis Heir. For some reason, the Deep Swamp didn't hurt him, but let him pass. Pa told me it even sent a guard of creeperscorps to protect him as he fled from Vane."

His finger sweeps across the map, past the heart of the swamp, to de Callis territory. "They managed to make a home for themselves here," he continues "In the place that became Marsh Wilds. They had children and their children had children, and occasionally outcasts and exiles would find their way here. The town grew, and people spread out and made other towns."

He shakes his head.

"The other families never recognized de Callis as a legitimate family, or agreed that our territory is our own. Both Vane and Jormund think we should become a vassal state of Vane's territory. Grayling would back Vane on anything it wants and Howl is staying out of it. Pa was a terrible tyrant, but he did manage a kind of peace between the de Callis territory and the other families. Now—"

He shrugs, and says nothing, closing the book.

"Now, Ruben is Heir," I finish.

Sheb flinches. "Yes," he says. "Though he hasn't come into his full power yet. Not all his brothers have sworn fealty."

I frown. "That's what he was on about on the boat, isn't it?" I say. "He wants you to swear fealty. He needs your pledge to come into his full power."

Sheb nods. "But I know him," he says. "I see him. What he's truly like. I know what giving him that power will mean. If he wants my pledge, the only way he'll get it is the way he got Jeelie's—through death."

He falls silent. I stare at him. At my friend who, until five minutes ago, I'd thought of as just a grubby, excitable man who happened to carry a harpoon.

Now, I know he holds an old, deep magic in his blood.

He's basically a kind of *prince.*

It explains a lot. But it also begs more questions.

I almost ask, *why didn't you tell me?* Then shut that thought off. There's loads Sheb doesn't know about my past. He never asks. I'm grateful that he doesn't. It's not fair of me to demand answers from him when I ain't willing to give them myself. Instead, I try to smile.

"Thanks," I say. "For ... sharing that. I know it ain't easy."

Sheb doesn't look at me. "No," he says softly. "It isn't. And something's ..." he chews his lip. "Something's not right," he says.

I frown. I mean, no shit. Something is very definitely *not right* with this place.

"We should go," I mutter.

At the same time, Sheb whips round to face me, says, "Can't you feel it? You must be able to, you're—" He stops himself, but I see the words start to form before he can stop them. I scowl.

"If you even *dare* call me murk-touched," I warn, "I swear, Sheb, I'll lose it."

The ghost of a smile plays on Sheb's lips. "Dark child or murk-touched," he says. "If I'm right, you'll be able to sense it. The wrongness. The thing that's broken. Listen."

He closes his eyes. I watch him, wondering what the hell he's on about. My legs still feel wobbly, my brain buzzes and I can barely stand up. I ain't got time for games.

Listen, Annie, Wriggler urges. *Stop stropping and just* listen!

He's so urgent, I glance down at him to make sure he ain't growing. He's not, thankfully, but his scales are a weird kind of sparkly.

With the history of magical families, wild swamps, and betrayed brothers whirling round my head, I sigh and do as Sheb and my lightning-snake demand. I close my eyes, open my mind, and listen.

It happens instantly.

A wave of nausea barrels through me. I feel it. That *wrongness* Sheb's going on about. It's like a shadow on my periphery that ain't there when I turn to look. Like the smell of lightning sizzling the damp air after a storm, when you know it's not quite over yet, the world is just taking a breath ready for when all hell breaks loose. I can smell it. The violence of this universe. Like teeth in the night. It feels like something's taken hold of my skull, squeezing. I crush my eyes closed, clench my teeth against the onslaught. My ears hum, then *thunder*, like a mighty swarm of insects has woken in my brain. I shake my head, hit the heel of my hand against my temple, but nothing gets rid of it. I feel ... death.

That's what this is. The roar of billions of flies come to feast on rotting flesh. The stink of necrosis. The hideous stillness of corpses, and the itch-inducing industry of bugs that call them home.

I feel them crawling on me. Their tiny, insistent jaws biting. Feel the poison of death. The stink. The closeness.

No. Get away from me!

The world pitches sideways. There's a crash, and the nausea is gone. I open my eyes and realize I'm sprawled on the floor, a throwing knife in each hand. The book's beside me, pages bent beneath the heavy cover. Wriggler is coiled on my chest, mantling me with his wings. He hums softly. The vibration sends a wash of calmness through my bones.

It's alright, Annie, he says, his voice in my head strangely comforting. *Open our bond wide. I'll dampen it. You're okay.*

Sheb offers me a hand, pulling me to my feet. His smile is so sad.

"Maeve will feel it, too," he says. "Whether or not the swamp is responsible for sending Wriggler to you, it's certainly the case that murk-touched—or dark children, as Maeve calls them—are more sensitive to those kinds of energies."

I taste bile in my throat, fight against the urge to gag. Sheb retrieves the book from the floor once again and smooths it on the table. He stares at the island in the map's center. The heart of the swamp. "It's my fault," he says. Tears film his eyes. "I caused this. I murdered my brother and then I ran. I left them to face the consequences. Whatever my father did—whatever Ruben did—maybe I could've stopped it. I could've—"

He's trembling. Pain bolts across his face like lightning. My heart stutters. What do I do? How am I supposed to save him from this?

Ask him what he sees, Wriggler suggests. *Always works for you.*

It's a good point. I grab Sheb's face with both hands. "Tell me something you see," I tell him.

Sheb's eyes meet mine, tears streaming down his face. "My best friend," he says. His face crumples. "My best friend who I brought into danger. I'm sorry Annie."

He starts to sob.

"No," I say. "That's not—" This isn't the way it's supposed to go. "You have to try to see good things!" I tell him. "That's the whole point!"

Annie, Wriggler warns. I feel my rage flooding him. It's not *fair!* How is Sheb able to calm me but I can't do the same for him? This is supposed to work!

"Tell me something good you see!" I demand.

But Sheb only shakes his head, backing away. He stumbles against a bookshelf, slides down it until he's on the floor. He drops his harpoon. I can't do anything except watch my best friend fall apart, my rib-cage tight with helplessness.

This ain't right. I'm failing, and I don't know why.

I sit next to him, trying not to let his pain infect me. There's nothing to do except wait for him to finish crying. Which he does, eventually. He looks raw from the effort, but he wipes his nose on his sleeve.

I don't know what to say, don't know how to fix this. So instead, I ask a ridiculous question.

"D'you think the bone crow is causing this?"

Sheb shrugs. "I don't know," he says. "There are rules to the swamp's magic, the balance between the Deep Swamp and the blood magic of the five families. If those rules are broken, the magic itself breaks. It would happen in the swamp's heart, first, but very few people can venture there and live to tell the tale." He pauses, frowning. "It feels like that's what's happened, though. Like the balance of the swamp has been upturned. Which means—" he stops himself, biting his lip. I frown, but don't push. Not yet.

"If we're right," Sheb says, "and the Corvos is a monster like Bear and Wriggler, it'll have a human.

It's one half of a murk-touched. Murk-touched are dangerous, but they don't break the magic."

I scowl at him. He smiles apologetically. "Look, Annie, I'm just telling you what I know, okay? For my people, the murk-touched are both a blessing and a curse. The five families have their magic—their warriors are the Heirs and their siblings. The swamp has its magic, and its own warriors. But the murk-touched are a bridge. They contain the magic of both the families and the swamp. They feel the energies of both. They shouldn't break the magic, they should mend it."

Right. Except I've just felt that hideous death-roar rip through my skull. So, if the bone crow didn't break it, what did?

We're here to fight a monster, Annie, Wriggler reminds me. *We know how to do that. Everything else is just noise.*

I take a breath. "Alright," I say. "Let's look at what we know. From what Einan described, d'you think the Corvos is a Serpentine or a Hot-Blood?"

Sheb frowns. "It's hard to tell without having seen it," he says. "Einan said it had scales on its tail, and it had wings. Wriggler has wings. Maybe a Serpentine? But Einan described it more like a bird. And its power ..." he shakes his head. "He said it showed him visions. That doesn't sound like Serpentines or Hot Bloods. Wriggler controls weather. Bear controls elements. The Corvos sounds like it controls—"

"Minds," I finish, my gut curdling. Holy Oak, this mess gets worse the longer we're in it.

Sheb nods. "Exactly," he says. "Maybe I'll have a clearer idea when I see it." He reaches for one of his notebooks, opens it, stares helplessly at a blank page. I can't take it. I grab his hand.

"We'll work it out," I say. "You'll know more when we ... when we find it."

Sheb nods but doesn't look at me. I lean my head against the bookshelf, close my eyes for. The smell of ink and old paper is a comfort. If I imagine hard enough, I can almost believe it's the smell of Nowhere. The trees, the leaf litter, the smoky smell of cracklemice poking about in the undergrowth.

But the image shatters as soon as I blink. I ain't in Nowhere. I ain't home. I'm somewhere dark, broken, dangerous.

"D'you think Einan's right?" I whisper. "D'you think the Corvos is Zuma's? She's …" I make myself say it. "Murk-touched?"

Sheb shrugs. "I don't know," he admits. "There's pain in my family. And they're good at inflicting pain on others. The truth is, Annie, it could be anyone."

Great. So, where the hell do we start?

There's a creak on the stairs. Me and Sheb glance up to see Maeve and Lin in the doorway, Bear stood between them with his tongue lolling out. He gives an excited yip when he sees me. I smile, but Wriggler rumbles in my brain.

Sycophant, he drawls. I raise my eyebrow.

Didn't know you knew such big words, I tease.

Wriggler swears at me, slams our bond closed to sulk.

I turn my attention to the girls. They both look pale, eyes glassy with sickness. Lin leans heavily against the door frame.

"Urgh," Maeve says. "I don't think this medicine is working."

"It won't be," I say. I explain what Sheb told me about the magic. Maeve flops to the floor.

"Well that's just bloody great, ain't it?" she says. "I want to go home."

Lin kneels beside her. They lace their fingers together.

"I do, too," I admit. I glance at Sheb. He says nothing, but I know that look. He might want to go home, might want *us* to go home, but he thinks this is his fault, so he'll stay to fix it.

I take a breath. "We'd best solve this mystery, then," I say bitterly. "And even if the Corvos might be anybody's, we got to start somewhere. We should find Einan's parents."

Maeve wipes sweat from her forehead. She looks exhausted but determined. "Alright," she says. "And if the little toe-rag is hiding anything, I'll—"

We all freeze at the sound of the front door opening. Soft voices drift up the stairs. I stiffen.

Nora's back.

Chapter Twelve

Eyes in the Water

Nora pauses in the doorway. There's a saber strapped at her hip, a crossbow across her back, and a pile of fresh, folded blankets in her arms. She stares at us in turn. Her jaw tightens, like she realizes what we've decided. None of us meets her gaze. She hands the pile of blankets to Maeve.

"One for each of you," she says. "The fireplaces are substantial, but the remnants are drawn here at night. Even the fires can't always get rid of the cold."

She unhooks a bag I hadn't seen from her shoulder, produces several vials of glowing medicine from her pocket.

"There's enough medicine here for a few days. Over time, your blood will get used to the water."

None of us answers. Nora's eyes rake the dusty shelves of books. My gaze lingers on the tooth pendant at her throat. I wonder who the hell this woman is. She doesn't seem like the meek wife I'd expect someone like Ruben to choose. "I won't discuss anything more with you in this room," she says. She stalks downstairs before we can answer. The rest of us exchange glances. Maeve shrugs, gets up to follow.

Downstairs, we gather in the living room. Maeve and Lin sink into the winged armchairs but Sheb remains standing, so I do, too.

Nora glares. "My advice is still to leave," she says. "You will die if you stay."

"No," I say, quietly. Something tells me we ain't got a choice, anyway. We're here now. We can't turn back. Not until we see this—whatever it is—through to the end.

Nora's eyes soften, like she's read my thoughts. She holds the bag out to me. I take it.

"There's food in there," she says. "Bread, some flasks of water—not swamp stuff. Pure. Make sure you eat and drink."

I open the bag and look inside, finding three flasks of water and two loaves of tough-looking bread.

"Thanks," I say, wrinkling my nose.

Nora turns and meets Sheb's gaze. "There's someone I'd like you to meet," she says, looks towards the open door. "Kai? Come meet your Uncle Sheb."

Sheb stiffens. I see a bunch of emotions fight each other on his face. There's a shuffle, and a diminutive figure appears in the doorway, clinging to the frame. A boy, maybe eight or nine years old. He's got the same light-brown skin as his mother, with silky, black hair that he keeps having to push back from his eyes.

Those eyes, though. I recognize that grey. Full of life and curiosity. He's got Sheb's eyes, only there's something not right about them. Where Sheb's eyes are usually full of laughter, this kid's full of suspicion. He watches us, unsmiling. He's wearing a shirt that's too big for him, tucked into black pants and boots, like Ruben's soldiers wear. There's a small harpoon strapped across his back.

Ice crackles through my veins. This is Ruben's firstborn son. Currently the only Heir to his power. Nora beckons him.

"It's alright," she says. "No need to be scared."

Kai shoots her a glare. "I'm not *scared,* Mama," he says. "De Callis boys don't get scared."

I tense, fists clenched. Nora folds her arms but says nothing.

At my feet, Wriggler flares his wings. *Arrogant little twerp,* he says. *Want me to—?*

No, I say, before he can finish. *You are not biting the kid.*

Wriggler huffs. Kai stares at him, then at me. His little brows bridge together. He points to Wriggler.

"He yours?" he asks.

"He's me," I say. "And I'm him."

Kai looks at me nervously. "You're a murk-touched."

I roll my eyes. "So I been told."

Kai scowls. "We don't need you here," he says, drawing himself up to his full two-and-a-bit feet tall. "My Pa will fix the swamp by himself. The de Callis way. We don't need swamp maidens and murk-touched to sort it for us."

Behind him, his mother stirs, but says nothing. I'm about to ask him what the hell he's on about, but Kai spots Bear, cub-sized, by Maeve's feet. He brightens. "Can I pet him?"

Maeve scowls. "I wouldn't," she says. Kai clenches his fists.

"Don't tell me what to do," he says, stepping forward. "I'll pet him if I want."

Maeve raises an eyebrow, her gaze locking with mine. I give the smallest shrug. Let the little know-it-all find out for himself what happens when he pets a monster.

"Kai," Nora says, warning in her voice. Kai ignores her, reaches for Bear. Lin signs frantically, but Kai ignores her, too. I notice Sheb hasn't moved. Has said nothing. He's watching Kai like he might watch a baby howler horse learning to conjure shadows for the first time.

Bear's lip wrinkles in a snarl as Kai's hand draws closer. "Calm down, cub," Kai commands.

On Sheb's shoulder, Bartok hoots nervously. Nora says Kai's name. Kai doesn't respond.

His fingertips brush Bear's fur.

And then Bear isn't a cub anymore. He's five times the size, rearing as he swipes the air with mighty claws. His fur is black as night, eyes burning. His massive horns catch on the ceiling and he roars, the sound catapulting through our minds. Everyone claps their hands over their ears.

Kai falls to his knees, screaming.

"Maeve!" I yell. "Get him—" I blink. "—under control," I finish lamely.

As quickly as he became the monstrous god-bear—the Krazka—that I met a few weeks ago, he's shrunk to cub-sized. He sits on his haunches, running his pink tongue over his teeth, staring at Kai as the kid curls into a ball and cries. Maeve folds her arms, a smile curling her lips. I glare at her.

Wriggler's laughter clatters in my brain.

It's not funny! I tell him.

It's hilarious, Annie, he counters.

Nora rushes to her son. She rubs small circles across his back until he pushes her off. "Stop it!" he snaps. "I'm not scared! I wasn't—"

"You were," Maeve says. "And you should'a been. Bear and Wriggler ain't pets. But you already knew that, didn't you? You don't listen to me in future, I'll let him bite you."

Kai glares at her, but his lower lip trembles. "I'm not scared of a stupid *murk-girl!*" he says. Maeve's jaw tightens. I fight not to let my growing rage flood Wriggler. It ain't working. He's dog-sized already, and sizzling.

"You should be," I growl.

Kai rounds on me, clearly intending to say something scathing, then he catches sight of my eyes and stumbles back. Wriggler grows until he's pony-sized. I know my eyes are glowing scarlet. Uncertainty flashes across Kai's face. He glances at his mother, then seems to remember he doesn't need her. He unstraps the harpoon from his back. It glows faintly.

"Don't come any closer," he growls. "I'll kill you."

I open my mouth to tell him to stop being such a rude little squit when the floorboards beside me creak. Without a word, Sheb strides onto the veranda. He disappears from view, though I still hear Bartok's grumbling commentary drifting back to me.

My heart kicks. I turn on Kai.

"The *hell* is wrong with you?" I growl. Kai's lips part in surprise but he holds his ground.

"Nothing's wrong with *me!*" he whines. "It's not my fault Uncle Sheb is such a loser—"

Anger ignites every nerve in my body. Bloody light from my eyes illuminates the dark floor. I take a menacing step towards the kid. Scarlet lightning snaps across Wriggler's scales. Lin's signing at me, trying to catch my attention, but I don't care.

"Call him that again," I growl, "And I'll—"

"It's not *me* that called him it!" Kai protests. He drops his harpoon and falls on his backside in his haste to get away. Nora steps in front of him, hand on her saber hilt. She glares at me. I peer round her, fixing my gaze on Kai.

"Who then?" I snarl. "Who says that?"

"Pa," Kai says, the thought clearly giving him strength. He gets to his feet, retrieves his harpoon. "Pa says it, and everyone knows he's right."

I dart past Nora, grab Kai's shirt before I can think what I'm doing. "Your Pa," I say. "Can go—"

"Annie!" Maeve barks, a warning in her voice. I blink, realizing I've got an eight-year-old kid by the collar of his shirt. Tears stand in the boy's eyes but he stares at me like he wants to kill me.

"Let him go," says a voice at my shoulder. It's Nora. She's got my arm in a vice-like grip, her saber now half-drawn. I forgot some mothers actually stick around to defend their kids. I drop Kai's shirt, step back.

Nora rushes to Kai's side, checking him for injuries. He glares at me, wiping angry tears from his eyes.

"I hate you!" he says, with the kind of petulance only a kid his age can manage. I raise an eyebrow.

"Yeah?" I drawl. "The feeling's mutual."

I don't look at Maeve or Lin, though I know they're staring at me like I've lost my mind. I'll deal with Maeve later for letting Bear off his mental leash. Silly girl. Dangerous. Reckless.

Still, she called him back down, didn't she? She wasn't the one who nearly hurt Kai.

No. That was me.

"Maeve, get our things ready." I fix Nora with a steely glare. "We're gonna talk to Einan's parents. You can help us or not. Your choice. But don't get in our way."

Nora blinks, smiling faintly, like she knows something I don't. I ain't fond of that look.

"I won't get in your way," she promises. "But I won't help you either. You've made your choice, and I have my own. I will find Xanni and help her in the Deep Swamp. That's all you need to know."

I frown. It's clearly *not* all I need to know, is it? I raise an eyebrow at her, but she doesn't elaborate.

Wriggler flares his wings in warning. Nora barely reacts. She touches her tooth pendant with one finger.

Whatever.

I stalk past all of them without a backward glance. My pulse thuds in my ears. The ever-present rage rolls in my core. I can't look at Nora, or her son. I can't look at Lin or Maeve. I need to find Sheb.

The only person who knows how to ground me.

Except, when I find him on the veranda, he doesn't look in any state to give me comfort. He looks far away. Broken. Lost. Leaning against the railing with his head bowed. On his shoulder, Bartok gives an anxious hoot, calling me over.

I hesitate. I don't know how to do this. I don't know how to be the one who grounds, rather than the one who needs grounding. But I can't just walk away from Sheb, can I? Not when he's hurting.

I check my throwing knives are in their sheaths. No idea why. For some reason, it gives me comfort.

"C'mon, Wriggler," I say.

Sheb doesn't look up when I approach, or when I lean on the railing beside him. We stand together, quietly. After a time, I reach for Sheb's hand.

"Hey—" I say.

But Sheb pulls away. I feel like the world has been torn from under my feet. I stare at my hand on the railing, waiting for Sheb to take it. But he never does.

My anger kicks again, that way it always does when I've got no idea how else to feel. I'm trying, ain't I? How am I supposed to help if he won't let me?

"Fine," I snap. "Have it your way."

He doesn't answer. My rage flares.

"I'm going with the girls to talk to Einan's parents. We're fighting your battle with you, Sheb. If you even care."

I turn to head back to the house. Furious with him. Furious with myself. Behind me, Bartok squawks indignantly. I feel Sheb's hand on my arm, trying to hold me back.

"Annie—" he says.

But whatever he's going to say is cut off. The water beyond the veranda explodes in a catastrophic silver spray, drenching me and Sheb. Bartok shrieks, bursts into the sky. Me and Sheb drop to the veranda floor, arms over our heads. A snapping, reptilian head crashes through the railings and clamps around Sheb's arm.

CHAPTER THIRTEEN

THE SWAMP BEAST

SHEB REACTS QUICKER THAN I've ever seen. With a war cry, he twists, ramming his foot into the beast's snout with such force that the thing lets go. Sheb whips his arm from between its teeth, cradles it against his chest. He leaps to his feet, reaching for his harpoon.

"Sheb!"

I scramble to my feet, palm a throwing knife in each hand.

"Stop!" Sheb yells, like that's ever worked with any beast we've fought. Then he says, "It's me! You know me!"

I frown. What?

The creature rears from the water, gaping its massive jaws. The size of it makes me freeze. It's like nothing I've ever seen (and I live in Nowhere. I've seen a lot). A huge, sinuous, lizard-like body, glittering with tough green and black scales that make it perfectly camouflaged in the swamp water. Its long, reptilian snout is wrinkled in a snarl. Those teeth, dagger-like, glint in the morning sun. My stomach twists. I've seen fangs like that before.

It rakes vicious claws across what's left of the veranda railings, snapping at Sheb. He jabs it with his harpoon. A blast of power throws me backwards. I crash into the wall as white light sears the back of my eyes. I blink, half-blinded, grope for my knives.

"What the *hell*, Sheb?" I groan.

"Little busy, Annie!" Sheb announces. He's trying to fend off the monster but, for some reason, he's not trying to hurt it. He stabs his harpoon but holds back a few inches so the barbed tip never touches the beast. Every time the tip gets near, his harpoon brightens and rings as if in warning.

"Stop it!" Sheb begs again. "You *know* me! I'm not my brother!"

The swamp-beast either doesn't believe him or doesn't care. It snorts steam. The putrid stench of rotting meat—what's left of its last meal, I reckon—makes me gag. I notice two sets of eyes in its head. Dark. Vicious. Mean. The creature hurls itself out of the water, stalks across the veranda. Sheb backs away, still jabbing at it, but I see his eyes widen.

There's a shriek from above and a fluffy, purple bullet shoots from the sky. Bartok collides with the beast's head, thumping his feet above its eye. The beast hisses, snapping at Bartok and narrowly missing his squirrel tail. Bartok hoots in fear and pulls away. He hovers, screaming in frustration.

I come to my senses.

Wriggler!

On it.

My lightning-snake is already a monster. Scarlet sparks crack off the huge crown of horns across his head. His scales have lightened to green and crackle with power. He beats his wings—now massive—and smacks the swamp-beast across the head.

Come and get me, you overgrown toad! He roars.

I've got no idea if the swamp-beast hears him, but it reacts like it can. Hissing, it rears back and slashes Wriggler's underbelly. My lightning-snake screams as the beast's claws split his scales. I suck in air, feel an echo of his pain across my ribs.

"Maeve! Lin!" I yell, throwing both my knives at the beast's head. "Stay inside! Keep Nora and Kai away!"

I don't know why I bother. Obviously, they all come rushing out.

One of my knives misses, but the other lodges in the soft flesh just behind the beast's second set of eyes. It yowls and arches back, giving Wriggler a chance to grab its throat. But the beast's too quick. It twists free, hurling Wriggler over the railings and into the water. It bats at the knife stuck behind its eye, but the blade's lodged in place.

"Holy shit!" I hear Maeve yell. Bartok takes another dive at the beast and, with a speed I hadn't thought possible, Lin manages to swipe him out of the air. She cradles him against her chest, despite his outrage.

The swamp-beast drops to all fours, fixes its beady eyes on its prey. Sheb.

I leap in front of my friend, flick my remaining knife into my hand and brandish it like a sword. "Come on then!" I snarl. "Come at me!"

The beast doesn't even look at me. With a massive, taloned paw, it swipes me aside. For a second time, I smack against the wall, the impact blasting air from my lungs. I crumple in a gasping heap. The beast keeps its eyes locked on Sheb as it advances. With what's left of my breath, I holler, trying to get its attention. It ignores me. It's after Sheb.

And only Sheb.

Wriggler! I scream. *Where the hell are you?*

He erupts from the swamp in a volcanic spray of water, wings spread wide, a vision of hell itself.

Poisonous green light falls across the veranda, and I turn to see Maeve's eyes glowing, face twisted in a snarl. Bear expands to monster form.

"Maeve!" I splutter. "Calm him down!"

She's never listened to me though, has she? She ain't about to start now.

The swamp-beast snarls as Wriggler crashes into it, twisting and grabbing the joint of Wriggler's wing. Wriggler shrieks, and so do I as I feel my snake's muscles tearing, flesh peeling from bone. Wriggler thrashes, but the swamp beast holds him fast. I leap forward, stabbing the creature's tail with my knife, but the blade skitters off its tough scales. It spares me a cursory, backward glance, then flicks its tail. It catches me in the gut. I go flying, crashing into the swamp water beyond.

I burst through the surface, my black curls plastered to my forehead. I swim for the veranda, haul myself up in time to see that Maeve's let Bear loose. Like Wriggler, he's monstrous. Green and white fire burns across fur so black it consumes the light. He shrieks, the sound crashing through my brain.

"Maeve!" I cry, clutching my head. "For Oak's sake, will you—"

I catch sight of Nora's face in the doorway. Hard. Determined. There's a saber in her hand as she strides onto the veranda, only looking over her shoulder to firmly tell Kai to *stay put.*

For once, he obeys.

"Nora!" I growl. Why is *everyone* determined to leap in front of flesh-eating beasts today? "Get back inside!"

Nora ignores me. Instead, she grabs my arm and pulls me to my feet as Bear crashes into the swamp beast like a battering ram. I hear a crunch of splitting bone. The swamp beast yowls, releases Wriggler's wing. Our monsters turn on the swamp beast, jaws agape.

"Call your creatures off," Nora says beside me. I stare at her.

"What?"

"You heard me," Nora says. She's not looking at me. Her eyes are fixed on the swamp creature, now gasping for breath at one end of the veranda, waiting for Wriggler and Bear to end it.

"But—" I start.

Nora shoves me behind her and strides across the veranda, placing herself between Wriggler and Bear, and the injured swamp beast. Wriggler and Bear look at us, confused. I hear Wriggler's voice in my head.

What the hell?

I scowl at Nora. *Your guess is as good as mine,* I mutter. *Just do as she says.*

Grumbling, Wriggler backs down. He shrinks, but not all the way. He's still pony-sized as he slithers across the veranda, mantles one wing over me. Bear shrinks, too, and wanders back to Maeve, no larger than a wolf. Maeve scratches him behind the ear. I glare at her. We will be having *words* about this, later.

Nora kneels beside the swamp-beast. Its black lips ripple in a snarl, but it doesn't try to attack her. She leans close to its head and—

My mouth falls open.

Is she ... *talking* to it?

Carefully, Nora grasps the hilt of my throwing knife, tugs it out of the beast's head. The beast snarls again. It aims a cursory snap at Nora's face, but she moves back to avoid it, and it's clear the beast didn't mean it. With a last, half-hearted swipe at Sheb, the injured beast slithers into the swamp.

We stare over what's left of the railings as the ripples on the water settle. The beast is gone. I round on Nora.

"What the *hell?*"

"Hell is right," Nora says, handing my throwing knife to me. She sheaths her saber. "We call those creatures hellgators. They are the keepers of the swamp. They are vicious, yes, but intelligent. And they're as old as the magic of the five families. They are the swamp's defenders."

I raise an eyebrow. Nora half-smiles.

"When the five families first discovered their power, you can imagine they were greedy, trying to take more than their share. They drained parts of the swamp so they could build cities, killing the creatures that live here. The swamp didn't like that. It fought back. It ... recruited ... some warriors of its own."

"The hellgators," I breathe, thinking that *recruited* seems a strange choice of word.

Nora nods. "Indeed, they are some of those warriors. They are the antidote to the magic of the five families and they uphold a tentative truce.

No Heir, or any member of his family, may kill a hellgator. And no hellgator may slay a member of the five families. If they do, the truce is broken, the swamp will release its magic, and there will be war."

"That sounds—" I start.

Glorious, Wriggler finishes. I glare at him.

"But that doesn't make sense," Maeve points out. For once, I agree with her.

"If the hell-things aren't s'posed to attack Heirs, why did it go for Sheb? *It* was going to kill *him!*" I point out.

Nora's gaze turns to her brother-in-law. A strange look crosses her face. I can't work out if it's hatred or pity. Maybe it's both. Sheb can't hold her gaze. He lowers his eyes as he straps his harpoon across his back.

Lin releases Bartok and the owl-squirrel swoops to his customary position on Sheb's shoulder. He glares at us all, as if we're to blame. Figures.

"Sheb—" I start, but Sheb raises a hand to silence me.

"Leave it, Annie," he says. He heads inside without looking at me.

I raise an eyebrow at Nora, waiting for an explanation. She doesn't give one.

"Let's go inside," she says. "You'll need more medicine."

I throw up my arms in frustration. Nora ushers Lin and Maeve into the house, then disappears to wherever-the-kitchens-are to retrieve more vials. We endure another dose of the awful stuff but it doesn't seem as potent as last time. Maybe it's the fight still blasting through my blood. My frustration at this whole, stupid situation. I don't know whether to cry or scream or break something.

Try doing them all, Wriggler suggests as he shrinks down. *One of them's bound to work.*

Maeve grimaces as she downs the vial of medicine.

"Well," she says. "I guess that could'a been worse."

I round on her. *"How?"*

I agree, Wriggler pipes up. *How?*

Maeve blinks at me. "I mean ..." she says. "Nobody died? The hellgator went away? I'm glad me and Bear were there to help."

I close the gap between her and me in two quick strides, only just manage to refrain from grabbing her by the collar. "You and Bear need to *pack it in!*" I snarl. Maeve holds up her hands.

"Woah! Okay! Last time I checked, it was Bear that got the hellgator to let go of Wriggler! We *helped*, Annie!"

"You put yourself in danger!" I shout, feeling the familiar rage coursing through me. It feels good. Comforting. Bloody light falls across Maeve's face as my eyes glow. At Maeve's side, Lin starts signing furiously. I think I catch signs for *fairness* and *calm* and *think* but my head's in too much of a muddle to work out what she's saying. I know I'm not being fair. Maybe Maeve did help, but it was such a foolish thing to do. She's still only a kid! And if I can't keep my family safe—if they have to step in to help me and Wriggler in situations like that—

Well, what use am I, in the end?

I could do with Sheb, right now. A gentle hand on my arm. A soft voice calling me *dear Annie*, asking me what I see and hear.

But there's no hand on my shoulder. No soft voice in my ear. Sheb's lost somewhere in his past. When I turn to him, there's such sadness in his eyes. How am I supposed to do this without him? How can I do *anything* without him?

Beside Maeve, Bear's fur bristles. He takes a swipe at my ankles and Wriggler hisses, striking at him. The pair fall to bickering, though neither are big enough to cause much damage. Maeve and I are too exhausted to flood them with rageful energy.

Maeve rolls her eyes. "Oak's sake, Annie," she snaps, adopting my usual curse. "*You're welcome, by the way.*"

She stalks past me, calling Bear to heel. Lin shakes her head at me. She follows Maeve as the two of them head upstairs.

Sheb drops into an armchair, head in his hands. Bartok hoots and turns accusing, tawny eyes on me.

Great. Once again, I'm everyone's favorite fuck-up. Like this day could get any worse.

I catch Nora watching me. Kai's hidden behind her skirts, still ashen-faced and silent after the attack. Nora clasps her hands, face inscrutable.

"Stay inside," she says. "Rest. I'll be back this evening with food."

I fold my arms. "If you think we're—" Nora holds up a hand and, to my astonishment, I shut up.

"I won't stop you searching for the Corvos," Nora says. "No-one will. But I will warn you again, if you stay, you will die."

She glances at Sheb. Their eyes meet and something meaningful—something I don't like—passes between them.

"It's not too late to turn back," Nora says. "This evening, I can take you to the portal."

She turns, Kai at her heel, and disappears. I hear her footsteps descend to the boathouse, the thrum of a boat engine as they leave. We're alone.

Great, I think into Wriggler's head. *That went so bloody well, didn't it?*

Wriggler oozes around my feet, checking the damage the hellgator left on his scales.

Oh yeah, he drawls. *So well. We smashed the hell out of that gator, you and me. Such a brilliant decision, Annie.*

I blink at him. Seriously? Is even my *monster* pissed off with me?

What's your *problem?* I demand.

Wriggler fixes me with his beady stare. *Annie, you're so clueless, sometimes,* he says. *So predictable. Let's fight the stupid swamp beast alone! What a great idea? Maeve and Bear can stand and watch like idiots while we wrestle a hell creature the size of a tree.* He butts his head against my ankle. *It's alright for you, you're not the one it scratched half to pieces.*

I scowl at him. *When you get hurt, it hurts me, too!* I point out.

Lucky you, Wriggler snaps. *Guess who's lost a bunch of scales and now has a torn wing? Is it you? No. What a surprise!*

He slinks into a corner to sulk. I'm left standing in the middle of this confounded house, no-one in my ridiculous family willing to talk at me.

Which means I can't even tell anyone that the stupid pendant at Nora's stupid throat is very definitely a hellgator tooth.

How the *hell* did she get one of those?

Chapter Fourteen

A Storm in the Family

No-one mentioned how bloody *hot* it is here when the sun reaches its peak. Biting things skitter in clouds above the water, sweat clings to me like a second skin. The air's so humid, I feel like I'm stewing alive as me and Lin fumble with the moorings of the boat Nora didn't scoot off with this morning. The knots are tight, unfamiliar, and I keep catching my nails in the rope.

"Dammit!" I yell, sucking at the finger where I've just torn the nail halfway off. "What the hell is wrong with this stupid rope?"

Lin rushes to my side, gently opening my hand so she can inspect the injury. She smiles at me. It's clearly not bad, is it? I've had worse. Lin cleans it with something that stings, then wraps a thin bandage around it. She signs. I catch the gesture for *fine* and one that I think means *clean* or *safe*.

"Thanks," I mutter, glaring at the rope.

Wriggler, lethargic in the heat, oozes across the wooden dock. *I'll sort it,* he growls, and starts tearing at it with his teeth.

Maeve appears in the doorway, stretching like a cat. "This heat!" she moans. "Are we nearly ready?"

Bear is at her feet. I glare at him, then her.

"You wanna help with these ropes?" I snap, then regret it. I close my eyes, take a breath. "Sorry," I say, more softly. "This bloody heat,"

Maeve quirks an eyebrow. "Yeah," she says. "It sucks. Sooner we catch whoever's driving the Corvos, sooner we can go home."

I clench my jaw, don't say anything. Maeve kneels beside me, helps Wriggler untangle the now shredded rope.

"Is Sheb coming?" I ask.

She shakes her head. "Says he's got stuff to do." She frowns. "He's not okay, is he? We should talk to him. Maybe if we—"

"No, Maeve," I snap. "Look, Sheb's got his secrets and that's okay. I never ask him."

Maeve rolls her eyes. "That's 'cos you're scared he'll ask you about *yours*," she says.

I bristle. "It is not!"

"It completely is," Maeve insists, ignoring Lin's frantic signing at her that she really ought to shut up. "And what good are Sheb's secrets if they're gonna get him hurt? We need to know, Annie. We should—"

"Maeve!" I bark, slapping the gunwale hard enough that my palm stings. Maeve falls silent. "Just ... *leave it*, would you?"

Maeve scowls at me, grumbles under her breath. I get the impression she very much is *not* going to leave it, but at least she stops arguing.

I look at Lin. She shrugs, then signs something that looks like she's coming with us. Probably a good idea. Me and Maeve might kill each other if we're left alone. Maeve goes to help her empty old netting out of the bilge. They chatter and sign, laughing together.

Bear paws at Wriggler's scales. Wriggler snaps at him. Me and Maeve both scold our monsters and our eyes meet. I realize how this has become an automatic response. We've spent so much time together these last two weeks. Learning together. Frustrating each other. Failing, then trying again. She gives me a small, embarrassed smile, then returns her attention to Lin.

It occurs to me as we clamber into the boat, that it's been less than three weeks since Maeve relived the murder of her mother. Since we tripped over the bones in the catacombs underneath her town. Since the truth came out about how the Order of the Dread King killed her parents to keep their vile secrets. I think back over that time—the time we've spent training together, learning together—and can't remember if I've asked Maeve if she's alright.

If she's sleeping okay. If she dreams. If she ever laughs sometimes, then feels guilty about it. If she walks alone in the woods of Nowhere so she can find somewhere private to scream and scream, knowing no-one will hear her.

Maeve tugs the engine chain. It roars to life. When she faces towards the swamp, the smile falls from her face. I see the echo of pain there.

Pain I know well.

"Are you—?" I start. But the word *alright* seems stupid. I clamp my mouth shut, avert my gaze. Maeve shrugs.

"Sometimes," she says. "Sometimes not. But that's okay, I guess." She puts an arm round Lin. "I reckon I'm allowed to be a mess after what happened." She pauses. "It ain't easy. Sometimes ... sometimes it really hurts, you know? My heart *actually* hurts. This throbbing ache in my chest. It hurts so much I can't get comfortable. Nothing will shift it and ... I just have to wait for it to pass. It always does pass, in the end."

I tighten my grip on the gunwale, keep my gaze fixed on the water.

"Yeah," I mutter. I mean, what else is there to say?

"How about you?" Maeve says. She faces me, one arm still round Lin's shoulder. Her gaze takes me in, appraising me. No idea why, but it makes my hackles raise.

"What about me?" I ask, gruffly.

Maeve gives a sad smile, shakes her head. "Annie," she says gently. "You know, you don't have to—"

I round on her. Can't help it. Something flares in my core and, for a moment, I think it's rage, but when I look at Wriggler, I see he's shrinking. This ain't rage I'm feeling, it's panic. Whatever she's about to say, I can't hear it. Can't take it.

"I'm *fine,* Maeve!" I snarl. "Holy Oak, why is everyone always *pestering* me? I'm fine! I'm completely alright. I'm totally, utterly ... *fine!* Okay?"

Maeve and Lin look at me like I've just sprouted a second head. Bear bats Wriggler's wing. Wriggler snaps at him. Me and Maeve don't say anything.

A darkness passes across Maeve's face. For a moment, I think she might yell at me. I square my shoulders, ready to feel the lash of her fury.

And it hurts that I feel disappointed when she holds up her hands in defeat.

"You know what?" she says. "Fine. Whatever. You don't wanna talk. No surprise there. Just ..." she looks at me, those eyes drilling into parts of me I've long kept hidden. I squirm under her stare. "I'm not a kid, Annie," she says. "I haven't been a kid for a long time. I've been taking care of myself most of my life, remember? You can trust me."

I roll my eyes. I've got a host of replies to that.

Things like, *Did you forget you almost killed Wriggler yesterday?*

Like, *When are you going to stop playing grown up and just do as you're told?*

Like, *Trust? I don't trust anyone.*

But Wriggler, back to his usual size, nudges my ankle before I can speak. Maeve shakes her head. "Let's just get this visit to Einan's out the way, yeah?"

I scowl, but she's turned away, whispering with Lin. I grip the gunwale as we push through the town, my pulse clattering in my ears.

Townsfolk pause to watch as we pass. Children throw things at us, which plop into the water, making our boat rock. They cackle, scurry away. I scan the bridges and walkways, and jolt when I see that old woman stood outside a small house. The same woman who glared down at us from a bridge as we entered Marsh Wilds. She's glaring again, now. I notice she has a fresh bruise across one side of her face, a nasty cut under her eye. She clutches a grey shawl round her shoulders, her silver-white braid sparkles in the high sun. Her gaze is sharp and unyielding, but I can't help looking at her throat, where that tooth pendant hangs.

The tooth I know belonged to a hellgator.

Her mouth moves. She lifts a finger, pointed at me. I think I see her lips form the words *murk-touched*. I drag my gaze away. I couldn't care less what she thinks of me. Daft old hag.

I scoop Wriggler up, drape him round my neck. He rasps his scaly head against my cheek. *Sometimes, Annie,* he drawls. *You really are an idiot.*

"Yeah?" I whisper, flicking the tip of his nose. "Well, you *are* me, Wriggler. So what does that make you, eh?"

Wriggler chuckles. I keep my gaze fixed on the water, occasionally glancing at the trees, where the remnant mist has thinned in the sun, but hasn't gone completely.

I tell myself I'm keeping watch over my ridiculous family.

It's got nothing to do with fear.

I'm Annie, ain't I? Monstrous and terrible and dark.

I'm not afraid of anything.

"Anyone actually know where Einan lives?" Maeve asks.

I blink. It's a very good point. But Lin smiles and signs something that looks like she's done her homework. Thank Oak for Lin. She takes us past islands with houses sprouting from them, down a left-hand tributary where the swamp splits into numerous, interweaving streams. Here, the houses cluster together, some nestled on top of each other, with steep wooden walkways leading between them. It looks like there's been a storm. Debris litters the water. Huge branches half-blocking the route downstream. Boats putter across our path and Lin has to concentrate to avoid crashing into any. I see men and women on the banks as well, hacking at branches and foliage that clog the water. They stop and stare as we pass.

I notice a few of Ruben's men strutting about, too. Their talismans shining at their thrust-out chests, their black uniforms and leather armor standing out among the loose cotton shirts and waxed overalls of the regular townsfolk. The soldiers don't wear overalls and seem keen not to get their precious uniforms wet. They shout orders, but never actually do anything useful. Lin guides us to the bank where one of the soldiers barks at a group of men and women clearing branches from the water. Maeve leans over the gunwale.

"Hey!" she says. "Sir?"

The soldier turns. I recognize him. The reedy blond man from Ruben's boat, who objected to *murk-touched* being aboard. I glare at him.

"What?" he says.

"We're looking for a kid called Einan?" Maeve says. "We need to talk to him."

The man scowls. "My son doesn't talk to murk-touched," he says. He turns away but one of the women clearing branches straightens, staring at us.

"Einan?" she asks. "Is he okay?"

The blond soldier snarls. "Hush, Yarella!"

Yarella throws him a filthy look. "Talk to me like that again, and we'll see which of us is the better fighter," she snaps.

My jaw drops in surprise.

Yarella abandons the branch she's been trying to shift, comes to stand beside the soldier. "What's happened to my son?"

I blink, my gaze darting from Yarella to the blond soldier and back again. Oak, is *she* married to *him?*

I stare at her. Her raven-black hair, secured in a loose braid, falls over her shoulder. Her face is weathered, but still sparkles with energy. Sweat shines on her black skin. Her eyes are so dark, I can barely see the pupils. Under her waxed overalls, she wears a long-sleeved blouse that looks like it was once white but hasn't been for a long time. I'd think she was a simple fish-wife, except she's got a saber strapped to her hip.

And a pendant at her throat. A hellgator fang.

Yarella smiles at me. "This is Lucius," she says, nudging her husband. "Yes, we're married. No, I'm not happy about it. Now, about my son—"

"He's fine!" Maeve says quickly. "As far as we know, he's fine. But he mentioned … he mentioned his sister."

Yarella's arms fall to her sides. Lucius shakes his head.

"I don't have time for this," he growls, turning his back on us. Yarella grabs his arm. Her grip is surprisingly strong.

"You'll make time," she says. She looks at him and her eyes seem to darken until they are pools of black. Lucius glares, but, to my surprise, does as she says.

Lin signs something and Maeve translates. "She wants to know what happened here."

Yarella shrugs, arms folded. "The swamp's getting angrier." She points beyond the mass of debris blocking the water. "Further out that way is Deep Swamp, beyond de Callis control. Ruben's magic can't reach that far. It's where the swamp's heart lies. Ruben keeps trying to push into it. The swamp doesn't like it. It fights back. But obviously, he doesn't care that branches smash houses and innocent folk are injured or killed. He doesn't care when Creeperscorps and fanged eels slither from the Deep and attack us. He couldn't give a flying f—"

"Yarella!" Lucius growls. He scowls at me. I scowl back.

"You one of Ruben's men?" I ask. I point at his talisman. He covers it with his hand.

"What of it?" he says.

I shrug. "Just interested. Those talismans seem powerful. I thought only the sons of the five families carried that sort of magic."

Yarella shoots Lucius a vicious glance. "They do," she says. "They *should.*"

Lucius snarls. "And Ruben believes that magic should be shared!" he snaps. "Among those he trusts. He's imbued these talismans with a sliver of his magic. They are a sign of that trust. It means we can carry his influence beyond him, get the swamp under control."

Yarella shakes her head. "Ruben is playing with something he doesn't understand—"

"Be still, Yarella!" Lucius hisses. He glares at us, like this is our fault. "You had questions about our daughter. Ask them and go."

Well, now I've got questions about a million other things, too. Like how Ruben managed to imbue those talismans with his family magic. Like what he's *doing* with them? Like why Yarella seems so offended by it? But the sooner we find Zuma, the sooner I can get my family home.

"Where is Zuma?" I demand. Might as well start with the obvious.

Yarella's lip wobbles. Her eyes darken, but she steadies herself. "Einan says she was taken by the Corvos, two nights ago."

Lin frowns, signing something. Maeve doesn't translate, but I catch the signs for *appearance* or *seeming, unusual,* and *calm,* and I agree. Most mothers are not this together after their daughters have been snatched by giant, mind-melting monsters.

Not that my own mum was the most shining example of parenthood.

"What d'you know about the Corvos?" I ask.

Lucius' hand tightens on his saber. "It's a vile thing," he says. "Appeared years ago, shortly before Deimos died. It keeps to itself, mostly."

I gape at him. "Wait," I say. "There's a vicious monster hanging around the town and it just *keeps itself to itself?*"

That makes zero sense.

Yarella kicks a loose stone. "It haunts the graveyard," she says. "We haven't been able to bury our dead there for years and if they don't go back into the swamp, they can't ... die properly."

She looks at me intensely until something clicks in my brain. "The remnants," I say. "They're the souls of those who haven't been buried?"

"Something like that," Lucius says. "Although we reckon it's disturbed the dead in the graveyard, too. But look, you can't fight that thing. Ruben sent men to deal with it years ago, after Deimos named him Heir. None of them came back. The graveyard's off limits. We don't know who it belongs to, which swamp-cursed murk-kid might be driving it, what the hell they want. Remnants are a small price to pay for not having to go near that thing."

He shudders and I see his eyes flicker skyward, like he's worried this talk might summon the bone crow. Yarella rolls her eyes.

"It doesn't come into the town," she says. "It has no interest in the living. At least ... it never did before."

Right. Because now, it's taken Zuma. A *living* girl.

"Any particular reason it might have an interest in your daughter?" Maeve asks.

Yarella shakes her head. Lucius mutters something about this being a waste of time.

"We're trying to find your daughter," I snap, my rage sizzling into Wriggler. "My friend got attacked by a hellgator this morning. We're risking our lives *for you*, so start talking!"

Yarella's hands fall to her sides. Lucius turns fully to look at us. "A hellgator attacked someone?"

"Yes," I drawl. "Sheb."

Lucius' jaw falls open. "Ruben needs to hear about this," he says. He tries to pull away but his wife grips his arm.

"Like hell he does," she says. "I need to know—"

"*No!*" me and Maeve snap at the same time.

"We're looking for Zuma," I remind them. "Your daughter. Tell us honestly, is there any reason she might have become—" I grit my teeth as I say it, "—murk-touched?"

Both Yarella and Lucius go still.

"No," Lucius says, gripping the pommel of his saber. "No, no child of mine—"

"Hush, Lucius," Yarella scolds. She lifts her chin. "Everyone has their reasons," she says. "And the swamp chooses those who know injustice. But Zuma has no pain in her past besides the ordinary pain of a child growing up in Marsh Wilds. She knows only the injustice that we all know. There is no reason for the swamp to choose her."

I hold her gaze, explore her face, but she seems in earnest. I believe her.

"And," she adds. "The Corvos has been with us for more than six years. Zuma is only eight.

I've never heard of the swamp calling a child that young. It's impossible."

I'm not sure it is, actually, but something about Yarella's face stops me arguing the point.

"Fine," I say. "But the bone-crow *is* a murk-touched monster."

"And we'd know," Maeve pipes up, pointing at Bear and Wriggler.

"Do you have any idea who might have summoned it?" I ask, flashing Maeve a disapproving look.

Lucius stares at his feet like a naughty child. Yarella shoves her hands in her pockets.

"No," she says.

Lucius shakes his head.

Neither of them looks at us.

Maeve thumps the gunwale, losing patience. She opens her mouth to speak. I turn to scold her into silence.

And Einan appears, sweat-soaked and panting, from between two of the stilt-houses. He pushes between his parents, and I see he's dressed like a miniature of his father. "Pa?" he says. "Atari sent me to tell you Ruben wants to push out east to-day and you have to—" he stops when he sees us. "What the hell are *you* doing here?" he demands.

I raise an eyebrow. "Looking for your sister," I say. "Like you asked us to."

"I—" Einan starts, then snatches glances at his parents. "I didn't mean you should—"

"We should what?" Maeve asks, a faint green glow in her eyes. "Actually *look* for her?"

Yarella puts a hand on her son's shoulder. "This is not his fault," she says. "And he's right, you shouldn't be here. Go and take care of Sheb. Even better, go back through the portal. Never come here again."

Einan wriggles free of his mother. "No!" he says. "Look, don't do that, just—"

"Just *what*, Einan?" I demand. My patience is wearing. Rage bucks inside me. Wriggler, now dog-sized, flares his wings.

Einan opens and closes his mouth several times, then hangs his head. "I need—" he says. "I can—look, go back to the de Callis manor. I'll find you later, okay?" He pulls at his father's jacket. "C'mon, Pa."

Lin steers us back from the bank, but I keep watching the family as they turn away from us. Yarella still grips her husband's arm. "Don't you dare go to him," she snarls. "You know what he's doing. You know what it'll cost."

"Get off me, woman!" Lucius hisses, ripping his arm free. "This is your fault. You involved our daughter in this!"

"And you involved our son!" she retorts. "Our children now fight on opposite sides of the same war!"

Lucius sneers at her. "That was true before they were born," he says. "It was true the moment I had to marry you."

I stiffen. *Had* to? Yarella doesn't seem like she'd bend to anyone's will. And after what I've seen of Nora, I'd say the same about her. So, who is forcing these women into such unhappy unions? And *how?*

Lucius stalks off, disappearing among the houses.

"I must speak to Imberg," Yarella announces. "Thank you for looking out for Zuma. My daughter is tougher than you think."

She crams her cap back onto her head and darts up the bank. I watch her go, frowning. What mother would assume her eight-year-old daughter could face something like the Corvos?

Lin turns our boat around. We putter back upstream, each lost in ourselves.

"Is it me," says Maeve, as the de Callis manor comes into view, Sheb stood on the veranda with Bartok on his shoulder. "Or was that weird?"

"It was weird," I confirm. "And all three of them know more than they're telling."

Lin nods, signing. Maeve translates.

"She says Einan was behaving strangely."

I nod, scowling back in the direction we've come. That kid's up to something.

Maeve sighs. "I guess it was too much to ask for it to be easy so we could all go home."

I clench my jaw, refrain from pointing out that everyone *except me* couldn't wait to jump through that portal and come hunt the Corvos. And *now* they want to go home? Typical.

I say nothing as we moor the boat, trudge back inside. I snatch a glance at Sheb. There's mud on his clothes and a fresh scratch above one eye. I quirk an eyebrow at him, but he avoids my gaze. I scowl. Too many secrets. Too many questions.

And even my best friend doesn't want to tell me the truth.

Chapter Fifteen

FROM OUT OF THE NIGHT

I SNAP AWAKE TO the sound of a soft splash outside.

Or was I dreaming?

My body prickles with sweat. It's dark, the house swathed in inky blackness. I lay still, waiting for my eyes to adjust.

My mouth's dry, neck stiff, shoulder numb. I realize my body's wrapped in something and flail, fighting my restraint. It takes a moment to remember I insisted I'd sleep on the massive sofa downstairs, wrapped in a dust sheet, while the rest of my family took one of the numerous, opulent bedrooms upstairs. I've dreamed of hellgators and swamp weed for however long, and now my heart's pounding like a war drum. There's a dull ache behind my eyes. The death-roar buzzes at the back of my brain.

After me, Lin, and Maeve returned from our chat with Einan and his family, the rest of the day was dull. Sheb refused to tell me what he'd been up to and wouldn't let me or Maeve back out in the boat. We argued. We sat in moody silence. Wriggler and Bear bickered whenever Bear got too close to Wriggler, or Wriggler deliberately antagonized Bear.

Lin signed something about going to visit the graveyard. I said I'd go. Sheb said like hell I would. Maeve yelled that we were a pair of morons and to stop treating her like a kid.

Everyone fell out and sulked in different rooms for a good hour. I took the library and rifled through the books on Sheb's family, looking for anything I could find about Deimos and the de Callis family power.

The more I read about him, the more I decided I loathed Sheb's father. Violent. Cruel. Callous. He reminds me of another father. One I poisoned and left for dead.

I wonder how Deimos died, in the end?

I wanted to talk to Sheb, ask him. Only he was in no mood.

Weirdly, I found myself thinking of Sasha. Of his arm around me. The musky, moonlit scent of him. How safe I'd felt—

I shook that thought away before it could go too far. He ain't here. He ain't coming. I'm a fool to think of him.

After a while, we got fed up with being angry at each other. We were tired. We needed sleep. Tomorrow we'd go to the graveyard, face whatever was waiting for us. I let the others traipse upstairs. I stayed down to keep watch. Only, I fell asleep.

Shouldn't have done that, should I? Not with hellgators prowling the swamp. Not with whatever's going on in this awful world.

Something brushes against my leg. I start, but it's only Wriggler. I scoop him up.

Finished sulking? I ask sullenly. He flicks his tongue at me.

Have you?

Fair point.

The hot, night air makes my skin prickle. Sunset brought a little relief from the humidity, but there's still a thin film of sweat coating my face. I lift my curls off the back of my neck, trying to cool down. But the air is too close.

I carry Wriggler outside. The veranda is battered from the hellgator attack, but it's massive enough that there's still plenty of it to stand on. I lean over the railing, trying to catch a stray breeze. There isn't one. I sit on the edge of the porch, stretch my legs in front of me, careful not to dangle them in the water.

Wriggler peers into the murk. *Disgusting,* he says. Then, there's a splash, a wet flapping sound, and Wriggler throws the ugliest fish I've ever seen against the wooden boards. It's no bigger than my hand, a vile, muddy green, with three bulbous eyes and a mouth full of misshapen teeth. Wriggler strikes it a couple of times to make sure it's dead, then lifts his head back and throws it down his gullet. My stomach turns.

Now who's disgusting? I ask.

Wriggler doesn't bother answering.

Moonlight reflects off the blackened water. The sky is studded with stars, but the trees are wreathed with remnant mist. The swamp stench makes bile rise in my throat. I breathe through my mouth.

Wriggler stiffens.

Annie! He says.

But I'm already scrambling to my feet. I heard it, too. Something snapping. Rustling undergrowth despite the still air. A ripple of water, like something large moving through it.

Coming towards us.

Without thinking, I've flicked a throwing knife into my palm, launched it into the darkness. Daft thing to do, seeing as I lost one when I fought the hellgator. I palm my remaining knife and hold it up like a dagger, ready for whatever's to come. The air tightens, like the swamp's holding its breath. I narrow my eyes, searching for signs of movement. I'm so focused on the swamp—the flick-and-splash of a fish tail, a shadow that might be a hellgator—that I don't see the huge shadow prowling across the veranda.

It's only when it's almost upon me, when Wriggler rears, suddenly five times his usual size, that I whip round to find two, amber eyes in a snarling, grey-furred face, inches from my own.

My throwing knife is clamped in its jaws.

I don't move. My lungs tighten. All I can do is look into the huge creature's face. It's a vast, cat-like beast with a mane of bristled fur running from its head, down to its shoulders. Its hackles are raised, quivering. Its sleek, grey fur catches the moonlight, muscles rippling beneath its pelt. Behind it, a long tail lashes in agitation. I can't take my eyes off that face. The tufts of fur along the jaw line. The black lips peeled back from curved canines. A jagged scar running just above one eye.

"Wriggler ..." I breathe.

The cat opens its huge jaws. My knife clatters to the veranda floor. I don't pick it up. The cat licks its black lips.

Then it says, *"You missed again."*

I can't help it. I let out a choking sob, throw my arms round the cat's sturdy neck. The cat gives a pained hiss. I hear the crack and pop of bones realigning, fur receding into skin, and suddenly, I'm not hugging a cat, but a man.

A man whose face has haunted my dreams for the last two weeks. A man I've hoped would come after me. A man I've feared might keep his promise.

Wriggler shrinks down. *Oak's* sake! He growls.

I tell him to shut up.

I pull back and cup the man's face. I'm smiling. I'm crying.

This is ridiculous.

"Sasha," I say.

He covers my hands with his, and I can't tear my gaze away. He's taller than I remember. Or maybe he's just standing straighter, no longer weighed down by the guilt of the priesthood he managed to escape. His dark black skin is flecked with cuts and bruises. But his deep brown eyes are full of light. He's let his hair grow—it was shaved last time I saw him—and there's a covering of tight, black curls over his scalp. Moonlight illuminates the thin scar across his eyebrow. He's wearing simple, black pants and a loose grey shirt, but no shoes. I glance at his bare feet, raise my eyebrows. He gives a wry grin.

"Bit difficult to skin-switch in and out of boots," he admits. "And I'm not—I won't wear my priest's uniform anymore."

He cups his hand under my chin, lifts my face. He leans in close.

"Annie," he says. I close my eyes, wait for his lips to find mine. "Do you have any shoes I can borrow?"

My eyes snap open. I shove him away, but I'm smiling.

"Insufferable ass," I say.

"Painful dark child," he shoots back.

Wriggler rolls onto his back and pretends to die of disgust.

"What are you doing here?" I ask Sasha. "You said—I thought—"

Sasha takes my hand, traces his thumb across the inside of my palm. I shiver.

"I almost didn't come," he admits. "But I—" he looks at me earnestly. "It was the strangest thing, Annie. Since you left me, it's like I've been able to sense you, even across worlds. I *felt* when you left Nowhere. I can't explain it. Like something in my core had shifted. And then I felt the world you'd entered and I—"

He looks away from me, face pained. I feel something roll in my gut and I'm suddenly nauseous. What the hell is this thing that everyone seems to know except me?

I wait for him to look back, then fix him with the most poisonous glare I can manage.

"Could'a done with your help earlier," I tell him. "When we got attacked by a giant swamp beast that tried to eat Sheb."

Sasha's eyes widen. He reaches for me.

"Are you hurt?" he asks. "Annie, I'm so sorry. I should've been there. I should've—"

I step back from him. "Oak's sake, Sasha!" I hiss. "Just *stop it,* alright?"

He drops his hands. "Sorry," he says. "It's just—" he clamps his mouth closed. Good move. I shift from foot to foot, my belly feeling both tight and weightless. I've wanted to see him for so long, dreamed his face, imagined him falling through the portal, into Nowhere and into my arms. Only, now he's here, all those old frustrations slither to the surface.

How he treats me like I'm made of glass.

How he looks at me like I'm his sun and his moon and the air he breathes.

How that was *why* he left in the first place. Because none of that is okay. None of that means we can build something that will last, even though him leaving left a deep wound in my core that still hasn't healed.

And I hate that the smell of him—incense and earth and a strange, ethereal fragrance that makes me think of howling at full moons—sets my skin tingling, my face flushing with heat. I hate that I want him close, that I wish he'd never come back. I fold my arms, ignore Wriggler nudging at my foot.

"Have you finished finding yourself yet, then?" I ask, half-smiling despite myself. Sasha dips his head, shuffles his feet.

"I—" he says. "It's not easy, Annie."

I soften, reach for his hand. He lets me take it and lifts his gaze to meet mine.

"I missed you," he says.

My lungs tighten. Warmth spreads through me and I can't help the wave of light-headedness that rolls through my head. "It's only been a few weeks, Sasha," I remind him. "But ... I missed you, too."

Sasha searches my face. "I wanted to come sooner," he says. "As soon as I felt you enter this world, but—"

There's a snap and a cry. The sound of a twig breaking, an animal in pain. Me and Sasha both jump. Sasha's eyes flash amber, his canines growing. He's preparing to shift. I flick a throwing knife into my palm as lightning cracks along Wriggler's scales. We peer into the dark, waiting.

I see a black shape ooze into the water from the opposite bank. It's too small to be a hellgator, but the moonlight glints off a pair of vicious pincers as long as my arm. A shining carapace and a tail, ending in a wicked sting. Creeperscorp, I think. I've got no desire to meet one of those at any time of day.

I keep hold of my knife, but Sasha relaxes once the beast has slithered into the depths. The amber in his eyes fades, though I notice his canines remain lengthened. He keeps his eyes fixed on the far bank. I touch his arm.

"Hey," I say. "Relax. That thing ain't nearly as bad as what we faced yesterday—"

As soon as the words leave my mouth, I realize.

"You're not worried about the 'scorp," I whisper. Sasha shakes his head.

"No," he admits. "I'm being hunted. Have been since I left Wilderness. They're still after me."

I chew my lip. I don't have to ask who he means. The priests. When we left Wilderness a few weeks ago, taking Maeve and Lin with us, Sasha denounced the Order of the Dread King, an army of skin-switching priests who were the last line of defense between the kingdom and the Wild Wood. I knew the Order didn't take kindly to Sasha leaving. I know they talked about stripping him of his powers.

But hunt him across *worlds?* Are they really so vengeful?

"How many?" I ask. Sasha finally looks at me.

"As far as I can tell," he says. "Just one."

My jaw tightens. "Alphonz," I say. "That back-stabbing snake—"

Hey! Wriggler says, affronted. I ignore him.

Sasha gives a mirthless smile. "He's always hated me. He probably leapt at the chance to chase me down."

I clamp down on my rising anger before Wriggler can feed off it. I remember Alphonz. Cruel, blue eyes, blond stubble across his shaved head, that smirk, the way he looked down on me, Lin, and Maeve, like we were bugs to be crushed beneath his feet. When I met them, he and Sasha were competing to be named Second to the town's highest-ranking Father. I thought, when Sasha denounced the Order, and when Wriggler ate Father Wystan (I still feel sick about that), Alphonz took charge of the remaining priests.

I underestimated his thirst for revenge.

"So," I say. "Let me get this straight. You wandered off to *find yourself* because you had no idea who you were without the priesthood, then, two weeks later, you come charging into Riverfell because you felt me enter this world. You were—what—scared I was in danger? And you thought the best way to help me would be to bring your vengeful nemesis through the portals with you to make my life more complicated, because you *missed me*." I raise an eyebrow. "Did I forget anything?"

Sasha opens and closes his mouth a few times. "I—" he splutters. "It's not—I didn't—"

I can see he hasn't thought this through. He's got no idea how to explain himself, and I'm half furious, half relieved to see him.

But this only makes things more difficult.

"Stay with us," I say before I can stop myself. Hope makes my ribs ache. "We can help you. We can—"

I can protect him. And I need him, even though I don't know why.

But he's already shaking his head. "I can't, Annie," he says. "I can't endanger you like that."

Holy Oak! Has he learned nothing? I shove his hands away, glaring.

"You already have, you ridiculous man-kitten!" I snap. "How many times do I have to tell you I can take care of myself?"

Clearly, I'm an idiot. I scowl at him. "Last time you tried to protect me," I say, "you almost sold Lin to a princeling and sent her to her death! Or have you forgotten?"

I get a wild satisfaction from the way guilt gleams in Sasha's eyes. He looks away. "I haven't forgotten," he says. "I could never forget."

"Did you forget Wriggler?" I ask. Sasha snorts.

"I could never forget him, either."

"Good," I say. "So, you can stop it. Stop trying to be the hero because it's nonsense—"

Sasha raises an eyebrow at me. "Stop trying to be the hero?" he asks. "Do you hear yourself, Annie?"

The scar across my back twinges. Rage floods my nerves. Wriggler expands until he looms over us. Scarlet lightning snaps off his scales. Sasha eyes my monster warily but, to his credit, doesn't step back. I'm almost impressed. Or I would be if I didn't want to smack him six ways to oblivion.

"Annie," Sasha says, raising a placating hand. "Please. I didn't come here to fight—"

"Yeah?" I growl, feeling Wriggler's power ripple through me. "Should'a thought of that before you showed your face."

I don't know why I'm this angry with him. I'm so glad to see him, but he's been such a fool. I've missed him so much, more than I should miss someone I've barely known for a few weeks, who almost betrayed me, nearly sent Lin to a certain death. I guess I just expected that, the next time I saw him, everything would be fixed. We'd be able to start again. Properly, this time.

Maybe that was too much to hope for.

Maybe it's not Sasha I'm really angry with.

Sasha drops his gaze. "We can talk about this later," he says. "For now, I came to warn you. There's something—"

He stops, gaze snapping to the opposite bank, though it's wreathed in darkness. Moonlight catches at the back of his eyes, so they shine like a predator's. I stiffen.

"What?" I hiss.

Sasha doesn't say anything. His face contorts with pain, but he manages to keep silent as he shifts into maned cat form. He casts me one last look—those amber eyes full of regret—before he melts into the darkness.

"Sasha, wait—" I start.

Annie, Wriggler growls, pony-sized and snarling. *Straight ahead, between the trees.*

I see them half a second later. Amber eyes gleaming in the dark. Maned cat eyes, narrowed in hatred. I know those eyes. Alphonz pushes his head into the moonlight so I can see him. The ragged grey fur, the vicious teeth. He stares at me, then withdraws and is gone.

"Sasha," I say again, but he's no longer there. He's slunk off, disappearing into the night like a ghost. Again. I didn't even hear a splash.

Chapter Sixteen

TO THE GRAVEYARD

Sasha doesn't reappear for the rest of the night. I don't go back into the house until the sun peeps above the tree line. When I poke my head round the door, I see Sheb's awake, strapping his harpoon across his back. I frown.

"Where'd you think you're going?" I ask.

Sheb doesn't look at me. "The graveyard," he says. "That's where Einan said he saw the Corvos. It might have a lair there."

I blink. It's a good point. Before I'd managed to get control of Wriggler, he did the same thing. As the Oraqua, he built a lair out of my rage and hate, almost trapped me in it. The Corvos may have done the same thing. Find the lair, and we find the person who summoned it.

"O-kay," I say slowly. "So ... what're you gonna do?"

Sheb keeps his eyes lowered. "I'm going to have a look."

I block his exit. "No you're not," I say. "Not by yourself."

"Excellent!" says Maeve, making both me and Sheb jump. She and Lin appear in the hallway, wrapped in blankets. Maeve throws hers off, stretches, then straps her dagger to her hip. "When are we going?"

Lin dashes upstairs, reappearing a moment later with her belt strapped to her waist. She checks her medical pouches, then pulls out a notebook, licks the tip of a pencil. They both look at me expectantly. Bear stands between them, tongue lolling.

I scowl. Why can't my daft little family just stay in one place and do as they're bloody well told?

"*We* ain't going anywhere," I growl. "You, Lin and Bear should stay here. Where it's safe. Bartok can keep an eye on you."

Bartok glances up from his perch on the veranda railing, looks at me reproachfully. He grumbles, pointedly hops onto Sheb's shoulder and fixes me with a tawny glare. I roll my eyes.

"*Fine.* Apparently, Bartok's coming with us. But the rest of you, *stay. Here.*"

Maeve folds her arms. Behind her, Lin tucks her notebook away and signs something. I catch the hand-to-shoulders gestures for *together* and *safety,* and then a fingers-interlaced sign that I think might mean *belonging.* Maeve looks triumphant.

"Exactly," she says, not bothering to translate. "We'll all fit in that boat in the boathouse—"

"No!" I yell before I can stop myself. "Just—all of you, stop *arguing* with me!"

Everyone freezes. Lin flushes scarlet. Maeve twitches an eyebrow. Bartok gives a grumbling hoot. Only Sheb makes no sign he's heard. Instead, he secures a dagger to his hip, begins unpacking things from his belt. I stare as he removes his handmade notebooks, pencils, vials for collecting supplies.

"Sheb," I say. "What are you doing?"

Sheb doesn't look at me. "I won't need these," he says. "They'll only weigh me down."

I tense. Wriggler winds himself round my ankle, tightening.

Annie, he says. *Stop him.*

Stop him doing what? My heart thumps against my ribcage. I can barely breathe. "They're your books," I say stupidly. "Don't you wanna study the Corvos? Add it to your categories? Work out if it's a Hot-Blood like Bear, or a Serpentine like Wriggler?"

I don't even know what I'm saying, but the words tumble out, won't stop.

"You need the vials to collect samples. Scales. Skin. Feathers. You gotta take them with you!"

Sheb shakes his head. "I won't need them," he says.

"Why—"

I choke on the last word.

Why not?

Because a hideous part of me already knows the answer. I can't bring myself to hear Sheb say it.

Wriggler says it for me, instead.

If he goes alone, my lightning-snake murmurs, *he won't come back.*

"Sheb—" I start, but I don't know how to talk him out of this. My fingers twitch towards my throwing knives, but this ain't a problem I can skewer to a wall.

Sheb looks at me, those kind, grey eyes meeting mine.

"You'll be alright, Annie," he says, quietly.

I shake my head. I don't know what else to do, how else to get him to just *stop it!* I rake my hands through my black curls, my scar burning.

"Sheb, what're you on about?" I demand. "What's going on?"

Sheb doesn't look at me. "There are things happening here you won't understand," he says. "I can fix this. I just need to go alone. I need to give the Corvos what it wants."

Ice clogs my belly. I can't breathe.

"And what's that, exactly?" Maeve asks. "Sheb, talk to us! We want to help! You're our family—"

"I'm not," Sheb says. I feel that like a dagger in the throat. I see Maeve and Lin do, too. Maeve's shocked into silence.

Sheb checks his harpoon. "I'm not your family as far as the swamp's concerned," he says. "My blood is de Callis. My power is de Callis. The swamp and the Corvos want recompense for what ... what happened before I left. I have to give it to them."

I try to grab Sheb's hand.

"Sheb, please. This is—"

Sheb pulls away, still not looking at me.

Wriggler expands to dog-sized. Bear responds in kind, pawing the ground while Maeve glances between me and Sheb.

What the hell do I do? Endanger my whole family? Take two girls who've barely survived one battle into what will almost definitely be another?

Or let my best friend walk into this fight alone?

Wriggler folds his wings, fixes me with a beady stare. *Crossroads, Annie,* he says, like that makes any sense. *One path or the other. Choose.*

I glare at him. *Yeah,* I think, sending splinters of frustration down our bond. *That was helpful. Thanks.*

I turn to Sheb, ready to argue with him. I see Maeve square her shoulders. Lin lifts her hands to sign.

Blood roars in my ears.

"If you think—" I start, then stop. Because a figure darkens the doorway.

It takes me a moment to realize it's Nora. She's dressed for battle. Crossbow strapped across her back, leather vambraces covering her arms. She's wearing a simple tunic with a leather breastplate, black pants with the hems tucked into heavy boots. She has a dagger at one hip, a holstered, ancient-looking pistol at the other, and her long, black hair is bound in a braid. She looks ferocious. I gape, until Wriggler tells me to close my mouth.

"Good morning," Nora says. "I take it we're going to the graveyard."

I hear the thrum of a boat engine, look past Nora to find a sizable vessel moored at the veranda, Kai sulking inside it, with Einan beside him. What're they doing here? I thought the graveyard was off limits to the townsfolk.

Nora doesn't seem to care, though. She gestures to the boat. "Shall we?"

· · · · ● · ● · · · ·

No-one says anything as we drift through town. I reach for Sheb's hand. He lets me hold it but doesn't look at me. I snatch accusing glances at Einan, but he won't look at me, either. I don't know why he's here, given how weird he was with us yesterday. He doesn't mention that stupid talk with his parents. It takes a lot of self-control not to swear at him, demand the whole damn truth.

I remind myself he's only a kid.

A foolish kid, Wriggler puts in, which doesn't help. *A kid who's put us all in danger.*

Yeah. Thanks.

Marsh Wilds is waking for the day. The jetties, walkways, and bridges creak with a steady traffic of feet. Children, barefoot, scamper across the spiderweb of wooden streets. Adults shouldering crates of goods yell at the kids as they scurry past. I notice how the doors and windows to the run-down houses are thrown open. Women hoist washing onto old lines, beat dust out of heavy rugs, hurl wastewater from chamber pots and washing buckets into the swamp. They stop when they see us. Or, more precisely, they stop when they see Sheb. A woman drops her basket in surprise, tears glistening on her cheeks. Two teenage girls on a bridge stop, pointing and whispering.

Someone calls, "Sheb? Is that you?"

Sheb stirs but doesn't answer.

A few of the men stop, too. Glaring. They seem less happy that Sheb's back. I notice the ones that glare and reach for their sabers wear Ruben's talismans. My scar prickles. I thumb a throwing knife into my hand.

The swamp is lively, too. Fish dart below the surface, shooting up to grab unsuspecting insects. Clouds of midges hang in the air and I slap them off my skin. The day warms. A film of sweat coats my arms, face, collarbone. I frown at the busyness around me. The *normalness*, how nobody seems afraid, even though they know the swamp could shoot up and strangle them.

And still—

It hasn't gone away, Annie, Wriggler points out. *Concentrate. You'll feel it.*

I resist at first, but Wriggler nudges my jaw with his blunt head. I take a breath, close my eyes. Listen.

And there it is. The death-roar. The necrotic soul of this world, simmering below the surface. I gasp and snap my consciousness back. Sheb casts me a sideways glance.

"You okay, Annie?" he asks. I nod.

"Fine."

Nora steers us through the town, beneath walkways where children point and stare, past a kind of town square, where boats have been lashed together, bobbing on the current, to create stalls, selling fresh fish, foraged fruit, fishing gear, bolts of fabric. Smaller boats scoot up and down this strange market, their passengers doing harsh and speedy business. We pass what looks like a town hall, its stilts raising it higher than the surrounding houses.

And then we're beyond the bustle of human life, out in the quiet of the wild swamp. The true swamp. I feel it thicken around me. Not just the damp air, the tangled trees, the dark water. But the swamp itself. Its spirit. The hair on the back of my neck rises. The swamp presses against my mind. Dark. Wild. Terrible. I try to shake it off, but the swamp just laughs, clings tighter. I squeeze my eyes shut. When I open them, I find Nora watching me.

"You're strong," she murmurs. "Even for a murk-girl. You sense it, don't you?"

I blink. "Sense what?"

Beside me, Maeve stirs, interested. Lin's already got a notebook out.

"The Deep Swamp," Nora says. "Its beating heart. The swamp as it should be. Untamable We're close to the de Callis border, here."

Her eyes widen in ecstasy. I think she looks like she's gone mad.

She doesn't, Wriggler argues. *She looks like she's gone sane.*

I don't know which is scarier.

I feel the swamp's tendrils in my head, searching. Feel its raw power, how it could tear me to pieces in a second. But it doesn't, because—

Because there's *love* there, too. Because it recognizes me. A dark, terrible thing connecting with another dark, terrible thing. I shake my head, raise an eyebrow at Maeve. She nods, looking slightly grey in the face. She feels it, too.

"Ruben has no power over the Deep Swamp," Nora says. "Though he wishes he did."

I say nothing, but scan the trees. It doesn't take long for me to see the symbol carved into the black trunks. The circle, the diagonal slash, the ever-staring eye.

He's trying to control it, ain't he? Trying to spread his influence. But the Deep Swamp won't let him.

I feel eyes on me again and the back of my neck prickles. Something shifts in the shadows. I startle, raise my throwing knife. A great, black eye peers at me from beneath a hanging tree branch, then closes and disappears below the surface. A huge shadow drifts under the boat. I make out the shape of a reptilian head, powerful legs with vicious talons, a rudder-like tail that propels it through the water.

"Hellgator," Nora says calmly. I glare at her.

"No shit," I say.

Nora gives a small smile. "She won't hurt you if you don't threaten her. These waters belong to her, remember."

I raise an eyebrow. I'm tempted to ask how she knows the hellbeast is female, but it occurs to me that these are questions Sheb would usually ask, and I can't get the words out. Beside me, by best friend sits utterly still.

I keep my throwing knife in hand. For some reason, Sasha comes to my mind. His face last night, half-lit by moonlight. My heart squeezes. I push the thought of him away, furious with myself.

Now isn't the time. I might be pleased to see him, I might've missed him until my heart ached, but his turning up has made things a lot more complicated.

I start at the glimpse of a shadow slipping between the trees. A cat-shaped shadow. Careful not to alert the others, I strain to catch sight of it again, thinking it must be Sasha. It *must* be.

But then I remember it could easily be Alphonz. I remember those murderous amber eyes glaring out of the darkness. I try to shake the thought of them both away, but I can't.

And that's just daft, ain't it? Because we've got bigger things to worry about.

I nudge Sheb's shoulder.

"What d'you think the Corvos is then?" I try. "I'm betting Serpentine, like Wriggler. Einan said it had scales."

Einan frowns. Sheb shakes his head.

"It's not Serpentine," he says. "And not Hot-Blood." He doesn't explain any further. The look on his face stops me from pressing.

Maeve, though, doesn't seem to get the hint. Typical. "Okay," she says. "But the big question is, who does it belong to? Do we still think it's—?"

She raises a pointed eyebrow at me, then twitches her head towards where Nora, Einan, and Kai sit at the back of the boat. They all see, obviously. I slap my palm to my forehead.

"The Corvos is a murk-monster," Nora says quietly. "Whoever summoned it, the swamp has a reason for it being here. We must respect that."

I glare at her. Maeve does, too. We catch each other's eye and Maeve quirks a small smile. I relent. Smile back. Lin reaches for my hand and squeezes. I feel some of my anger drain, though notice that Wriggler doesn't shrink.

Which means it ain't really anger I've been feeling, is it?

It's fear, Annie, Wriggler pipes up. *Learn the difference.*

I throw him a withering glare. He chuckles.

Nora steers us off the main river, up a small tributary where dragonflies zig-zag across the water and birds dart between the banks. She cuts the engine, grabs an oar from the bilge, and guides the boat to the bank, where a half-rotten jetty pokes from the weeds. The press of the swamp in my head intensifies. Nausea rolls through me. The death-roar hums behind my ears.

"Einan," Nora says, and the boy jumps ashore to moor the boat. Nora steps onto the jetty with Kai, who unstraps his harpoon.

"Stay quiet," Nora says. "And stay alert. Let's go."

Chapter Seventeen
LOST SOULS

THE MOMENT I STEP from the jetty, I feel it.

The death-roar. It's like being run through with white-hot steel. I groan, double over as my vision stutters. My bond with Wriggler spills open. Immediately, he's pony-sized and snarling. He mantles his wings over me while I fight to control my treacherous stomach. I feel the swamp pulling my mind. Its anger. Its pain. For the first time, I imagine it as a great beast, harpooned and dragged ashore. It's *dying,* I realize, with a gurgling gasp. Whatever Ruben's doing, it's killing the swamp.

But the swamp ain't done yet. If it goes, so does everyone that lives here. It'll go in a roar of vicious beasts and strangling weeds. Of rot, disease, rushing water. I feel it happening, feel the fetid water sloshing into my mouth, sliding into my lungs, choking off my breath—

"Annie?" It's Maeve, her hand on my back. "It's awful, ain't it?"

If I open my mouth, I'll puke, so I just nod. She ain't wrong. It's appalling. After a while, my body gets used to the onslaught. The nausea subsides. I'm *not* drowning, and I'm able to straighten up, though I still feel like if I move too quickly, my stomach will empty itself. I lean against Wriggler. If Maeve feels what I feel, she's dealing with it scarily well. Her skin looks grey, and there's a glassiness to her eyes, but she's upright, alert. Maybe she's just better at hiding it than I am.

"You should go back," I say to Maeve. "This ... whatever it is ... it's awful."

Maeve rolls her eyes. "Pack it in, Annie," she says. She unsheathes a dagger, trudges up the bank, where the reedy grass is flattened into a narrow path. I stare at her as she goes. How the hell does she do it?

I cast a sideways glance at Lin. She looks faint, too. Her eyelids flutter. She stumbles sideways, but Wriggler stretches a wing, catches her. He gathers her close to his side.

Humans, he hisses. *You're such a pathetic bunch.*

Yeah, whatever. I ain't fooled. I don't miss the way he looks at Lin with concern, the way he tucks us both close to him, supporting us up the bank. Apparently, my ridiculous monster has a soft side.

I do not! Wriggler protests.

I smile to myself.

Tendrils of mist swirl around our ankles. I feel its cold brush my skin. There are faces in it. Staring eyes and gaping mouths, hands reaching before dissipating into nothing. The remnants are active, here. I feel their pain like I feel the swamp's. Holy Oak, I want to be sick.

Maeve waits at the top of the bank, rushing to help Lin when Wriggler guides us both onto the path. Lin's head lolls. I see her wave her hands in front of her face, like she's trying to shoo away swarms of flies. Maeve hugs her.

"It's okay, Lin," she murmurs. She looks at me. "She can sense something. A disturbance of ... I don't know."

I try and steady the rolling in my gut. "A soul?" I ask. "I mean, 'cos there are bloody loads floating about."

Lin's soul-reading power—her ability to sense and show the true nature of another living thing—was what saved us two weeks ago, when Maeve almost killed a lot of people with Bear. Lin might be a gentle, quiet girl, but I've learned not to underestimate her.

Maeve shrugs. "It's a graveyard, ain't it?" she says. "It's full'a souls. I dunno if Lin can feel ... dead ones, the same as she feels living ones."

We both look at Lin, who sags against Maeve and covers her mouth with a hand. Looks to me like she can sense dead ones just fine and it ain't something she's used to.

Good. New territory for all of us then.

Territory in which there lurks a giant, flesh-eating monster that kidnaps younger sisters. Bloody great.

Nora leaps up the bank in two quick strides. She unclips her crossbow, unholsters her pistol. I blink. I can't square this furious, warrior-woman with the quiet wife I met yesterday.

Einan and Kai stay close to her, their weapons drawn. They scan the bank with the practiced wariness of kids who've grown up in the jaws of danger. Einan, in particular, looks ashen. His eyes are huge, wild with fear.

"Okay," Nora says. "Keep your wits about you. Let's—"

"Wait," I say. I peer down to the jetty, where Sheb is still stood. He hasn't moved since we stepped ashore. Hasn't drawn his harpoon. His breath comes in shallow gasps. His eyes stare beyond us—*through* us—like he's looking into the distant past.

He's shaking.

On his shoulder, Bartok nudges his face. But Sheb's lost. Reliving nightmares.

My pulse clatters in my ears, almost drowning out the death-roar. I can't take my eyes off him. My best friend. The man that so often grounds me. He's falling apart, and I don't know what to do.

"Sheb?" I say.

He flinches but doesn't look at me.

What do I do? How do I fix this?

The sight of him losing it, crumbling in front of me, makes me splinter, too. I can't do this without him. I can't—

It's Nora who heads down the bank, grips Sheb's shoulder.

"Brother," she says softly. She doesn't say it like Ruben says it, with a sneer that makes the word sound like a subjugation. It's soft, reaching through the folds of Sheb's fear until it pulls him back. Slowly, he turns to her. She holds his gaze. "This is your choice," Nora says. "Face it or turn back."

Sheb swallows. Pain clouds his face. "I can't—" he starts. "You don't know—"

"I know what this costs you," Nora says. "I know *exactly* what it will cost you." She cups his face. "And I know that you are stronger than your brothers. Than your father. I know who *should* have been Heir. Your choice."

I stare, unspeakable things clawing at my throat, as Nora's words settle Sheb. His trembling calms. He unstraps his harpoon.

"Okay," he says. "Let's go."

He strides up the bank, walks past me without a glance.

"Sheb—" I say, reaching for him. He flinches away.

"It's okay, Annie," he says, though everything about his voice tells me that's a lie. "It's my fight. No-one else's."

I don't know what to say, so I close my mouth, press my hand against Wriggler's scales. We head up the narrow path. The trees either side thin out. I see grassy clumps and mounds sprouting from the ground. Some block the path, and we step around them.

It's only when I trip over one, dislodging dirt and moss from its surface to reveal mottled stone underneath, that I realize what they are.

Gravestones.

"Shit," I mutter, rubbing my sore ankle as I peer at the exposed stone. There's a name carved into it, weathered by time and neglect. It's barely legible, but— "Luana," I read. "Luana de Callis."

I frown. I know that name from somewhere, don't I?

Ahead, Sheb stops dead. Oh hell.

"What ..." he whispers. "What did you say?"

"Sheb," I say. "I'm sorry, I—"

He lets out this sound. It's like a howl and a groan and a sob at the same time. An animal cry from beneath his ribs, wrenching out of him, like a giant has reached down his throat and torn his insides out. I stare at him, every part of me clenching at the sound. My throat closes. I can't breathe. His pain is so violent, it rockets through me. Bartok beats his wings in panic, pressing his face against Sheb's cheek.

"Sheb—" I say again, but he can't hear me.

Then Lin and Maeve are beside us, crouched over Sheb, rubbing his back, saying soothing words. Bartok nuzzles Sheb's neck, gently beaking away the tears.

I just kneel there, no idea what to do, my hand frozen halfway to Sheb's shoulder. For some reason, I feel that if I touch him, it'll make everything worse. He'll break apart in front of me. I can't handle that. I can't.

Sheb lifts his tear-stained face as Nora approaches.

"A year after I left?" he says. I remember the brutal way Ruben had told him about the death of their parents. My anger bucks. Wriggler's scales sparkle.

Nora nods. "Yes," she confirms. "And Deimos, a few months after that."

Sheb's saying something, but I've stopped listening. There's something else written on the headstone under Luana's name. I can't quite make it out, but it looks like … *swamp … swamp maiden*. That's a weird epitaph. I reach out to brush the headstone with my fingertips.

Annie, Wriggler growls. But I don't listen to his warning until it's too late. My fingers connect with the rough stone. Pain shoots up my arm. I cry out, knees buckling. I'm vaguely aware of someone shouting, hands gripping my shoulders, but I fight them off.

I know what this is. It's happened before, back in Maeve's world, when I touched the smashed altar in the old prayerhouse. This is a memory, slithering to the surface.

Light flashes behind my eyes. Shadows swim just out of sight. There are voices.

"Foolish woman! Don't you realize what you've done?" The rough voice of a man.

"I'd do it again. I'd do it as many times as it takes to save him." A woman, fierce but afraid.

"Then he'll be your death!" The man bellows.

"And I'll be yours, Deimos."

There's a terrible cry, a sharp shout cut hideously short.

Then silence.

I snatch my hand from the stone, blinking through tears. "He ..." I gasp. "He killed her."

The others look at me in horror, but Nora only nods. "He did," she says. "Though he knew what it would mean. He knew the swamp would destroy him for it. He thought—" she stops, shaking her head. "Well. It doesn't matter what he thought."

I struggle upright, intending to point out that it might matter *very much* what he thought, but the look on Sheb's face silences me. This is his history. His family. The pain is written deep in his bones.

Sheb shakes his head, hands balled into fists. "He never thought the rules applied to him," he says bitterly. "Always thought he was above the law of the swamp. This is his fault." His voice deepens. "And hers. How could they let this *happen?*"

Nora reaches for him. "Sheb—"

He shrinks away.

"No!" he growls. "She's to blame, too! Everything he put us through. All the trials. All the competition and punishment. She could have stopped it and she never—she waited until—"

His face crumples. I can't take it anymore. I shove Nora away, draw my knife.

"Get off him!" I snarl. "You're making it worse!"

Sheb sobs behind me. I can't bear to turn around. Can't see him like this. Can't cut his pain out of him and kick it to dust like I want to. I just stand there, glaring at Nora, trying not to think how mine and Sheb's stories are so similar it hurts. Broken by our fathers, abandoned by our mothers.

I want to tell him he can't blame his Mum, that she was a victim like he was. She had no choice.

But I think about how much I blamed my own mum. I couldn't get past it. I never trusted her to love me the way I needed. She never forgave me for being my father's girl.

And she left me again, in the end.

Maybe Luana would have done the same. Maybe we can't blame them, really. But we do anyway. Blame's easy, ain't it? Means it's not your fault.

It lets you keep going the way you always have.

After a while, Lin persuades Sheb to stand. Tears run down his face, but we keep moving. We head deeper into the graveyard and the headstones become taller, more clustered. Beside me, Wriggler flicks his tongue at the putrid air. Everyone keeps their heads bowed, but their weapons ready. I notice Kai slip a hand into his mother's. He reddens and snatches it away when he sees me looking. Something inside me cracks.

Einan hangs back. He brings up the rear, keeping his distance from us. His eyes scan the sky, and he gives the headstones a wide berth. Mostly, though, he watches Sheb. His eyes tracking my best friend's movements. He never lets Sheb out of his sight.

And I don't know why, but it makes me frown.

CHAPTER EIGHTEEN

UNDER THE BLACK ASH

THE GRAVEYARD IS MASSIVE. Considering dry land for burying bodies is limited in a swamp, the town have made good use of this patch. Now I know what to look for, I see how the headstones extend beyond the clearing, into the trees. Some are huddled in clumps. I realize the same plot has been used for several bodies.

But I notice other things about this place, too. The birds don't fly over it. They don't sing. The air's more chill here. Mist hangs at ankle-height and doesn't clear, even when the sun reaches its peak. The death-roar hums in my brain. The only thing keeping me from vomiting is sticking close to Wriggler.

Maeve seems okay, though her face is greyer than normal. She keeps a hand on Bear's side. Like Wriggler, her monster has grown. The beginnings of his white-and-green fire flicker along his spine.

Lin, though, looks like she's about to scream. She stumbles, her skin almost green with nausea. Her eyes have that faraway look. Maeve steadies her. The back of her neck is shiny with sweat.

Once we reach the center of the graveyard, Nora stands aside.

"Show us where, Einan," she says.

Head bowed, Einan takes the lead. He hasn't spoken since before we set out across the swamp. Something about his silence disturbs me.

He did almost get eaten by a monster here, Wriggler points out. *And that same monster might have eaten his sister. Cut the kid a break.*

I turn to him, eyebrows raised. Wriggler looks as sheepish as it's possible to look when you're a giant, winged lightning-snake.

What? Doesn't mean I care.

I allow myself a smile. *'Course not.*

We follow Einan, weaving between the crumbling, moss-covered headstones. He leads us to the edge of the clearing, then plunges into the trees. I hesitate on the tree line, but Wriggler slithers after the kid, so I force myself to follow. We fight our way through tangled branches until we come to a clearing. It's not really a clearing, it's just that the tree in the center is so bloody massive, its canopy so thick, that nothing can grow within at least ten meters of its trunk. The ground is littered with leaf mulch and damp earth. Around the tree's base, there's a cluster of headstones that are larger and better kept than the others. Maeve helps Lin to sit against the tree. Sheb makes a strange noise. I go to stand beside him. I touch his arm. This time, he doesn't flinch.

"Hey," I say softly. "Are you ... I mean ...?"

Why is it so hard to ask him if he's alright? Maybe I'm scared of the answer. Holy Oak, I'm such a coward! I'll fight monsters without a thought, but show me my best friend falling apart and I don't know what to do. I steel myself.

"You alright, Sheb?" I say in a rush.

I see his jaw tighten. "I'm alright," he says. "Don't worry, Annie. It's just ... this is where ..."

He doesn't need to finish. I stare at the tree with new understanding. Suddenly, its thick, black trunk seems soaked in years-old blood. The wind through it leaves sounds like the echo of a death-cry.

This is where Sheb murdered his brother. Right here.

He's only told me that story once, five years ago, and I never asked again. I don't know much. Only that Sheb's father and brothers drove him to it, that he didn't want to do it, and he escaped to Nowhere shortly after. He's never been back since.

I want to ask him about it now. But the words glue themselves to my tongue. He looks so desperate. So lost. I know pain like that. I know what it costs to talk about what you've done. So, I don't ask.

Sheb shakes his head. Bartok gives his ear a gentle nip, trying to rally him. The owl-squirrel turns and glares at me because, like always, he blames me for this, doesn't he?

I glare back.

Nora comes to stand on my other side. She holsters her pistol but keeps her crossbow ready. She turns to Einan.

"This is where you saw the Corvos?" she asks. "By the de Callis graves?"

Einan nods.

I flinch, cast Sheb a sideways glance. He murdered his brother on land under which his ancestors were buried.

I leave his side, wander among the headstones. There are five of them, all larger than every other headstone in the graveyard. There's one for a baby girl who died shortly before her first birthday. There's not even a name on it, she's just remembered as *Baby Girl*. For some reason, that makes my heart thunder.

There are a couple for older men that I guess must be Sheb's grandfather and great grandfather. They have ridiculous, warrior-like epitaphs, like, *he faced death and laughed,* or, *may his war cry sound in the hearts of his sons.* I roll my eyes.

The fourth headstone is difficult to make out because something has gouged great claw-marks across the name. I throw a questioning glance at Nora. She shrugs, her fingers absently touching the tooth pendant at her throat. "Hellgator," she says. "They get ... angry, sometimes. That's Deimos' grave."

My eyebrows shoot up. I look at the headstone.

It's hard to make out any of the engraving, and my letters aren't the best anyway, but it looks like it's just his name carved there. No title. No warrior epitaph. His headstone is mostly blank.

And the same man that was killed by a hellgator—a rare event, apparently—just so happened to have the engraving on his headstone obliterated by one?

Fishy, Wriggler says. I smirk at him.

Talking about the situation or the smell?

Both, Wriggler says, wrinkling his blunt snout.

I don't look at the final headstone, mainly because I know who it belongs to. I can't bring myself to read his name out loud. It's Maeve—clueless Maeve—who does that. Leaving Lin to sip water, she wanders up beside me.

"Who's the final grave, then?" she asks, peering at the waist-high headstone. "Jeelie de Callis. *His battle was in his blood.*"

I see Sheb flinch. Maeve doesn't notice. She wouldn't, would she? Sheb never told her his story. How lonely he was growing up. How the bullying, the isolation, drove him to do something awful.

To murder his brother.

His battle was in his blood.

Sheb sure looks like he's battling his blood right now. Like an onslaught of memories holds him prisoner. His breath quickens. Maeve stands back, folds her arms.

"These epitaphs are so weird," she says. "What the hell does this one mean? *His battle was in his blood?* It sounds like—"

I whirl to face Nora, blurt the first question I think of. Anything to get Maeve to shut up.

"Why isn't Luana's grave with the rest of her family?" I ask.

Everyone looks at me, except Sheb, who closes his eyes as if in pain.

"Annie!" Maeve hisses, like I've said something unkind. I glare at her. Painful girl.

"No," I say. "I want to know. Why is Luana de Callis back there, with a tiny headstone, and everyone else in the family is here?"

Maeve throws her hands up in despair. I ignore her. I fix my gaze on Nora. She meets my eyes and, for some reason, it's hard to hold her gaze. Those deep brown eyes are like blades sliding into my mind. Feels like they can see everything. I blink against the intensity of her stare.

"Luana de Callis was never part of that family," she says.

I open my mouth to protest, furious that she could say something so heartless in front of Sheb, but something in her voice stops me. There's an undertone. A softness to the way she speaks that makes me feel like Luana's death was more than a town tragedy to Nora.

It was, in some way, personal.

"Were you there?" I blurt. "When she—?"

I clamp my mouth closed before I get myself into more trouble, but it's too late. This time, Sheb's head snaps up. He fixes Nora with a pleading gaze. Maeve has frozen with her back to us. I realize that the subject of mothers is raw for her, too.

Hell, it's raw for *me.* It might have been years since my own mum abandoned me for a second time, but the ache still sharpens into something unbearable some nights. I wonder what it is about all these bloody worlds that snatch mothers away, throw them to the jaws of the universe like meat thrown to starving dogs.

Nora smiles sadly.

"I wasn't," she says. "I wish I had been. I wish we all had been."

I blink at her. *All?*

She hesitates. I think she might be about to say something else, but Lin stands up, drawing our attention. She starts signing, her eyes staring somewhere past me. Her skin is slick with sweat. Maeve rushes to her side.

"Lin?"

But I whirl round, searching the area where Lin was looking.

The area beside Jeelie's grave.

I see it immediately. The thickening mist that lifts against the breeze and forms a shape. A remnant boy. A boy I recognize. It's ... hell, it's *Sheb!*

No it isn't, Annie, Wriggler drawls. *Look again.*

I narrow my eyes as the remnant drifts towards me, a strange frown on his insubstantial face. He blinks, and I still see Sheb. Those grey eyes. That flop of hair. But he's different, too. There's a swagger in him. A tilt to his chin, a slant to his shoulders. There's the ghost of a harpoon gripped in one hand. It's not Sheb. It's his twin.

It's the brother he murdered.

"Is anyone ..." I breathe. "Is anyone else seeing this?"

Maeve grips Lin's shoulders as the other girl's eyelids flutter. Sheb and Nora are silent behind me, staring.

Jeelie reaches out a hand, palm upturned, beckons to us. His eyes narrow.

Then he disappears.

"Shit!" I say, rushing forward, as if I could catch him. "We've got to—"

Lin collapses in a heap, spasming violently. Froth spews from her mouth. Suddenly chasing Jeelie's remnant doesn't matter.

"Time to leave," Nora says.

Once we're in the boat, I realize I've got no memory of how we got there. Maeve alternates between sobbing and crying Lin's name. Wriggler curls up so Lin can use him as a pillow. Bear scratches at the bilge in agitation. Nora has an arm round Kai as she powers us back through the swamp.

I sit close to Sheb as he shakes his head, eyes still leaking tears.

"I should never have let you come," he says.

I open my mouth to protest, then freeze.

"Sheb," I say. "Do you hear ...?"

Wingbeats.

Huge, powerful wingbeats.

"Get down!" Nora bellows.

We throw ourselves flat in the boat, but it's not enough. The death-roar batters through me. I feel like I'm being torn apart. I'm a warzone, a fortress under siege. I am nothing but the horror of death blasting through me. My mind is so loud, I almost don't hear it.

The shriek.

It comes from overhead, slicing the skies. It takes me a moment to realize it's not in my mind. It's real. And whatever made that sound is huge, violent, coming this way.

Birds erupt from the trees. Bartok joins them, exploding from Sheb's shoulder in a flurry of panic. A shadow passes over us, blotting out the sun. The shriek sounds again. Sheb throws himself over me as whatever-the-hell-it-is sweeps low overhead. A huge shadow, wingspan reaching from one bank to the other, a whiplash tail that slashes the water ahead of the boat, sending up spray. I feel its wind against my face.

There's a white-hot knife in my head, slicing my mind. I scream. The creature's shriek fills my skull.

You shan't have him! I won't let you! He's mine mine mine!

It goes on and on, getting louder and louder until I feel something burst. A hot, metallic taste fills my mouth.

Lin moans fitfully. Her eyes roll and Maeve only just manages to lift her in time for her to throw up over the gunwale. Her fingers twitch like she's trying to sign but can't.

Nora unstraps her crossbow, aims skyward as the thing comes back for a second pass.

"Kai!" she yells. "The tiller!"

To his credit, the kid grabs it with steady hands, keeps us on course. As we hurry away from the graveyard, the death-roar eases in my mind. I gasp as its hold on me weakens. The nausea subsides.

But I make the mistake of glancing back to the jetty. Something has landed by the water. A vast, dark shape with a lashing tail, a crown of vicious horns. It draws its wings down and leans on the wrist joints, watching as we speed away. Its voice fills my head again, distant this time.

Don't take him from me. Don't take him! I'll kill you! I'll kill you all!

Wriggler ... I think.

Here, my lightning-snake says. He's grown, dived off the boat, and now swims beside us, ready to defend us if he needs to. I hadn't even noticed my rage flooding him.

"What was that?" I ask.

"That was the Corvos," Nora says, her eyes fixed on it. "I'm sure of it."

I don't reply. Can't. *How ...* I ask Wriggler. *How do we fight that thing?*

I don't know if it's just a trick of the morning light, or my vision is still blurry, but I think Wriggler looks scared.

No idea, he says. *It's strong. Really strong. I'm not sure I can fight it by myself.*

We have to find a way, I say. *We have to find out who it belongs to and what the hell they want.*

Wriggler glares. *Easy for you to say,* he drawls. *It'll be me that thing tears to pieces, won't it?*

You're me! I point out. *So, it'll be both of us.*

Wriggler grumbles, slithers below the surface without answering. Fine. Let him sulk. I ain't got the energy to argue. I let my head drop onto the gunwale, close my eyes.

"Mum," I hear Kai say. "How come Einan didn't get in the boat with us?"

CHAPTER NINETEEN

A SONG OF DEATH AND SHADOW

I BOLT UPRIGHT. A scan of the faces in the boat confirms Kai is right. Einan isn't here. Surely, a life lived in Marsh Wilds has taught him the water ain't safe to swim in, which means there's only one place he can be.

I stare at the disappearing bank, where the winged shadow still looms.

Why doesn't it take to the air? Come after us?

And where the *hell* is Einan?

"Turn the boat around," I say. I mean to sound commanding, but I splutter, hacking something foul out of my lungs. "Turn around!"

Nora doesn't look at me. Her hand is on the tiller. "No."

I blink. "What d'you mean *no?*" I demand. "We just left a kid on his own on the bank with a giant *monster—*"

"Exactly," Nora says. "You want me to turn this boat around, with my *son* inside, and take us back to that graveyard, with the Corvos lurking there? I will not."

"Einan is someone's son!" I blurt, smacking the gunwale with my fist. "He's just a kid—"

"He's not just a kid," Nora interjects. "He's the child of Lucius Kanzpatrick, Ruben's most loyal lieutenant."

I raise an eyebrow. "What's that s'posed to mean?"

Nora doesn't look at me. "It means he can take care of himself," she says. "He'll make his own choices. In many ways, he already has."

I have no idea what she's talking about.

"He's Yarella's kid, too," I point out. "And she's ... she's one of you, ain't she?"

Nora chews her lip. "Einan is smart," she says, softer this time. "He'll find somewhere to hide. Once my son is safe, we can go back."

"This is crazy," I growl.

"It is," Nora agrees. "All of it. A form of terrible insanity. Isn't that what all monsters are? A murk-touched would know."

Now she looks at me, and I wish she hadn't. The intensity of her stare makes me flinch like I've been stung. "Or perhaps," she says, "it's the opposite. Maybe the swamp only sends monsters to people who are terribly sane. The ones who see the evil in the world and know what it can do."

I thump the gunwale. "Whatever," I say. "Turn this boat *around!*"

"I will not," Nora says.

My scar twinges. Rage simmers down the invisible threads to my lightning-snake. His sinuous form scythes through the water, sparks flicker across his scales. He lifts his head, baring his fangs at Nora.

She's completely unmoved.

"Let your snake attack me," she says, "and you will both regret it."

A hand grasps my shoulder.

"Annie," Sheb says. His voice is gruff. When I look at him, I see tears in his eyes. "It's okay. We can't ... there's nothing we can do."

I shove him off. I'm not sitting in this boat while Einan gets mauled to death by the bone crow.

Wriggler, I think. *Can you go back for him? Find him?*

But my lightning-snake sends waves of concern back to me. *Once you're safe,* he says. *The water feels strange. Hungry. No way I'm leaving you.*

I clench my jaw in frustration. *But Einan—*

Has lived here his whole life, Wriggler points out. *He'll find a way to survive. Now shut up and let me concentrate.*

I almost ask, *on what?* But then I remember the hellgators, the creeperscorps, the strangling weeds. I shut up.

Maeve swears, and Lin retches, emptying her stomach into the inky water. No-one says anything. Kai whimpers, and Bartok calls from above, where he's still circling us.

No-one mentions the appalling strength of the death-roar in the graveyard, or the fact it seemed to be centered around the graves of Sheb's family.

No-one mentions Luana de Callis. Or the vast, winged shadow we saw at the edge of the bank.

No-one mentions Einan.

I clench my jaw, trying to forget the movement of the boat, how it makes my gut roll. The death-roar buzzes in my head, though it's reduced to muttering. The mist in the trees thickens, forming remnants that swoop across the water. I flick a throwing knife into my palm, scanning the trees.

My breath catches when I see his face. He stares through the milky glow of his own mist, blinking those grey eyes. Sheb's murdered twin. He doesn't drift across the water like the others, doesn't wail or cry. He just ... watches. He watches *me*. He drifts quietly alongside us, occasionally disappearing and reappearing further up the bank. I reach for Sheb, trying to draw his attention, but Jeelie's remnant presses a finger to his insubstantial lips.

My mouth falls open.

Then he's gone, and I don't see him again. Holy Oak, I need to sleep.

There's an ache behind my eyes. Every breath feels like an effort. I'm concentrating so hard on trying to catch another glimpse of Jeelie, I don't notice when the boat bumps against something in the water. I don't hear Nora swear, or Kai gasp. I barely feel someone shaking my shoulder. It's Wriggler that finally snaps me out of it.

Annie! He hisses. *Pay attention, for Oak's sake!*

I jerk to attention, knife raised. Nora cuts the engine, her face deathly pale. "Don't move," she says. I don't know whether she's talking to her son, or to all of us, but everyone stays put while Nora peers over the bow. Her shoulders tense, a strangled cry escapes her. I'm immediately alert.

"What the—"

Nora returns to the tiller. She tugs the engine chain and it rumbles to life. Her mouth is set in a grim line but—

She's shaking. Her fingers are barely steady enough to hold the tiller.

"Don't look," she says.

So, of course, we all do. The boat rocks as we lean over the starboard gunwale, trying to work out what we're seeing. It's a vast, mangled lump, floating in the murk, easily as long as our boat, if not longer. It's mottled green, brown and black, but parts of it look like they've been hacked with a dagger. It could be the rotting trunk of a fallen tree. Driftwood, nothing more.

Except—

It takes a moment to realize this thing used to be *alive*. It's a hellgator. Or it was. A front limb has been torn off and floats a short distance away, leaking black blood into the water. Half its reptilian head is missing. One eye has been gouged out. Its tail is torn in at least seven places and there are huge, bloody marks down its back. It drifts in the swell from the boat, bobbing like a log on the waves. I stare at the wreckage of its vast, powerful body, try to reconcile this destruction with the thing that attacked Sheb last night. The thing that it took both Wriggler *and* Bear—and Nora—to see off.

How the hell did this thing die? And it didn't just die. It was killed, wasn't it? *Butchered.* Someone—or some*thing*—tore it to pieces in a frenzy, not because it was hungry—damn thing didn't eat any of its kill, did it? No, it killed because it was fun. Because it *delighted* in death. In pain and ruin.

"What did this?" I breathe. Sheb covers his mouth. He looks like he's about to vomit.

"Nora," he says, reaching for her. "I'm sorry. I'm so sorry."

I frown. What the *hell?*

But there are tears drawing tracks down Nora's cheeks. Sheb's face is ashen. I notice his harpoon glowing faintly.

"This can't happen," he says. "This *cannot* keep happening. It's making everything worse."

I don't understand. I can't tear my eyes away until the remains of the hellgator disappear around a bend in the river. I flop down into the boat beside Sheb.

"You think the Corvos did that?" I ask.

Sheb says nothing.

Wriggler lifts his head, fixing me with a beady glare. *Still want me to abandon you to go find the kid?* He asks.

I shake my head slowly. It's not refusal. I just ... Can't process what I saw.

A strange keening sound starts from the back of the boat. At first, I think the engine's failing, but when I glance back, I realize the sound is coming from Nora. Her eyes are crushed closed. There's pain on her face. Her lips are parted and she's making this sound, halfway between a song and a scream. Beside her, Kai tugs her sleeve.

"Mama," he hisses, face flushed. "Mama, *stop it!*"

I stare, my muscles bunched. "What the hell's wrong with her?" I ask. Sheb stirs.

"Nothing," he says, in a way that makes me think it's absolutely *something*. "Beyond grief. That's a lament. We call it the song of death and shadow. It helps carry the spirit into the depths of the swamp, where it will nourish the fish and keep monsters at bay."

I look at him. The heavy slope of his shoulders, the way his eyes stare into some distance I can't fathom. And that smile ... I haven't seen that smile of his since before we arrived. I miss him. I miss him so much it hurts.

"Why's she singing for the gator?" Maeve asks. "Didn't one attack us yesterday? It's just a swamp beast, right?"

Sheb shakes his head. "Like she said, they're sacred. And this—" he sets his mouth in a grim line. I get what he means.

Instinctively, my mind reaches for Wriggler.

Whatever this thing is, I say. *Whatever it wants, we have to kill it.*

Wriggler huffs. *You mean* I *have to kill it,* he grumbles. *And I feel so much joy at the prospect of being left a bloody mess at the bottom of the swamp, Annie. Thank you and fuck off.*

I glare at him as he pokes his head above the water again. *Scared, are you?* I challenge, expecting him to argue, insist monsters aren't afraid of anything.

Instead, he says, *yes, you idiot. I'm scared. Did you see that thing? Did you not feel the darkness it resonates? That's not just a monster, Annie, that's an old monster. Whatever—whoever—is driving it, they have enough pain to infect an entire universe. Yes, I'm scared. And if you're not scared, then you're a fool.*

Good. That fills me with confidence. I snap our bond closed. Wriggler disappears back into the murk as our boat drifts into town.

He's right though, ain't he? I hate it, but he is. I heard that death-roar, I saw that huge, winged shadow on the bank. I felt the sickness at the heart of this world.

I can't get the image of the hellgator out of my mind.

Nora's wailing song drifts on the still air. Sheb prepares a cloth and helps Maeve dab Lin's brow. Poor girl's collapsed in the bilge, eyelids fluttering. After a while, Bartok swoops down and lands on Sheb's shoulder. None of us speaks.

CHAPTER TWENTY

SECRETS WITHIN SECRETS

THE MOMENT NORA MOORS the boat outside the old de Callis house, I pull at my bond with Wriggler.

Yeah, yeah, he grumbles. *I'm on it. Stop pestering.*

He pushes his head above the water, though, nuzzles my shoulder, before heading for the graveyard. I lean over the port gunwale as everyone disembarks, watching him go. I want him to find Einan, bring the kid back safely. But I *need* him not to get hurt. Or worse. Me and Wriggler can be pretty far from each other without any consequences, as long as we're in the same world. I reckon—though I ain't tested the theory—that my death would mean his death, too, but I'm not sure what his death would mean for me. It would hurt, no doubt about that. But I'm our anchor. If Wriggler died in this form, I think he'd find a way back to me.

But something tells me the Corvos is a different enemy. It doesn't just kill, it shatters. Destroys. And if it destroyed Wriggler. If it obliterated him, like it did that hellgator …

I ain't convinced I could survive that.

Stop worrying, Annie, Wriggler thinks. *It's distracting. I'll be back soon.*

I roll my eyes as I clamber out of the boat. Nora ushers Maeve and Lin inside. She tries to wrap a blanket round Kai but he wriggles out of it.

"I'm not hurt, Ma!" he complains. "Stop *fussing* me!"

I scowl at him. Something tells me that's language his father uses. It clearly works. Nora's cheeks redden but she says nothing. Instead, she beckons me and Sheb inside, leaving Kai to sulk on the veranda.

We get Lin upstairs. She looks tiny in the huge four-poster bed in one of the guest rooms, her black hair plastered to her forehead.

"She's burning up," Maeve says. "What the *hell* happened back there?"

I go to them, sit beside Maeve on the bed, feel Lin's forehead. She's a furnace. She looks half dead. Strange colors swirl around her. A gentle mist of purples, blues and lilacs. If I hadn't seen it before, I reckon I'd be unsettled, but I know what this is.

Lin's power means she can show people the true color of their soul. She showed me mine two weeks ago, helping me to see I'm not the evil thing I thought I was. She showed Maeve her soul, too. It was what allowed Maeve to accept her bond with Bear. It saved us, Lin's power.

Except, now, it seems like it's killing her.

My throat tightens. "Sheb?" I say, hating how my voice wavers.

He's by our side in moments. "I'm only guessing here," he says, "but I think her sensitivity to energy means what's … what's going on here af-fects her deeply."

I watch him as he talks, rummages through his supplies. There's a glimmer of my Sheb back. He's got a mystery to solve, a problem to study, a kid to care for. All the things that make him *him.*

"I'll give her bluewort for the fever," he says, un-stoppering a bottle with a twisted, blue moss inside. "And Bartok's saliva can take the edge off any pain."

Bartok obliges, hopping onto the bed. He gives Lin's ear a sharp nip. She frowns, then relaxes with a sigh.

"I'll need to observe her for a bit," Sheb says. "I don't know enough about her powers, yet, to diagnose what's happening, but—"

He reaches to his belt where he keeps his note-books, then seems to lose courage. Pain clouds his face. A shadow sweeping all the hope from him. I can't take it. I grab his hand, as if it'll somehow help. I glance at Nora, imploring, but she remains silent, watching. Bloody useless. I turn back to Sheb.

"What about the bone crow?" I ask, saying the first thing that comes into my mind. "What category do you think it is? A Serpentine like Wriggler? Or a Hot Blood, like Bear?"

At Maeve's feet, Bear paws the ground. I will Sheb to look at me, focus on what he loves. Caring. Learning.

"We need to know," I tell him. "We need to understand it. And no-one does that like you, do they? We need you."

I need him. I can't bear it if he drifts away. Not again.

But I can't say that, even though the words claw my throat. Sheb takes a breath, like he's trying to ground himself.

"Neither," he says. "It's difficult to tell from one glimpse ... but ... it's different. Serpentines are linked to rage and hate. They pull at a person at their most desperate. The Corvos has hate, but it's ... deeper. It's a kind of violence that even Wriggler isn't capable of. And I don't think it's a Hot-Blood. From what I've observed of Bear, his link with Maeve isn't the same as yours and

Wriggler's. There's anger. But there's something different, there."

I catch Maeve's eye. Neither of us says anything. We let Sheb talk.

"The Corvos has love, too, but it's tinged with darkness. Betrayal, maybe? It's an anger born of deep pain. Maybe even madness. I don't think it knows what it wants. It's full of confusion. I can't …" his face crumples. He covers his eyes. "I can't work it out."

I stare at him, frozen. He's leaving me again, ain't he? I reach for him, but I'm scared. It's like he's shrouded in mist.

Maeve frowns at me, then drops to her knees beside Sheb. "Hey," she says. "It's okay. We'll figure it out."

I watch as she holds him, rocking him gently, glaring at me all the while like this is somehow on me. I tear my gaze away, scowl at the wooden floor. Maeve huffs, disappointed, and returns her attention to Sheb. She lets him cry into her shoulder, and I don't get how this kid—orphaned when she was six, starved of love—can listen to Sheb's sobs and not feel them blast through her. Each terrible, desperate noise he makes is an earthquake inside me. The physics of the world shifts as he cries. It takes everything I have not to run. Get away from those awful sounds, find somewhere to *breathe.*

A noise from the door makes me glance up. I see Kai staring at us, a frown bridging his brows.

"Why's he crying?" he demands. I open my mouth to say something scathing, but Maeve gets there first.

"Because he's sad," she says, still holding Sheb . "It's okay to cry when you're sad."

Kai wrinkles his nose like he's not convinced. "No it's not," he says. "Warriors don't get sad."

Maeve blinks at him. "You never get sad?" she asks. "You never feel lonely? Or frightened?"

Kai stiffens. "No," he says.

"I'm sorry to hear that," Maeve says. I gape at her, but she ignores me. "It's important to feel everything. We can't feel love if we're never afraid. We can't feel joy if we're never sad. If you don't feel the bad things, you can't feel the good things."

Kai chews his lip thoughtfully, then clearly decides he doesn't want to talk about this anymore. He goes to his mother. He lets her wrap him in a blanket, then curls up in the corner. I can't stop staring at Maeve.

Is that true, what she said? And what the hell does she know, anyway?

She keeps casting me glances, like she expects me to do something about the way Sheb's crying.

Like *what*, Maeve?

Sheb wipes his eyes, pats Maeve's shoulder. "I'm alright," he says. "I'm okay. Thank you."

He gives her a sad smile. She squeezes his arm. I don't know why that makes me feel such a failure. Maeve helps Sheb to his feet.

The door slams. Voices sound downstairs.

Sheb's brothers are here.

· · · · ● · ● · · ·

I'm relieved when neither of the two figures lounging in the doorway is Ruben. We left Lin upstairs, still unconscious. Nora heads out to the veranda. Me, Maeve, and Sheb trudge into the front room, Bartok swooping after us. We find Locke and Cheran waiting. Locke lounges against the wall, a cruel smile on his face. He tests the tip of his harpoon with one finger, fixing Sheb with a glare.

"Ruben's running out of patience, brother," he says. "He wants a decision."

Sheb stiffens. "I know what Ruben wants," he says. "He won't get it."

I frown, catching Maeve's eye. She raises an eyebrow at me. I shrug, but flip a knife into my hand, ready to defend Sheb if I need to. Maeve unsheathes her dagger.

The smile drops from Locke's face. He goes to grab at Sheb but Cheran snatches his arm. Holding his brother back, Cheran looks at Sheb, his gaze imploring.

"Please," he says. "Just give him what he asks for. No-one wants you to get hurt." He gives Locke a pointed glare. "Ruben's ... you don't know what he's capable of."

Sheb raises his head, meets Cheran's gaze. "I know exactly what he's capable of," he says. "And I'm giving him nothing."

Locke wrestles free of Cheran's grip, squaring up to Sheb. Cheran splutters excuses.

"Oi!" I yell, levelling my knife at Locke's face. Wriggler and Bear start expanding, but Locke's gaze drifts past me as Nora enters the room.

"There you are," he says. "Ruben's looking for you, woman."

Nora tenses. "What of it?"

Locke bares his teeth. "So, you should go home!"

I bristle and, though Sheb tries to grab my hand, I'm ready to tell the brothers to go to hell, only someone else gets there first.

"Not yet, boy," says a cool, female voice from the veranda. "We have business to discuss with Nora before you send her back to that oaf brother of yours."

My mouth falls open as two women push past Cheran and Locke. They're both in heavy, grey cloaks, clasped at the front with silver brooches.

Underneath, I'm surprised to see they're wearing the same battle-dress as Nora. Leather vambraces and tunics, crossbows across their backs and pistols at their hips. The first woman meets my gaze. A jolt goes through me.

"It's you!" I blurt. "I've seen you! On the bridges and walkways, watching us ..."

The woman raises an eyebrow. "Have you, now?"

I scowl because I definitely have. I recognize her silver hair, her piercing eyes, and that cut under one eye, swollen and bruised. She has deep wrinkles around her eyes, but a stern set to her jaw. She touches the hellgator-tooth pendant at her throat as she appraises me, Maeve and Bear.

"Hmm," she says, stalks past us without another word.

"Imberg," Nora says urgently. "I was coming to find you, I need—"

The older woman—Imberg—puts a finger to her lips and gestures over her shoulder at us. Nora falls silent, which makes me frown.

I sneak a glance at the second woman, still in the doorway. She's red-haired and ferocious-looking. Locke has grabbed her arm, holds it in a claw-like grip. As he does, his sleeve rides up. I see a livid bite mark on the back of his hand. A human bite mark. He pulls the woman towards him.

"What the hell are you doing here?" he growls.

The woman yanks her wrist from his grip. Something slips loose from the collar of her dress and I realize she's wearing a pendant like Nora's and Imberg's. A hellgator tooth. "It's not your business, Locke," she says.

Locke's eyes flash. "It *is* my business if my wife—"

"Wife in name only," the red-haired woman says. "The whole town knows I only married you because ..." she pauses, but her gaze is fierce. "The thought of you near me fills me with disgust," she says.

Locke's fists clench. I think he might be about to hit her, but he glances at the bite mark on his hand and seems to think better of it. I can't help but smile. I hope his wife drew blood when she sank her teeth into him.

The red-haired woman turns her back on Locke and strides into the room. She stops when she sees me. Her gaze flicks between me and Maeve. Her fingers twitch towards the pistol at her belt.

"What're you doing here?" she demands. "You can't be here. Nora—"

"I know, child," Nora says sharply. "But there's not much we can do about it. When the swamp summons, we must listen."

"But murk-touched—" the red-haired woman protests. She falls silent at a sharp noise from Imberg.

She lifts her chin. "I'm—" she starts, then her gaze falls on Sheb. Something strange happens to her face.

"Sheb," she says, her voice no more than a whisper. "I thought you were ... Imberg said ..."

I frown. Why the hell would Imberg say anything about Sheb? She hasn't seen him in eight years. I stare at Sheb. A soft smile plays across his lips.

"Hey, Allise," he says. "It's good to see you."

My glance flicks between them. Sheb, Allise, and back again. Why does the air feel so charged? Why are they both blushing like—

Oh.

I don't know why, but I step forward, positioning my body so I'm half shielding Sheb. I glare at Allise. Whatever their past, whatever their feelings for each other, she wasn't there for Sheb when he needed her, was she?

Or was she? Did she see what his brothers did to him? Did she see what *he* did to Jeelie?

Allise looks at me. Her jaw sets. "Are you two—?" she asks.

Sheb grabs my hand, squeezes, gently guides me aside. "No," he says. "I love Annie. She is my family, but there has never ... been anyone else like you."

I can't work out why that makes my heart break a bit, but I know why those words make me think of Sasha. I wish he was here, even though he'd make everything a hundred times more complicated.

Allise steps forward, but Sheb backs away, gaze lowered.

"No," he says softly. "Not anymore. I'm sorry."

"Allise!" Imberg hisses. "Stop wasting time!"

"I'm not—" Allise protests. Nora cuts her off.

"Xanni's dead, girl," she says.

Allise pales.

"Xanni's—" she says, then covers her mouth to stifle a sob.

I frown. Hasn't Nora mentioned Xanni before?

Yes, Wriggler rumbles in my head. *She once told you she would help Xanni in the Deep Swamp.*

What does that mean? I demand.

I feel Wriggler rolling his eyes in my mind. *How should I know?* he drawls.

Allise hurries to Imberg's side, whispering urgently with the other two women. I frown as I watch them.

Maeve appears at my shoulder. "Funny," she whispers. "These women don't strike me as the kind to be forced into marriage with brutes like the de Callis brothers."

I nod. Can't help but agree. They have sabers at their hips, crossbows at their backs. And *hellgator teeth* hanging at their throats. These women know how to handle themselves. What has Ruben got over them that allows him to control them like this?

Locke's still lounging in the doorway, watching Sheb with smug amusement.

"I forgot about that," he sneers. "That you used to moon after my girl."

I snap my attention back to him and Cheran. "Careful," I growl, raising my knife.

Sheb says nothing. Locke smirks.

"What are you going to do, murk-girl?" he asks. "Skewer me to the wall? I'd like to see you try."

"I'll do worse than that," I snarl. Part of me is glad Wriggler isn't here, though I feel my anger fuel him.

On my way, Annie, he says. *Couldn't find Einan. No sign of him, or the Corvos.*

I don't know whether to be relieved or terrified by that, but I'm a distracted by the fact that Locke is a jerk and I want to break his nose. He seems to sense my anger. His smile widens. He pushes himself off the doorway, coming to stand inches from Sheb's face. Bartok growls, flying onto Sheb's shoulder and lunging at Locke's eye. Locke laughs.

"Trust you, Shebbie," he says. "Trust you to gather all the misfits. You were always like that, weren't you? It's why Allise would never have married you, in the end. Our mother might have fawned over you like your ass was coated in gold, but Pa knew. He knew your magic was weak. He knew you'd never make a good Heir."

Sheb flinches. I bristle.

"Talk to him like that again," I growl through gritted teeth. "I bloody *dare* you."

Locke's wicked grin widens, but Cheran steps in front of him, hands raised. "We're not here to fight," he says."

I glower at him. "Why the hell *are* you here?"

Cheran reddens, lowers his hands, and says nothing.

Locke's thoroughly enjoying himself. He pushes past Sheb, into the middle of the room. "So, the unwed swamp maiden is dead, is she?" he says. "Good riddance."

My eyebrows shoot up to my hairline. Swamp maiden? That was written on Luana's headstone ...

I cast a sideways glance at Sheb but he's glaring at Locke.

"You're making a mistake," he says. "You all are. Can't you feel it? The swamp—"

Locke grips his stomach, makes a mock gagging noise. "Brother, you make me *sick*," he says. "You and your damn feelings. Ruben was right. You'd have had us all holding hands, singing songs, letting the swamp do whatever the hell it wants."

Sheb doesn't answer. I step between him and Locke, seeing as Cheran's too much of a coward to intervene.

"Give me an excuse, Locke," I say, aiming my blade between his eyes. *"Please."*

Locke laughs. "That's the swamp's problem," he says, looking me up and down in a way that makes my skin crawl. "Its Maidens, its murk-touched ... it always picks the weak."

Beside me, Maeve stiffens. Bear yowls. I see him beginning to grow, white flames sparking from his paws. The women stop talking and turn. Imberg's gaze falls on Bear, the white fire, and her eyes widen. I see her shrink back.

That's interesting. Bear's white fire doesn't burn, but it has other powers. It saps the will to fight. How does Imberg know that, though?

"Control it!" she hisses.

"Maeve," I bark.

Her eyes glow. "I'm fine, Annie," she says, glaring at Locke.

He seems to be enjoying himself. He nudges Sheb with his shoulder. "The bone crow'll make short work of you, brother," he says.

Cheran's eyes widen. "Locke!" he barks. "We're not threatening him! Ruben said—"

"I don't give a shit what Ruben said," Locke sneers. "We all know he won't give in. Sooner Ruben realizes what he has to do, the better."

Icy cold washes through me. What the hell? I bare my teeth at Locke.

Wriggler!

Nearly there, he says. I feel him powering through the swamp, ten times his usual size. *Try not to kill him before I get there.*

I narrow my eyes at Locke. *No promises.*

"The Corvos won't get anywhere near Sheb while I'm around," I say. Locke's blue eyes fix on me. He grins. It's a hideous, wolfish smile that makes my hackles prickle.

"You're an idiot," he tells me. "You all are. You've got no idea, have you? In the end, Ruben will win. He'll win *because* of you, murk-girl. You'll help him and you've got no idea!"

My gut clenches, but I hold his gaze. The smile on Locke's face stutters as he looks at me. I know my eyes are glowing red.

"I'll kill him before I help him," I growl. "Whatever's happening, I swear I'll put a stop to it."

Lock chuckles, like he sees the doubt in me.

Because, holy shit, that dead hellgator, the feel of the Corvos in my mind, that relentless death-roar ... whatever's going on, it runs deeper, darker than the bone crow and whoever summoned it.

"Good luck, girl," Locke whispers. "There are consequences to killing a monster."

I can't tell if he's talking about the Corvos, or Ruben, so I say nothing. Locke stalks forward until his face is inches from mine.

"I'm going to enjoy watching you die," he says.

And, like a dancer waiting for his cue—a big, brutal dancer with massive red wings and sizzling lightning—Wriggler appears. He bursts from the water just outside in a shower of spray. He snarls as he slithers onto the veranda. He's only just small enough to fit through the door. Nora and the other women shrink back when they see him.

"What in the—" Allise exclaims, tripping over Kai in her haste to back away. Wriggler chuckles in my head, but his attention is fixed on Locke. Scarlet sparks zap across his scales. The crown of horns around his head sparkles with red light. He lowers his head so it's level with Locke's. Locke's bravado falters. He looks from me to my monster and back again. Wriggler shows his teeth.

Pathetic, he rumbles. *Tell him he's too scrawny to taste good, but I'll eat him if I have to.*

I smile and relay the message. I'm ashamed to say I get a pulse of satisfaction when Locke's face drains of color. Good. Let him feel what it's like to be the one on the ground, rather than the one kicking.

"That's enough now, Wriggler," I say aloud, to make sure Locke knows this monster is mine. Wriggler snaps at empty air.

Are you sure? He complains. *I'm enjoying myself.*

I cast him a sideways glance. *Pipe down.*

Grumbling, Wriggler shrinks to his usual size, winds round my legs. I lower my knife.

"Now we've got that out the way," I say, glaring. "Why don't you piss off?"

Locke's face twists. He makes to come towards me. I raise my knife, ready to fight him. Turns out, though, I don't have to. A hand grabs Locke's arm, holding it tight enough that he winces. I blink, lowering my knife. It takes me half a second to register that the hand holding Locke belongs to Maeve, that she's stepped in front of me. Her eyes glow that vivid, brutal green.

"Annie ain't the only one with a monster," she growls. As she speaks, Bear pulses and white fire blooms across the floor. He yawns, showing his teeth. "You wanna fight?" Maeve says, "you fight both of us. Gonna take that chance?"

What the hell does she think she's playing at? Painful girl! I glare, but she ain't looking at me. Locke wrenches his arm free. I see the defeat in his face. He's backing down, and he hates it.

And because he can't take it out on the murk-girls who have just put him in his place, he turns on the person he reckons is the weakest.

"You ain't changed much, have you Sheb?" he says, sullenly. "Still need women to defend you. Too soft to be of use to anyone."

Me and Maeve both react like lightning. Maeve's dagger and my throwing knife cross blades at Locke's throat.

"Go on," Maeve growls. "Finish that thought."

Locke raises his hands, but he's still smiling.

"I'm done," he says. "For now."

Sheb pushes past us, strides out onto the veranda. He disappears around the corner before I can call him back. I feel my heart squeeze.

Rage. Rage is the answer.

Always, Wriggler agrees, flaring his wings. I round on Locke, grabbing him by the shirt. He laughs as I wrench him close enough to spit in his face. I'm sorely tempted.

"If you *ever*—" I start, but Maeve's hand lands on my shoulder.

"Annie," she says.

"What?" I snap. "A minute ago, you were—"

But she's not looking at me. She's looking towards the door. I drop Locke and turn, fearing that Sheb's done something I might need to save him from.

But the figure that appears in the doorway, sopping wet, with haunted eyes, ain't Sheb.

It's Einan.

CHAPTER TWENTY-ONE

THE DISTANCE BETWEEN US

I SHOVE MY HANDS on my hips and glare.

"Where the hell've you been?"

Wriggler expands to dog sized, echoing my anger. Einan shrinks back with a whimper. Something in me softens.

"Come here," I say, frowning when he shies. "I ain't gonna hurt you. Just let Sheb look at that cut."

The slice across his forehead is deep enough that it's bleeding into his eyes. He wipes it away as Sheb comes back inside.

Sheb dabs at the cut, wraps a bandage over it. Einan's gaze slides to meet Locke's and Locke twitches an eyebrow. Something passes between them. My frown deepens.

The women fall silent, stalk past us. Kai rises to go after his mother but she glares at him. He sits back down. My eyebrows shoot up. Seriously? I ain't babysitting her brat while she runs around not telling us anything. I open my mouth to tell her so as she passes, but her fingers brush my wrist. Her breath tickles my ear.

"Don't believe everything you see," she murmurs. Before I can ask what the hell she means, she's gone, the other two women following. Locke tries to catch Allise's arm but she snatches it away, striding outside without a backwards glance. He reddens.

"Allise!" he yells, running after them. "Don't walk away from me!"

A boat engine roars to life. Locke shouts louder. Cheran casts us a last apologetic look, then follows his brother.

"Thugs," Maeve says.

For once, I agree with her. I round on Einan.

"Well?" I growl. "Where've you been?"

Einan winces as Sheb ties off his bandage. "I need to show you something," he says. "You gotta come with me."

I shove my hands on my hips. "Why—"

"Quick!" Einan pleads. "Before they come back. I shouldn't be—"

He falls silent, but it's enough to convince me. Anything the brothers don't want us to know is something I *absolutely* want to find out.

"Maeve," I say. "You stay—"

"Like hell," Maeve says.

I bristle, but Sheb touches Maeve's shoulder. "Maeve, Lin is upstairs, very vulnerable to the death-roar. We need someone strong to stay and care for her. And there is no-one better than you. Let Annie and I go with Einan. We will tell you everything we find. I promise."

Maeve wilts. "Fine," she says. "But what about him?" she jerks a thumb at Kai. It's an excellent point. Kai throws Maeve the filthiest look he can muster, and Maeve returns it in kind. If we leave them alone together, I'm pretty sure only one of them will be alright when we get back. Sheb sighs.

"My nephew can come with us," he says.

I snap round to face him. "He can *what?*"

He can what? Wriggler cries at the same time.

Sheb smiles softly. "He's a de Callis boy," he says. "No-one is better equipped to handle the swamp, are they, Kai?"

Kai blinks at him. "I—" he says. "You—"

Sheb winks. "Come on," he holds out his hand. "I'll let you hold Bartok."

Bartok turns his accusing tawny glare on his favorite human. I wouldn't want Kai holding me, either.

We leave Maeve scowling after us, pile into a boat. Einan busies himself making it ready and Sheb settles Kai on one of the benches. The kid unclips his harpoon, but Sheb shakes his head.

"You look like you're going to battle with the swamp," he says. Kai looks at him.

"I am going into battle with the swamp," he points out.

Sheb smiles. "No, you're not," he says. "Your pa might not have told you this, but your magic is born from the swamp. It's old and wild, just like this place is. And if you use it right, it can work *with* the swamp, not against it."

Kai frowns. "I'm not a swamp maiden," he says sullenly. His gaze lands on me. "I'm not a *murk-touched*."

I clamp down on my bond with Wriggler before my lightning-snake senses my rage.

Sheb sits beside the boy. "Those people just have different kinds of magic," he says. "The swamp needs the maidens and the murk-touched because we fight it. If we didn't fight it, it wouldn't need to fight *us*, would it?"

Kai seems to think about this for a moment. He lets Sheb sheathe his harpoon across his back. I smile as Einan fires the engine. We scoot out onto the water. Sheb would've made a great dad. He'd make a great Heir, too, by the sounds of things.

He catches my eye. I smile at him. "You're good at this," I mouth. His smile falters.

"I'm not," he says, staring at his hands. "I used to be, but I ..." his fingers curl into fists. "I don't know, Annie. I feel so weak. So useless. What am I doing here?"

I reach for him, then think better of it. I don't know what to say. It's Kai who speaks as we pass under the bridges and past the walkways of the town.

"The swamp likes you," he points out. "It's weird. Look."

He points to the banks. I ain't surprised to see birds hopping from tree to tree, following in our wake. Or that the trees reach their branches towards Sheb, like they're desperate to touch him. I'm reminded again of the story Sheb told me about Everyn Vane de Callis, how his magic was stronger than anyone had ever seen. It makes me wonder ...

Sheb catches my eye. I quirk an eyebrow.

"Nowhere's like that, too," I remind him. "It loves you."

"It loves you, too," Sheb says, waving a dismissive hand.

I shake my head, laughing. "It puts up with me," I say. "It's afraid of Wriggler."

My lightning-snake huffs. *So it should be.*

"But it *loves* you, Sheb. It follows you. It wants to be near you. It don't surprise me the swamp is the same."

Sheb stares at his hands. "Something's different," he says. "I don't feel it like I used to. Something's blocking it. Something ..." he drifts off, staring at nothing. Kai fidgets.

"Pa said you were weak and useless," he says. I've a mind to cuff him round the head, but he looks embarrassed when he says it, like he's no longer sure it's true.

Sheb shrugs. "He would say that."

"Is it weak when you don't fight?" Kai asks. He's looking at me, like I might have the answer.

"I—" I stutter. Wriggler nudges my palm. I scratch the scales on his blunt head. I think back to a few weeks ago when we rescued Maeve and Lin. How Maeve had fought for so long. How I helped her learn not to, because she was mostly fighting herself.

And how I'd fought Wriggler for so long. Held him down, locked him tight. But we're so much stronger now we're *not* fighting each other.

"No," I say. "You got to learn what are the right battles. Sometimes, we fight 'cos we're scared."

Kai chews his lip and thinks about this. "You don't fight," he says to Sheb. "Even though Pa says you should. It annoys him that you don't."

Sheb smiles. I see a cheeky gleam in his eyes. "I know," he says. I snort into my hand.

Sheb hold out his arm and encourages Bartok onto Kai's shoulder. Bartok takes some serious persuading but, in the end, he does it for Sheb. He clings to the kid's shoulder, leaning as far away from him as he can manage.

I watch Sheb as he guides Kai's fingers to stroke Bartok's soft belly feathers, explaining about the owl-squirrel's anesthetic bite, what he eats, how Sheb found him. Kai even asks questions. He shuffles closer to his uncle. There's a light in his eyes I ain't seen before. Curious. Gentle.

He'd be so different if he was Sheb's son.

Annie, Wriggler says. I realize he's grown. I glance up as the world darkens. The trees thicken around us, tangled branches blocking the light. At the back of my mind, the death-roar buzzes louder than before. The air feels suddenly close. I stare at the water. Is it me, or are there strange black streaks in it, like some oozing poison?

Sweat prickles on my skin. My clothes cling to me. Einan guides us up a narrow tributary, around small islands with clumps of grass and reeds. Remnant mist drifts between the branches, shaping into hands or faces before falling formless again. A face flashes in the trees. Jeelie's here. He catches my eye, frowns, then vanishes. I clutch the sides of my head as the swamp probes my mind. Its questioning presence darkens my vision. I shake my head, trying to free myself of it.

"Einan," Sheb says, alert. "You didn't say we were going to the Deep Swamp."

Einan says nothing, stares straight ahead. Sweat gleams on his forehead, but his eyes are determined.

"It's okay, Sheb," I say, as I feel the swamp recognize me.

Sheb doesn't answer. Beside him, Kai shivers, moans, flops against his uncle. Sheb puts an arm round the kid.

"What's wrong with him?" I demand.

Sheb swallows, his face drained. "It's angry," he says. "I feel it."

I frown. "No, it ain't," I say, sensing that same love I felt before. The connection between me and this place. Its wildness gently holding my wildness.

"Not with you," Sheb says. "With *us*. With the de Callis family."

I open my mouth, then shut it again. *Us.* I hate that he's put himself with them rather than me. He's not theirs. They don't deserve him. And the swamp doesn't get to be angry with him. Not after what he's been through.

I reach for the swamp in my mind, grip it in mental fists. I push my anger into it, show it Sheb's kindness, his gentleness. Show it how he hasn't even *been* here for eight years so how can it blame him?

He left, it replies. The buzz of its voice sends nausea rolling through me. *He left us …*

Right. Ain't much I can say to that.

"Einan," Sheb says. "We need to turn back. We're heading towards the heart. We can't—"

"A little further," Einan says.

I notice the black streaks in the water thickening. The stench of infection stings my nose.

Einan moors the boat to a tree stump, cuts the engine. The noises of the swamp intensify. The hum of heat-loving flies. The chatter-hiss of rushing water. I see eyes in the murk, a huge, sinuous shape sliding through the water. The reeds tremble, reaching towards us like grasping fingers, but they fall shy of grabbing us. Maybe they sense me and Wriggler. Maybe it's Sheb they don't want to attack. Either way, they do nothing but threaten for now. I blink in the gloom, resist reaching for my throwing knife. The canopy is so thick I can barely see a thing.

But Wriggler can.

Look through my eyes, he says.

What? I demand. We've never done that before. *How?*

Well close yours for a start, he drawls.

I grumble but do as he says. Immediately, I feel a tug behind my eyeballs and gasp. I can see *with my eyes closed.* Wriggler's vision is sharp and strange, brighter, but with fewer colors. Reds and oranges are sharper, with greens and blues muted. There's a thread of gold running through everything. He sees in the colors of my soul.

Wriggler rears in the boat, growing so he can lift himself up, show me what he sees. He scans the trees.

You seeing this? He demands. I can.

Tree after tree after tree, each stump and sapling and towering giant is marked with the de Callis symbol. That circle, slashed through, with an eye in the center. Through Wriggler's eyes, they glow faintly, but I also notice there's a red tinge to some, like a cut that's become infected. The death-roar grows louder. My fingers tighten over the gunwale. I feel the swamp in my mind, silently screaming. It writhes, thrashing against invisible restraints. Ruben's been here, and he shouldn't have been.

"What the hell has he done?" I breathe.

My eyes snap open as something brushes my arm. I glance down to see Einan's hand gripping me. I wrench free.

"What the hell is all that?" I demand.

Einan blinks at me. "All what?" he says. "You're looking the wrong way. You should look *that* way."

He points over my shoulder to where Sheb and Kai are looking. Next to where Einan moored us, a huge tree leans over the boat, its roots—as thick around as my torso—plunging into the inky water. There's something carved into its trunk. A message. I lean further out of the boat.

Wriggler, can you see?

I close my eyes again. Wriggler's vision replaces mine. I instantly wish it hadn't. The writing on the trunk is clear as day.

For the swamp. For the fallen. For Luana. The bone crow is coming for you, de Callis.

It looks like it's been slashed into the trunk with a knife. Except it hasn't. I know it hasn't, because the thing that has been used to slash the message is plunged into the trunk below the final word. It's a tooth. A hellgator tooth.

I reach out, tug it free.

"What the hell?"

"The swamp maidens," Einan says. He spits into the water and, for some reason, this makes me want to smack him. "Ruben knew they'd been plotting. It's one of them, I reckon. They've got the bone crow. They've stolen my sister to punish Pa. It's them, it's—"

"Shut up a minute," I snarl. To his credit, he shuts up. "I keep hearing these swamp maidens mentioned. Who are they?"

Sheb stares at the tooth in my hand. "They're warriors of the swamp," he murmurs. "Because the family Heirs are only ever men—no, I know it's ridiculous, Annie," he says as I start to protest. "The families misuse their power. They always have. So the swamp recruits its own soldiers. And it always chooses women. Mothers. Wives. Daughters."

"It takes them—" Einan starts. I round on him but Sheb gets there before me.

"It doesn't *take* them!" he hisses. "It never takes what does not want to be taken! The women offer themselves. They're volunteers!"

Einan falls silent, but he stares at Sheb with fire in his eyes. It looks a lot, to me, like hatred. Sheb ignores him.

"The swamp maidens live among the families. They marry. They have children. They appear perfectly human. But they aren't. They are the swamp's messengers. Its army. When it is angry, it calls on them to fight."

I gaze at the tooth in my hand. Something icy prickles the back of my neck. "You think a swamp maiden called the bone crow?" I ask.

Sheb shrugs. "I don't know, Annie," he says. "But that tooth is a sign of the swamp maidens."

I'd worked out that much. The pendants the women wear now make a terrible sense. Nora. Imberg. Allise. Yarella. Three of those women are married into the de Callis family or its warriors. Is it an infiltration? I remember Allise snarling at Locke as she stormed out of the house. Doesn't seem like she's happy to be his wife. If these women have magic from the swamp, if they're that powerful, how is Ruben forcing them into marriage?

And if the swamp still sees Sheb as a de Callis, how much danger is he in?

I think of the hellgator that attacked him at the house. My fists close over the tooth.

"We need to talk to Nora," I say.

"If she's betrayed us—" Einan starts. I glare and let Wriggler rear in front of him. Einan yells, falls back into the bilge. He stops talking though, which is a relief. He scowls at me. I raise an eyebrow.

Kai glances up at his uncle, eyes wide. "Is Ma in trouble?" he asks. "Did she hurt Pa?"

Sheb looks at him. I see a familiar battle in Kai's face. A battle of allegiance between warring parents. A battle I've felt too many times. And one Sheb also knows well.

Sheb puts his arm round his nephew. It's okay, Kai," he says. "You know you've done nothing wrong, don't you? Whatever is happening between your parents, it's much bigger than you."

Kai doesn't look convinced. He strokes Bartok's soft belly again, and this seems to give him comfort. Bartok fluffs himself up, summons his sweetest self and nuzzles Kai's cheek. Kai giggles—actually *giggles*—and hugs the owl-squirrel tenderly.

"Time to go," Sheb says. Einan unmoors the boat, starts the engine.

None of us speak. I grip the tooth so tight its serrated edge cuts my palm.

As we glide towards Marsh Wilds, I see eyes in the murk. Eyes of unfathomable black, set in faces of brown-and-green scales. Huge, reptilian bodies drifting beneath the water.

Hellgators. Dozens of them. And they're watching us.

Chapter Twenty-Two

Annie, Do You Want This?

This bed is stupidly big. I hate it. I can't sleep. I kick the sheets off, throw an arm over my forehead. Both my arm and forehead are slick with sweat.

Sheb insisted I sleep in one of the guest rooms, rather than on the sofa. No idea why. I said yes, for him, but now I wish I hadn't.

I can't stop thinking about the de Callis crest carved on those trees. The hellgator tooth. The swamp maidens—whatever they are. The hellgators watching us as we left.

And Einan. The hatred in his eyes as he'd looked at Sheb. Despite the heat, a chill ripples through me.

Wriggler slithers out from under the sheets. He flicks his tongue against my nose.

It's too hot up here, he says. *Let's get some air.*

I don't need telling twice. I scoop Wriggler into my arms, grab a throwing knife, and creep downstairs. We head onto the veranda, where a faint breeze brings some relief from the heat. I close my eyes as it cools my skin. Moonlight illuminates a light haze over the water. The remnants are out in force tonight, drifting in packs across the darkness. I scan their faces. Old and young. Parents, children. They wander aimlessly, appearing to search for something they can't quite remember. I don't see Jeelie among them. Don't mean he ain't here, though.

Wriggler nudges my foot.

What's on your mind?

I frown at him. *You know what's on my mind. You're in my head.*

Wriggler shuffles his wings. *Yeah,* he says. *But it's nice to pretend you've got the choice, isn't it?*

I suppress a snort. *I'm thinking about Einan.*

Wriggler flicks his tail. *Oh,* he says. *Him.*

I chew the inside of my cheek. *Why do you say it like that?*

Wriggler nuzzles his blunt head against my cheek. *That kid isn't telling us everything.*

Yeah. No shit. And his hatred for Sheb seems to run as deep as his hatred for the swamp maidens, despite the fact his mother is one. Why would the de Callis brothers marry swamp maidens if Ruben is determined to go to war with the swamp?

And where the hell does the Corvos and its master fit into all of this?

Wriggler tucks his head under one wing. *More secrets,* he grumbles. *So tedious. Anyway, who d'you think it is?*

I roll my eyes. *How the hell am I s'posed to know?* I snap. *At this rate it could be bloody anyone! But that message on the tree ... and Nora said Xanni's dead, whoever she is. The swamp maidens seem angry. Maybe one of them is angry enough to summon a monster?*

Wriggler chuckles like I've said something daft. I scowl.

Alright, genius, I say. *Who do you think it is?*

Wriggler gives a strange shudder, halfway between a sigh and a shrug. *Haven't the faintest.*

I roll my eyes. *So helpful.*

Wriggler huffs. *I'm just the monster,* he points out. *You're the monster hunter, aren't you?*

I don't know why, but his words make me feel strange. Is that what I am? And what does that mean?

"I just want to keep my family safe," I murmur.

I expect Wriggler to reply with something scathing, but instead, he rears up, glares at the water. Immediately, I'm alert.

What? What is it?

Company, Wriggler says, sparks skittering from his tongue.

I scan the dark. *What kind of company?* I ask.

The splintered boards of the veranda creak with the weight of something big. A shadow rears in front of me, rumbling a growl. I raise my knife.

Then lower it. "Dammit!"

Wriggler curls around my legs. *Nothing to worry about,* he chuckles, as Sasha shifts from maned cat to human. *It's only Sasha.*

Wriggler, I growl in my mind. *You useless—*

If you need me, he interrupts, *I'll be here, trying not to listen to you two moon over each other so I don't choke on my own vomit.*

I scowl at him, trying to think of a mean enough insult, but Sasha pulls me into a fierce embrace. I forget everything except his warmth, the scent of earth and incense and that ever-present, ethereal smell I've come to realize is the tang of his power. I struggle against him for a moment, still furious with him.

His voice sounds in my ear. "I was at the graveyard," he whispers. "I saw the Corvos. You could've—" he holds me tighter. "I'm sorry."

All the anger goes out of me. I wrap my arms round him, close my eyes.

Wriggler makes gagging noises in my head. I tell him to piss off.

"You were at the graveyard," I say aloud, registering what this means. "You didn't come to help?"

Sasha draws back from me, a wry grin on his face. "Do you remember how angry you get every time I say anything about saving you?"

Oh yeah. Fair point. My face heats. Sasha chuckles. He lifts a hand, brushes his fingers across my face. I close my eyes. Can't help it. I don't know why his touch makes me feel so powerful and so vulnerable at the same time. Why I long for it when he's not nearby, fear it when he's right in front of me.

"Don't take this the wrong way," he murmurs. "But are you hurt?"

I snort a laugh. "No," I say. "It didn't come after us. I just ... I can feel something in my mind. This death-roar. I don't know what it is, if it's the Corvos doing it, or if it can hear the awful thing too, and that's why it's come."

Sasha frowns. "You think something's called it?"

"I reckon some*one* has," I say. "Like Maeve did with Bear. Like I did—"

I bite my lip, lower my gaze. In my head, I feel Wriggler doing the mental equivalent of an eye-roll.

Yeah, yeah, he grumbles. *You're mortally bound to a monstrous lightning-serpent, your undying rage made manifest. Get over it already.*

I shove him out of my head, but not before I feel him laughing.

"I can't work it out," I say. "Ruben and his brothers are waging war against something they don't understand. The world feels broken. These remnants ain't natural. I think ..." I trail off, not sure how to explain. "I might need your help with something," I say.

Sasha takes my hand, laces his fingers through mine.

"Always," he says. "I'm with you, Annie. Whatever you need."

My lips quirk into a smile. I feel Wriggler in my head pretending this is killing him.

"I need to ask some questions," I say. "Flush people out, make them scared. They won't tell me the truth, but—"

"But you're hoping, if I'm watching, I might notice something," Sasha says.

I nod. "Exactly."

He holds my gaze and I feel something shift under my solar plexus. I let myself fall into the silky light of Sasha's gold-flecked eyes, those pools of darkness I never tire of gazing into. Maybe he gets this now. What I need from him. Maybe this is where we start to work.

Sasha chews his lower lip. "It would be safer if the others didn't know I was here," he says. "Alphonz is still hunting me. He's likely watching us now."

I tense. "If he comes anywhere near you—" I growl. Sasha looks at me, amusement dancing in his eyes.

"Oh, he knows," Sasha says. "That's why he doesn't come anywhere near me."

I'll eat him if he does, Wriggler offers.

I suppress a smile. *I knew you liked him really.*

I do not, Wriggler insists. *It'll just be annoying if he gets hurt and you get sad.*

I don't reply, but I know Wriggler feels my amusement.

"I'll watch from the shadows tomorrow," Sasha offers. "I'll try and see the things you can't."

I nod my thanks. We fall silent, staring over the darkened swamp. I'm aware that his hand still holds mine, our fingers laced together. His thumb gently strokes the back of my hand. It feels good. A comfort I so often get from Sheb—my best friend—and I hadn't realized how much I've missed it. That touch from someone who only wants to make you feel loved.

Only it's different from Sasha, ain't it? Sheb holding my hand doesn't electrify me like this. Doesn't heighten my awareness of my own heartbeat, the quickening of my breath.

I don't deserve this.

"I'm ..." I start. "I know I'm hard work. I'm angry a lot. I know I ain't always been ..."

Sasha chuckles quietly, leans closer to me. "It's kind of refreshing," he admits. "Back in Wilderness, as a priest, the townsfolk were always so deferential. Averting their eyes. Bowing. Stumbling over themselves to thank me for defending them from the Wood. No-one ever challenged me."

"Maeve did," I point out.

Sasha shakes his head. "Maeve barely spoke to me. She was too angry. I could convince myself what I was doing was right. And then you came along—"

"And messed everything up," I say bitterly.

Sasha grabs my other hand, turns to face me. "No," he says. "You showed me the truth. You aren't easy, Annie. I won't pretend otherwise. But you ... you make me want to be better."

I raise my eyes to meet his. Those dark, gold-flecked pools, reflecting moonlight. I should pull away. This is too soon. It must be. We'll only shatter each other, leave the broken pieces strewn across each other's hearts. We can't do this. Not yet.

"Sasha," I murmur. "We should ... I can't ..."

Sasha cups my chin, lifts it so I'm looking at him. Into those deep, brown eyes, flecked with gold and green. He holds my gaze, gently pushing hair back from my cheek.

"Annie," he says, and my name on his lips is like a spell, stealing my breath. "You are ..." he starts.

I quirk an eyebrow. "I'm what?"

He smiles. "Exceptional," he says. His gaze drops to my mouth. I feel my lips tingle. How often have I lain awake at night, imagining this? Wanting it? How often have I stood by Nowhere's portal tree, yearning for Sasha to appear, gather me in his arms and—

He leans towards me. "Is it okay if—?"

I close my eyes. Yes. Yes, it's okay. More than okay. I tilt my head up, gather the front of his shirt in my fists, pulling him closer.

ANNIE!

Wriggler's voice blasts through my head, sending dizzying jolts of pain down my nerves. I jerk suddenly, pull back from Sasha, clutching the sides of my head.

"Dammit, Wriggler!" I growl. "What was that—"

"Quiet," Sasha says beside me. He's tensed, scanning the water, then the sky. He bares his teeth. I see his canines elongate, eyes flashing with amber.

"Call Wriggler," he snarls. "Now!"

My lightning-snake is already monstrous. His eyes flash red, and mine mirror the glow. Lightning zaps across Wriggler's scales as he coils himself around me, snarling at the sky. Sasha yowls as his body changes.

I have just enough time to see Maeve and Sheb rush onto the veranda. "Annie?" Maeve asks. "What the hell—"

And then the world is noise. Something spikes in my head. The death-roar is so intense I can't see. The stench of necrosis. A deep, dark, violence echoes behind my eyes.

Screaming. Deep and cruel. Murderous.

You will not take him from me! Not again. He's mine. Mine, always!

I stagger against the sound, clutching the veranda railings.

And that's when a shadow detaches from the sky. With a shriek like the end of the world, it crashes into us.

CHAPTER TWENTY-THREE

THE BONE CROW

I'M BLASTED OFF THE edge of the veranda, and only Wriggler's outstretched wing stops me from plunging into the water.

You're welcome, he rumbles. He sets me down, rounds on the monstrous thing now perched between me and my family. It lifts its head. The sight of it steals my breath.

It's vast. Of course it is. It's a monster, fueled by rage. It stands on two, powerful legs, talons splintering the boards beneath. It balances its weight on the wrist-joints of two, huge wings, covered in black feathers. Feathery down coats its whole body, even the long tail lashing behind it. It tosses its massive head, snapping a cruel, hooked beak. Moonlight catches on the frill of horns sweeping from its head, and its eyes ... I can't tear my gaze away. There's no light in them, but even in darkness, their intense emptiness pulls me. They're so devoid of life, they suck at my soul, slow my heartbeat. It throws its head back and *shrieks*.

The inside of my mind explodes with pain. My vision blurs. I clutch the sides of my head, scream, feel myself rattle out of reality. Everything around me disappears and my legs buckle. I don't feel my knees hit the veranda boards. No-one tries to drag me to my feet. All I can think is that this thing is in my mind, needling through my memories, rooting around in my darkness. It tears open scars I've long tried to heal, until the inside of my head is a wild, shredded mess. Spasms jerk my body. Something foul stings the inside of my mouth. I'm being sick. I collapse into a twitching heap, too weak to call for help—

And, as quickly as it came, it stops. I'm left gasping, spluttering bile.

I push myself up. Soil shifts beneath my hands.

I'm not on the veranda anymore.

I scramble to my feet, whip round in a circle. I'm alone. The frigid night air stings my nose. A pale mist obscures my view, but it's clear where I am. Headstones loom from the dark. Trees entwine their branches overhead. The graveyard. How the hell did I get here?

I reach for a throwing knife but my fingers close on empty air. My belt isn't there. In fact, I'm not even wearing the flax shirt and pants I always dress in. The clothes Sheb made me from the trees and plants of Nowhere. When I look down, I see …

I'm in the yellow dress I was wearing when I murdered my daddy, then ran from him. But that was five years ago. I burned this dress. It doesn't exist anymore, yet I'm wearing it. It's torn where I crashed through the window to escape the mayor and his mob. It's stained with the blood I lost when I cut my foot. Grimy with sweat and soil, where I collapsed under a tree, feverish, convinced I was going to die.

Before Bartok and Sheb found me.

What the *hell* is happening? How am I in the graveyard, wearing this dress?

Wriggler? I reach for our bond, try to send rage flooding to him. Give him power—

But I can't feel him. The bond isn't just closed. It's *gone.*

I panic.

As my heart thunders, a strange, calm voice in the back of my mind points out this is completely irrational. I've spent five years battling Wriggler, hating that he's tied to my darkness, but now he's gone, loneliness spears my heart. We were just starting to understand each other and—

I need him. He's part of me. A part I can't escape and don't want to, anymore. I *am* him, and he's me. How the hell has this piece of me been torn away?

The answer stalks out of the shadows, its laughter ringing in my head. Its movements are slow, deliberate. It knows I have nowhere to run.

The bone crow prowls in a circle around me. Its long tail drags in the soil, its lightless eyes fix on me. It opens its beak. I see a red, lashing tongue, a row of wicked fangs. Its darkness curls in my mind, trying to unspool me.

I have nothing to defend myself with. No knives. No lightning-snake. I'm just a furious, frightened woman desperate to survive. I raise my fists. The Corvos snarls, stops in front of me, lowers its head so its vast, cruel beak is inches from my face. I hold its gaze, defiant. Rage floods me, like it always does when I'm scared, only this time, there's no Wriggler to defend me. My scar sears with pain, but I glare into the bone crow's violent eyes. If I'm going to die here, I'll die fighting. I'll let this vile thing know that Annie doesn't fall easy. I lift my chin, though all I can hear is the roar of blood in my ears.

"What did you do with Zuma?"

The Corvos tilts its head, considering me. I frown, still holding its stare. There's a pulse in my mind. I feel …

I don't know what I feel. A tangle of darkness and pain. A lifetime of oppression. Cruelty. But there's something else beneath it. Something I recognize.

Yearning.

It wants something. But I can't work out what.

There's something about it that doesn't feel right. Doesn't feel ... *alive.* I notice there are holes in its wings, its feathers are bent. The down in some places has fallen away, revealing black flesh teeming with flies. Its bird-like head is gaunt, skin hanging off in folds, as if the muscles beneath have wasted away.

"Who are you?" I ask. "Who summoned you?"

The Corvos draws itself up to its full height, mist curling around its massive form. Remnants appear beneath its wings, turning their pale, sightless eyes on me. I step back before I can help myself.

"What have you done?" I demand. "Where's Wriggler? Sasha? Where's my family?"

The Corvos snaps its beak at me. *"Here,"* it hisses, its voice like a serrated blade sawing my mind. *"They're here, beside you. Talking with me, just like you are."*

I bare my teeth. "Don't lie to me," I growl. "I know where I am. I know—"

I fall silent, suddenly understanding. I'm not in the graveyard. Not wearing this dress. I haven't left the veranda.

This is in my head. This vile thing's found a way into my darkness, making it my reality. And whatever the hell it's doing to me, it's doing to the others.

The Corvos rumbles a laugh. *"You're a clever one, aren't you?"* it says, circling me again. *"I can see why he likes you."*

I frown. "Who?"

It ignores me. *"So full of doubt, though. And that's why he can never be yours."*

Something cold blooms in my gut. "For Oak's sake, w*ho?*" I hiss. "Who're you talking about?"

The bone crow snarls, tossing its hideous head.

"My family," It growls. *"The ones you will never destroy. I will not let you. I'll kill you first."*

It leaps.

A wave of vicious energy tears through my brain. I'm screaming. My mind is on fire. My scar alight with agony so intense I fall to the ground, thrashing. Something bursts in my nose.

I'm bleeding. I claw at the ground, tearing my nails. I feel every blow my daddy ever dealt me, the loneliness after Mum left, both times. I feel the eyes of all those others in my town, watching. The ones who knew what Daddy was like, knew how desperate I was, but did nothing. How they came for me when I finally killed him. I feel it all, as fresh as it's ever been. And I do something I haven't done since I was seven years old.

"Mama!" I yell, as if she's ever come to save me. "Mama, please!"

The pressure in my head withdraws. For a quiet moment, I realize I'm curled up like a fetus, shivering and crying. I open my eyes. The Corvos watches me, head tilted.

"Mama," it repeats. *"Why do you call her? She is gone."*

I don't know why, but this makes my eyes burn. Hot tears spill down my face. "I know," I sob. Dammit, why can't I get a hold on myself? I wipe my face, force myself to stand. This thing is tearing me apart. I need to escape it.

"Mothers don't save us," the Corvos says. *"Mothers are wounds others can use against us. Mothers disappoint us. Mothers make us weak."*

I frown, but don't answer. Let the vile thing keep talking. My fingers twitch. I scan the ground, searching for a weapon. This isn't real. Somewhere nearby, my friends are fighting, too. I have to get back to them.

I reach again for Wriggler, pushing through the fog, frantic to find him. The air around me sizzles, shimmers. For a moment, I think I feel him, somewhere far away.

Annie!

His voice is like an echo of an echo, so faint I wonder if I'd imagined it. But it's enough. I know he's close.

"Let go ... of me!" I cry.

The Corvos snarls. *"Never,"* it hisses. *"He's mine! How dare you try to take him from me!"*

What?

The Corvos steps closer. I feel its breath on my face, putrid with death. Its tail beats the ground as it spreads its wings, screeching to the night. It's so dark, it drinks the moonlight. Everything about it pulls life from the world. I reckon I see the trees wilt, the grass wither. This thing is death. Death on wings. Death in my heart.

And I ain't having it.

I open my mouth as wide as it'll go and scream. Not in fear, or even in rage. It's a scream of life. A scream that says, *I am here and I will not leave.*

I charge. I've got nothing but my hands, but I grab fistfuls of its feathers, wrench them out, then claw at the flesh beneath. I kick and snarl and punch. The Corvos thrashes under my attack, but I hear it laughing.

"You won't take me!" I yell. "Or my family!"

"He is not yours," the Corvos sneers. *"He never was."*

Those words punch the air from my lungs. It's talking about Sheb. I reach for Wriggler again. It's like reaching for the lip of a cliff I've just tumbled off. One, last, desperate grab for life.

Annie! His voice is loud in my mind. *Annie I'm here! Fight it!*

I grasp the thread that ties me to Wriggler.

Follow my voice, Annie. I'm here. Always here. Fight it, for Oak's sake! FIGHT!

I roar. Imagine I'm clawing my way from deep underground and there's light. Imagine that my lightning-snake is fighting to free me as hard as I'm fighting to free myself.

There's a shift somewhere beneath my solar plexus. Something twangs free. I gasp, fall forward onto all fours. My knees hit wood. I smell the swamp, hear a battle raging around me. I'm back to myself.

Don't just sit there! Wriggler yells. *Get your ass up and help me!*

I look up, finally take in the chaos around me. Wriggler and the Corvos have locked jaws, beating each other with their wings. Black blood pours from Wriggler's scales. I feel the echoes of his wounds on my own body. They bite and claw each other, wild and furious. The veranda can barely take their weight. Bits fly off it. Chunks of the house itself blast off in different directions. If they don't stop, they'll bring the whole place down.

Hold it off! I tell Wriggler, flooding him with fury.

Great advice, Wriggler drawls. *I hadn't thought of that. Move, Annie!*

My friends are strewn on the veranda. Sheb lies over the threshold of the door. I see his legs, bent at an awkward angle. He's too far away for me to reach. Beyond him, Maeve's collapsed in a heap, too. She's clutching her head, eyes squeezed closed. Bear, still in cub form, mewls and paws at her. Beside her, is Lin, also unconscious, with one arm thrown over Maeve, like she was trying to wake her. I can't reach any of them with Wriggler and the Corvos carrying on like that, so I drag my shaking body over to the nearest person I can find. Sasha.

He's in human form again, though I see his canines are lengthened, claws still curving from his fingertips. His eyes roll feverishly under closed lids. His mouth moves, forming silent words I can't follow. I shake his shoulder.

"Sasha! Wake up!"

But obviously, he doesn't respond. He's not asleep, is he? The Corvos has got him. It's got them all.

CHAPTER TWENTY-FOUR

IS THIS REALITY?

I SHOUT SASHA'S NAME, shaking him roughly. He won't wake.

The Corvos needles my mind. I clench my jaw, shove it away, but it's persistent. Like a rolling dizziness that won't be quelled.

Stay with me, Annie! Wriggler rumbles, locking his jaws around the bone crow's throat. His voice keeps me grounded.

The Corvos thrashes, raking its talons down Wriggler's belly. Wriggler shrieks, lets go, beating the monster with his huge wings. He opens his maw and lightning shoots from his throat, catching the Corvos in the shoulder. The hideous thing takes off, its wings throwing a foul downdraft against the veranda. I'm pushed flat against Sasha's chest, digging my fingernails into the wooden boards to avoid being hurled off. The Corvos rises into the night.

Let me have him! It screams. *He's mine! How dare you take him!*

I hear it circling, the rhythmic thrum of its wings disturbing the air. Wriggler keeps his own wings flared, jaws agape.

It's after Sheb! I tell Wriggler. *Keep close to him. Don't let it have him!*

Wriggler snarls. *It'll come back for another attack,* he says. *Wake the others, Annie. Now!*

Thick, black mist curls around my hands as I shake Sasha. His eyes roll, his mouth keeps moving, but he's lost to me. The black mist thickens until I can barely see. It tastes putrid. I splutter.

"What the hell is that?"

The Corvos, Wriggler says, glaring into the sky. *It's got some sort of psychic power. It's trying to pull you back under.*

I slap the side of Sasha's face hard, leaving a red hand print I'm sure he won't thank me for later. He doesn't stir. Panicked tears sting my eyes.

I scramble across the veranda to Sheb. Bartok's perched protectively on his chest and fixes me with a wide, terrified glare. Weirdly, he doesn't lunge at me when I shake Sheb roughly.

"Sheb, please ..."

But it's no use. Like Sasha, he's pulled so far under, he can't hear me. I see how his face contorts in pain, mouth moving soundlessly. Sweat beads on his foreheads. My gut lurches. It's him the bloody thing wants What the hell is the Corvos *doing* to him? Why can't I reach any of them?

My whole family. All the people I love, lost in the miasma of the bone crow's power. Helplessness washes over me. For a moment, I'm paralyzed, the breath squeezed from my throat.

I finally force myself to move, trying to wake Lin, with the same pathetic results. Nothing.

The death-roar buzzes behind my ears. I feel the feet of a million flies scuttling across my skin. I squirm, slap them away, but they're not there. When I touch my face, there's only my skin, slick with sweat and tears.

Not real, Annie, Wriggler tells me. *It's the Corvos. Stay awake. Stay with me.*

His voice is clarity in the madness. I watch him, poised for the bone crow's attack. Lightning sizzles along his scales.

Wake them up!

How? I howl, clutching my head as the death-roar intensifies. I can't do this. Wriggler fixes me with a glare. His eyes glow red, like mine do, and our beams of bloody light lock onto each other. Immediately, the death-roar quells. The panic subsides. I feel only what I need to feel. Rage. Fury that this vile thing thinks it can hurt my family.

How *dare* it?

Wriggler feels my rage, rumbles with approval. *How did you pull yourself out?* He asks me. I clench my jaw.

I didn't, I admit. *You did—*

My gaze snaps to Bear, pawing at Maeve's prone form. Maeve. She's under, just like all the others, but I see her fingers twitching, her muscles tensing. She's fighting it. She's trying. Really trying. And she might just succeed.

Because she's got an anchor, like I have.

The Corvos can't get into the minds of our monsters.

I scramble to Maeve's side, grab Bear by the scruff of his neck and force him to look at me. His gaze sputters with green light. He's trying to find Maeve's fury.

"Remember when the whole town was after Maeve back in Hollow Creek?" I growl. "Remember how helpless she felt? How *angry* you were?"

Bear's lips peel back in a snarl. Good.

I lean down so my lips are level with Maeve's ear. "Remember when you thought Lin would be married to a princeling who'd kill her?" I whisper. "Remember how you fought?" I feel Maeve stiffen, her breath quickening. "Remember how *furious* it made you?"

I can't believe I'm doing this, calling Maeve to throw herself into her rage without abandon, when I've spent the last two weeks teaching her to do the opposite. But what choice have I got?

The bone crow's wingbeats change. I feel the death-roar creep into my consciousness again.

Annie, Wriggler warns. *It's coming back. Hurry!*

The black mist is so thick, now, I'm choking on it. Wriggler hisses as it touches his scales. His lightning sputters out. A terrible shriek fills my mind.

I grip Maeve's shoulder. "*Fight!*" I yell.

The Corvos bursts out of the mist, blasting into Wriggler. The pair crash off the edge of the veranda in a vicious heap of wings and fangs. Swamp water explodes over us as they battle. The Corvos locks its jaws around Wriggler's head, squeezes. I feel my own skull contract under the pressure. Wriggler's anger turns to panic.

I clutch the sides of my head, screaming. It hits me all at once that if Wriggler dies, it might kill me, too.

And Maeve's eyes fly open.

They glow so green, the light penetrates the mist as she rises, her face twisted in a vicious snarl. She turns her gaze on the Corvos.

"*Get it!*" she roars.

I blink, and Bear is enormous. White and green fire bursts down his spine as he rears back, almost the same height as the house. He opens his vast maw and *screams,* the sound reverberating through my skull. His black fur drinks the moonlight, stirring in an otherworldly wind.

The Corvos pauses, releasing Wriggler's head as it meets Bear's enraged gaze.

Bear charges.

With the Corvos distracted, Wriggler lunges, grabbing its beak in his own jaw, crunching down. There's a sickening crack as beak and bone splinters, pieces falling into the water. The Corvos shrieks, beating Wriggler with its wings, trying to pull free.

But then, Bear's upon it, his claws sinking into the bone crow's side, raking huge gashes across its ribs. Wriggler wraps the thing in his coils, squeezing. Bear tears at its head, leaving bloody slashes across its jaw.

I realize my friends are stirring. Sasha sits up with a gasp. Sheb's eyes flicker open—to Bartok's delight—and Lin pushes herself upright.

Bear and Wriggler wrestle with the Corvos, but hell, it's strong, even with the two of them on it. It thrashes. I see how Wriggler's attack has left its beak split and broken, revealing bloody gums and cracked fangs. Bear punches at it. Wriggler squeezes. But still, its sheer power is almost too much for them.

At last, the thing breaks free, shoving Bear and Wriggler off. It gives one last, hideous shriek, then rises into the night.

I will take him! It cries. *He's mine!*

Black blood spatters the veranda as it swoops away, heading for the graveyard.

There's a moment of impossible silence. I hear nothing but our breathing. Then Bear and Wriggler shrink, scramble back onto what's left of the veranda. Maeve throws an arm around Bear and kisses Lin fiercely as the other girl blinks away her daze.

I stay kneeling, my body trembling. I can barely draw breath. My vision swims. Strong hands grip my shoulders, pull me upright.

"Annie?" It's Sasha. "You're in shock. We need to keep you warm."

I try to stand but stumble, grabbing Sasha for support. He pulls me against his chest. His sturdiness is comforting. I feel my chest rise and fall in time to his, find my eyelids fluttering closed to the steady rhythm of his heartbeat.

"It almost—" I murmur. "I couldn't—"

The full weight of what just happened—what *could* have happened—hits me like a charging howler horse. My knees buckle. Sasha catches me, lifts me off the floor and carries me inside. I register, dimly, that one wall has been almost destroyed. The living room is strewn with debris and Sasha picks his way over it. He carries me to the sofa and lays me there. He ignores my protests and wraps me in the sheets, then lays behind me and wraps his arms round me. I'm dimly aware of heat stirring inside me at his closeness, at the rightness of it. Something about that scares me, but I'm too exhausted to dwell on it.

Wriggler slithers onto the cushion beside me, curls up. His tongue flickers against my forehead.

Well done, Annie, he says. He sounds exhausted.

Bear trots inside, followed by Maeve and Lin, supporting each other. Everyone is dripping wet, their eyes wide and wild in the dark. I try to push myself upright.

"Wait," I say, ignoring Sasha's attempts to get me to lie back down. "Where's Sheb?"

"I'm here, Annie," he says softly. I spot him by the door, leaning against the wall with his head bowed. His face is in shadow. "I'm right here."

Something about his voice makes me freeze. The sadness in it, like a piece of him has been ripped away. He lifts his head, looks at me.

"Sheb," I say, trying to rise. Sasha pushes me back down. "It's after you. It's—"

"I know," Sheb says quietly.

"It must be one of your brothers," I insist. How can he be so calm? Maybe he doesn't get it yet. I've got to make him see. "Ruben," I say, then remember the note slashed on the tree in the Deep Swamp. "Or maybe Nora." But that doesn't feel right. Why would Nora call Sheb her family? "Allise!" I blurt, talking faster when he frowns at the sound of that name. "It could be her." My voice slurs. I know I'm in shock. "Someone wants you dead, Sheb. We can't let them. I won't—"

"Hush, Annie," Sheb says. He kneels beside me, brushing my sweat-slicked curls from my forehead. I look at him. My gut tightens with fear.

He looks haunted, like part of him is lost in the bone crow's power. I can't help wondering.

What the hell did the Corvos show him?

What does it want with him?

Chapter Twenty-Five

YOUR MOVE, ANNIE

W\E SPEND THE REST of the night huddled in the living room in shivering, frightened silence. Every screech of a night bird sends jolts of fear shooting through my body. Sasha hushes me, stroking my sweat-soaked hair. I'm aware of Maeve's eyes on us, a frown bridging her brows.

"So," she says eventually. "How long's *he* been here?"

I push myself up.

"Why don't you ask him yourself?" I suggest. Maeve and Sasha have history. I ain't getting in the way of that.

Sasha sits up, too, looking everywhere but at Maeve. Her frown deepens.

"Hi, Sasha."

"Hi, Maeve," Sasha mumbles.

Maeve quirks an eyebrow. "So?"

Sasha fidgets beside me. When I snatch a glance at him, I see his cheeks darken. "I ... err ..."

I roll my eyes. "He came through just after we did," I say. "He ... was worried."

I don't know why I hold back that weirdness about how he *felt* me come through the portal. For some reason, that feels private. I feel his hand brush mine. Maeve's frown deepens into a full-blown scowl.

"Two days," she says. "He's been here *two days,* and didn't think to show himself?"

Sasha's eyes meet mine, then snap away again. But Maeve's too quick. She's seen. She barks an incredulous laugh.

"Oh, *perfect!*" she blurts. "You two've been sneaking about in the dark while we've been trying to fight the bloody Corvos. This is *great!*"

Me and Sasha start protesting at once.

"It ain't like that, Maeve—"

"We haven't been sneaking—"

Maeve holds up a hand. I hate that we both fall silent. "I don't wanna hear it," she says, so imperious I want to smack her. "Especially seeing as you couldn't even be bothered to let me and Lin know you were here. You know, your *friends?* The ones you grew up with? The ones you nearly betrayed?"

I stiffen, glaring. That's hardly fair. Sasha did nearly make some bad decisions, almost helping Lin's awful stepfather marry her off to the princeling. But when it came to it, he fought on our side. He turned his back on everything he knew, sacrificed his freedom and safety, to help his friends escape.

Sasha bristles. "*Nearly* being the operative word," he bites back. "I made the right decision when it counted, didn't I? And for that, I've spent the last two weeks being relentlessly hunted—"

He cuts himself off, but Maeve's alert now. Bear's eyes flash green. Lin pats at her shoulder, trying to get her to calm down. Maeve's not having it.

"Hunted? By who?"

Silence. Sasha glares at her and she glares back. Stalemate.

It's Sheb that breaks the silence.

"Who do you think?" he says. His voice is gentle, but it makes us all jump. I glance at him. He stands by the door, where he's been all night, staring out over the swamp with a distant expression on his face. His cheeks are pale, eyes sunken into dark craters. "It's good to see you, Sasha," he says sadly. "But this does complicate things."

"It's Alphonz, ain't it?" Maeve says quietly. "Alphonz is after you. That conniving—"

"Maeve!" I say sharply. "Not helping!"

Maeve falls into a moody silence. I sigh, massaging my temples. Clearly there's no time for rest, is there? Never mind that we've just been attacked by the most terrifying monster I've ever seen, one that even mine and Maeve's monsters combined can't best.

I get to my feet. "We've got work to do," I say.

Everyone immediately wilts. Of course they do.

The sofa behind me creaks as Sasha stands, taking my hand. I glance into his face—those deep, brown eyes, flecked with green and gold—and find myself steadied. He smiles, squeezes my fingers. The meaning is clear.

I'm with you.

And I don't know why that makes my eyes sting, but it does. Maybe, because I've missed him so much. Maybe, because Sheb feels so distant. Maybe, because I feel like I'm buckling under the weight of all this.

Wriggler slithers off the pillow. I scoop him up. He twines himself round my wrist.

I'm with you, too, he huffs. *Just because Sasha's got pretty eyes ...*

I bite back a smile. *Jealous, much?*

Wriggler flicks his tongue at me. *Monsters don't get jealous,* he says, though something about his voice tells me that's far from true.

Lin gets up and fetches the bags Nora brought when we first arrived. She starts handing round bits of bread and cheese. I almost refuse but the smell of the bread makes my belly gurgle. I guess she's right. We can't fight this on empty stomachs. I grab the bread and tear into it. I'd feel embarrassed, but everyone else is doing the same. We eat in silence for a moment, staring at nothing.

"Okay," I say at last. "Let's just ... start at the beginning. What do we know?"

Lin's eyes light up as she lifts her hands to sign. I catch the hand signs for *different* and *new* and can guess what she's saying, though Maeve's translation helps.

"She says we've never seen anything like this before," Maeve explains. "The Corvos doesn't have powers like Wriggler or Bear. It's different."

I glance at Sheb, who's chewing his lip, nodding. "A new kind of monster," he agrees. "If Wriggler and Bear are anything to go by, we can expect Serpentines to have weather-related powers and Hot-Bloods to have elemental powers. The bone crow has neither, as far as we can tell."

I nod. "But it *does* have power," I point out. "We all felt it."

"Psychic power," Sasha says quietly. A collective shudder passes through us.

"So, it's something we've never seen before," Sheb murmurs. "A winged monster with psychic powers."

"*Furious* psychic powers," Maeve grumbles. "I don't know what you all saw, but—" she bites her lip, shakes her head. My heart cracks.

I see an old light sparkle in Sheb's eyes. The corners of his mouth twitch upward. I catch a glimpse of my best friend, still in there somewhere.

"A winged fury," he offers. I clamp down on the temptation to roll my eyes. Naming the bloody thing won't help us beat it, but it does mean Sheb's finding himself again. For that, I'm grateful.

"Fine," I say. "Good start. What else?"

Maeve bites her lip. "Yarella and Lucius said the Corvos don't come into town. It sticks to the graveyard."

I nod. "Well it came into town for us, didn't it?" I point out. "So, something's changed. Now to the main issue." I take a deep breath. "Who in this Oak-forsaken town might want Sheb dead?"

Maeve and Lin exchange glances. Sheb stares at his hands. My heart kicks. Sasha squeezes my hand.

"My brothers," Sheb says quietly. "Especially Ruben. He's always been concerned by how the swamp behaves around me."

I nod. "Okay," I say.

Annie, Wriggler needles into my mind. *Remember me. Remember Maeve and Bear.*

I frown. It's a good point. In Maeve's world, we'd suspected Lin's stepfather, Krogan, of controlling the Krazka. But the monsters we know don't behave that way. They don't respond to the calls of those who already have power. They respond to the impotent rage of the helpless. Like me. Like Maeve. Like—

"I think it could be one of the swamp maidens," I blurt. Sasha stiffens, I feel his fingers loosen around mine.

"The *what?*" Maeve says.

I fill her in on what Sheb told me in the Deep Swamp, show them the tooth we found that I now suspect belonged to the dead Xanni, whoever she was. Maeve's eyes widen.

"That makes sense!" she cries. "If the monsters in this world come from the swamp, of course the swamp would choose one of its own warriors! Someone it knows will be on its side. And they're angry, ain't they? But ..." her face falls. "Why would they be angry at Sheb?"

We all turn to look at him. He shrinks under our gaze. Absently, he strokes Bartok's soft belly. The owl-squirrel fluffs his feathers, glares at each of us in turn.

"I left," Sheb says quietly. He pauses for a long time, then adds, "When my father was deciding which of his sons should inherit his power, the swamp maidens made it clear they wanted me as Heir. They knew if any of the others inherited Pa's power, it would mean war with the swamp. They wanted me to play Deimos' awful games, competing with my brothers for his approval. I refused. Some of the swamp maidens ... will feel that it's my fault, what's happening here."

I stare at him. "That feels like quite impor-tant information, Sheb," I say. "That maybe we could've done with knowing earlier."

Bartok growls. Sheb's gaze snaps up to meet mine. There's a ferocity in his eyes I've never seen before. "I didn't ask you to come with me, Annie," he says, his voice harsh. "I didn't ask for any of this. I've never demanded you tell me anything about your past and its pain. This is mine. Mine alone."

I open my mouth to reply, can't think of any-thing to say. There's such agony in his face. How do I deal with that?

The way I always do, apparently. I get angry.

"What d'you expect we would do?" I demand. "Sit on our hands back in Nowhere while you fight the Corvos alone? Have you even *met* any of us? We're here now, fighting beside you, so stop keeping your damn secrets. Tell us the truth!"

"Annie," Maeve says. She reaches for me. I shrink back.

"Holy Oak, Sheb!" I keep going. "You think the rest of us ain't ever suffered? Hell, everyone here has darkness in our past! We get it! Let us help!"

Lin signs something at me. I deliberately don't look at her. Maeve tries to grab me again. I slap her away.

Sheb holds my gaze, but his own is guarded, like a wall has gone up behind his eyes. "You don't," he says, standing. "And you can't."

He marches out. I hear the front door slam behind him. I kick the sofa hard.

"Dammit!"

No-one says anything for a long time.

Then Lin signs, *what now?*

Right. We can't just stop, can we? If the Corvos belongs to someone who wants Sheb dead, we have to find out who. And I still can't work out what *any* of this has to do with Einan and his sister.

"We should talk to the swamp maidens," I say. "They're our best suspects."

Maeve nods. Lin signs affirmative. But Sasha snatches his hand from mine.

"No," he says.

I stare at him. "What do you mean *no?*"

He doesn't look at me, backs away. "I mean I can't help you with that. Not against them."

I clench my fist. "Why the hell not, Sasha?" I demand. "What's wrong with you?"

"This is wrong," Sasha says. "I won't be part of exposing the swamp maidens. Whatever they want, we can't stand in their way."

Ice creeps through me. "Even if what they want is my best friend dead?"

Sasha averts his eyes. "You don't understand," he says. "I can't ... it's ..."

His canines lengthen, eyes flashing amber. He turns away.

Rage crashes against my ribcage. Wriggler responds, growing huge as lightning zaps off his scales.

"Annie ..." Maeve says. I hardly hear her.

I stare at Sasha's back, willing him to turn and face me, at least explain why he's going back on his promises. What happened to *I'm with you, Annie?* What happened to *Whatever you need?*

I think about my mum, disappearing through the portal two years ago, without saying goodbye. I think about the first time I had to leave Sasha, how long I've wished he'd come through the portal after me. What is it with him? He makes promises and then he breaks them like they're nothing. Just like everyone else. My rage builds.

"Get out," I snarl. "Before I let Wriggler do something I might regret."

Wriggler towers over my shoulder, almost too big to fit inside the room.

Sasha meets my gaze. "I'm sorry, Annie," he says. "I want to help. I do. I wish I could explain ..."

"Out," I repeat.

Sasha's at least smart enough to do as I say. He goes. On the veranda, I hear the stifled yowl of his transformation, then he melts into the swamp.

Wriggler shrinks. I realize I'm shaking. Beside me, Maeve shakes her head.

"He's always been an idiot, Annie," she says. There's a note of sympathy in her voice I can't bear. "You're better off without him. Really."

I don't reply. Can't trust myself to speak. I'm furious, but the way Sasha reacted, it feels like there's more to that decision than I understand. Lin gets up, teetering—she's still affected by the death-roar—and comes to put her arms round me, but I shrink back. I can't bear to be comforted. I need to hold onto my rage. Rage is safe. Rage is familiar.

The sound of a boat engine cuts through my thoughts. It takes me a moment to realize what's happening but when I do, I dart outside, heading for the boathouse. I'm too late. A boat shoots out onto the swamp, a single passenger manning the tiller.

"Sheb!" I yell. "For Oak's sake, where are you going?"

But he's too far away. Or he doesn't bother to hear me. On his shoulder, I see Bartok's head swivel to face me, tawny eyes huge and frightened.

But he doesn't fly back, does he? Of course not.

He doesn't abandon Sheb. He never would.

Even though that's exactly what I've done.

CHAPTER TWENTY-SIX

ALL FAMILIES FIGHT

THE NEXT FEW DAYS feel like a constant battle. Sheb keeps sneaking off to Oak knows where. Either Sasha or Wriggler follow him, try to keep an eye on him. Often, infuriatingly, he gives them the slip. They come back, shrugging apologetically. On the occasions they do manage to stay with him, they tell me he goes to see Nora and Kai. He talks with Nora, then kneels with Kai while they dip for critters in the swamp or identify bird calls.

It's so bizarre, Wriggler tells me after the third time this has happens. *The kid spends so much time pretending he's tougher than a howler mare, but when no-one's looking he's soft as anything. Doesn't make sense.*

I can't help smiling quietly to myself. *Sheb has that effect on people,* I say.

Wriggler huffs. *He doesn't have that effect on me.*

He shuffles into a corner to peel leeches from between his scales. I feel a pulse of guilt. He's working hard to keep Sheb safe, to keep all of us safe, and it's hurting him. Waves of exhaustion thrum from him. I feel the aches and bruises on his body like they're on my own. Once he's removed the leeches, he curls up, grumbling himself to sleep.

Macvc, on the other hand, is so desperate to help I genuinely consider tying her up and shoving her in a cupboard to keep her safe. Still, there are times when she's useful. She works out a schedule for the swamp medicines that means Lin can stand without throwing up for more than an hour. Poor girl still looks grey and nauseous most of the time, but she's at least able to sit on the veranda now.

I watch all of this like I'm far away. Sheb's so distracted trying to give us all the slip that he barely acknowledges I exist. Sasha keeps giving me sad eyes but we're not talking. We tried, yesterday, but he still refused to help me with the swamp maidens without telling me why. He kept starting and stopping, them got frustrated with himself and transformed, darting away into the dark. We haven't spoken since.

Maeve's been busy with Lin. My family don't need me. They don't *want* me.

So, I do the only thing I can think of. On the fifth day after the attack, I take the second boat from the boathouse and go to find Nora.

I hold my breath against the stink of fish as we pass through the main town, with its throngs of fishing boats. Remnant mist hovers in the trees but remains mercifully formless in the sunlight. I notice Ruben's men stalking the walkways, barking at wayward children. I spot Lucius on one of the bridges. He catches my eye and scowls, a hand automatically going to the glowing pendant at his throat. I scowl back. Wriggler hisses a warning. Lucius' lip curls but he turns his attention elsewhere.

It takes me a while to navigate the narrow tributaries to Ruben's house. When I get there, it's obvious it belongs to the de Callis Heir. It's larger than any of the other run-down houses we've passed, set high on stilts with a wooden ramp leading up from a nearby walkway. The skins of hunted animals—deerlike creatures, something that resembles a bear—hang out to dry on the veranda. A huge sword hangs above the door and there are two small boats moored in a boathouse outside, next to a long jetty where I reckon Ruben moors his bigger boat. Right now, it ain't there. Small mercies.

The door is closed, though the shutters are open. I see movement beyond the windows.

And someone waits for me on the jetty.

I frown as Sasha grabs the rope I throw him, sets about mooring my boat.

"Hi," I say.

"Hi," Sasha says back.

We're silent for a minute. "Aren't you s'posed to be with Sheb?" I ask.

Sasha looks sheepish. "I lost him," he admits. "I followed him as far as the graveyard, but—"

"The *graveyard?*" I splutter. "He can't be there alone!"

Sasha holds up his hands. "Relax, Annie, I don't think he's—"

I silence him with a furious look.

Wriggler? I think.

My lightning-snake lets out an exasperated sigh as he oozes into the water. *Oh yeah, great idea,* he grumbles. *Send Wriggler to the graveyard where the giant, nightmare monster lives. He won't mind at all.*

I send him a pulse of gratitude. *Thank you.*

Wriggler mutters under his breath as he disappears beneath the murk. I pointedly ignore the hand Sasha offers me, clamber out of the boat without his help.

Sasha sighs, meets my gaze. "You said you'd like me to help," he reminds me. "So ... I'm here. I came to talk to Nora. To try and ..." his face contorts as if with pain. He takes a deep breath. "Anyway, she said no. So that's that."

I don't look at him, but the inferno in me dampens a bit. "You know I'm still gonna talk to her, right?" I say.

Sasha nods. "I can't ... it's complicated, Annie. I'll help where I can."

My heart feels like it's made of rocks. "But you can't help with them."

"No." He looks so lost when he says it. "Annie, I ... it's ..." he voice cuts off again. He lets out a frustrated yowl, turning away. I watch him for a moment, but he doesn't turn back.

Right. So, we're back to where we were before. I feel like he's leaving me again, watching me disappear through the portal, not even trying to come after me. I don't know why this makes me feel so alone. His fingers brush mine. I snatch my hand away, cling to my anger. It's the only thing stopping me falling apart.

"Should you be out in the open?" I ask Sasha. "What if Alphonz—"

Sasha shakes his head. "I've not seen, heard, or smelled him since the night the Corvos attacked," he says. "Maybe it scared him off. Maybe he's given up."

I frown. Instinct tells me that ain't true. Alphonz's desire for vengeance is stronger than his fear of the Corvos. But I don't argue the point. I realize, weirdly, that I don't want to be alone here, even if my only option for company is the ex-priest I'm furious with.

I sigh. "Let's go, then."

"Hang on," Saha holds up a hand. I frown, then I hear it too. Another boat engine. I whirl on the spot in time to see Maeve bring her boat up alongside mine, moor it, and hop out with Bear at her heels. I can't believe this.

"What the hell are you doing here?" I demand.

Maeve grins. "Came to help!" she says, jogging to meet us. "You need back up with the swamp maidens. And we all know how useless *he* is when it comes to having your back," she adds, jerking her head at Sasha. Sasha's face flushes, but he says nothing.

I sigh, hating the fact I'm actually glad Maeve's here. "Fine," I say. "Just ... keep Bear under control, okay?"

Maeve gives me a mock salute, which I decide to ignore. I lead us up the walkway, rap my knuckles on the door.

For a moment, I think no-one's home, then the door flies open. Nora stands before us. Her jaw slackens and she blinks at me, nonplussed. Behind her, I see the room is full of women. Some, I recognize. Yarella paces like a caged animal. Allise lounges in a rocking chair by a window, looking ill. Imberg's there, too. I meet her gaze and see her stiffen, a muscle in her jaw twitching. Her fingers light on the saber sheathed at her hip. What's she worried about? Why's she looking at me like I'm some agent of the Corvos, come to wreak havoc?

But I'm more interested in the other women. There's at least half a dozen, each with a crossbow strapped across her back, a saber at her hip. They're wearing the same leather breastplates and vambraces that I've seen Nora and Imberg wearing.

And every one of them has a hellgator tooth pendant at her throat.

Swamp maidens.

I square my shoulders, meet Nora's gaze. "Hello Nora," I say. "Can we come in?"

Chapter Twenty-Seven

THE SWAMP MAIDENS

Nora doesn't move immediately. She keeps one hand on the door handle, places the other on the door frame, like she's blocking us from entering. She manages to regain enough composure to close her mouth, fixes me with a fiery glare.

"Kai?" she calls, without taking her eyes off me.

There's a scuffle, and her little boy appears from a corner of the room, his face sullen.

"What?"

"Go and play," Nora says, still staring at me. Kai fidgets reluctantly.

"But isn't Uncle Sheb—"

"Now," Nora snaps.

Kai huffs. He disappears for a moment, then reappears, strapping his harpoon across his back.

He mutters, scowling as he ducks under his mother's arms. "Papa will be angry you've got all these—" he starts. Nora cuts him off.

"I couldn't care less about your Papa's anger," she says.

Now it's my turn for my mouth to fall open. I stare as Kai shoots his mother one last, furious frown. He turns his glare on me.

"You ruin *everything,*" he pronounces, then stalks down the wooden ramp. I'm too stunned to watch him go. I just stare at Nora, confusion a roiling tumult inside me.

I turn to Sasha, try to catch his eye, but he won't look at me. His face has gone grey. He's staring at Nora with his lips slightly parted. I feel how his breath quickens. His hand still rests against mine, and I sense his pulse accelerate.

What is happening?

Nora holds the threshold, lifts her chin. "To what do I owe the pleasure?" she asks, as if *pleasure* is the exact opposite of what she's experiencing.

Maeve, ever the diplomat, shoves her hands on her hips. "Are you gonna let us in or what?" she says. I duck my head to hide my eye roll and think, not for the first time, that life would be so much easier if Maeve would just *do as she was damn well told.*

Nora blinks, face impassive, then slowly moves aside. Maeve shoots me a smug look as she stalks into the house. I grumble something about painful teenagers as I follow her.

Sasha grabs my hand, holding me back. I look at him, my brows bridging in confusion. He's still staring at Nora, the color leached from his face.

"Annie," he murmurs, a pleading note in his voice. "I have to leave. I can't."

I scowl, twisting my hand free. "Fine," I say. I ain't even angry, now. Just disappointed.

Sasha stares at me for a moment, then leaves without another word.

My throat tightens and there's a pain in my chest I can't explain. I clutch my belly, feel Wriggler's concern in my brain.

You need me? He asks.

I don't know, I admit.

Wriggler shoots his resolve down our bond. I feel my spine straightening.

Call if you do, Wriggler says. *I'm at the grave-yard. No sign of Sheb. Or the Corvos. I'm going back to check on Lin.*

I hear a boat engine thrum to life, know that Sasha is heading away, breaking his promises again.

Like I care. I don't care. I blink back the sting in my eyes. I don't bloody care.

I lift my chin, stalk into the house. Nora closes the door behind me.

"We were expecting Sheb," she says. "He's been coming over most days to spend time with Kai."

I decide not to mention I already know this. Admitting I'm spying on my best friend might not go down well.

With the daylight shut out, the house darkens, illuminated only by the sputtering, yellow light of a few candles. The house is smaller than Sheb's old family manor and I've walked straight into what looks like the main living space. I see a tidy kitchen through an open door in the far wall, and other doors leading off to what I guess must be bedrooms and washrooms. There's a big staircase winding up out of sight.

The room isn't rich, but cozy. There's a rug—some sort of animal skin—thrown over the wooden floor, a long, heavy table dominating the center of the room, with six chairs placed round it. Squashy chairs are arranged around a hearth in one wall, and I see signs of family life strewn around. A pair of pants hanging over the arm of one chair, waiting to be patched. Blankets folded in a corner, a wicker basket filled with clothes to be washed. Mugs on the table, herbs hanging by the door.

It should be calming, but something doesn't feel right. The blinds on the windows are drawn, there are towels strewn on the floor beside Allise's chair, next to a bucket from which I can smell something sickly. Imberg flashes me a scowl, then returns her attention to Allise. She gently dabs a cloth against the younger woman's brow. Allise looks unwell.

Maeve folds her arms, opens her mouth, but I get there first.

"What's going on?" I demand.

Maeve blinks at me. I hear Wriggler chuckling down our bond, clearly listening through me.

Subtle, Annie, he jibes. *Keep going. They'll never suspect you're on to them.*

Shut up, I snap, then clamp our bond closed.

Yarella throws her hands up in frustration. "We're wasting time!" she pronounces, apparently to the six unfamiliar women stood together in predatory silence. "Are you going to help us or not?"

One woman blinks, lip curling. She's taller than the others, hair falling in a thick, blond braid over her shoulder. Freckles dot her face. She can't be much older than me, but her green eyes are hardened, angry.

"On what grounds?" she demands. "You want us to go to war with the de Callis Heir? You know what that could mean. We need proof."

I frown. Proof of what?

Nora puts down her cloth. "Xanni's body has gone back to the swamp," she says. "As is right. I have no proof for you other than my word, and the darkness you can all sense."

The unfamiliar women murmur among themselves. I'm getting sick of being ignored.

"You're talking about the death-roar?" I ask.

No-one pays me the slightest bit of attention.

"You know what Ruben is doing," Nora says. "You've seen his marks in the Deep Swamp. You know he's trying to extend his territory, and the swamp is angry. Its magic is breaking. If we do nothing, he will win. This will get worse. The remnants will grow more powerful, the swamp will become sicker—"

"And the Corvos—" Maeve starts.

"Quiet, girl," Imberg snarls. "Don't speak of what you don't understand."

Maeve falls silent. I throw Imberg a filthy glare. I'm more convinced than ever that whoever's controlling that damn Corvos is in this room. Maybe I'm looking right at her.

"Our sister is dead," Nora says again. "By law of the swamp, the swamp maidens are duty-bound to—"

"On. What. *Grounds?*" the blond woman says again, thumping her fist against the table with each syllable. "We have seen no proof that Xanni's death was anything but natural." Her eyes soften, she takes Nora's hand. "I know you're struggling," she says. "Come with us. There is always room for you at Maiden's Creek. You don't have to stay here—"

Nora snatches her hand away. "You know that's not possible," she says. Her hand goes to the tooth pendant at her throat. "You know what Ruben's done! We're bound."

I catch Maeve's eye, see her raise an eyebrow. I nod agreement. I'm so sick of these cryptic secrets.

Nora's still talking. "We have no choice. We need you to go to war with us, Petya!"

The blond woman—Petya—frowns again. "We can't," she says. "And you know that. Without Xanni's body, we can't prove what you say Ruben has done. We can't prove any of what you say she saw!"

Wait ... does Nora think *Ruben* killed this Xanni? Why is no-one answering me? I'm so fed up with this stupid conversation. I snatch Xanni's hellgator tooth from my pocket, slap it on the table. Everyone stares at it.

"Found this in the Deep Swamp," I say. "Under a message carved into a tree."

Funny. No-one's ignoring me now. I tell them what me and Sheb saw in the Deep Swamp. I see Nora's mouth twitch with the hint of a smile and, not for the first time, wonder who the hell this woman is. It's no small thing to start a war against your own husband.

Yarella glares at Petya. "Satisfied?" she demands.

Petya says nothing. With shaking fingers, she scoops up the hellgator tooth, cradles it to her chest.

"I trained her," she whispers. "She was one of mine."

I stare. There are tears in her eyes.

"It will go on like this," Nora says. "Forced into marriage. Stolen. Murdered. Just like Luana." She puts a hand on Imberg's arm. I see how the older woman trembles. But not with fear, I reckon. With rage. I frown.

"You *know* he won't stop," Imberg says. Is it me or is there an edge of pain to her voice?

"And another of ours has been taken," Allise says, her words slurring. "A youngster. Not yet of age. But promising."

Maeve nudges my arm. "They're talking about Zuma," she murmurs. "Aren't they?"

She's right. Einan failed to mention his younger sister is a swamp maiden-in-training. And this doesn't add up. If Yarella is a swamp maiden, if one of these women is controlling the Corvos, why would they take Zuma? She's one of their own.

Petya's fingers tighten over Xanni's tooth pendant. "I'll take this," she says. "I'll go back to Maiden's Creek, talk to Olha and Hadri. I'll see what I can do."

"Make it happen," Imberg says, eyes flashing. "Or we're all doomed."

Allise chooses that moment to throw up.

Petya slips Xanni's tooth into her pocket, heads for the door. "I'll be back as soon as I can," she says. "With whatever resources I am granted."

The other five women follow her. They leave without a backward glance. Me and Maeve wait while Imberg cleans up Allise. Nora goes to fetch water and Yarella resumes pacing.

I admit, this ain't exactly what I had planned.

Nora returns with water for Allise, sets down two glasses in front of me and Maeve.

"Drink," she says. We do. Nora folds her arms. "Allise is pregnant."

Imberg throws her a scowl, which Nora ignores.

I look between the women in the room, their grim faces and funeral-stiff mannerisms, and realize this ain't good news. This ain't a room of celebration, but mourning. My gaze flicks towards Allise as she wipes her mouth, sips water. I remember how she and Sheb greeted each other, the tenderness in their gazes, and how Allise had flinched away when Locke came near her. His predatory possessiveness. How he'd gloated over Sheb, having claimed Allise for his own.

"Oh," is all I manage. I'm not sure what else to say.

Imberg looks furious. Her hands tremble as she dabs the cloth against Allise's forehead. I hear how her breathing quickens, see a flash of fierce energy in her eyes. "These de Callis boys," she spits. "Trying to dilute our bloodlines. Hoping our daughters will be powerless and our sons will be their Heirs. It's disgusting. Time we fight back."

"Someone *is* fighting back," I point out. "With a monster. Did you hear the note Xanni left? *The bone crow is coming for you, de Callis.*" I look at them each in turn. "*What* is going on? Who is Xanni? What did she find?"

Nora and Imberg exchange glances. Yarella says, "You can't tell *them!* They're murk-touched!"

Allise is sick again.

Me and Maeve wait.

Nora rubs circles into her temples. "They are murk-touched," she says. "And I think that's exactly why we tell them."

Imberg and Yarella start to protest.

"Chosen by the swamp," Nora points out. "As a bridge. A place between. Both of the human world and of the swamp. They have a right to know."

Maeve opens her mouth. I elbow her sharply in the ribs. This ain't the time to point out that neither of our monsters come from their precious swamp.

Imberg throws up her hands, turns away. Yarella folds her arms.

"It's my daughter's been taken," she points out. "My son who's been brainwashed by those bloody de Callis brothers."

"And we're here to help, actually," I snap. "But we can't unless you tell us the truth."

No-one speaks for a bit. The silence clangs in my ears. Nora sits down.

"Xanni was one of us," she says.

"Yeah," Maeve mutters. "We got that."

Nora shoots her a mean look and continues, "She was our youngest, but one of our bravest. Ruben talked of marrying her off to Cheran, but Xanni was smart. She never let Ruben close enough to ..." A noise from Imberg stops her. Nora clears her throat. "They want to control us, the de Callis men. Want our children under their power. Xanni wasn't having any of it. She ran."

"To Maiden's Creek," Allise puts in, her voice thick with nausea. "It's the refuge of the swamp maidens, out in the Deep Swamp, and no member of the five families may enter there uninvited. To do so would be an act of war. But Xanni didn't abandon us. She was investigating Ruben's magic, so she explored the swamp, travelled right to its heart, where she said—" She retches again. I wince at the sound of spattering inside the metal bucket. "She said there's darkness stirring."

Nora nods. "Still, she kept searching. And she found things."

I nod. "Ruben's crest marked on the trees," I supply. "He's trying to influence it, ain't he? Trying to extend his power beyond its borders."

"Yes," Nora says. "Xanni felt how the swamp hated it. If it was stronger, it would throw off his influence easily, but it's weak. Sick. We all feel it. The death-roar. It's where the remnants come from. It's what weakens the swamp and makes Ruben so strong."

I frown. "Did he cause it?"

"We don't know," Imberg says. "No-one does. All we know is the death-roar, the sickness, the remnants ... and the Corvos arrived at the same time. It's been this way since Jeelie de Callis died." She pauses. "Since Sheb fled through the portal and never came back."

I freeze.

"You can't think Sheb—" Maeve starts. I elbow her again, hard enough that she winces.

Could Sheb have done this? Was it his act—*murdering* his brother—that caused this darkness? It doesn't matter which way I turn it in my head, I can't make myself believe it.

"Xanni was determined to stop Ruben from taking the Deep Swamp," Yarella puts in. "And now she's dead."

"You think Ruben killed her?" I ask.

Imberg and Nora say nothing, but the glance they exchange answers my question.

"Look," I say. "Monsters come to those who are angry. Frightened. Powerless. They ... we don't really know where they come from, only that they don't exist one moment and the next, there they are. Something sparks them. Something triggers the summoning ..."

Everyone looks at me expectantly. I chew my lip, staring at Bear as I think. "What's going on with the swamp, how Jeelie died, Ruben's war, all of it is enough to make someone summon." I glare at each of them. "And right now, it sounds a lot like it's one of you."

Nora raises an eyebrow.

"Why the hell would any of us summon a monster that kidnapped my daughter?" she demands. "Our *youngest* maiden?"

It's a good point. I can't think of an answer.

"Who took you to the Deep Swamp?" Imberg asks suddenly. "Who showed you Xanni's message, made you think it might be one of us?"

Maeve glances at me.

"Einan," I say, quietly.

"And when you saw that message," Imberg continues, stalking towards me, "who did he blame?"

Yarella grabs her arm. "Imberg, it's not him—"

Imberg tears her arm free, still looking at me.

I lift my chin. "He blamed the swamp maidens," I say. "He wanted me to think it was you."

"Interesting, no?" Imberg says. "His own mother is a swamp maiden. He knows that."

"But he also showed us Ruben's signs ..." I trail off. Because he didn't show us those, did he? I don't reckon he meant for us to see. And it was so dark. The only reason I saw them was because I could look through Wriggler's eyes.

The thing he'd wanted to show me was Xanni's message. He wanted me to think of the swamp maidens.

"That little—" I start. Yarella growls and I remember it's her son I'm talking about. "He's hiding something."

"Of course he is," Yarella says, though there's no anger in her voice now. "He loves his father. Wants to be just like him. And he hates me."

No-one speaks for a bit. Then Allise sighs, her eyelids drooping.

"I think she's settling," she murmurs, rubbing her belly. Nora goes to her, drapes a damp cloth over her forehead.

"These brothers," she mutters. "They think they can get away with anything."

Allise rubs the subtle hump of her belly. "I hope it's a girl," she says. "I hope she's strong like we are. I hope she kills him when she grows up."

I flinch before I can help myself. All eyes land on me. Nora and Imberg don't know. How could they? But I feel Maeve's hand on my arm, holding me steady.

"Find a way to escape him yourself," I growl. "Don't leave it to your kid to do. Trust me. That ain't the way."

Allise's eyes flash. "What would you know, murk-girl?" she demands. I decide not to answer her question. I'm not sure *I killed my own daddy years ago* is going to make me seem trustworthy.

I remember something then. Something the Corvos said.

Mothers don't save us. Mothers are wounds others can use against us.

Weird thing for a monster to say.

Unless whoever drives it hates their own mother. Unless they've wounds of their own.

I glance at Maeve. It wouldn't be the first time a kid came to us crying for help, with no idea the monster they were running from was their own.

Could Einan be the bone crow's master? Is that where this is leading?

Imberg strokes Allise's flame-red hair out of her face. "Easy, child," she says. "Your daughter's a strong one, clearly."

Nora takes the bucket to the kitchen, then returns to wipe the sweat from Allise's forehead. I watch all this, rage and puzzlement roiling like a hurricane inside me. I'm more confused now than I was before we came.

But it's clear these women ain't what's causing the death-roar. They didn't summon the Corvos.

None of this makes sense.

"Okay," I say. "Why would anyone in this town want to harm Zuma?"

Imberg blinks at me. "Harm her?" she says. "There's no sign it did that. It took her, sure. But there was no blood. No body. She was in the grave-yard, and then she wasn't."

"According to Einan," I point out. "Who we all agree ain't been telling the truth."

I huff a frustrated sigh.

"It might've killed that hellgator," Maeve says shakily. I see how all three women flinch at the mention of this. Allise looks away, like she's about to be sick again. Nora's face twists in agony. I remember her horror at seeing the huge creature so brutally broken. A muscle in Imberg's face twitches.

"A hellgator is dead," she says. "We do not think the Corvos killed it."

Allise doubles over, vomiting again.

"It's time for you to go, now," Nora says. "Allise needs care."

She ushers us out, ignoring our protests, shuts the door firmly in our faces.

"Well," Maeve says, rubbing her nose where the door clipped it. "That was a barrel of laughs."

I scowl at her. "It was a waste of time was what it was," I mutter.

Maeve shakes her head. "I ain't so sure," she says. "Those swamp maidens might not have summoned a monster, but they're up to something. Ain't a small thing, starting a war."

"No ..." I decide to keep quiet about the suspicion growing in my mind. I ain't sure yet. And Maeve's not exactly the subtlest person I know.

"Whose side is the Corvos on?" I demand as we head to our boat. "Is it fighting for Ruben, or the swamp?"

"If we knew that," Maeve says, "I feel like we'd know who was driving it."

I clench my fists. Wriggler's curled up in the bottom of our boat, no longer than my forearm and wearing a painfully smug expression.

Good trip? He asks. *Useful? Did they tell you everything?*

I tell him to shut up. He chuckles. *Thought not.*

We unmoor the boat, head for the old de Callis house. Maeve's silent for a long time, her hand resting loosely on the tiller. I watch the remnant mist in the trees. Shapes form and dissipate, hands reach for nothing.

And there's a face. The same face I've seen so many times. A mirror of my best friend with hate in his eyes.

I blink, and Jeelie's ghostly form is sitting in a tree branch. He reaches out, beckons.

"Maeve—" I start, but when I blink, Jeelie's gone. "Never mind."

Maeve looks at me questioningly but doesn't ask. Small mercy. I try to calm the turmoil inside me. Wriggler drapes himself around my neck, his weight oddly soothing.

"We should get back to the house," I growl. "I need a word with Sasha."

CHAPTER TWENTY-EIGHT

TOUCH THEM, I'LL KILL YOU

WE HEAR THE COMMOTION before we reach the house. Yelling, the crash-and-grunt of a fight. I catch Maeve's gaze, her eyes wide and frightened. Lin's eerie soul-mist swirls frantically outside the door. We moor the boat, pelt down the jetty. Maeve grits her teeth.

"It's Ruben," she says, pointing to the huge boat moored in the boathouse.

The door to the house is thrown wide. Shouts echo from inside. There's a cry of pain. It's Sheb.

Rage bucks through me. My scar sears. At my feet, Wriggler expands. Lightning cracks along his scales. The glow in Maeve's eyes intensifies as she floods Bear with rage. Our monsters grow powerful as we leap onto the ruined veranda, burst into the house.

Inside is chaos. Blankets and sheets torn from the furniture, tables upended, shards of smashed vases scattered across the floor. Ruben has Sheb by the collar, shoved against the back wall. Sheb's eyes are wild, darting.

Cheran stands at Ruben's shoulder, blocking Sheb' escape, though he doesn't look happy about it. Locke, on the other hand, looks delighted. He has both his and Sheb's harpoons aimed at Lin as she huddles in a corner.

Sasha's nowhere to be seen. I don't know why this makes my rage flare. He's *supposed* to be with Sheb. He's *supposed* to have our backs, and he's off somewhere, sulking. Coward.

Ruben bares his teeth. "You can either walk out this door with me, brother," he says, "or I'll drag you out by your hair. Your choice."

Sheb tries to choke out an answer. Can't.

"Just do as he says, Shebbie," Locke drawls. "We'll take you either way. Time to finish this now."

My breath catches. Whatever the hell they're doing here, these brothers are finishing *nothing*.

I growl. Ruben turns, noticing me and Maeve. I see his smile falter. Good.

"Get him!" I yell.

Wriggler moves before I've finished speaking, lightning snapping off his scales. His massive jaws gape. Ruben glances over his shoulder, eyes widening as he sees Wriggler's massive form crashing towards him. He dives aside just as Wriggler's teeth snap closed on where his head had been. Behind me, Maeve roars. Bear's fur darkens and he expands, white fire bursting down his body. He bats Locke away from Lin, then leaps between them, snarling.

I grab Sheb's arm and pull him behind me, flick a throwing knife into my palm. Wriggler bears down on Ruben. Behind them, Cheran grabs his harpoon. I throw my knife. Just a warning. It misses Cheran's nose by less than an inch, embeds itself in the door frame. Cheran stumbles back with surprise, his gaze finding mine.

"Don't," I growl, raising my last knife, "or this time, I won't miss."

Cheran drops his harpoon and raises his hands. He looks a bit relieved, actually.

"Cheran, you filthy coward!" Ruben rages, jabbing his own harpoon at Wriggler. Pain sizzles my skin as the barb touches Wriggler, along with a strange sensation I've not felt before. Dizziness. Weakness. I shake my head, trying to throw the feeling off. Wriggler snarls but holds back. He could splinter Ruben's harpoon, swallow the insolent bastard whole if he wanted, but he's done that before, and it left me shivering with nightmares.

Vengeful as my Wriggler is, he doesn't like it when I suffer. That's the point of him, ain't it? So, he dodges Ruben's jabbing harpoon, sending just enough lightning to make Ruben yelp.

It looks like Maeve doesn't have any such reservations. A howl from behind draws my attention. I whirl to find Maeve standing over Locke, eyes gleaming green as Bear raises a massive paw.

Maeve kicks Locke viciously, ignoring Lin's attempts to hold her back. "You touch her," Maeve snarls, "and you die!"

White fire explodes from Bear's claws. He brings his paw down in a crushing blow towards Locke's head.

My heart gives a sickening squeeze.

"Maeve!" I yell. "No!"

Wriggler responds in a blur of movement. With a flick of his tail, he sends Ruben flying across the room, then surges towards Bear, knocking him clean off Locke. The pair of them tumble in a snarling heap against the far wall. Locke lays against the floor, chest heaving, his hands half raised, as if he can't believe he's still alive.

"Lin!" I yell, rushing towards our battling monsters, "calm her down!"

I see Lin grab Maeve's face in both hands, green soul-mist curling from her fingertips as she taps her power into Maeve. I sheathe my last knife, curl my fist and drive a punch into Bear's flank. He turns burning green eyes on me. It's enough of a distraction that Wriggler manages to wrap him in tight, restraining coils. Bear howls, thrashes for escape, but Wriggler holds him. I see the fight sputter out of Bear's eyes as Lin gets through to Maeve. He shrinks to cub-form, mewling sorrowfully. Wriggler glares at him.

This cub, Wriggler mutters, *does my head in.*

I stifle a laugh as the last of the adrenalin trembles through my body. I feel echoes of Wriggler's pain. The bloody jabs from Ruben's harpoon, the oozing scrapes left by Bear's claws.

You and me both, I say.

Lin pulls Maeve into a tight embrace. Wriggler lets Bear go, and the cub trots to Maeve, pawing at her for comfort. Ruben goes for his harpoon, but Wriggler's there, snarling him into submission. Locke doesn't move from the floor. I can tell the fight's gone out of him. Cheran's retreated to the door.

"Now," I say, glaring at them in turn. I grab Sheb's hand. It hangs limp in mine. "What the *hell* was that about?"

And where, I think furiously, *where* is Sasha? If he'd been here, he could've prevented this. When I get hold of him …

Focus, Annie! Wriggler reminds me.

Right. I'll deal with this nonsense first. Then I'll find Sasha and yell at him for being such a pain.

I whirl on Ruben, holding a knife to his throat. "Well?" I demand. "Speak!"

Ruben sneers. "You think you're doing the right thing," he growls, "protecting *him*." He thrusts a finger towards Sheb, who tenses behind me. I grip my friend's arm tighter, hoping he understands what that means. That he *is* worth protecting, and I'll never stop. Maybe I should say these things, but I ain't ever been great at talking about feelings. I just grip him tight, hope he understands. Ruben's cruel smile widens.

"You bloody murk-touched," he snarls. "Think you're clever, don't you? But I'm patient. I can wait." His eyes narrow. "I know you've sensed it."

"Sensed what?" I demand, though I already know the answer.

For a moment, the mean smile on Ruben's face freezes. I think I see something like fear pass across his eyes. "The death-roar," he says, his voice lowering, like he's scared he'll wake the awful thing up. "And the bone crow. I know you feel where that thing comes from. You can tell it isn't alive."

A look of shock must pass over my face because Ruben smirks.

"It's looking for something," he says. "And you know what it is."

"Revenge," I breathe. Because it makes sense. I think of the face in the mist. The remnant who's haunted me since we arrived here.

I think of how I knew, as soon as I saw it, that the Corvos was a creature of death ...

"The death-roar, the Corvos and whoever drives it, is the swamp's last stand," Ruben says. "It's fighting me when it should bow to me."

"Right," I drawl. "And for some reason, beating up your brother is going to sort that out, is it?"

Ruben's jaw tenses. "The de Callis Heir should inherit his father's power," he says. "That's the way it is. The way it's *always* been." He thrusts an accusing finger at Sheb. "If he would just re-linquish his share, I'd have the swamp under my command. I'd have everything. But he's selfish. He's always been so bloody selfish!"

He steps towards us. "And now," he says. "I'm done asking. I will take your share of the power, brother."

He raises his harpoon, but I'm ready for him. I throw open my bond with Wriggler. Rage spills into him. I blink, and he fills the room, his crown of horns knocking against the rafters, wings crackling with red lightning. He bears down on Ruben, fangs sizzling. Ruben freezes, glaring with barely concealed fury.

"Come any closer," I snarl. "And I'll let him eat you."

Don't tell him that, Wriggler protests. *Then he won't come any closer, will he?*

Pipe down, I retort.

Wriggler fixes me with a sparking, scarlet glare. *But I'm* hungry.

I ignore him. I'm busy watching Sheb's brothers. The weird look that passes between Ruben and Locke, the way Cheran's cheeks redden.

"I have none of my power, Ruben," Sheb murmurs. "You know that. You've seen. The swamp doesn't respond to me the way it used to, and I'm glad. I never asked for that power. I never wanted it."

"Don't want me to have it either though, do you?" Ruben shoots at him.

I try to shield Sheb with my body but he steps round me, facing his brother. "No," he says. "You don't deserve it."

Ruben's face contorts. He raises a fist but I step in front of Sheb, Wriggler towering behind me.

"If I were you," I say. "I'd leave. Now."

Ruben casts Wriggler one last glance. I see the muscles in his arms tensing, his fingers twitching like he's considering a fight. Wriggler gives a rumbling laugh, lowers his head, fangs flashing.

Go on then, he goads, though obviously, I'm the only one who can hear him. *I dare you.*

"He'd *really* like me to let him eat you," I say.

Ruben's jaw clenches. I see how furious it's making him that a little woman, half his weight, has him trapped by the sheer power of her rage. Smug satisfaction lights my blood. Wriggler flares his wings, basking in our victory. Finally, Ruben relents.

"Locke," he grumbles. "Cheran."

He throws me one, last, filthy glare, then stalks out. Cheran and Locke follow. Locke dumps Sheb's harpoon on the floor before he goes. They don't look back, and none of us move as we listen to their boat drift away.

Wriggler shrinks to his usual size. Maeve turns her tearful face towards Lin, cups her cheeks, kisses her, demands to know if she's alright, and if she's *sure* she's alright.

I feel my family let out a collective sigh, but our fear still tornadoes round this ruined house. I steel myself and look at Sheb, then wish I hadn't. The look of devastation on my best friend's face is enough to splinter my heart.

"Sheb," I start, then realize I've got no idea what to say.

Sheb hugs himself. Wordlessly, he flops into a chair, staring at nothing. I frown as I realize someone is missing. There's a distinct absence of a certain, indignant, fluffy companion.

"Where's Bartok?" I ask.

"He flew off," Sheb says vaguely. "When my brothers came. He was flapping around their boat, making an awful racket, but he wouldn't come back inside. I don't know where he is."

My eyebrows fly up. That's not like Bartok. I've known that daft owl-squirrel to face off against Wriggler before. He's attacked Maeve, while she was in the throes of rage, to stop her from strangling me. He'd *never* abandon Sheb.

I'm suddenly exhausted, pain throbbing behind my eyes. I sag against the wall. Wriggler winds himself round my ankle.

You need to sleep, he points out.

I sigh. Yeah, right. I need to find Sasha. I need to find Bartok. And something tells me time's running out.

"We need to go back to the graveyard," I say.

Everyone looks at me. Lin groans, clutches her head, as if just the idea of the graveyard makes her sick.

"Have you lost your mind?" Maeve demands. "Did we forget how hard it was to fight the Corvos the first time? And anyway, after what Nora told us, and with Allise the way she is—"

I wince at the sound of Allise's name, casting Sheb a sideways glance. His eyes snap to mine, challenging.

"What's happened to Allise?" he murmurs.

Panic flares in my gut. "Maeve—" I warn. She ignores me.

"What's happened to her?" Sheb insists, his voice gaining strength.

"Well, she hates being married, don't she?" Maeve goes on. "Was that a forced marriage? Like Lin was s'posed to have?"

"Maeve!" I snap. "I don't think—"

But Maeve ain't done. When is she ever?

"And she's pregnant," she blurts. "Clearly don't want to be, that awful Locke—"

"Maeve!" I shout.

At the same time, there's a crash from behind me, making Lin jump. We turn to find Sheb standing over an upturned side table, the leg of which he's just torn off. Shards of a broken vase litter the floor. Sheb lifts the leg, brings it crashing down on the already shattered vase. Pieces fly across the room.

"I'll kill him!" he yells. "How dare he hurt her? *Stop saying her name! Leave her alone!*"

I go to him, but he flails, batting me away, as he brutalizes the vase, the upturned table, the floor. I watch, a sickly hollow opening inside me. I've never seen him like this. A wild, furious thing, blasting rage into the universe. I feel the pull of it. Understand its strength.

"Sheb," I say. "Sheb, stop ..."

But he doesn't. Can't. He picks up what's left of the table, hurls it against the wall. Bits snap off. I throw my hands up to shield my face. Splinters of wood whizz past me.

"What the—" Maeve cries, ducking as a table leg flies overhead. "Sheb!"

He can't hear us. He's gone. Lost in the hurricane of his own rage. I feel the world pulse, the death-roar intensifies at the back of my mind until I'm doubled over, fighting off sickness. I know what this is. A rage so strong, so potent, it's shaking the foundations of the world. Pulling something wild and dangerous from that place where darkness dwells.

This is what it looks like when someone is about to summon a monster.

"Grab him!" I yell, ducking under Sheb's arm, snatching his wrist. Maeve leaps to help, but Sheb's too strong. He flings us both away, throws his head back, roars. Rageful tears streak his face. I feel his pain pulsing through my body. Wriggler and Bear respond to our anger.

"Don't hurt him!" I warn, as our monsters rush to help.

Sheb grabs his harpoon, jabbing at Wriggler's side as my lightning-snake tries to wrap him in restraining coils. *"Get away from me!"* Sheb yells. The tip of his harpoon grazes Wriggler's side. I yelp as I feel an echo of that pain, as I register that Sheb is the person who caused it.

Gentle, kind, beautiful Sheb. My compass. My shelter. My home. What's happening? What is this awful world doing to him?

"Lin!" Maeve cries, as the other girl stumbles over. She's still affected by the death-roar. Her skin is waxen from nausea, but she struggles to Sheb's side, pushing Wriggler and Bear away. Somehow, she manages to grab Sheb's wrist. He freezes. Mist bursts from the point where Lin's fingers grip him. Soul-mist. She pulls it from Sheb's skin, a riotous rainbow of swirling color, shot through with threads of darkness, just like everyone is.

Sheb freezes at her touch, watching the colors of his soul swirl around him, reminding him what he is.

I've seen Sheb's soul-colors before, but never in this much detail. I notice the reds and blacks are more prominent. And the threads of color are arranged strangely. Rather than floating freely like they should be, they look tangled, like someone's grabbed them, knotted them together.

"Is his ..." I say, starting forward. "Is he alright? This don't look like it's s'posed to."

Gently, Lin releases Sheb, but holds his soul-colors steady. She signs at us. Maeve translates.

"It's like someone's tied his soul," she says. "I think it's trapped his family power, stopped him from using it. He's hurting."

Sheb collapses into a sobbing heap.

I feel my heart crack as it reaches for Sheb, trying to absorb some of that pain. But, of course, it can't. I drop to my knees, hold him fiercely, glare at everyone else.

"Who did this to you?" I demand as Sheb cries into me. "What's happening? Is it the Corvos? What do we *do?*"

Lin looks at me helplessly, shakes her head. She doesn't know. This is new to her, too. I grip Sheb, hoping my arms are enough to shield him from whatever this agony is. I want to kill whatever did this to him. I want Wriggler to decimate it. But it's *inside* him, ain't it? This terrible, knotted pain. All I can do is hold him as he cries.

And it ain't enough.

"We need," I say, through gritted teeth, "to go to the graveyard."

This time, no-one protests. Wriggler slithers to my side, nudges me with his head.

Someone should stay here, he suggests. *With Sheb.*

I'm about to respond when there's a familiar cry. I look up as a purple shape swoops through the open door, landing beside Sheb. Bartok glances at the chaos, then fixes me with an accusing, tawny glare.

I leave you for five minutes, that glare seems to say. *And this is what happens.*

But I'm too distracted to be annoyed. I'm distracted by the thing Bartok's clutching in his beak. It's a shoe. Small enough that it can only belong to a child, slender and off-white. Or it used to be. The tip and the heel are both stained red with blood. The sole is torn open. What clearly used to be a little black bow on top is shredded.

Annie, Wriggler says, reaching up to sniff it. Bartok growls and his feathers spike. Wriggler ignores him. *Annie, something about this is familiar.*

I don't answer, but I can't help feeling he's right. I stare at the shoe. Something nags in my brain. I can't think what.

"What the hell?" Maeve breathes.

I hear a boat engine approaching. Maeve rushes outside.

"It's Einan!" she reports. Her face darkens. "He ain't alone." She shoots me a meaningful look. "Sasha's with him."

Chapter Twenty-Nine
NO WAY BACK

I STAND ON THE veranda, arms folded, as Einan moors the boat. Sasha steps ashore.

"Annie—" he starts, like I might be glad to see him. Like I don't want to smack him six ways to oblivion. If he'd been here, like he was supposed to, Sheb wouldn't be in this state.

"What?" I snap. "Finished sulking, have you?"

Sasha's face falls. I feel a pang of regret, which is quickly dispelled by an owl-squirrel flying in frantic circles around my head. Bartok shrieks at the top of his little lungs, lands smartly on my head and wallops me repeatedly with the blood-soaked shoe.

"Ow!" I cry, flapping my arms at him. "Get off, you ridiculous thing!"

Bartok screams, smacks me once more, then flaps away from my flailing arms. He goes to pester

Maeve, still hollering like he's being murdered. While he's distracted, I lead Sasha and Einan inside.

Lin's there with her arms folded, glaring. She starts signing. I suppress a smile.

"She wants to know where you've been," Sheb translates. I snatch a glance at Sasha and see his face darken with shame.

"I—" he starts. "I needed—"

"Oh shut up," Maeve drawls. She stalks inside, having finally managed to catch hold of Bartok. She has her hands clamped over his wings while he struggles, still clutching that damn shoe. Maeve throws Sasha a filthy glare. "Always with your excuses."

I expect Sasha to snipe back but he does, actually, shut up. His eyes scan the chaos of the room, worse now than after the bone crow's attack. Sheb sits limply on the floor, blood trickling from a cut on his temple.

"What happened here?" Sasha demands. He's beside me in moments, cupping my face, hands tracing my shoulders, my arms down to my elbows. I shiver at his touch, at the way it quickens my heartbeat. But I fix him with the fiercest glare I can manage.

"I'm fine, Sasha," I say. I jerk a thumb towards Wriggler, who's still pony-sized and sizzling. He flares his wings for dramatic effect. "I ain't helpless, remember?"

Sasha's lips quirk, but he doesn't let go of me. "I know that," he says. "You've shown me enough times."

I feel my anger cooling, and I don't want it to. I cling to it, push him away from me. "It weren't me they were after," I tell him. "It was Sheb. Who *you* were s'posed to be with."

Sasha reaches for me again, then thinks better of it. "You're right," he says. "I'm sorry. But listen, we're running out of time. I've been at the graveyard. Something's shifted. We—"

Bartok screeches and breaks free of Maeve's grip. We duck, but he doesn't go for me, or Maeve, or even Sheb. Instead, he makes a dive for Einan. He lands hard on the boy's face, thumps a foot into his nose, then starts whacking him round the head with the bloody shoe.

"Bartok!" Sheb cries. Einan yelps, going down in a whirlwind of arms. Bartok keeps up his assault until Sheb grabs him, though he still won't give up the shoe.

"What's his obsession with this thing?" Maeve demands, rubbing her face where one of Bartok's thumper feet caught her in the jaw.

Sheb doesn't say anything. He simply cradles Bartok to his chest, then looks at Einan, whose face is grey.

"This is Zuma's, isn't it?" Sheb says.

Einan lets out a choked sob and nods. "I'm sorry," he gulps. "Zuma, I'm so sorry. I'll try harder. I—"

He stops, blinking away tears as Lin kneels beside him, rubbing his back gently.

"Where did he find it?" Sheb asks. We exchange glances, but no-one has the slightest idea where Bartok's been.

"I found him at the graveyard," Sasha says.

I raise an eyebrow, finally register what he's saying. "What were you doing at the graveyard?"

Sasha opens his mouth to respond, then casts Einan a sidelong glance. The boy kneels, staring at his sister's bloody shoe. "He was following me," he admits.

I sigh. "And what were *you* doing in the graveyard?"

Einan doesn't answer. I throw my hands up in frustration. "Fine!" I snap. "We're only looking for your sister, Einan! We're only here because you asked us to be! If you won't tell me what you were up to, I'll go and find out for myself."

Maeve starts strapping her dagger to her belt. "I'll come with you—"

"No!" I say, more forcefully than I meant to. Maeve frowns. I close my eyes. I can't deal with another argument. I just need her to do as she's told for once! I need my family here, safe. Together. While I sort out whatever nonsense we've got ourselves into.

"Maeve," Sasha says. "You're needed here. We don't know where the Corvos is, but it's attacked you all here before. Bear made the difference last time, didn't he? You and he should guard the others. Keep them safe."

I glance at him, trying not to let my shock show. Sasha's gazing earnestly at Maeve. I watch as her shoulders square, pride coloring her cheeks. "What about Annie, then?" she points out. "If Wriggler needs Bear to fight the Corvos, what happens if she finds it at the graveyard?"

Wriggler hisses over my shoulder. *I do* not *need that oversized cubling to fight my battles!*

I nudge him in the belly. *Quiet!*

He grumbles but does as he's told. Sasha glances at me, and I allow him a small smile. He returns it, and some tightness in my chest loosens a little. I let my hand brush his.

"I'll go with Annie," Sasha says. "I might not be as strong as you and Bear, but I'll keep her safe."

I frown. Oh *really?* Are we back to that nonsense again? And why the hell is Maeve so concerned about my safety? She's always half desperate to get away from me!

Maeve scowls, eyes darting between me and Sasha. She sighs. "Fine," she says. "But you better not get hurt. Either of you."

I hear the slight catch in her voice. Something tightens in my chest.

"We'll be careful," I promise. "Just ... look after the others, okay? Keep everyone safe."

Maeve nods, chewing the inside of her cheek. "What're you looking for?" she asks.

I shrug. "Dunno," I admit. "I guess we'll know it when we find it."

Einan glances up, his tear-streaked face tensed with worry. "Maybe you should take Sheb with you?" he says. "He knows the swamp. He's good with a harpoon. He could—"

"No," I say. I ain't even entertaining that idea. "Sheb stays here. So do you."

Einan's face falls. "But—"

"No arguments," I say, turning away before Einan can protest further.

I go to Sheb. He's staring at his harpoon across his knees. It glows faintly. I crouch in front of him, hold his face in my hands. "Sheb?" I say. He lets me lift his chin but doesn't raise his eyes. I try to hold his hand, but it stays limp in his lap. I dab the blood away from his temple. He doesn't respond to that either. I don't know what to do. Don't know how to fix this. I hug him close, tightening my hold when he doesn't hug me back.

"Whatever the hell's going on," I say fiercely. "I ain't leaving you. I ain't *ever* leaving you. If that thing's after you, it'll have to get through me first."

I feel him stir and step back as he finally raises his eyes to meet mine. Deep sadness clouds his face. "I know, Annie," he says sadly. "I've always known."

"Annie," Sasha says. "The sun will set soon. We should go."

I check my throwing knives, tell Maeve one more time to *stay here*. Lin signs at me that she'll look after Einan, keep an eye on Sheb. I tell Bartok to stay, too, but he's having none of it. To my surprise, he flaps to my shoulder and flags his tail, apparently impatient to be off. Weird creature.

Sasha sits at the tiller as I hold Wriggler on my lap. Deep, evening gloom leaches what little color the swamp has. As the darkness washes over the house, obscuring the faces of my family on the veranda, I can't help this feeling that leaving them is the worst thing I could do.

Chapter Thirty

DEEPER INTO THE DARK

ME AND SASHA ARE silent as we drift through the murk. Marsh Wilds is settling for the evening. Parents gather children inside, lock their doors and shutters tight. A few cast us suspicious glances as we scoot by.

"Creeperscorps'll be out soon!" someone calls. "Best get inside, miss!"

We ignore them. Creeperscorps be damned. I'd like to see one try it on with Wriggler. My lightning-snake flicks his tail.

So would I, he hisses.

"I dare them to attack us," I growl through gritted teeth. "I *want* them to. I'm angry enough that I'd kill a hellgator with my bare hands right now."

Behind me, Sasha stiffens. "We'll leave the hell-gators alone, I think," he murmurs, ignoring the scowl I shoot him. "Nora says they're sacred to the swamp. They should leave us be as long as we show them the same courtesy."

I raise an eyebrow. "Oh yeah?" I drawl. "You forgotten one attacked Sheb outside his own house?"

Sasha's mouth tightens, but he doesn't say anything. I frown, searching his face. My suspicions are deepening. I open my mouth to ask but Sasha holds up a hand.

"Don't, Annie," he says. "Please. It ... you don't understand. It hurts not to tell you. I can't. Just ... I'm trying, okay? Please."

I huff a frustrated sigh, and make a show of being cross with him, but the way he looks unsettles me. It's like these conversations cause him physical pain. So, I can't ask him, even though I half-know what he's keeping from me. Wriggler drapes himself round my neck. I'm weirdly comforted by his weight.

Sasha guides the boat upriver, past Ruben's huge house. For some reason known only to himself, Bartok loses it entirely when he sees Ruben's boat moored outside. He shrieks like a cherish screamer, beats me round the head with his wings. He's still clutching Zuma's lost shoe in his beak. He wallops me in the jaw with it.

"Ow!" I say, flailing at him. "Get off you stupid creature!"

Wriggler snaps at the owl-squirrel, but Bartok's too fast. Sasha tries to grab him. Bartok dodges aside, kicks Sasha in the face for good measure and swoops to Ruben's boat. He sits on top of the cabin, beating his wings, screaming ferociously.

"Shut *up!*" I hiss at him. But Bartok's not having it.

"What do we do now?" Sasha asks.

I glare at the owl-squirrel. "Leave him," I say. "Let's go before he alerts Ruben."

Bartok screeches after us, but I'm done dealing with his meltdowns. We need to get to the graveyard, preferably without Ruben or his men on our tail. Bartok knows his way back to Sheb.

Sasha opens the engine. We pick up speed before Bartok lets everyone know we're here. We pass out of the town and the swamp thickens around us. I see the silhouettes of fanged eels oozing beneath the water, hear the chitinous clicks of creeper-scorps somewhere on the shadowy bank. I shudder, feeling that familiar pressure on my mind. The swamp, trying to dig into my brain. We're right on the edge of de Callis territory, and the Deep Swamp is calling. I peer through the dark, can just make out Ruben's crest carved into the trees, glowing a faint, eerie green. The swamp slips into my mind. I feel its pain. Its fury. I press my fingers to my temples, trying to ease the pressure.

Wriggler shunts his head against my cheek, in that way I've come to realize is a kind of affection. A monster's love for his girl. I close my eyes at the rough brush of his scales, feel soothed.

The roar is loud tonight, he points out. *Listen.*

I shudder at the thought, but close my eyes, attune myself to that sickly frequency. Wriggler's right. It is strong tonight. It sets my skin crawling, my head whirring. I gasp at the power of it, feeling Wriggler pull me back.

Maybe don't do that again, he suggests. I groan and lean forward, breathing deeply through a roll of nausea.

"Annie?" Sasha asks. I feel his hand on my back, warmth spreading through me at his touch.

"I'm okay," I say, still a little breathless. "It's just—"

It's just *what* though?

"We're here," Sasha says, as the boat's prow bumps against a jetty. It's utterly silent. There's nothing but tangled branches clutching at the ink-dark sky. A bright half-moon illuminates the swampy water. I can just make out the narrow path leading into the graveyard.

The death-roar pulses in the back of my brain. Wild, furious. I grip the sides of my head again. Wriggler drops from my shoulder, now dog-sized. I feel his hold on my mind tighten, fending off the worst of the death-roar's effects.

We should be quick, he says. *Something's happening here.*

Yeah, I say, suddenly thinking how coming to the lair of the Corvos at nightfall may not have been the best idea. Too late now.

I clamber ashore, help Sasha moor the boat. We both stare up the path. Sasha's fingers intertwine with mine.

"You ready?" he asks.

I cast him a sideways glance, realize he ain't looking well. His skin has a waxy sheen to it, sweat beads on his upper lip.

"You okay?" I ask. Sasha nods.

"It's just ..." he clamps his mouth closed for a moment, clearly trying not to be sick. "That roar. It's strong tonight."

Wriggler scoffs. *What's this?* He drawls. *Big, strong Cat-Boy struggling with the buzz?*

I throw him a filthy look. *He don't have a monster to shield his mind,* I point out. *And don't ever call him Cat-Boy again.*

I shunt a shoulder under Sasha's arm, help him stand.

"I got you," I tell him. "Even when you don't got me. Which is always."

He smiles faintly. "I know you have," he says. "And ... I know the other thing, too. I really am sorry."

I bite down on the urge to tell him that just being sorry ain't enough. Everyone's always sorry. Mum was sorry, too. She was so sorry she left me the first time that she did it again.

I don't know why I'm having these thoughts. Now ain't the time.

I steady Sasha against me. "Come on. Let's get this over with."

We trudge up the bank, pausing sometimes to let remnants drift across our path. They've got form in the dark. Weeping parents, crying children, lost lovers searching for each other. They call and gesture over and over, like they're stuck in a loop. I avert my eyes, embarrassed to witness this repeated pain. Occasionally, one comes too close, brushing against us, and sends a hideous, icy thrill through my body.

"I hate those things," Sasha grumbles.

"Yeah," I say, scanning their faces. I'm looking for one in particular. "Me too."

I see him hovering between the headstones, his face so familiar and yet so ... not. Jeelie hangs in the air, watching me. Unlike the other remnants, he doesn't cry, or reach out, or repeat some endless pain he felt in life. He just drifts, his eyes fixed on mine. He quirks an eyebrow, opens his mouth like he's about to say something. But then a breeze kicks up and he's nothing but mist again. I shudder.

We find the moonlit track, follow it through the hunched silhouettes of headstones. I pause at some, trying to trace the epitaphs with my fingers. I'm looking for one. Small, worn, wreathed in moss and barely legible.

She's here, Annie, Wriggler says. Our bond pulls me off the path towards the almost-not-there gravestone that belongs to Luana de Callis. I kneel beside it, breath hitching as I lift my hands. Sasha stands behind me, moonlight catching the amber in his eyes. His canines are elongated.

"What're you doing?" he hisses. "We shouldn't linger."

"I need to know," I say. "Something about this whole mess is linked to Sheb's family, and she's a key part of it. I need to know."

Sasha goes still, watching me. I remember he was there the first time I discovered I could do this, back in the old prayerhouse of his home world. He kept trying to pull me off the altar as I read its memories.

"Last time you did this," he says. "It hurt you."

"It always hurts me," I growl. "But what am I s'posed to do, hmm? Turn around and walk away?"

Sasha doesn't answer. Instead, I hear a strangled hiss, the pop-and-crack of bones as he shifts. When I glance behind me, a huge, grey cat is staring back. Sasha's amber eyes meet mine. He shows his massive teeth.

"I'll keep watch," he rumbled. He sets to prowling around me and the gravestone. Wriggler lets out a derisive huff.

Yeah, yeah, he drawls. *Big, brave Sasha can protect poor, defenseless Annie and her completely help-*

less lightning serpent, who's definitely never eaten anybody whole before.

I roll my eyes, but I'm too distracted to argue. I need all my focus. This ain't going to be pleasant. Best get it over with. I press my palms against Luana's headstone.

At first, I feel that same darkness I felt when I touched the stone before, shrinking from me, like a cornered animal. I feel its threat and its fear. "Come on," I murmur, closing my eyes. "I ain't trying to hurt you. I ain't gonna judge. I just need to understand."

The memory still resists. It's like what's left of Luana can't bear to remember. I frown.

She sends me the same memory she showed me before. Deimos' cruel voice roaring.

"Foolish woman! Don't you realize what you've done?"

I grit my teeth. "I know this already," I tell the gravestone. "I need something more." But the memory holds back, sending me waves of pain. I groan, sag against the gravestone, but don't let go.

"She's still fighting me," I growl. Wriggler nudges my side.

Tell her why you're here, then, he says.

I scowl at him. This is so weird, talking to the memories of a dead person. I'm sure I've never seen Luana as a remnant, but that doesn't mean she ain't one. And this memory, the way it's pulling me, somehow feels conscious. Like it's *deciding* to fight me.

"I did tell her why I'm here," I protest. "I need to understand."

Wriggler throws me a withering glare. *Turn your brain on, Annie,* he says. *Why are you here? Who for?*

Oh. Yeah, okay. He's got a point.

I shoot him another scowl, just so he knows he's being annoying, then focus on the echoes of Luana's memories again, the shadows of shadows leaning away from me.

"Luana," I whisper. "I'm here for Sheb."

Immediately, I feel Luana's darkness stir, a tendril of energy probing at my fingertips. Questioning. There's a stab of strange energy, like a mix between fury and yearning. I frown, pushing through.

"He's hurting," I say. "He's in pain. He needs you."

I feel her relent. I resist glancing at Wriggler, who I know is wearing his *I-was-right* face.

"I'm worried he's in trouble," I say, pushing the sentiments through my fingers to that tendril of Luana's energy. My fear. My confusion. How desperately I want my friend back, though I don't know how to reach him. "I need to know the truth. To help him."

Luana's energy rushes me all at once. A torrent so forceful I bite my lip against crying out. She sizzles through me, igniting every nerve. I throw my head back as lightning snaps through my veins. I try to pull away, but it's like Luana has fused me to the stone. I hear Sasha growl, rushing to my aid, hear Wriggler darts into his path.

Stop interfering, you idiot! My lightning-snake snaps. Not that Sasha can hear him. But he doesn't say it for Sasha. He says it for me. To let me know I ain't in danger. To hold on.

So, I do. Whimpering through the pain, I open myself to Luana's onslaught. To whatever this blast of emotion is. I steel myself for her pain. Her rage. The terrified riot of her last moments.

What I don't expect, is the flood of *love* that hurtles through me. So potent, it's painful. An inferno of raw devotion. Images battle in my mind, and I'm pulled, one after the other, into a series of memories. I stand on the edge of the visions, like a remnant. I watch, but can't interfere, and it's excruciating.

Sheb, three years old, fighting his brothers for table scraps. A huge, bearded man stands over the squabbling boys. I recognize him from the family portrait in the de Callis library. Deimos. He smiles with pride as the brother with mean, blue eyes knocks Sheb on the head, steals his bread. Sheb cries as the others laugh. The boy beside him, his twin, tries to comfort him, but Deimos glares. Luana gathers Sheb into her arms, only for Deimos to shove her away.

"Stop coddling him. It's your fault he's soft—"

Sheb, five years old, crouched on the floor with his twin. They're playing with a set of wooden creeperscorps, scuttling them across the floor. They giggle with each other, their shoulders touching, heads together. At the end of the room, Deimos watches. He's scowling.

Sheb, seven years old. Running to keep up with his brothers and their game, but they don't wait. They never wait for him.

"Jeelie!" he calls. "Wait for me!"

His twin hesitates a moment, glances from Sheb, back to his retreating brothers. He shakes his head, turns, and darts after the others. Sheb totters home, sobbing. Luana hugs him. Sheb struggles free. "Pa doesn't like it when you do that."

Sheb, eleven years old. He's learned not to follow his brothers into the graveyard, now. He's at home with Luana, watching over a little cat as she gives birth to four kittens. He checks each one carefully, talking constantly to the mother, reassuring her he won't hurt her babies. His own mother looks on, smiling gently. "I love you, my Sheb," she says. Sheb beams, his own love for her clear in his face. But his father's in the next room, so he doesn't say it back.

Sheb, thirteen years old. He chases his brothers between the headstones, screaming at them to come back, to return what they've taken. The brothers howl with laughter. One of the kittens—now two years old—is tied in a sack on Ruben's back. It was the youngest. The smallest. Almost died, but Sheb refused to let it. It became his shadow. Followed him everywhere. And now his brothers have taken it. Because it's his. Because they like it when he begs them. He stumbles after them, past the boundary of the graveyard, fighting through the tangle of trees until he comes to the huge, black ash, with its broad canopy and sturdy limbs. By the time he gets there, it's already done. Sheb kneels by the remains of his kitten, his only friend, sobs over its broken body. His brothers don't care. One of them even kicks him for good measure. Sheb turns his tear-stained face up to the brother who struck him. The brother who mirrors him in everything but kindness. "Was it you?" he demands. "Was it you, Jeelie?"

His twin sneers.

"Now you know how it feels," he snarls. "To have something precious taken from you."

Sheb's eyes sparkle with tears. "I don't know what you're talking about—"

Jeelie kicks him again.

I'm thrown out of the memory, fall backwards with a yelp. Wriggler catches me with an outstretched wing. I massage my palms where the echoes of Luana's onslaught stings. Sasha waits nearby, tail lashing.

"That was—" I murmur. "That was awful."

Hmm, Wriggler says. *Not what you needed, though.*

No. He's right. Still, I can't help the knot of rage that tightens in my chest at the sight of my dearest friend in such pain. His tear-stained face. His loneliness. And how Luana ached for him. How she knew he was too gentle for the family he'd been born into. She'd tried to nurture him but couldn't.

I wonder if my own mother felt the same. Did she try to love me the way I needed, but couldn't? Is that what drove her away from me twice? I wonder if her memories would echo love for me as strong as Luana's is for Sheb? Or would my mother's echoes be fearful, accusing? Did she look at me and see my father?

I shake those thoughts away. Wriggler's right. Whatever's happening with Sheb, it links to Luana. To Deimos, his father. To the way his brothers treated him. I need more. I need to know why Deimos turned on Luana in the end.

Because something tells me it was to do with Sheb, the son who murdered his brother a year before Luana died, and vanished from their lives without a trace. And Jeelie's words sting the inside of my mind, too.

Now you know how it feels to have something precious taken from you.

What did Sheb take? At that point, he hadn't taken Jeelie's life, so what the hell is his twin talking about?

I steady my breathing, reach, again, for Luana's headstone. "I need more," I say.

The memories are a trickle, now, rather than a torrent. It's still only pieces, but it doesn't set my nerves on fire. This time, though, I live the memory through Luana's eyes, as if I am her.

Footsteps. Someone running through the grave-yard. I hear her breathing. The ground squelches under her boots. There's a shadow chasing her. The sound of huge wings thumping the air.

The black ash. She's hiding, hand over her mouth. She squeezes her eyes closed. The scent of damp earth mixes with the metallic tang of blood. Heavy boots draw closer. A gruff voice. "Come out, foolish woman! Don't you realize what you've done?"

The wing beats draw closer. There's a rush of foul air. Luana opens her eyes. There, towering over her, its hideous bulk blotting out the sun, is the bone crow. She's frozen, trembling as the crow's tendrils of power spiderweb through her mind, plugging into every painful memory, every shameful secret. Luana clutches her head and screams.

Strong hands grab her, jerking her to her feet. Deimos shoves his face into hers, teeth bared like an animal. He points towards the Corvos as it prowls closer. "This," he says. "This is your fault."

His hands close around her throat. Her air cut off. Panic as she claws at his fingers. He won't let go. Her skin burns. She thrashes but can't get loose.

Another voice from somewhere distant. A woman. "Deimos! Stop!" It's Imberg. But she's not going to get here in time. The light is leaving the world. Luana's body is heavy with impending death.

Imberg's voice becomes a growl of rage. She's running. Running for Luana. For the woman she loves. Luana's heart hurts, but she doesn't have the strength to turn and meet Imberg's eye. To say those last words she was so desperate to shout to the world, but never could.

"I love you. I love you."

It's too late now. Maybe it always was. And all this time, the Corvos crouches over them, rot penetrating every pore, and just watches. Watches her die.

Beside it, stands her son. The murdered one. He drifts in moonlit mist, one hand pressed against the bone crow's side, and he stares, unmoving, as his father murders his mother.

I snap back to myself, tumbling back again. Wriggler doesn't catch me this time. I land hard on my backside, gulping air, still clawing at my throat as if it was me Deimos was throttling.

Sasha's by my side, half-shifted back to human. He cradles me against his chest while his long, cat's tail curls protectively around us. His eyes are amber, grey fur lining his jawbone.

"Breathe, Annie," he says. "You're okay. Just breathe."

After a while, the panic subsides. I slump against Sasha's chest, trembling. I feel him kiss the top of my head. I close my eyes, clinging to his arms.

"Tell me what you saw," he says.

I do. Haltingly, still touching the base of my throat where I felt Deimos' fingers shutting off Luana's air.

Sasha stares at me. "Hell," he says. I don't think I've ever heard him swear before. "I should've guessed. Who would most want revenge against Sheb?"

I splutter, still pressing fingers to my sore throat. "How can a dead person summon a monster?" I rasp. "It don't make sense."

"I don't know," Sasha says. "But the swamp's broken. Somehow, it's not letting spirits settle. People can't die properly, so some part of Jeelie still lingers in life. He must've summoned the Corvos as Sheb was killing him. Maybe it helped him cling to life. Maybe that's what broke the swamp."

I shake my head. This is too many maybes. But I can't get that image of Jeelie and the Corvos out of my head. Sasha's right. No-one would want to punish Sheb more than the brother who died at his hands.

Wriggler? I say, as Sasha helps me up. *What d'you think?*

But Wriggler doesn't answer. Instead, he peers at the star-studded sky. *We should find cover,* he says. *There's something overhead.*

My throat tightens. We dash for the nearby trees, their skeletal branches obscuring the moon's glow. Sasha scans the sky, his shifter-sharp eyes glowing in the pale light.

"C'mon," I say. "We should check out the black ash again."

Sasha blinks but doesn't resist. "Why?"

I shrug. "Dunno," I say. "Just ... I have a feeling. If Luana died there, if Jeelie saw it, maybe ... maybe the tree has memories too."

Sasha casts one last glance towards the sky but says nothing. We both hear it. The distant sound of huge wings. Wriggler bares his fangs. He's still dog-sized, but I feel him straining for more power. We're running out of time.

CHAPTER THIRTY-ONE

MEMORY TREE

THE OLD TREE'S LARGER in the dark. I don't know why, but it feels quieter, too. Like it's grieving. When we reach the clearing, I stand for a moment, staring at its massive limbs.

The ground's firmer here, but there's a slight give. The leaf litter doesn't crunch, it squelches. I try not to look at the headstones arranged under the tree's boughs, though I feel ice on the back of my neck. Something tells me Jeelie's not far away.

I draw closer to the tree. Some instinct urges me to turn and run.

There are memories here, Wriggler says. Like I need telling.

Sasha's back in maned cat form, tail lashing.

"*This place feels vile,*" he growls. He ain't wrong.

"Let's get this over with then," I say.

A rustle somewhere to my left. I snap to attention, palming a throwing knife as Wriggler expands to pony-sized. Sasha's ears flatten. He hisses a warning. A twig snaps. I feel eyes on us.

"Something's here," I say.

Wriggler folds his wings, lightning crackling in his eyes. *It's not the Corvos,* he says.

I raise an eyebrow. *Should I be worried?*

Wriggler flicks his tongue. *Not overly. I'll eat it if it gets annoying.*

I let out a nervous guffaw, then clap my hand to my mouth. Sasha's mane bristles. His amber eyes scan the darkened foliage. Wriggler shoots him a glare, then looks at me.

Your boyfriend's paranoid.

"He's *not* my boyfriend!" I squeak before I can stop myself. Heat floods my cheeks. I snatch a glance at Sasha. Wriggler sniggers behind one wing and Sasha refuses to meet my gaze. My face is on fire as I stumble closer to the black ash. My lightning-snake is a pain.

My fingers brush the tree's rough, ivy-covered trunk, skim the soft bellies of fungi blooming over its surface, the prickle of lichens, the mossy cush-ions. This close, I feel sadness emanating from the tree, like it's absorbed all the pain it's witnessed. I scrape away some of the mosses, trying to get to the bark beneath. Wriggler curls his tail around me. His gaze snaps to some point in the darkness.

Annie— he says, but I ain't listening.

There's a split second where I register his tug on my anger, like he's getting ready to fight.

But then my palm presses against the tree's bark. It's instant, this flood of memories. Such a tor-rent that my head snaps back, eyes rolling. My legs buckling, knees hitting the damp earth. Then the memories take over, and I'm peering at the scene from above, as if I've become the ash.

Sobbing. Desperate, and wild. A girl, no more than fifteen with flame red hair splayed across her shoulders. She's kneeling, her arms thrown up against the tree like she's praying to it, begging. "Don't let him take me. I can't—I can't—"

The memory shifts slightly. The same girl, an-other day.

She's kneeling by the tree again, this time with an older woman with raven-black hair and steely eyes. It's Imberg. Years ago, before age silvered her hair, lined her face. She hooks a finger under the girl's chin, lifts it so the girl meets her gaze. I see a flash of green in the girl's grief-stricken eyes. It's Allise.

"I won't let him take you," Imberg says.

"You can't stop them," Allise whimpers. "His power's growing too strong even for us. I—I have to!"

Imberg grips Allise's shoulders. "You can't," she growls. "And you know it. He's taken Luana—" her voice cracks as she says that name. "—and he's taken Yarella and Nora. He's controlling the swamp maidens. He's suffocating the swamp. He must not have you, too." She pauses. "We'll run. We'll hide. Anything."

Allise's face crumples. "But Sheb—" she says. "It'll mean leaving him."

She covers her face, weeping. Imberg watches, a hard set to her mouth.

Another shift. The suddenness makes me dizzy.

Evening. Wisps of white cloud drift across a sky aflame with dusk. Allise crouches by the tree's roots, waiting. Imberg appears, carrying sacks heavy with Oak-knows-what. She hands one to Allise. "Change your clothes," she says. "We've got a long journey."

Allise rummages through the sack. "Did you leave my letter for Sheb?" Her voice breaks as she says his name.

Imberg opens her mouth to speak, but another voice cuts her off. "She did, yeah."

Imberg and Allise whirl to face the newcomer. A young man, wiry and proud. For a moment, I think, it can't be … because the young man looks like Sheb. That dark, tangled hair framing his face. The grey eyes, the sinuous muscle of his arms. But it's not Sheb. Jeelie saunters into the clearing, holding the crumpled remains of torn up paper. Allise blanches.

"Planning to run, Allise? Wait until my father hears about this."

A hand grabs my arm. I remember where I am. Sasha's voice calls my name, trying to pull me back. With what little control I have over my body, I wrench free of his hold. I need to see this. This is the truth.

Jeelie reaches for Allise. Imberg steps into his path. Her eyes flash with otherworldly light.

"Stay away from my daughter!"

My lips part in surprise. *Daughter?* Oh Oak, it's starting to make sense …

Jeelie laughs. "Not yours anymore though, is she? She's mine. Pa's orders, and he owns the swamp."

"No-one owns the swamp," Imberg snarls. Suddenly, there's a dagger in her fist, raised, ready to strike. Brief fear flickers across Jeelie's face, but then that smirk is back. He brandishes his harpoon, which glows with a faint, green light. "I'm not afraid to kill a swamp maiden," he says. I feel the waves of fear, of regret, of anger, pulsing from the branches of the ash—my branches—as Jeelie lifts his harpoon, the tip glinting in the sunlight.

Imberg hesitates, teeth bared. She looks like a cornered animal, eyes darting for escape. Jeelie's grin becomes a grimace. "I'll kill you quickly," he says, like that ought to be a comfort. "It's what Pa would like—"

A shape barrels into him from the side, blasting the air from him. The tree—the one I've be-

come—shivers as waves of anger pulse from the ground. Jeelie splutters, fights his attacker. The gangly boy with the same tangles of dark hair, the same grey eyes.

"Let them go!" Sheb growls, punching Jeelie square in the jaw. Jeelie falls limp under Sheb's weight. Sheb stands. He unclips his harpoon from his back, steps in front of Imberg and Allise. "Run," he says. "Go! Now!"

Imberg sheaths her dagger, grabs a sack in one hand and Allise's wrist in the other. Allise fights free.

"Come with us," she says to Sheb.

Sheb shakes his head, glaring as Jeelie struggles to his feet. "I'm a de Callis," he says. "They'll sense my magic. They'll hunt us."

"They'll hunt us anyway!" Allise protests, voice trembling with desperation. Sheb finally turns to her, a sad, loving smile across his face.

"But they'll find me," he says. "They'll always find me. I have their blood. Their power. It calls to them. If I go with you, you'll never be safe. And you cannot fight him. Even with all your power, my *love, fighting him will destroy everything. You know this." He meets her gaze, his own softening. "Go."*

Allise lets out a bitter sob but lets Imberg drag her into a run. She looks back, trying to catch a last glimpse of Sheb. The boy she loves. The boy who saved her.

Or tried to.

Jeelie roars, charging after the fleeing women. Sheb steps in his way, swinging his harpoon. Jeelie stumbles back, snatches his own harpoon from the ground. "Let me pass!"

Sheb growls. "Never."

Jeelie's face twists. "It's always you," he snarls. "You take everything from me! She loves you more. They always love you more!"

"I can't take what doesn't belong to you," Sheb murmurs.

"I hate you!" Jeelie roars. He attacks, rage burning bright in his eyes. "You don't get to take her!" he yells. "She's mine! Pa said!"

He feints left. Sheb lowers his harpoon to block the attack. A powerful pulse of magic rockets through the clearing as the brothers clash. Jeelie throws a vicious punch into Sheb's face. Sheb staggers, harpoon falling from his grip. Jeelie's on him in seconds. "I'm ten times the de Callis you'll ever be!" he growls, abandoning his harpoon as his fingers close around Sheb's throat. Sheb thrashes, clawing at Jeelie's hands. Shouts sound in the woods beyond. Harsh, male voices. I recognize them. Ruben. Cheran. Locke. Jeelie must have alerted them. They're after Imberg and Allise. Those two will never escape.

Sheb's eyes widen, both with fear for himself and fear for Allise. His mouth opens, trying to gasp air through his closed throat. Something wet spatters his cheek and I realize Jeelie's crying. Sobs rack his body as he squeezes Sheb's throat. "What do I have to do?" he stutters. "Why does she love you so much? You're so weak! *It's not* fair!"

The shouts from the woods intensify. I hear a woman scream, someone pleading, then silence. Sheb thrashes, fumbling in the leaf litter.

Jeelie roars. "It would be better if you'd just die! You don't deserve it! You're not one of us!"

Sheb's body slowly falls limp, his eyelids fluttering, but the tree—the one I've become—sees something Jeelie doesn't. Sheb's hand closing around Jeelie's abandoned harpoon. In one, desperate arc, Sheb's brought the harpoon up, punched it under Jeelie's ribs. Jeelie gives a grunt, his eyes widening. His grip on Sheb loosens. Sheb rolls, shoving Jeelie off him. He gasps, clutching his throat. Jeelie collapses, the leaf litter beneath him darkening with blood. He blinks, surprised, his fingers pressing against his wound. Sheb crawls to his side.

"I'm sorry," he says, pulling the harpoon free. "I can't let you take them. I can't."

"Traitor!" Jeelie hisses, blood bubbling between his teeth. He's dying.

Sheb touches Jeelie's face. "My brother," he says, tears rolling down his cheeks. "We were so close once. I don't want this. If you'd just let them go. Just let us be."

Jeelie bares his bloody teeth. "Never," he says. "Have your forgotten whose side you're on?"

Sheb stands, angles the harpoon over his brother's heart. "There shouldn't be any sides," he says.

"There doesn't have to be a war. The swamp wants to co-exist."

Jeelie spits blood into Sheb's face. "Who gives a shit what the swamp wants?" he demands. "Pa will take it. All of it. You've chosen wrong. You always do!"

Sheb shakes his head. He meets his brother's gaze. "I'm sorry, Jeelie," he says. "I don't want this. I love you, brother. But you won't stop. I know you won't stop. This is the only way."

Jeelie tries to speak, but it's beyond him. Blood trickles from his mouth. Sheb slams the harpoon into Jeelie's chest. Jeelie spasms once and falls still.

Sheb leans heavily against the black ash as his brother's blood drips from his hands. His eyes are wild. He stares, half seeing, at his murdered brother's body. Then, he grabs his harpoon, staggers into the forest.

I feel the tree relinquish its hold on me, but I cling tight, hoping I'll see what happened to Imberg and Allise. I need to know—

The hand on my arm tightens, wrenching me back. I gasp, lose connection, barely have time to register what's happening. I fly across the clearing, landing hard on my back. The air punches from my lungs, my vision blurs. Wriggler is beside me, colossal, lightning searing down his scales.

Get up, Annie! He hisses.

I stagger to all fours, gasping for breath. It takes me a moment to realize I hear a battle. The yowling-spitting-snarling of two powerful predators going at each other. My vision clears. In the glow of the moon, I see what's happening.

Sasha is in maned cat form, on his back, kicking his rear legs into the belly of a second maned cat that has him pinned, snapping at his throat.

Alphonz.

Chapter Thirty-Two

THE CAT AND THE CROW

I STUMBLE TO MY feet, rage kicking through me. How *dare* he? This prideful ass who hid Maeve's past from her, who threatens my ... whatever-Sasha-is-to-me. Who's chosen *now* to attack us when we were getting somewhere!

I roar. Wriggler unfurls, monstrous beside me. Tendrils of smoke curl from his wings. I flick a knife into my palm, point it at Alphonz.

"Get him!"

With pleasure, Wriggler rumbles.

He surges forward, mouth agape. Alphonz turns, takes in Wriggler barreling towards him. Beneath him, Sasha kicks, dragging his back claws down Alphonz' belly. Alphonz howls but manages to dodge aside. Wriggler's jaws close on empty air. He growls in frustration. Sasha struggles to his feet. His head hangs low. He's got a nasty gash running along one shoulder, vicious claw marks rake his ribs. I dodge aside as Wriggler chases Alphonz in circles. I heft my shoulder under Sasha. His eyes shutter with pain.

"Annie ..." he growls.

"Shut up," I tell him. "Help me!"

I know it's harder for him to transform when he's injured. Still, he tries to take a little of his own weight as I half-carry, half-drag him from under the black ash. We stumble to the edge of the clearing, heading towards the graveyard. Wriggler and Alphonz make an awful racket behind us. I scan the skies, wondering if their caterwauling will attract something bigger.

Deadlier.

Sasha groans, falls limp against me. It's all I can do to scramble from under his weight. He sinks to the ground, cradled between the tangled roots of a tree. I crouch beside him, a hand on his shoulder. He's trembling, fur slick with blood. I feel that tightness in my throat at the idea of him in pain, never getting up again. I sink my fingers into his fur, fighting the fear that burns the back of my throat. Sasha opens one amber eye.

"*Get ... to the boat,*" he whimpers.

"Don't be an idiot," I hiss. "We ain't leaving you."

Sasha snarls but knows better than to argue. Ain't like I do what he tells me, anyway.

The racket of Wriggler's battle with Alphonz cuts short. I strain to listen in the sudden quiet. I close my eyes, trying to feel any echoes of Wriggler's injuries, but there's only the odd scratch. Nothing serious.

A rustle, squelch of leaf litter, and Wriggler's beside me, no bigger than dog-sized.

He got away, Wriggler says, flicking his tongue indignantly, *which is boring.*

I round on him. "What the hell?" I hiss. "Did you know it was Alphonz out there? You said we shouldn't be worried!"

Wriggler sticks his nose in the air. *No, I said* you *shouldn't be worried. I didn't say anything about Sasha.*

I roll my eyes. Great. We're stranded in a haunted graveyard in the dark, being stalked by a murderous, skin-switching priest, and I'm arguing semantics with my bloody lightning-snake.

"You," I say, smacking him on the nose, "are awful."

Wriggler fixes me with a beady stare. *Like you'd want me any other way.*

I can think of a lot of things to say to that, but we ain't got time. I'll lay into him later, when we're back at Sheb's house. All of us. Alive. That means Sasha, too.

"We need to get to the boat," I say. "I need your help to carry Sasha."

Wriggler shoots me a withering stare. *Can't he carry himself?*

I scowl, point at Sasha, half conscious on the ground. Wriggler huffs.

Fine, he grumbles. *But tell your boyfriend he's being a pain.*

"He's *not* my—" I blurt, then clamp my mouth shut. This is a stupid conversation. "Just *carry* him!"

Wriggler mutters under his breath but draws power through our bond, expands to pony-sized. He spreads his wings, helps me roll Sasha onto his back, then folds his wings around Sasha's body, holding him secure. We pick our way through the darkened trees, heading—I hope—towards the graveyard, and the boat. I hesitate at the tree line, scan the sky again. The graveyard is open ground. Exposed.

"Is Alphonz still out there?" I ask.

Wriggler snaps his jaws. *Probably.*

Great. I glare at him. "This would've been so much easier if you'd just *told* me it was Alphonz."

Wriggler chuckles. *Where's the fun in that?*

I resist the urge to smack him. I focus on the main graveyard, checking the path to the boat is clear. It is. For now.

"C'mon," I say. "We should—"

Wait, Wriggler growls. *Something's coming.*

I stiffen, going for my throwing knife as I strain to pick up whatever Wriggler's sensed. Then I hear it.

The thump of air beneath huge wings. And something else, too. The distant sound of a boat engine. The bone crow's coming, but someone else is, too. My fingers tighten around my throwing knife. Great. We've got the Corvos above us, Alphonz at our backs and Oak-knows-who coming from the swamp. The boat engine cuts. Feet on the jetty.

Above, the wing beats grow louder. I feel pressure in my skull. The stabbing psychic energy of the Corvos needling my mind. It knows I'm here. Wriggler bares his teeth. He's feeling that same psychic blast.

"We've gotta risk it," I say. "If we stay here, we—"

My gaze snags on the three figures who appear up the graveyard path. The words die in my throat.

The smallest figure leads, moonlight highlighting how his black skin has blanched grey. His eyes scan the sky. His tongue flicks over his lips. Einan stops in the middle of the path, trembling. He points upward. I don't need to look to know he's spotted the Corvos above. The figure beside him tilts her head, squints into the sky, then nods. The moon is bright enough to catch her silver hair. Imberg. What the hell is *she* doing here?

But I ain't got long to wonder, because the third figure steps from behind her. I want to scream, but there's no air in my lungs.

"No ..." I breathe.

Sheb lifts his eyes, follows the line of Einan's arm. His harpoon's across his back, but he doesn't draw it. I see the moment his gaze finds the Corvos, the sadness in his face. Einan's voice cuts the silence.

"Alright!" he calls. "He's ready!"

I wince. What the hell is he doing? *Who's* ready for w*hat?* And if he keeps yelling like that, he's going to attract—

The Corvos lands with a thud on the grass, towering over the figures of Einan, Imberg, and Sheb.

Annie— Wriggler says, warning in his voice. I'm half stood, one foot planted outside our hiding place, ready to charge.

"What the hell is he doing?" I hiss.

But I already know, don't I? I've always known.

The bone crow's tail lashes. I feel its cruel psychic power in my mind. It folds its wings, lowering its hideous head until its level with Sheb. And then.

Then ...

Holy Oak, it speaks.

"Sheb," it says. *"The other half of me. We can be together again. Forever, this time."*

Einan has frozen. His eyes clamp shut and he whimpers. Imberg steps forward. Her face is ash pale but her voice is steady.

"He is willing to give himself to you if you stop this," she says. "Once and for all."

The Corvos rumbles a laugh. *"Like I have that power,"* it snarls.

Imberg stiffens. "This is where it ends," she says. "The death-roar, the soul-infections, the foulness in the water. The killing of my kin—"

Her *kin?* Who—?

"It ends now," Imberg insists. "With him."

The bone crow levels its necrotic head with Imberg. *"I am not what you think I am,"* it says.

To her credit, Imberg doesn't flinch. She holds the Corvos' gaze for an eternal moment. I see her eyes widen.

"Forgive me," she breathes, reaching towards the thing's vile beak. "I didn't know ... I didn't realize ..."

The Corvos draws its head back, snapping at empty air. It spreads its wings, one talon lifting, stretching towards—

Annie! Wriggler says again. Lightning sizzles from his mouth. I ignore him. I burst from hiding and run, a throwing knife in each fist. Tears blur my vision and, though Wriggler roars in my head, though I feel him expanding, I can't turn back.

Sheb steps forward, spreads his arms. The Corvos screams as it seizes my friend around his waist. Einan falls to the ground, covering his head.

"What about Zuma?" he sobs.

The Corvos ignores him. With a last blast of psychic power, it shoots skyward. I skid to a halt beneath where it had stood, screaming into the darkness. My gaze meets Sheb's as he's torn away. Those grey eyes, usually full of love and life.

Now shining with terrible fear.

CHAPTER THIRTY-THREE
TAKEN

WRIGGLER APPEARS AT MY side as my knees give way. His wing catches me, cradles me close. I roar into the darkness, howling with everything I have. I can't get that image out of my mind.

Sheb, gripped in the bone crow's talons. The terror in his face as darkness swallowed him.

"No, no, *no!*" I scream, beating Wriggler's side. Like just hoping hard enough will change everything. Like it ever has.

Annie, Wriggler says, his voice in my head no more than a growl. *No grief, Annie. Find your rage.*

He's right.

And ain't it easy to reach for it? My old friend. The fury of the damned. Of the heartbroken. I push away from Wriggler and round on the two people still here. The ones the Corvos didn't take. Einan trembles on the floor, clutching his head, whimpering Zuma's name. But Imberg watches me with a cold light in her eyes.

"Bring it back," I snarl. "Bring him back *right now!*"

Imberg blinks. "I can't."

Tears sting my eyes. I palm my throwing knife, level its blade at her face.

"I'll kill you," I tell her.

Imberg says nothing. Fine. The Corvos ain't hers anyway. I stagger in a circle, aiming my knife at every stray shred of mist.

"Where are you?" I roar. "Come out, coward! Show yourself!"

He does, immediately, which I don't expect. Mist converges a few feet away and there's Jeelie, hovering just above the ground. I aim my knife at him.

"Bring it back."

Jeelie's eyes narrow. My rage bucks. I hate how he's stolen my friend's face, twisted it to something vile and cruel. I can't help it. I shriek, lunging for him. But, obviously, he's only mist and memory. He dissipates as soon as I get near him.

I fall face first into the ground, swamp muck spattering my face.

"Come back!" I scream. "Bring him back, you worthless worm! Bring him *back!*"

Images swirl in my mind. I remember the monstrous lair Wriggler made when he was the Oraqua. The terrible, sheer-walled cave he'd trapped me in. Has the Corvos created something similar? Has it taken Sheb to a place like that?

My lungs tighten. I can't breathe.

A hand grips my arm, pulls me to my feet.

"Calm down, girl," Imberg says. "You won't bring him back with your yelling."

I throw her off, aim my knife at her throat. My eyes shoot bloody light across the ground as Wriggler looms above me.

"You," I snarl. "You brought him here. You *sacrificed* him." For the first time, I see a fearful light enter Imberg's eyes. Good. "I'll kill you!" I roar again.

I go for her.

I flick my wrist, hurl the knife. My aim is true. I watch it wing through the air, blade singing, and know it should slam home in Imberg's left eye, killing her instantly. But it doesn't. Because with a speed I would never have thought possible, Imberg swings aside, drops to the ground. She reaches for her fang pendant, lifts it to her lips. Her eyes flash wide, pupils expanding until they blot out the whites. She bares her teeth. I watch something both horribly familiar and desperately alien. Imberg's shape changes. Bones pop and crunch as her skull elongates, teeth protruding to vicious, dagger-like points. Scales pucker her skin. Her joints dislocate, shift, then relocate. The yowl of pain becomes a snarl and I'm not staring at Imberg anymore, but at a hellgator.

A hellgator with partially healed slashes across its face and jaw.

The same hellgator that attacked us at the house a few weeks ago.

Wriggler's wings droop. *Well,* he says. *That was unexpected.*

Funny. I'm not as surprised as I should be. Instead, a whole load of things now make terrible sense. Sasha knew, didn't he? I stare at the wild, snapping thing in front of me. The thing that was Imberg.

"Come on, then," I say, flipping another knife into my hand. "I dare you."

Imberg lunges. Despite her size, her speed is terrifying. Wriggler knocks me aside and I fall into the grass, out of Imberg's reach.

I need anger! Wriggler roars. *Now, Annie!*

I let our bond spill open, my fear and rage flooding down it. Wriggler gasps with the onslaught, pupils dilating. For a moment, I wonder if I've overdone it, but then I hear his heady laugh. Too fast to register, he's huge. Dominating the graveyard, wings blotting out the moon. Lightning cracks along his scales.

Come at me, then!

But Imberg doesn't seem the slightest bit interested. I meet her gaze. Two sets of void-black eyes, glaring. She charges. But not at me. Instead, she darts into the foliage at the edge of the graveyard. Into the undergrowth we'd been hiding in when we spied the Corvos.

Where I left Sasha.

My heart stutters. "Wriggler ..."

On it.

Wriggler surges after Imberg. I hear his vicious monologue in my head.

Get back here and fight me, you overgrown swamp gecko!

Imberg disappears into the undergrowth. I'm running, even as I hear the feline howl of something in pain. The snarling of two powerful beasts squaring off. Then there's a cry cut short, the rustle of foliage as if something darts away. Imberg emerges, dragging Sasha behind her.

"Get off him!" I growl. I charge, throwing knife raised. Wriggler rears, lightning snapping off his fangs. Imberg side-eyes Wriggler, seems to sigh, and gently lays Sasha in the grass before me. She shuffles back, as if to show she means no harm.

I fall to my knees at Sasha's side, running my hands over his silver-grey pelt.

"Sasha ..."

The world tilts at the sight of him. That cruel slash on his shoulder, the claw-marks across his ribs. Has she hurt him? I aim my knife at her, mindless of the fact she's now three times my size and the whole of her head is a weapon. That my measly little knife is the same length as one of her many, vicious teeth.

"If you touch him—"

Imberg snaps at empty air. Then, in a strange, guttural voice, she bloody *speaks*.

"Calm down, child. I'm not your enemy,"

I blink, my mouth flapping open and closed. "You *what?*"

Beside me, Wriggler droops with confusion. He's still massive, could take on Imberg, but now he's looking at me like he's waiting for permission. Which ain't like him.

Imberg looks at me out of one eye.

"We should leave here," she growls. *"The Corvos draws remnants. This place will be overrun in an hour. And I don't think that the other skin-switcher will stay away for long."*

I gape at her. Alphonz. She chased Alphonz off. While I was fighting and screaming, Alphonz came for Sasha. She saved him.

"But ..." I say weakly. "The Corvos." I feel my face crumple. "Sheb ..."

Imberg lowers her head. Is it just me, or does she look guilty?

"I was wrong about that," she says. *"Wrong in a thousand terrible ways. I see that now. But you must trust me when I say the Corvos is not what you think it is."*

I shake my head. What the hell is she on about? It *took* Sheb. She gave him to it. How did she think that was right?

"We need to leave," Imberg insists. *"You're in no condition to fight."*

I get to my feet, rage flooding me again. It ain't so much rage at Imberg now, as at the whole bloody business. "I'm not leaving without Sheb." I say. I picture his face again, the way his eyes met mine as the Corvos took him. "I'm not leaving."

Imberg rolls her eyes. *"Fine."*

In a flash of her huge jaws, she's grabbed my leg. I fall on my backside and roar, expecting pain, but there is none. Apparently, Imberg ain't interested in hurting me. Just humiliating me. She drags me, kicking and cursing, through the graveyard to where we left Einan.

"Get *off* me!" I rage, stabbing with my throwing knife. The blade skitters harmlessly off her toughened hide. She doesn't look round. "Let me *go!* Wriggler!"

But my lightning snake gently gathers Sasha in his jaws, slithers along beside us like this is all perfectly normal.

She's right, he says. *We should get to safety.*

I glare at him. Traitor.

Imberg nudges Einan where he's still cowering. He looks up at her touch, balks when he finds a hellgator staring at him, then seems to remember something.

"Bloody swamp maiden," he mutters. Imberg growls.

"Watch your mouth, little soldier," she says.

Einan's got enough sense not to answer back. Shakily, he falls into step beside Imberg, snatching glances at me as I roar, thrash, swear. But Imberg doesn't let go. Not even when I twist onto my belly, clawing at the earth.

"Sheb! *Sheb!*"

I know I'm making a racket. Good. Let the Corvos come. Let it show its hideous face. Let me fight it. I want it dead. I want my friend back.

But the Corvos doesn't come, and Imberg doesn't release me. At the jetty, she tosses me into the boat, then slides into the water behind it. Wriggler lays Sasha beside me, shrinks down and slithers onto my lap. I shove him off.

"You're s'posed to be on my side!" I mean it to sound harsh, but it comes out as a sob. Suddenly I can't hold it back anymore. My ribs heave. The tears come in great, choking gasps. Wriggler flicks his tongue, hurt, then slithers close to me again.

I am on your side, he says. *Even when you're being an idiot.*

I'm furious. Part of me wants to hurl him over the gunwale. Instead, I gather him into my arms, hug him as I weep. Wriggler curls against me, extends one wing, and hugs me back.

Einan says nothing as he unmoors us, hops into the boat, and throws the engine into life. We drift away from the graveyard. Without Sheb.

Something in my core twangs loose, like a thread has snapped. My friend is gone. Walked willingly into the bone crow's talons. Had he been planning that all along, and I didn't know?

And what the hell does Jeelie plan to do with him?

Chapter Thirty-Four

A Delicate Balance

Back at the house, we find chaos. Bear has almost become the Krazka, rampaging through the living room. Bartok has found his way home and flies in frantic, shrieking circles, knocking ornaments from every surface. Below them, Maeve struggles to regain control. Her eyes glow green, her face twisted in a snarl as Lin tries to hold her back.

"They took him!" she screams. "He shouldn't have gone! They made him go!"

I guess that was expected. What I didn't expect is that Nora and Allise are here, too, with Yarella half-transformed and ready to attack Maeve if necessary. I stare at the scales across her cheeks, her darkened eyes.

"I should'a guessed," I mumble. So many things suddenly make sense. Imberg's fear of Bear's white fire—the fire that has stopped Sasha from being able to skin-switch before—and the tooth pendants they wear.

This is why Sasha didn't want to investigate the swamp maidens, ain't it? He knew they were skin-switchers. He knew they were the hellgators. I throw him a filthy glare. This would've been so much easier if he'd just *told* me!

Sasha manages a few steps into the living room, then collapses. All the anger goes out of me. I kneel beside him.

"Sasha ..."

He bares his teeth, eyes glassy with pain. *"Now you know,"* he says. *"I'm sorry, Annie. I couldn't tell you ..."*

I clench his fur in my fists. "Why not?"

Nora stands over me. "Our power comes with rules," she tells me. "No matter which world we're in. We can sense each other. There's a scent, something undetectable to any but our own kind, but part of the magic is that no skin-switcher may reveal the secrets of another. Telling you, even trying to do so, would have caused him immense physical pain."

Oh.

And I've been so angry with him. I press my cheek against his forehead, feel tears burn my eyes.

"Get up, girl," Nora says. "There will be time for that, later."

I sit up, wipe my eyes. I notice Kai, cowering in a corner. Nora and Allise hardly notice him. Einan runs to his mother, tears staining his face. She wraps him in a fierce hug.

"It's okay, my son," she says. "It's okay."

It's anything but okay. But before I get a chance to tell them so, Allise fixes her glare on Imberg, rages towards her.

"*You!*" she growls. "How could you? I told you not to do this! I told you it wouldn't work. And now—"

Her words dissolve into a mindless scream. Her pupils dilate, the black of them blotting out the whites. I see her skin shimmer as scales pucker on its surface. Her elongated jaw snaps empty air.

Imberg has shifted back to human form and helps me carry Sasha—still a maned cat—to the tattered sofa. She doesn't look at her daughter.

"I did what I thought was right," she says. "Had I known ... Allise, I—"

Allise swipes a dust-coated vase off its stand. It shatters like a heart. There will be nothing left unbroken in this house by the time we leave. *If* we leave. Because I'm not going without Sheb.

"It won't work!" she snarls. *"You've doomed him for nothing!"*

My lungs tighten.

"We have to go back," I breathe. "I need to find him, I have to—"

Imberg grabs my wrist. "It won't hurt him," she murmurs. "You must trust me on this. I know, now."

I wrench my arm away, glaring. Funny how that brings me no comfort whatsoever.

"Why would I trust you?" I hiss. "You attacked him! You tried to kill him!"

Imberg's jaw tightened. "I did not," she says. "I did not wish to hurt him. I wished to return him to the portal, where he could not pledge his power to Ruben."

I stare at her, the anger draining from me. "Oh," I say.

Of course she wouldn't want him dead. If he died, Sheb's power would flow to Ruben. Then, *why* give him to the bone crow?

"What the hell have you done?" I demand. Imberg doesn't reply.

Allise becomes a woman again, turns her tear-streaked face to her mother. "You've only made it worse," she hisses. "And you know it!"

Imberg doesn't answer. I see her gaze flicker up, meet her daughter's. She says nothing, but her face is lined with guilt. I can't stand it.

Sasha shudders, snarling in pain. I go to him, stroke the matted fur from the wound as carefully as I can.

"Stay with me," I say. "Please, I—I *need* you right now."

I choke on the words, hating that I've said them aloud. Hating that they're true, especially after everything he's kept from me. Everything he's put me through. Sasha stares at me. He sets his jaw and nods.

"Medicine," he hisses. *"Something for the pain, so I can ... change back."*

I stand, wondering if Nora's swamp medicines might help. But I can't think about anything clearly with this racket going on. I gaze at Bartok, winging his screaming circles around the ceiling. I look at Lin, trying to get Maeve under control, at Bear, destroying everything, at Nora trying to manage Allise, and Imberg ignoring her, and Einan who's gone to sit with Kai. All this chaos. I've got to do something. There's no-one else to fix this but me.

Like bloody always.

"Wriggler," I murmur. "Sort Bear out, would you?"

Wriggler gives me a side-eye. *Do I* have *to?*

I glower at him. he sighs. *Fine. But just so you know, I hate this.*

You and me both, I think but don't say. He knows. He can feel it pouring off me in waves.

I blink and he's huge enough to wrap Bear in his vast coils. *Stop it!* I hear him chide. *Pipe down, you oversized cub.*

Bear roars, manages to free a paw and rakes it across Wriggler's scales. I wince as I feel the echo of Wriggler's pain across my ribs. Wriggler snaps at Bear's ear until I tell him off.

Wriggler fixes me with an accusing glare. *He hit me first!*

I raise an eyebrow. He flicks his tongue at me, then squeezes Bear just tight enough that Maeve gasps. The fight goes out of her. She drops to her knees, the green light sputtering from her eyes. Bear shrinks and Wriggler releases him.

I turn to Nora. "Medicine," I say. "For Sasha. Will the swamp meds work?"

Nora's still trying to calm Allise.

"In the pantry," she says.

I kneel beside Maeve, rub circles into her back.

"Can you get the meds?" I ask Lin. The other girl nods, glad to be doing something, and scurries away. Now that Bear's stopped smashing things and Maeve's been reduced to sobbing,

Bartok lands on my shoulder. I realize he's still clutching Zuma's bloody shoe. He croons into my ear. When I look at him, his tawny eyes are wide and scared. He glances around, searching. But the person he wants ain't here.

My fury builds again. Wriggler sparkles with energy. But I can't solve this by raging. Not this time. I meet Nora's eye.

"Let her go," I say, jutting my chin at Allise.

Nora's eyes widen. "But she'll—"

"Let her," I say, turning my glare on Imberg. "Ain't like her mother can't handle it."

Nora hesitates, but Imberg doesn't protest. Nora lets go. Allise flies at her mother, pummels her shoulders, screams in her face. Imberg just holds her daughter's wrist, waits until she dissolves into a weeping mess. Then, Imberg hugs her close.

"It's all over," she sobs. "All of it. Everything. He'll win, now. *They'll* win, just like they always do."

I blink, frowning, as Lin returns with the medicine. Nora helps me tilt Sasha's head, pour the fluid down his throat. We steady him while he shifts back. He falls limp and shivering against the sofa cushions, injured, but alive, and human again. He reaches for my hand. I take it, brush his hair back from his face, then turn and meet Imberg's eye.

"Think it's time you told me a few things," I growl. "Without lying, this time."

Chapter Thirty-Five

BONDS AND PROMISES

Nora and Imberg exchange a glance I don't understand. Nora opens her mouth. I can tell she's going to give me platitudes. Tell me it's best if I go home. Take what's left of my ragged family. Leave and don't look back.

Ain't happening.

"You gave my best friend to a monster," I remind her. "I have no idea what it'll do to him. If he's even still alive—" I bite back a sob, hating how my hands tremble. "Tell me the truth!"

Nora closes her mouth again. Imberg drifts towards the huge window, stares out over the swamp. A grey dawn lights the town. Fat droplets of rain disturb the water's surface. Even after everything, they're still not going to tell me, are they? I can't believe how secretive and selfish—

"Sheb was always different from his brothers," Allise says, making me jump. Yarella snarls. Imberg and Nora round on Allise, but she glares them down. "Don't!" she snarls. "They have a right to know. They're his family!"

Damn right, we are. I fold my arms, nod at Allise to go on.

"The swamp and the families have been in uneasy alliance for centuries," Allise says. "The families' magic tempers the swamp enough so that communities can flourish, and the swamp maidens make sure the families don't damage the swamp. It's a delicate balance. If one or the other gains too much power, the magic we rely on would collapse.

"Normally, the swamp and its maidens tolerate the Heirs of the families, keeping their power in check, but years ago, Deimos ... discovered a way to control us."

She looks pained, touches the tooth pendant at her throat. She turns it, holding it out to me.

On the underside, I see a symbol carved into it. A circle, a diagonal slash, a crude eye. The de Callis crest. Around the carving, the tooth is blackened and cracking, as if rotting. Allise looks pained.

"If you take the tooth of a skin-switcher," she says. "You hold some of their power. To an extent, you can control it. When Deimos stole Luana's tooth, he carved his power into it, and forced her to marry him. He thought his magic would dilute the power of the swamp maidens. He planned to control all of us that way, marrying us to his sons. But when Sheb came along ..." she pauses, composing herself. "When Sheb came along, something was different. The swamp loved him. He could walk through the trees and they'd lean towards him. He'd draw birds from the branches. Creeperscorps would eat from his hands. It was unheard of. It was like the power of the swamp and the de Callis magic had blended in him."

I nod, remembering how Nowhere responds to Sheb. How it loves him, defending him from the night predators, making paths for him where previously there were none.

"His power was beyond what any of us had known but it was different," Allise continues. "He was like a new Everyn. Had that same, unquenchable power. And his brothers were jealous. The swamp maidens wanted Deimos to name Sheb as Heir, thinking it would soothe tensions between the de Callis family and the swamp, that it might release us from Deimos' bonds."

"Deimos was a fool," Yarella growls. She prowls the room, still half-hellgator, which is doing nothing to calm my frayed nerves. "And he loved watching his sons compete. He loved their rivalry, how they all vied for his attention."

"It's his fault Sheb did ... what he did," Allise says. "And when Sheb killed Jeelie, the swamp was so stricken with grief that it just ... broke."

"The death-roar," Maeve says, finally glancing up. "Sheb caused it?"

"Deimos caused it!" Allise insists. "And when Sheb had to flee, everything fell apart. Sheb's magic was stronger than any we'd known and it turned out it was holding both Deimos and Ruben back. Without him, everything went to shit."

"Ruben was named Heir," Nora says bitterly. "But Luana—" she stops, glancing at Imberg as the older woman covers her hand with her mouth. She trembles, then composes herself.

"Luana knew Ruben would never fully come into his power unless Sheb accepted him as Heir," she croaks. "And Sheb would never do that. So, there was only one thing Deimos could do."

My heart lurches. "Deimos wanted him dead," I say, remembering what Sheb's memory had said under the black ash.

They'll always find me. I have their blood.

I frown. "But Sheb's been in Nowhere for eight years," I point out. "If the brothers could always find him, if Deimos and Ruben control the portal, how has it taken this long?"

Imberg sinks onto the sofa. "It was Luana," she says, eyes shining. "Brave, brilliant woman, she found a way to shield Sheb. She bound his magic to hide it, blocked Sheb's brothers from going through the portal. That's why Deimos killed her, thinking her death would release the magic. It didn't."

"So we killed him," Yarella says. Everyone looks at her, but I find nothing surprises me anymore.

"When Sheb returned, Ruben hoped to talk him round," Allise says. "But Sheb would never give in. The moment he returned, we knew he was in danger. His magic was still bound, and Ruben was getting stronger. He's found a way to bypass the swamp's rule, and has imbued talismans with his power, granting them to his followers. He's using the de Callis crest to spread his magic."

I frown, thinking of Lucius and the warriors, of the crests carved into trees in the Deep Swamp.

"That's what Xanni was investigating," I say. "And she—" I stop, realizing something. "That dead hellgator we saw, that was Xanni, wasn't it?"

The swamp maidens don't say anything. They don't need to. I remember the hellgator's torn body, its limbs ripped off, its hide slashed open. Holy Oak, did Ruben do that to her? I clutch my belly against sickness.

Nora's jaw tightens. "You understand now," she says, "What we're up against. Still, Ruben isn't able to gain full power. Even bound, Sheb has more magic than Ruben ever had. And the swamp is getting sicker. Sheb's return only made its grief worse, and he refused to go back to Nowhere."

"So we thought—" Nora starts.

I feel myself bristling, my ever-present rage bubbling to the surface. "You thought if you gave him to the Corvos," I say, "that the death-roar would stop. Jeelie wouldn't kill him, that wasn't what he wanted. He wanted to make him suffer, but to do that, he had to keep him alive. Sheb's power wouldn't pass to Ruben, but the remnants would die properly. The swamp would heal enough to resist Ruben." I glare at them each in turn. "You thought Jeelie would be appeased."

It makes sense now. If Imberg couldn't return Sheb to the portal, she could at least use him to appease the swamp. She must have drawn the Corvos to us, too. And Sheb, my brilliant, brave best friend, risked everything to return, to fight a war that almost destroyed him. I glare at the swamp maidens. The women at least have the decency to look ashamed.

"We were wrong," Imberg admits. She covers her face with her hands. "Nora, Yarella ... we were *so* wrong. If we'd just—"

"It's too late for that, now," Nora says. There's urgency in her voice. She turns to me. "You and Maeve, you have to leave. Now. Go back to Nowhere."

I fix her with a hateful glare. "I ain't leaving without—"

"Yes," Nora says firmly. "You *are*. If Ruben can't have Sheb, there is another way he can break the swamp enough to gain control over it. Did you see the way he looked at you both when you arrived? How delighted he was that two murk-touched had landed in his boat?"

My insides squirm. I remember what he'd said to me.

Maybe the swamp is hungry for you.

"His magic strengthens by the day," Nora says. "He's already dangerously powerful, and he's getting impatient. If he returns even one murk-touched to the swamp, it will shatter what's left of the swamp's power. But two ..."

"What do you mean, *return?*" I ask. Though I reckon I already know.

"Death," Yarella says. "Both you, and your monsters."

Maeve finally stands. "Let him try," she growls. "I dare him."

Yarella rounds on her. "He will come for you," she says. "It's a matter of time. And you cannot fight him. His power is growing. He can use it to cut off your bond with your monster, if he chooses."

Maeve freezes. I see the horror in her face. It's my horror too. Can he really do that?

Wriggler?

If he dares ... my monster snarls, but I hear the uncertainty in his voice.

Nora's face is fierce. "If you want to survive," she says. "If you do not want to be responsible for dooming this world, our families, you will *leave.* You will let us find Sheb and handle the Corvos."

"Like *hell* we will!" I yell. Wriggler rears, his vast wings cracking against the ceiling. "You handed him over! You *gave* him to the brother he was forced to murder!"

Allise seems to lose all control, throws her head back and howls. Her legs giving way beneath her. Nora catches her before she hurts herself. Yarella stops pacing. She and Imberg watch me, eyes full of regret.

"If we'd known," Imberg whispers. "I swear ..."

"You've killed him," I say. As soon as I say it, I know it's true. He'll die in that lair. Maybe not today, or tomorrow. But eventually, he will. Frightened. Alone. "No, more than that. You've *destroyed* him. Jeelie hated Sheb even when he was alive. He'll rend him apart. He'll—"

My voice fails. A hideous buzzing takes hold in my head. I've failed him. My Sheb. My heart, my soul. The world tips sideways as my vision swims. I clutch the edge of the sofa but can't stop the dizziness that slams my brain. Strong hands grip my shoulders. The air thickens. Someone says my name from very far away. Bartok launches off my shoulder and flies to the mantelpiece. Wriggler darts off my lap, slithers to the far end of the room.

Dammit! I hear him think.
And I vomit all over the floor.

CHAPTER THIRTY-SIX

YOU SHOULD BE SCARED

I GROAN AS MY legs give way. Sasha catches me before I collapse, wincing as his injured arm takes my weight.

"Annie ..."

I cling to him. Can't help it. Though he's hurt, he holds me, hushes me. Something inside me splinters and I'm sobbing, pressing my face against him. His arms encircle me, lips brushing my forehead.

"He's gone," I choke out. "He's gone and it's my fault. I should've— I didn't—"

Sasha hushes me. "Annie, it's okay—"

"It's *not okay!*"

I ball my hands into fists, trying to find the rage that's always a heartbeat away from tearing me apart. But it's suffocated beneath a well of grief. Sheb. My Sheb. I can't get his face out of my head. The way he'd looked as the Corvos snatched him skyward.

Something nudges my finger. I glance down to find Wriggler beside me. Small. Harmless. Useless. Like I am. What the hell good am I if I couldn't comfort my friend when he was suffering? If he didn't trust me enough to tell me what he was planning?

Another hand touches my shoulder. It's Allise. She kneels beside me, face puffy and tear-streaked, but set in determination. Her hand is pressed to her belly, absently protecting the child she didn't even want. She meets my gaze.

"It won't kill him," she tells me.

"How do you know?" I demand.

"She's right," Imberg butts in. "It won't. Look, girl, I'm sorry. I thought—anyway, I was wrong. The only thing to do now is get you away from here before Ruben—"

"No!" Einan yells.

We all turn to stare at him. Nora folds her arms.

"What do you mean, *no?*" she demands. "You're outnumbered here, kid. You've no idea what Ruben is capable of."

Einan paces furiously. "You know nothing about me!" he growls. He runs angry fingers through his curls, drops his arms to his sides. He's breathing heavily, eyes wild and searching. Bartok swoops back to my shoulder—Zuma's shoe still clamped in his beak. He fixes Einan with a tawny glare, growls. The feathers on his back rise into sharp spikes. A hideous cold settles in my gut.

"Einan?" I say. "Something you want to tell us?"

Einan's face changes. He looks hunted. "No."

Which means there is *absolutely* something he's keeping from us. Finally, the rage bucks in my core. Wriggler flares his wings, sparkling with the strength of it. I make to stand, but Sasha grips my wrist, holding me. He cups my face, puts his mouth close to my ear.

"Wait," he murmurs.

I scowl at him. *Wait?* For *what?* For my friend to be broken by the Corvos?

But it turns out, he's right. Lin moves to Einan's side, places a gentle hand on his arm. And my mouth falls open when I see Kai kneel at his other side. Kai touches Einan's shoulder.

"It's okay," he says. "It's okay to tell the truth. You should *tell* them!"

Imberg and Yarella perk up.

"Einan?" Yarella says. "What's he talking about?"

Kai looks at her sorrowfully. "About Pa," he says. "About—"

He stops, clamps his mouth closed. His face drains of color, gaze drifting to the window, where a boat engine thrums outside. Footsteps on the jetty. My heart thumps, even as I push away from Sasha. I let my rage flood to Wriggler, let him expand to dog-sized, don't tell Maeve off when she lets Bear grow, too.

The front door slams open. Ruben marches into the room, looking so triumphant it's all I can do to resist clawing his hateful eyes right out of his head. Locke and Cheran follow in his wake and, behind them, are five of Ruben's men. I recognize Lucius among them.

There's another figure that makes my heart clench and my rage spike. Blond stubble dappling his scalp, cruel blue eyes gleaming, light catching those sharp canines as he grins at me. Alphonz.

"Hello Annie," he says. "Maeve. Lin. Seems I can punish three traitors today." He fixes Sasha with a victorious smirk. "Instead of just one."

Sasha growls, eyes flashing amber. The swamp maidens are on the verge of shifting, too. Yarella bares her teeth at Lucius.

"Bastard," she growls.

His lip curls. "Traitor," he shoots back.

"Quiet," Ruben drawls. He leans against the door frame, smirking at me. "Right where we left you," he sneers. "You should've taken Nora's advice. Too late now, though." I clench my fists, eyeing the harpoon strapped across his back.

"What've you done with Sheb?" I demand.

Ruben barks a laugh. "What have *I* done?" He says. "I haven't done anything, have I? It wasn't me that delivered Sheb to the Corvos. But you know that, girl. You were there."

Annie, Wriggler hisses. He tents his wings, bares his teeth. *Let me bite him.*

I'm sorely tempted. But Locke's unclipped his harpoon from his back and now eyes Wriggler with cold disdain. These men have no idea who they're messing with.

But Alphonz does.

"Careful," he warns. "She's explosive, this one."

At least he's sensible enough to look nervous. Not nearly nervous enough, though. I'll kill them all. Bloody light from my eyes falls across the wooden floor. Wriggler expands until he's pony-sized, larger, filling the whole room with his mighty presence. I feel a sickly thrill when Ruben and Locke step back.

Behind me, Maeve stands. Her eyes flash green. "Stand down, Maeve," I growl. "This ain't your fight."

"The hell it ain't," Maeve snarls. "Alphonz is mine."

Bear's five times his usual size, white fire bursting down his back. I see Nora's and Imberg's eyes widen, know they see the fire for what it is—it'll stop them transforming, rendering their power obsolete.

Cheran whimpers at the two monsters looming over him. Even Locke's gone pale, but Ruben laughs.

"Oh you!" he roars. "You'll both be perfect. The swamp will weep over you for a long, long time." He turns to Alphonz, delighted. "You've kept your word, priest, persuading my idiot brother to go with the Corvos," he says. My throat tightens. Did Alphonz find Sheb one of the many times my friend gave Wriggler and Sasha the slip? I glance at Einan, who stares at the floor, shame in his eyes. He knew! Treacherous little creep!

Ruben gestures to me and Maeve. "I'll take the murk-girls," he says. "The traitor is yours."

Alphonz' smile widens.

Wriggler hisses. *Annie, seriously, let me eat him.*

I hold him back. But only just. I can feel his want, the way he drinks my fury. I turn blood-red eyes on Ruben, stepping between Sasha and Alphonz. "I'll kill you," I tell him. "I'll kill all of you if it means getting Sheb back."

Ruben's cold smile widens. "Try then, murk-girl," he says, lifting his harpoon. "See where it gets you."

I let my rage loose. Let all the hurt and fury spill like blood from collapsed veins. Wriggler gasps with the onslaught. Lightning cracks off him, smashing into the chandelier above us, which explodes in a violence of glass. Bartok shrieks, takes off. He darts through the open front door, still carrying Zuma's shoe. Sasha throws himself over me, trying to shield me. I push him away, feeling glass nick my face. The pain is quickening. I raise my arms, feel the flood of my anger racing through my monster. Wriggler's wings open, smashing the plaster in one wall, and shattering the window in the other. He headbutts the ceiling. Plaster rains down. I splutter on the dust. Ruben launches his harpoon. Wriggler knocks it out of the air. Ruben's eyes widen as he realizes what my monster is doing. Then he runs.

Good. Let him fear me. Like he's made everyone fear *him*.

I'm smiling. Laughing. And then my rage is so great, so violent, I can't see anything. Someone shouts. Hands grab my wrists. I thrust them off. Let them try and contain me. Let them bloody *try*.

Something whizzes past my head. Wriggler's taken the sofa in his jaws and now shakes it like he's trying to kill it. Stuffing flies out of it. The cushions split. The wooden frame splinters and it falls into a misshapen heap. He turns to the fireplace, tears it out of the wall. Soot and ash explode into the room. He lashes his tail, smashes a door. He brings down the entire wall between the living space and the hall. He reaches his massive head through the hole in the ceiling, bites out a piece of floor from the upper story. He smashes his way through the rest of the floor. A wardrobe crashes from above, narrowly missing Einan's head.

That brings me to my senses, but I've let the rage loose now. I can't rein it in. My vision returns, I blink as I see Bear crash into Wriggler, clamping his jaws around Wriggler's throat. Maeve throws an arm around Lin, rushes her out of what used to be the front door. Nora has Kai under one arm and bundles Einan under the other, covering their heads as she, too, flees for the jetty. Imberg and Yarella grab Allise, shielding her head, dash for the door.

Alphonz transforms, lunging for Sasha. I slash at his face with my knife, leaving a bloody gash across his cheek. He howls, but he's not stupid. His eyes flick towards the groaning ceiling, then he bounds for the door.

Wriggler thrashes against Bear's hold, wings battering the floor, smashing the boards, exposing the foundations beneath.

Get off me, cub! Wriggler roars. Bear does no such thing, but he clearly retorts, because Wriggler roars, affronted.

You *calm down! I'm smashing this house to smithereens, then I'm filling it with so much lightning it'll burn for a week! Get* off!

But Bear holds fast. His claws rake Wriggler's scales. I wince as the echo of his pain flares across my ribs. Wriggler twists free, opens his maw, and shoots lightning at Bear's head. Bear dodges it, grabs the wrist-joint of Wriggler's wing, and pulls. Wriggler bellows.

"Let go of him!" I yell, a knife in my hand.

Maeve reaches for me. "Annie," she begs. "Annie, enough. We have to get out—"

I shove her away, screaming until my lungs ache. Fingers grab my wrist, an arm across my collarbone. Sasha's lips are close to my ear. "Annie, don't," he says. "Please don't."

I thrash against his hold. I'm strong, and he struggles to hold me, but he doesn't back down. He presses his cheek to mine. "Annie, I'm here," he says. "I'm here. Please stop."

A sob escapes me. "Sheb ..." I whisper.

"I know," Sasha tells me. "I know."

The strength goes out of me. I crumple against him. He takes my knife, sheathes it in my belt.

Bear's let go of Wriggler. They face each other, panting, blood dripping from their jaws. Wriggler glances at me, sorrow in his eyes.

Annie, he says. But my rage has ebbed, replaced by a hollow yearning that seems to swallow all the light. Wriggler shrinks to dog-sized as the last intact wall in the room buckles. The whole house groans, lurching sideways.

"Run!" Sasha yells.

We do.

Furniture crashes from above. I have a strange sense of déjà vu. This ain't the first building I've let Wriggler destroy. Or even the second. Back in Maeve's home world, he brought down Krogan's manor, then smashed what was left of the old prayerhouse at the edge of town.

Seems we're getting good at tearing down houses.

Sasha bundles me into the last boat. Wriggler and Bear—now back to normal size—tumble in after us. Maeve throws the engine to life. We power onto the swamp as what's left of Sheb's family house—that huge, dark, memory-laden mansion—crumbles in on itself. The last of the windows burst. Furniture smashes through the platform, takes out one of the stilts. Then all the stilts buckle and split. The house falls into the swamp. We bob on the waves caused by the collapse, watch as the house sinks. The water around it bubbles, as if delighted to devour the de Callis legacy. Bits of timber float on the dark water.

Bartok's shrieking draws my gaze towards Ruben's huge boat. The owl-squirrel flies in furious circles above it. My gaze falls to the deck, where the swamp maidens are grappling with the brothers. Allise has managed to shove Locke overboard. Yarella and Nora try to transform but Alphonz pounces, pinning Yarella to the deck. Ruben stabs his harpoon into Nora's shoulder. She shrieks.

"Ma!" Kai yells. He tries to wrestle his father, but he's so small. So helpless. Imberg howls and in a flash of scales, she's a hellgator. She throws Cheran overboard to join Locke, then dives at Ruben, but the de Callis Heir fends her off with his harpoon. She turns on Alphonz. I see his ears flatten. He knows he's outmatched. He leaps over the gunwale, paddling frantically for the shore.

Bartok finally abandons his vigil and swoops to my shoulder, whacking me over the head with

Zuma's shoe. I bat him away. He hops down to sulk on Lin's lap.

"Faster, Maeve," Sasha says, wrapping an arm around me so I can no longer see the battle.

"Like I need you to tell me," Maeve growls. She drives the boat so fast we crouch in the bilge to avoid being blown overboard. She takes us out of Marsh Wilds, past the graveyard, past where the trees grow thick and wild, where Ruben's crest is carved into the bark. She takes us out to the tree where Xanni left her message.

Maeve cuts the engine. Everyone is silent, our faces wreathed in shadow.

"Great," Maeve says finally. She glares at me. "Now bloody what?"

Chapter Thirty-Seven

MONSTERS ON ALL SIDES

While I appreciate her effort, it's obvious Lin's cooking ain't quite up to Sheb's standard. We've finally stopped, mooring the boat to a tree, and staggered ashore. I've no idea where we are, apart from that it's far into the Deep Swamp. The death-roar snarls in my head. Remnant mist swirls around us, shaping into hands and faces. Sometimes, fully formed remnants drift among us. I shudder as they brush me. Their touch doesn't harm us but Holy Oak, does it hurt! It sends freezing needles of pain through our skin, quickening our heartbeat and filling our noses with a necrotic stench. Ruben's crest glows everywhere on the trees, here. I swear, there are more of those awful carvings than there were last time I ventured into the Deep Swamp. The trees creak and groan as if in pain.

Wriggler, still massive, curls around our pathetic little camp, snapping at remnants when they come to close. Bear prowls the perimeter. We huddle together, shivering. No-one speaks.

The fire we've built is meagre, sputtering in agitation. We've cleared as much of the leaf litter as we can and set out a makeshift fire pit. Lin, who luckily kept her pots and other supplies strapped to her belt, boiled some swamp water and found some mushrooms she claimed to recognize. She set about cooking, signing something about how no good rescue ever happened on an empty stomach.

The sentiment made my eyes sting. I mumbled something about checking for danger, stalked off on my own, just to stuff my fists into my mouth, muffle the scream clawing its way up my throat. When I came back, Sasha was watching me with concern in his eyes. He didn't say anything, which I was grateful for.

Lin, with a deflated-looking Bartok clinging to her shoulder, scoops watery mushroom soup into a bowl, hands it to Maeve. She hands me a second soup-filled bowl. I take it absently, noticing the sheen of sweat layering Lin's face. She's paler than normal. Whatever cruel energy infects the swamp, it affects her more than the rest of us. I watch her, frowning, as I lift the bowl to my lips. Something tangy and acrid stings my tongue. I recoil, trying not to pull a face. Lin watches me anxiously, though, and Maeve's looking at me like if I upset the girl she loves after the stunt I've just pulled, she can't be held responsible for her actions. Slowly, I lift the bowl to my lips again, take a tentative sip.

It's foul, but luckily, not anywhere near as foul as it smells. Mostly, just water and bits of mushroom. It's warm, at least.

"It's good," I lie. "Thanks, Lin."

She smiles, like she knows I'm lying, and scoops a bowlful for Sasha.

Somehow, I manage to finish my meal. The soup simmers uncomfortably in my stomach. I try to distract myself from the nausea by scanning the trees. Faces appear and disappear in the remnant mist, like the souls they belong to can't hold their shape.

Except for one. He's been sitting among the branches ahead of me for some time, fully formed, watching us. I glare at Jeelie's ridiculous face but, for some reason I can't work out, I haven't mentioned to the others he's there. Whatever he's here for, I can't shake the feeling it's between me, him, and Sheb. He tilts his head, eyes narrowing.

"Annie?" Sasha's voice makes me jump. "You okay?"

I feel him looking at me, asking permission. A part of me is still angry he didn't tell me the truth about the swamp maidens, but I know that's unfair. I realize, now, that he tried. It hurt him to try. And he's here, ain't he? For a change, he's here. I'm grateful, even though I can't bring myself to trust it.

He'll leave again the moment he gets a chance, won't he? He can't wait to get away from me. Just like everyone else. Still, I let myself lean into him, don't protest when he wraps an arm around me.

It's different to Sheb's touch. Me and Sheb are close without expectation. Affection to show the simplest, gentlest love.

Sasha's fingers drawing soft circles on my bare shoulders sends electricity shooting through my veins. It feels wrong, given everything that's going on. Still, it ain't like he's asking anything of me. He lets me nestle against him. His touch is light, unassuming. He just wants me to know he's here.

For now.

"Your shoulder okay?" I ask him.

He nods into my hair. "Much better."

We managed to bind the worst of his injuries. Lin boiled some bandages and Maeve helped me cauterize the wounds with branches from the fire. It stopped most of the bleeding and we cleaned the wound, strapped it up. It'll likely hurt for a while. I'm hopeful he'll be able to shift if anything happens.

Like if the Corvos descends on us. After all, Jeelie knows where we are. If he wants vengeance against Sheb, coming after his family might be the next step.

I shudder, hug my knees tighter, watching Lin snuggle into Maeve's side. Maeve kisses the top of her head. Bartok hops onto Lin's knee, making forlorn, crooning noises. He's still got Zuma's shoe, but thankfully he hasn't hit anyone with it for a while.

Bear lumbers over to them, currently the size of a regular bear. His horns brush the lower branches, white fire licks his fur. He sits behind them and cleans his paw.

Despite everything, I feel my eyelids sliding closed. I shake myself awake.

"You should all get some sleep," I say. "I'll keep watch."

Sasha looks at me, frowning. "Annie," he says. "You're exhausted—"

I wriggle out from under his arm, force myself to stand. "I'm fine," I say. "But you're injured, Lin's suffering from the death-roar, and Maeve's—"

"Maeve's *what?*" Maeve snaps, cutting me off.

I glance at her, see the beginnings of that tell-tale green glow in her eyes. Bear's lips peel back in a snarl. I sigh. I ain't got the energy to have this argument right now, but Maeve seems determined to start it, so ... hell. Let's get it over with.

"Maeve's still not got enough control over Bear," I say, resigned to her inevitable burst of anger.

But it doesn't come. Maeve just shakes her head, sadly.

"Annie," she says. "Is that still what you think?"

Her sadness startles me more than her anger would have. I stare. "It ain't just what I *think*," I say. "It's what I *know*. You lose it, and Bear's huge. I can never tell what you're ... if it's ..."

I trail off, because everyone—including Wriggler, is looking at me with the sort of face that says, *go on, Annie. Keep digging that hole.*

Wriggler flicks his tongue. *We gonna keep going with this nonsense?* He drawls. *Or you ready to face the truth?*

I shoot him a glare, but he's right, ain't he? They all are. It wasn't Bear who tore Sheb's family house to pieces. It wasn't Maeve who lost control of her monster. And if I really think about it, I've watched Maeve show admirable control over Bear recently. I've been cross because I think she keeps going faster than she should. But if I'm honest, it's because she's learning faster than I did. She's pushing me because she's ready. She accepted Bear more quickly than I did with Wriggler. I watch the pair of them now, Maeve sat cross-legged between Bear's paws while he nuzzles the top of her head. They're so well aligned. Their bond so clear that it makes me glance sideways at Wriggler with shame.

Wriggler side-eyes me. *What?*

I don't know what to say. Even if Maeve does have more control than me, even if she's strong, fearless, full of fight, I'm still not okay putting her in harm's way. The thought of any of them—*any* of them—in danger punches the breath from my lungs. I can't stop the image of Sheb's face whirling round my mind. His eyes, how frightened he was as the Corvos snatched him.

And Sasha's still injured.

And Lin's ill.

And Maeve's just ... *Maeve.*

I ain't risking them. I shouldn't have risked them as much as I already have. The truth is, there's only one person I'm willing to risk. I never realized how much it hurt to have a family you love this fiercely. To feel how that loss would crush you, leave you skinned and bleeding with no-one to put you back together.

I can't. I *can't.*

I shake my head. "Maeve, it don't matter how good you are with Bear. Or that Sasha can turn into a giant cat, or that Lin's got a power stronger than anything I've seen. I'm not—"

"Not *what?*" Maeve demands. She's on her feet, a hand on Bear's shoulder. He shows his teeth. Maeve's eyes flicker with green light. "Why d'you think it's only you who gets to make decisions about us? Don't we get a choice?"

Sasha reaches for me. I snatch my hand away. Wriggler's pony-sized behind me, hissing and sparkling. "No," I say. And I bloody mean it. "You *don't!*"

And I ain't explaining myself. Because I can't, can I? How am I supposed to tell her Sheb's loss is like a thorn in my heart? That every time I think about him, the thorn pushes deeper? Or that I see her and Lin snatched away like that when I close my eyes? That the sight of Sasha torn open under Alphonz' claws made fear roar through me like a hurricane? I ain't got the words.

I feel Wriggler's energy crackling, frustration building until my nerves are aflame.

Wriggler turns glowing scarlet eyes on me. I know my own are glowing too.

Annie? he says. I hate the concern in his voice. My monster, my darkness, is afraid. Tears burn my eyes. I turn away.

"I'm gonna do another patrol," I say. "Stay *here*, all of you. I'll be back in a minute."

I ignore Sasha as he struggles to his feet, trying to grab me. I ignore Lin signing at me. I ignore Bartok screaming in protest, Maeve's indignant voice yelling, "Don't you *dare* run away, Annie! Not from us!"

I storm away from camp, set off at a brisk stride. I ain't running away.

I'm *walking* away.

Which ain't the same.

Chapter Thirty-Eight

TO FACE THE WORLD ALONE

SASHA FINDS ME CROUCHED against a tree, sobbing my heart out. He kneels beside me.

"Breathe, Annie," he says. His hand rubs gentle circles on my back. "It's okay. Just ride it out."

Oh yeah, because he's the expert at keeping me calm. I try to shove him off, but I end up grabbing his hand instead.

"I hate this," I tell him.

"I know," he says.

"All you do is let me down."

"I know that, too."

I blink. Fresh tears burn my eyes. "I miss Sheb."

Sasha strokes his thumb across the back of my hand. Wriggler curls around me, hissing empty threats at Sasha, which he ignores. Instead, he does the thing Sheb always does.

"Tell me something you see," he murmurs. I blink in surprise, turn my tear-streaked face towards him. His eyes are soft with concern.

"What?"

A smile quirks his lips. "You know what," he says. "I know it's normally Sheb. I know you're furious with me, but right now, I'm here, so you'll have to make do. Tell me something you see."

I face him. My heart thuds, but it feels different now. A breathlessness that comes when I hold his gaze. I want to be furious with him. I *am* furious with him. But those dark, gold-flecked eyes send a wave of calm through me.

"You," I whisper. "Your face. Your eyes. I see you."

Sasha nods, scoots closer to me. Our knees touch. He takes my other hand. "Something you hear."

I close my eyes. "Your voice. How calm it makes me."

He leans closer. I smell the musk of him. Back when he was a priest, it was incense, mixed with that strange, mystical scent that made me think of dark nights and full moons. Now, the incense fragrance is dimmer, the dark, full moon smell is stronger. I breathe him in. My lips part.

"Something you feel," Sasha says. His face is inches from mine, his breath warm against my lips. I open my mouth.

"I ..." I say.

But Sasha doesn't let me finish. He catches my mouth with his and I'm electrified. I feel Wriggler's power fall dark with shock. I don't care. Sasha's arms are around me, his mouth on mine. He pulls me against him. I clutch at his collar, let my head fall back as he kisses me.

Weird how certain thoughts burst into your head at moments like this. I realize I'm twenty-two years old and this is the first time anyone's kissed me.

I realize I expected it to be rough, cruel, possessive, but it's nothing like that. Sasha's urgent, yes, but gentle. His hands around my waist tighten and release. He pulls back, inviting me to lean in, keep our lips together. It's a language I hadn't realized I knew how to speak. A language of constant asking.

May I?

And I can't help myself, because even though I'm still angry, my answer is, yes. Yes, always.

Finally, Sasha pulls away. My lips burn with the memory of his. I open my eyes to find him staring at me, his forehead gently resting against mine. He's smiling, and I can't help smiling too.

"I wasn't expecting that," I admit.

Wriggler flicks his tongue. *Neither was I,* he grumbles.

Sasha strokes hair from my face. "But you ...?" he says. "I mean, I wasn't ...?"

I see his cheeks darken with embarrassment and laugh. "No," I say. "And yes. I mean, I wouldn't mind you doing it again." I can't believe I just admitted that. Can't believe I have no intention of taking it back. "It wasn't ... what I expected."

Sasha chuckles. "I figured," he says.

We stare at each other for a bit, but neither of us leans in for a second kiss. Maeve and Lin are by themselves. Sheb's still missing and I ain't got the first clue how to find him. That fear flowers in my gut again but, somehow, Sasha's touch stops it spilling over.

"Sorry I ran," I say. "I ... it all gets a bit much sometimes. I can't ... I'll try harder."

I make to stand, but Sasha's grip on me tightens. "Not yet," he says. "Maeve and Lin are fine. They've got Bear. And *you* need some space."

I frown at him. "I ain't got time for what I need," I say, trying to squirm free. Sasha doesn't hold me this time. He lets me push him off but holds my gaze.

"And that," he says, "is half the problem."

That pulls me up short. I raise an eyebrow. "What's that s'posed to mean?"

Wriggler, expanded to dog-sized, winds around my ankles. *Exactly what it sounds like,* he says smugly. *I hate to admit it, but Cat-Boy is right. You are your own most irritating problem.*

I scowl at him. *We agreed you'd never call Sasha Cat-Boy ever again.*

Wriggler chuckles. *I didn't agree to anything.*

Sasha gets to his feet, wincing as he does. I reach for him, but he bats me away. "I can do it," he says. "I'm okay. But you're *not*. You keep pretending you can keep going, be the lone hero. It's going to end in disaster. It already has."

I bristle. "So now this is all my fault?"

Sasha grabs both my shoulders. His eyes flash amber.

"It's like you can't see how much you're hurting us!" he growls. I blink. What the hell's he on about? "You try and do everything by yourself! You won't let us help! Maeve's tearing her hair out with worry for you! Lin doesn't know how to convince you, and Sheb marched straight into the bone crow's claws because he'd rather endanger himself than see you hurt! Don't you *get it*, Annie?"

I blink again. Because I don't get it. What's he trying to say? That my entire family are a bunch of reckless chaos-mongers that can't see danger when it punches them in the face?

But it turns out, that's not the point he's making.

"We *love you*, Annie!" he says, his voice fierce. I go very still in his arms, staring at him.

"What?"

"We love you!" he says again. "You think we can bear to watch you clawed to pieces by a monster? Or drowned? Or buried? Or murdered by Ruben?"

I shake my head, feel the way tears burn my eyes again. "I can't lose you," I say. "Any of you. You don't understand—"

"No, *you* don't understand!" Sasha says. He's so angry his canines have lengthened. "Annie, you've been so afraid of losing all of us, you can't see how *we're* terrified of losing *you*. You are amazing and brilliant and brave, but you're not an army. You're one woman. One *exceptional* woman, but still only one. Unless you let us help. Unless you let your *family* stand by your side. Do you see?"

I stare at him, open-mouthed, wonder why his words make my whole body feel limp with fatigue. It's hard to believe him when he uses words like *brilliant* and *brave*. All I feel is exhausted and terrified. And it's even harder to believe him when I remember how often he's shut me out, kept secrets from me.

But maybe he's right. Maybe I don't have to do this on my own.

It's not that you don't have *to do it alone, Annie,* Wriggler drawls. *It's that you bloody can't! You saw the Corvos. It took both me* and *Bear to see it off. You seriously want me to face that thing by myself?*

It's a fair point, but it still makes me smirk. *You saying you and Bear can work together?*

Wriggler covers his head with one wing. *If I have to,* he grumbles. *But only if he does as I say.*

I can't help it. I let out a guffaw, then feel my face crumple. The sobs come again. I thought I'd cried out all the water in my body, but apparently not.

Sasha holds me until the sobs subside, kissing the top of my head. Eventually, I pull away from him.

"Okay," I concede. "Point made. We should get back to the others."

Sasha nods, smiling. "And *I* will take first watch," he says. "You need to get some sleep. If Nora and Imberg are right, the Corvos won't hurt Sheb. We can work out what to—" He trails off, peering over my shoulder. Wriggler hisses. I whip round, a throwing knife in my hand.

A shape detaches from the shadows, prowling towards us. Dusk-light shines in its amber eyes. Wriggler snarls. In a flash, he's pony-sized, baring his fangs over my shoulder. I raise my throwing knife, ready to loose it at the hateful, smirking face in front of me.

"What the hell do you want?" I demand.

Alphonz yowls as he shifts back to human form. He's an absolute wreck. Half his face caked in blood, a split lip. He holds one arm awkwardly and favors one leg, but his cruel, blue eyes flash with amber light. There's enough cruelty in that smile that I know he's still dangerous if he wants to be.

"You know what I want," he says. His gaze meets Sasha's and his grin widens.

Sasha growls, shifting, but I step between them. Wriggler tents his wings over me.

"Piss off, Alphonz," I say. "You think I'm gonna let you take Sasha?"

Alphonz shrugs. "No," he admits. "Because you're an idiot. But Ruben is searching for you. And now, I've found you. Perhaps I can't take Sasha on my own, but I have the power of the de Callis brothers behind me. And when Ruben finds you, Annie," he laughs coldly, "you and Maeve won't be able to come after me. He has his own plans for you both." He taps his chin thoughtfully. "Perhaps I'll take Lin back to Hollow Creek with me, too. Reckon Princeling Jax might be *delighted* to have his runaway bride returned."

I raise my knife, my eyes glowing.

Wriggler snarls. *Shut up, kitten,* he rumbles, snapping the air inches from Alphonz' face. *You're getting boring.*

Alphonz steps back, but the smirk doesn't leave his face. "You can't run forever, Brother," he says. "And you, dark-child, your days are numbered."

"I'm not your brother anymore," Sasha snarls, swiping at Alphonz. The priest sidesteps, but he's too slow. Sasha leaves a bloody graze across his thigh. Alphonz bares his teeth.

"I will take you back to the Jewel City," he says. "And the Sovereign will strip you of your powers." He grins. "It will hurt, Brother. And then it will kill you. I've been patient this long."

Wriggler beats his massive wings, sending a foul wind towards Alphonz. The priest covers his head, dashes for cover. I hurl my knife at his retreating back, but Wriggler's wind sends it off course. It thuds into a tree.

By the time I've retrieved it, Alphonz is gone.

We stare at the place where he stood. I feel fatigue weigh on me again.

"We'll fight him," I say.

"No," Sasha murmurs.

I turn to him. "What the hell d'you mean, no?"

Sasha brushes a loose curl from my cheek. I close my eyes at his touch.

"We can't fight him and the brothers alone," Sasha says. "And if I stay, it puts you in more danger. We need help, Annie. We need Riverfell to fight alongside us."

I glare. "And how're we s'posed to do that?" I demand. "The swamp maidens had a hand in delivering Sheb to the Corvos. They want us gone. And anyway, they're four women, all under Ruben's power."

"They aren't four women," Sasha says. "They're Riverfell's warriors. They range across the five territories."

My lips part. I remember the blond swamp-maiden we met at Nora's house. Petya. How Nora and the others had implored her to fight alongside them. Petya's mention of a haven. Maiden's Creek.

"You don't even know where to find them!" I protest, grabbing Sasha's shirt. Panic claws my ribs. I can't have him walk away from me again.

Not when I've just realized how much I need him. How much I need them all.

Gently, Sasha untangles my fingers from his shirt. He lifts my hands to his mouth, kisses them each in turn, then kisses my forehead. He's leaving again. Like always. I bloody knew he would.

"I'm coming back, Annie," he says, like he can read my thoughts. I shake my head. Can't bring myself to believe it. Sasha's eyes soften. He nods at Wriggler. "It's not like you need me to defend you, is it?"

Wriggler draws himself up to his full height. *No, it bloody well isn't!*

Sasha cups my chin. "Let Maeve and Lin help you," he tells me. "Keep moving. Find Sheb. I'll come back." He presses his lips to mine again. "And I'll bring an army."

I close my eyes, lean into his kiss. Then he lets me go. When I blink, he's gone.

I don't give myself time to think. "Come on, Wriggler," I growl. Then, I run back for the girls.

Chapter Thirty-Nine

THE LAST BROTHER

I CRASH THROUGH THE trees and stumble back into camp, making so much noise that Lin and Maeve jump. Bear flashes to twice his usual size. Maeve rolls her eyes when she realizes it's me.

"What *now?*" she demands. "Where's Sasha?"

I lean on my knees for a second to catch my breath.

"Alphonz found us," I gasp. Still snatching my breath, I tell them what happened, where Sasha has gone. "We've gotta go!" I say. "Now!"

The girls scramble to pack up camp. Lin snatches Bartok from a tree branch, shoves him, squawking, into my arms while she and Maeve stamp out the fire, pour out the rest of the soup, and gather our pots.

Finally ready to go, Maeve draws her dagger.

"Right," she says. "Where to?"

They look at me expectantly. My gut sinks into my boots. My plan took us as far as *we've got to get out of here,* but I realize we've got nowhere to go. What are we supposed to do, keep running in circles until Ruben catches up with us?

"I ..." I stutter. "I don't ..."

Maeve lowers her dagger. Lin wipes sweat from her forehead. I sink to the ground. A wave of tiredness knocks me sideways. "I don't know," I admit.

The girls say nothing.

Wriggler slithers to my side, extends a wing over me. *Breathe, Annie,* he says.

I refuse to look up. I don't want to see the disappointment in Lin's eyes, hear the derision in Maeve's voice.

But neither happens.

Hands grab me under the arms and haul me to my feet. The girls hold me until I'm steady. Lin dusts me down, then touches my face and smiles.

"Right," Maeve says, winking. "We need a plan."

Something kicks at my ribs. I realize I'm still clutching Bartok. I release him and he clambers onto my shoulder, nuzzling my neck. He still won't let go of Zuma's shoe.

Lin glances over my shoulder, then starts signing.

"Maybe our plan should involve him," Maeve translates, then frowns. "Involve who?"

We both turn, and I leap backwards in shock. Jeelie hovers a few meters behind me, watching in silence.

"Holy *shit!*" Maeve exclaims, aiming her dagger. "Who the hell is—" I see her eyes widen as she takes in those familiar eyes, that floppy hair. Her face pales. "No," she says. "No, Annie, it can't be—"

"It isn't," I say quickly. "It's not Sheb, remember? It's his brother. The one he murdered."

Both girls stare at me, aghast. I realize exactly how much I've been carrying alone. I sigh, filling them in on what I know, including the vision I had of Jeelie's death at the black ash.

Maeve glares at me. "Reckon it would've been real useful to know that *forever* ago," she drawls.

There's no argument to that, really. "Yeah," I say. "Sorry."

Maeve makes a derisive noise, then turns back to Jeelie. "Reckon he can help?" she asks. "All the other remnants just wander around like ... well, like lost souls. They don't seem to remember much."

Jeelie scowls at me. I scowl right back.

"Oh, he can help," I growl. "He has Sheb. The Corvos is his monster."

Lin smooths her shirt and signs. I catch the main element as she points behind me.

Shall we follow him, then?

Me and Maeve whip round in time to see Jeelie evaporating into a cloud of mist.

"Shit!"

I lunge for him, but obviously, he's got no substance. My fingers sting as they claw through the remnant mist. Laughter echoes through the air.

"Little weasel!" I grumble. "How're we s'posed to—"

Maeve grabs Lin's hands. "Can you track him?" she asks.

My heart stutters painfully. Of course! Lin's power is linked to souls. If we act quickly, perhaps he isn't lost to us after all. Lin closes her eyes, fingers flexing. Sweat beads on her forehead and she teeters, leaning against Maeve. For a moment, I think it's too much for her. Then, a thin, silver thread appears in the air, leading from Lin's chest and weaving through the trees. When she opens her eyes, she looks as shocked as me and Maeve do, but there's no time to dwell on it. Lin signs something. Maeve nods.

"She says she's tethered him," Maeve explains. "Whatever that means. If we're quick, we can follow his trail. Let's go!"

There's no time to ask what the hell *tethering* is, or how Lin knew to do that. We rush for the bank, bundle into the boat. If Alphonz is alerting Ruben to our location, we can't stay here, and following Jeelie seems like as good a course as any.

We follow the silver thread as it weaves through the swamp. Dusk has Riverfell in its grip and the trees above are so thick that only the dimmest moonlight filters through. But the silver thread of Jeelie's tether gives off its own light. It leads us out of the Deep Swamp, towards Marsh Wilds, then jinks sharply at a crumbling old jetty I've come to know only too well.

"The graveyard," Maeve grumbles. "What a surprise."

We moor the boat, hurry ashore. Both Wriggler and Bear are pony-sized.

"We should hurry," Maeve says. "This place is gonna be the first Ruben's cronies will look."

She shunts her shoulder under Lin's arm, helping her onto Bear's broad back. Bear nuzzles Lin's leg. She smiles and scratches under his chin. Wriggler sticks his nose in the air.

Just 'cos he's a better shape for riding, he scoffs. *She'd be far safer with me.*

I raise an eyebrow. *Are you jealous?*

Wriggler spits sparks. *No,* he says sullenly, which means he completely is.

I suppress a smile, but we don't have time to waste on teasing. I turn to Bartok on my shoulder.

I try to extract Zuma's shoe from him, but he ducks and weaves his head, growling until I give up.

"Fine," I say. "Want to help Sheb?" Bartok gives me a look that suggests I'm daft for asking. I stroke his fluffy tummy. "Get into the air," I tell him. "Stay low but keep an eye on the skies. When you hear wingbeats, yell. Got it?"

Bartok blinks. I've no idea if he does get it, but I know he'll do anything to help Sheb. Bartok turns his worried gaze towards the skies, chirps once, then swoops into the darkness. I peer after him, trying to see if he's doing as he's told, but his flight is silent. I can't make out his shape against the night sky.

He's sticking close, Wriggler confirms. *He'll help.*

I touch my lightning-snake's side with a smile. Wriggler makes a show of pretending my gratitude doesn't please him, though I feel his happiness jangling in my head. He knows, as well as I do, we'll need each other for what's to come. Wherever Jeelie has taken Sheb, whatever the Corvos is doing to him, this is going to be a vicious fight.

But it's for Sheb. My Sheb. No, that's not fair anymore, I think, looking at Maeve and Lin. They're fighting just as hard for him, ain't they? It may only be a few weeks they've been part of my little world, but they haven't run. They haven't abandoned Sheb. Or me.

So he's not my Sheb anymore. He's *ours.* I gulp down the truth of what that means. That I'm walking into terrible danger with two teenage girls at my side, not doing anything to protect them.

Annie, don't be ridiculous, Wriggler scolds. *They wanted to come. And who says they'll need protecting? Maybe* they'll *protect* you. *Maeve's got a gigantic icefire bear at her command and Lin's one of the most powerful humans I've ever met.*

I scowl. "Until a few weeks ago, the only humans you'd ever met were me and Sheb," I point out.

Wriggler fixes me with a beady-eyed stare. *So?* he says. *I'm an excellent judge of character.*

I roll my eyes, but don't respond. We fall silent as we follow the silver tether across the graveyard, heading for the black ash. Beneath it, the de Callis graves stand silent, shrouded in remnant mist. On Bear's back, Lin groans, slumps forward. I feel a pulse of energy, that sickening death-roar growing louder at the back of my mind. My gut rolls.

"Is it here?" I ask, frowning. The silver thread goes past these graves, weaving around the black ash.

Annie, Wriggler says. *Look.*

I blink through my blurred vision, peer around me. Ghostly light drifts from the damp earth, twisting into faint shapes that drift slowly between the headstones. They follow some half-remembered path. Remnants. There are more than I've seen here before. Little kids chasing shadows through the graveyard before they pause, as if they've forgotten their game, and turn their shimmering faces to the sky. Men and women wandering aimlessly, or standing, gazing at nothing. Even in their misty form, their faces are so sad. So frightened and lost, it makes me want to reach out to them.

They won't feel you, Annie, Wriggler reminds me. *They're just echoes.*

I shake my head. "It ain't right," I say. "It shouldn't be."

No, Wriggler agrees. *It shouldn't. So, let's fix it.*

The black ash looms above us, darker than the night itself, its limbs stretching skyward. The silver thread of Jeelie's tether is wrapped around the tree's massive trunk. I notice the area immediately around the tree is ominously empty of remnants, like the other souls are afraid to come close.

"Jeelie?" I say. "Come out, then. Come face us."

Maeve draws her dagger. Lin slides from Bear's back. I flick a throwing knife into my hand. For an agonizing moment, nothing happens.

Then, remnant mist oozes from the tree's branches, forming into a fog so thick I can't see through it. I feel the buzz of the death-roar in my brain, the sickening hum of a thousand flies. Nausea crashes through me. I double over, grabbing Wriggler to steady myself.

Maeve and Lin buckle, too. Maeve flops against Bear. Lin collapses altogether and vomits.

The remnant mist roils for a moment, then forms into that same shape I've come to know so well. Jeelie hangs inches above the ground, his hair and clothes drifting as if he's under water. He meets my gaze.

I'm struck, again, by those eyes. How similar they are to Sheb's. In another world, under the gaze of another father, maybe my best friend and his brother might have been comrades, laughing together, exploring this amazing world they were born into.

But I see the jealousy, the hurt in Jeelie's face. I see the echoes of want and fear. A legacy carved into his soul by his father.

And don't I know what that feels like?

I reach for him.

"I need your help, Jeelie," I say.

Jeelie watches my hand as it extends towards him. Unlike the other remnants, he looks like he's aware of us. Still—

"He won't be able to feel you," Maeve whispers. "There's no point—"

Jeelie's ghostly arm flashes out, grabs my wrist. *Grips* it. Terrible, burning cold bites my flesh. It's all I can do not to scream. I stare at his hand, clasping me. *He shouldn't be able to do that.*

There's something weird about his fingers, too. It takes me a moment to realize that the tip of his little finger is missing. But I ain't got time to think about it.

"He said you'd come," Jeelie says. His voice sounds like gathering storm clouds, rushing swamp water and blood spilling from an open wound. "He said you'd never stop fighting until you found him." He smiles. "And now, you're mine."

The world around me evaporates into darkness. I hear Maeve scream my name. Wriggler roars. I struggle, but Jeelie's grip is too strong. He drags me down, down, down.

Into a darkness like none I've ever known.

CHAPTER FORTY

JEELIE'S DARKNESS

WRIGGLER SHRINKS, BARELY HAS time to wrap himself round my ankle before the graveyard, the night, and the swamp all vanish.

I fall into darkness so thick it swallows my scream. A foul scent clogs my throat. I gag, pressing my hand over my face, but there's no getting rid of it. The necrotic buzz of the death-roar sounds in my ears, grows until it rattles my skull. It's all I can do not to vomit.

The only light comes from Jeelie, still gripping my arm tight enough to make my fingertips tingle. Tendrils of mist curl off him. His form stutters, like whatever strange magic keeps him tethered to the graveyard loses some of its power down here.

If here is even down.

If here is even *anywhere*.

I reach for my bond with Wriggler, trying to flood him with power, but I can't. That knot of rage that's normally so easy to draw on feels dark and distant.

Wriggler's voice echoes in my brain, like it's coming from far away.

The death-roar, he says, his voice no more than a whisper. *It's linked to Jeelie.*

I reach for my knives, but what's the point? Even though he's holding me, what's the betting my blades will go straight through him? Wherever he's taking me, I know Sheb's down here, too. Trapped in the vile lair the Corvos must have built from Jeelie's anger. That's what they do, these monsters. They build worlds from our darkness. I remember my own, five years ago, how close I'd come to being trapped there forever. The deep, unfathomable darkness, the walls, almost impossible to scale, the way Wriggler—the Oraqua, back then—had lanced through my brain, until I almost turned on Sheb, almost killed my own mum.

I stare at Jeelie as the wind tears at my hair, as we fall and fall and fall.

Finally, our descent slows. The air thickens until it feels like water. Strange black and silver mist swirls around my wrists and ankles. The thick, fungal stench makes me gag again. And the death-roar intensifies until something pops in my nose. A stream of blood stains my face. Disembodied fingers reach from the mist, grabbing at me. I shy from them but Jeelie still has me in a tight grip.

Then my feet hit something solid. My knees buckle. I'm on all fours, choking against the foul smell of ... wherever we are.

Wriggler slithers from around my ankle. He draws what little of my rage he can reach, expands to dog-sized. He mantles me with one wing, snaps at Jeelie's fingers, still clutching my arm.

I almost tell him not to bother, but then his fangs catch on the mist of Jeelie's thumb. Jeelie gasps, snatching his hand back. He looks at it, flexing his fingers, then fixes Wriggler with an accusing glare.

"You bit me!"

He sounds so petulant, I almost laugh, except if I open my mouth, I'm sure I'll throw up. Wriggler flicks his tail.

I'll do it again, too, he hisses. *Just try it.*

Jeelie scowls, though I doubt he can hear my monster talk. Interesting, though. Something about this broken magic means Wriggler can touch Jeelie. Hurt him. That's useful. I push myself upright and peer around.

There's barely any light, but what little comes from Jeelie and the strange, black-and-silver threads swirling a few feet above us show an earthen chamber. We're underground. Or at least, that's what the Corvos wants us to believe. Jeelie's rage-cave is similar to mine. Vaguely round, with sheer walls that would be all but impossible to scale. But where my cave was made of jagged rock that would cut you if you touched it, Jeelie's feels suffocating. Layer upon layer of packed earth, with tangled roots poking out here and there. The floor is an impossible tangle of vast roots. I see roots reaching over my head, too, forming what look like rafters and balustrades. My mouth falls open as I realize.

We're under the black ash, I think to Wriggler.

He flicks his tongue. *Makes sense,* he says. *That's where he died.*

Shakily, I get to my feet, facing Jeelie. He's recovered from Wriggler's bite and stands a few feet from me, glaring. He wafts his misty hand in the air and the ghostly shape of a harpoon appears there. He snatches it. I flick a throwing knife into my palm. Jeelie's smirk widens.

"That won't work down here," he says.

I ignore him, lift my knife. "Where's Sheb?" I snarl. "Give him to me or I'll—"

I pause. I'll *what?* The boy's already dead! I lower my knife. What can I possibly threaten him with that would make him return Sheb to me?

Jeelie must see the fear in my face because he laughs. His misty form shimmers. "Swamp's sake," he scoffs. "He told me you were *smart.*"

I lower my weapon, touch the side of my head. The death-roar thunders at the back of my mind.

"What do you want?" I ask.

Jeelie's face twists. "Want?" he repeats. "What do I *want?* I want to live my life! I want my brother not to have murdered me!"

I can't help it. I roll my eyes. "Okay," I drawl. "Well you can't *have* that, can you? And anyway, I saw what happened—"

Jeelie lets out a noise like an animal in pain, twitches towards me. I shrink away as Wriggler slithers between us, fangs bared. He's still no bigger than a large dog, but lightning sizzles down his scales. Jeelie doesn't notice. He stares at me with a strange, forlorn expression.

"You saw?" he says.

I nod. "Everything," I say. "You say he murdered you, but you'd have killed him, right? Sheb's carried the burden of your death since it happened. It ain't as simple as he makes out. Or you. He was trying to save the girl he loved."

Jeelie shakes his head. "I wasted so much time," he says. "So much time on that bloody jealousy." His harpoon evaporates. He covers his face with his hands. I see again how the little finger of one hand is missing. "Poor Allise," he says. "She didn't deserve any of it. None of them did. Especially not Sheb."

I blink. Wasn't expecting that.

"You—" I start. "You ... *don't* want revenge?"

Jeelie lifts his face, meets my gaze. Holy Oak, he looks so much like Sheb.

"What would be the point?" he whimpers. "Being dead gives you a lot of time to think. Hurting Sheb, making him suffer, it wouldn't change a thing. I'd still be in the ground. Along with Pa and my ... my ..." he buries his face in his hands again.

I glance at Wriggler. He gives me one of his weird, serpentine shrugs.

Don't look at me, he says. *I've got no idea what's going on.*

I look at Jeelie, this dead kid who's made so many mistakes, and I realize I've been so wrong. All those looks, those frowns and narrowed eyes that I thought were sinister ... they weren't, were they? He was trying to reach me. Trying to explain. And like bloody always, I wouldn't listen.

Jeelie finally manages to compose himself. "It was her," he says. "It was always her. I wanted her to love me so much, but she only had eyes for Sheb. She loved all the things about him Pa said were weak. His kindness. His joy. His gentleness. I couldn't understand it."

I sheathe my knife. "Yeah, well," I say. "Turns out, Allise has good taste."

Jeelie scowls at me. "I'm not talking about Allise!" he snaps.

I gape at him. "Then who—"

"I'm talking about our mama!" Jeelie bursts out. "The others, they were all desperate for Pa to be proud of them, to claim them as his Heir. But Sheb never cared, and that's what Mama loved about him. I wished she'd look at me like that. I wished she kept a lock of *my* hair in that stupid ring on her finger, but she never did. She never would. And when I died, all she took of me was my bloody fingerbone!" He holds up his hand, showing me the missing finger. He sobs. "She only did that because of him, too! Bind his power to the swamp, keep it small and quiet so his brothers couldn't find him. Stop them going after him through the portal. She only took a part of me so she could save *him!* It was always about him!"

I feel a stab of something in my gut. An echo of old pain. Don't I know what it's like, to have a mother who doesn't love you like you need? I remember what the Corvos said to me.

Mothers are wounds others can use against us.

All this, the breaking of the swamp, Sheb's dampened power, Ruben's greed, it's all from Jeelie's wound. Suddenly, I realize I'm not angry at this dead kid anymore. I can't be, can I?

Jeelie doesn't look at me. He stares at the shimmering swirls of mist where his feet ought to be, shrugs helplessly.

"It's all so broken," he says, like I don't already know that.

I sigh. "Jeelie" I say, "Ruben's getting stronger. I need to understand how all this happened, and I've only got pieces—"

"He's spreading his power," Jeelie interrupts. "I know. I've felt it. It started before Pa died. It started with Mama. With Nora."

I frown, then it hits me all at once. "The swamp maidens," I breathe. "The brothers have been forcing them into marriage, using them to control the swamp. That's how Ruben's sharing his power, ain't it? Somehow, he's using the swamp maiden's magic to split his power into those talismans."

"Their teeth," Jeelie says. "They link him to the swamp. Pa did it first with Mama. She's the root of it all. He marked her tooth, and then he had her under his power. Her tooth was buried with her when he killed her, to stop the other maidens getting hold of it. Ruben's terrified someone will find it, use it to free the other maidens. If Ruben controls them, he gets to spread his influence." He covers his face with his misty hands. "It's all so wrong,"

He looks up suddenly. "But there's time to stop it. When Pa named Ruben as Heir, the others had to pledge their service to him. When they do that, most of their power passes to him. I didn't matter, 'cos I was dead. My power was his already. But Sheb? Sheb was alive. He'd run, hadn't he? After he killed me."

I nod. "Yeah," I say. "To Nowhere. To me."

Jeelie shrugs. "Ruben needed to find him, either force him to pledge his service, or kill him. But Mama would never let that happen. She was a swamp maiden, and she knew things about the swamp's magic that the families don't know. She took the lock of Sheb's hair, and she did something to it, bound it to something that belonged to the swamp."

"Your fingerbone," I whisper.

"A thing of death," Jeelie says. "To smother Sheb's power. To keep it quiet, so Ruben would never sense it. Whatever she did, it kept him from going through the portal. Ruben couldn't go after Sheb. None of my brothers, could."

I press my fingertips into my temples. "That's why Deimos killed her," I remember. "She stopped Ruben gaining his full power. She protected Sheb, and Deimos killed her for it."

"And sealed his own death," Jeelie spits. "He was an arrogant man, my pa. Thought he could do what he liked. He forgot that when an Heir kills a swamp maiden, the swamp comes for them.

Those hellgators, they ripped him to shreds." He shudders. "I felt it. Even down here. I felt the swamp's fury. It's grief for Mama." He fixes me with sad eyes. "It was Imberg who gave him the fatal bite. She tore out his throat. Ripped it like paper. I felt him die."

Well, that sounds horrific. I can't help the wave of sympathy I feel for Jeelie. He was a fool in life, but death seems to have taught him a few things.

"Where's your fingerbone now?" I ask.

"Mama has it, still," he says. "I don't know where. I don't know how—" His face crumples again. "I ruined everything," he says.

Wriggler folds his wings, looks at me.

He's a bit pathetic, my lightning-snake says. *I feel sorry for him.*

My eyebrows shoot up. *You* what? I say.

Wriggler gives his weird, serpentine shrug. *Maybe you're rubbing off on me,* he says.

I roll my eyes. *Ain't nothing we can do for the kid now. And he's got Sheb. He summoned the Corvos, remember? The one that took Einan's sister? The one it took both you* and *Bear to see off?*

Wriggler shuffles uncomfortably. *It got lucky,* he grumbles, though we both know that's a lie.

I step closer to Jeelie. Oak knows none of this is going to plan, but maybe there's a way to free Sheb and Zuma without bloodshed.

"Jeelie," I say, keeping my voice soft. "I get it. I do. My daddy, well, he was a piece of work, too. I guess you could say he made me what I am. And my mum … she couldn't love me, either. I reminded her too much of Daddy. Bad stuff happened to both of us. But it don't mean we have to be the ones who make bad stuff happen to other people. We can choose better. I'll find a way to heal the swamp. I promise. But I need you to release Sheb and Zuma. Einan needs his sister back and … I can't do this without my best friend. So, please … where are they?"

Jeelie blinks at me. "They're not here," he says.

I feel rage bucking in my core again. The death-roar pulses behind my eyes. "Okay," I growl. "Then where are they? I need you to release them—"

Jeelie's eyes widen. "I can't."

"You *can!*" I say, stepping closer.

Jeelie drifts back, eye wide. "No, you don't understand. I can't because I don't have them!"

This is getting ridiculous. "Of course you have them!" I yell. "That's why Einan came tumbling into Nowhere looking for us! I *saw* the Corvos take Sheb, I—"

The words die in my throat as I look at Jeelie's face. "Aw hell," I say. "It's not yours, is it? It's not bloody yours!"

This ain't a monster's rage cave. It's just a dead kid's sanctuary. And Jeelie? He's just a frightened boy trapped in the most terrifying moment of his short life. The Corvos ain't his!

But how is that possible? The Corvos was summoned at a moment of pain and fear. A moment of death. I *know* this. I felt it. I'd always thought if a monster-bonded human died, their monster would die, too, but maybe it don't always work like that. Maybe something about the monster could hold the human halfway between life and death. Keep them in stasis, prevent their energy from scattering.

Create remnants.

And if Jeelie's remnant isn't at the heart of this, then—

I stagger sideways as a wave of nausea blasts through me. The death-roar bellows in my mind. Through the haze, I hear a cry. A voice I know.

"Annie! Don't come back! He's here!"

It's Maeve.

I reach for Jeelie, somehow manage to grip his wrist. My heart gallops like a howler horse. "Jeelie," I say. "You need to take me back to the surface. *Right now!*"

CHAPTER FORTY-ONE

BACK FROM BENEATH

Jeelie looks at me, aghast.

"I can't," he protests. "I promised. I said I'd keep you safe—"

"*Jeelie!*" I burst out. The remnant boy jumps, even though he's got no body to startle. I close my eyes, trying to compose myself.

"Sheb's been coming to talk to you, hasn't he?" I realize. Jeelie hesitates, then nods. I find my heart hurting more than normal. Along with getting to know his nephew and, apparently, being persuaded into foolishness by Alphonz, my dear friend has found time to reconcile with the brother he murdered. I scowl at Wriggler.

It would have been really useful *to know a lot of this stuff before we came charging into the grave-yard!* I tell him.

Wriggler huffs. *I wasn't the only one on Sheb duty,* he points out. *Sasha was rubbish at it, too.*

Now is not the time to have this argument. I look at Jeelie.

"The swamp's in danger," I tell him. "Ruben will get what he wants. I need to get out of here. I need to get to Sheb. He's the only one who has the power to stop Ruben from destroying every-thing."

Jeelie chews his insubstantial lip. "But I told him I'd protect you," he says. "I made a promise."

"So did I," I tell him. "And I bet the promise Sheb asked of you weren't just for me. He asked it for Lin and Maeve, too. They're up there, waiting. Ruben's coming for them, Jeelie. He's gonna hurt them, sacrifice Maeve to get the swamp to surren-der." My heart feels so tight I can barely breathe. "*Please.* For Sheb. For the swamp."

Jeelie stares, shimmering in and out of focus. "Alright," he says.

I grab hold of Wriggler just as Jeelie's form dispels completely. His mist wraps around me in freezing coils. I gasp as the icy cold burns my skin. But I don't have time to scream. Jeelie's mist lifts me. We race upwards, away from ... wherever this is. The surface looms, and I see the sprawling limbs of the black ash, dark against the night sky. Jeelie's grip on me loosens. He cries out as if in pain.

Then the cold of his mist is gone. I'm on all fours under an inky sky, coughing up my guts into the leaf mulch.

Annie! Wriggler says, then falls quiet with a strangled yelp.

Pain—an echo of Wriggler's—blasts through my shoulder. I'm thrown against the ground. My head snaps up. Locke stands above me, his harpoon plunged through Wriggler's wing. Wriggler's body shimmers as he reaches for my rage, but can't find it. Locke's harpoon, the de Callis magic, blocks us somehow. Nora was right.

Locke grins. "Found you," he says.

Someone chuckles and I glance behind me. Ruben's here, too. He's got Maeve on her knees in front of him, Bear, in cub form, bound and muzzled beside her. I see a wound in the monster's side, presumably where Ruben stuck him with a harpoon, dampening his and Maeve's bond, too. I remember the strange dizziness I'd felt last time Ruben jabbed Wriggler with his harpoon. In just a few short days, his power has grown enough that he can cut me off from my monster. Panic claws my insides. How is that possible?

Cheran stands back with two of Ruben's men, trying to contain a struggling Lin.

"Please," he begs her. "Just ... I don't want to hurt you."

I see Locke roll his eyes.

Bartok's nowhere to be seen. Bloody coward. More of Ruben's cronies surround the black ash, their talismans glowing, sabers drawn. I ignore them. I've seen something else.

Prowling around the perimeter is a snarling maned cat. My throat squeezes, but the moment those amber eyes meet mine, I know it ain't Sasha. The cat lunges at me. I scramble aside but Locke's magic surges through me. I collapse on my back. The maned cat pins me beneath his massive paws.

"*Where is he?*" Alphonz demands.

I spit in his face.

Ruben kicks Alphonz off me. "Don't you damage my murk-girl," he says. "Your traitor isn't here. You want him? Go look for him elsewhere. Stop getting in my way."

Alphonz snarls but says nothing. Instead, he continues circling the tree, like he expects Sasha to appear from the foliage. I glare at him, but then my eyes fall on another figure. The world around me falls deathly silent.

Beside Ruben, looking thoroughly shamefaced, is Einan. He avoids my gaze. Ruben's grin widens.

"Good work, kid," he says, clapping Einan so hard on the shoulder that the boy stumbles forward. "You did well."

Einan still avoids my gaze. "Everything you asked," he mumbles. "So now ... will you give my sister back?"

It takes a minute for Einan's words to sink in.

"Give—" I start. My eyes snap to Maeve's, then to Lin's. I see realization hit all three of us at once.

"Excuse me, *what?*" I blurt. Rage bucks under my core and Wriggler yowls. Locke's harpoon holds both him and our combined power pinned down. Wriggler hisses, snapping at Locke's feet.

I ain't paying attention. I'm staring at Einan, trying to believe what I'm hearing. A few things snap into place in my head. Bartok obsessing over Zuma's shoe with its little black bow. I suddenly remember where I've seen that bow before—I found one stuck between the planks of Ruben's boat that first night here, didn't I? Has Einan been lying to us this whole time? The bloody Corvos never took his sister, did it? The de Callis brothers did, and used her to lure Sheb back. Because whatever the hell Luana did to Sheb's power, it somehow stopped Ruben from traveling through the portal. So, he sent Einan instead.

"You snake!" I roar.

Wriggler glares at me. *Hey!*

But I ain't got a moment to spare for my monster's affront. This kid—this *treacherous* little weasel—has cost me my best friend!

Einan doesn't look at me. My rage flares hot.

"All that shit about seeing the Corvos kidnap your sister," I growl, remembering the story he told us. "You were lying!"

Einan glances up. "Not all of it!" he protests. "I really did see it! I just—"

"But it didn't take Zuma," I snarl, glaring at Ruben. "Another monster did that."

Ruben shrugs. "Whatever," he says. "The girl's been a pain in my ass anyway."

"And mine," Locke growls. He scoops up Wriggler, his harpoon still in my lightning-snake's wing. As he does, his sleeve falls back. I see that bite mark again, along with fresh ones further up his arm. Not Allise after all, I realize.

Zuma's been fighting her captors like the hellgator she'll one day become. I can't help my smile. Locke doesn't take kindly to that.

"Get up," he tells me, twisting his harpoon into Wriggler. Like my body is a puppet on a string, I do.

Ruben marches us to the jetty. Me and Maeve struggle the whole way, though it's obvious the brothers' hold on our monsters is affecting us. Lin, weirdly, is silent. She walks calmly, but scans the trees, searching the mist. I see her eyes catch on something, widen.

I feel it a moment later. The whisper-sting of a remnant touching my skin, something pressed against my palm. Jeelie's voice murmurs in my ear.

"Take me with you," he says. *"I can help."*

I close my hand around whatever he's given me. It's faintly damp, but tough under my fingers, rough to touch. A piece of bark. Black ash bark. A talisman from his death-place. I tighten my fist so the brothers don't see.

Lucius and a few other men meet us on Ruben's boat. They bind our hands and feet, throw us to the deck. I kick out and manage to catch Lucius in the shin. He yells, kicks me back. Locke takes Bear and Wriggler to the bow, where Maeve and I can't see them, but we both feel the moment harpoons are skewered through our monsters' flesh, pinning them to the deck. I feel it in my shoulder again—Wriggler's wing—and Maeve roars, clutches her hand where Locke's harpoon has pierced Bear's paw.

Ruben stands over us, smirking. "Can you feel that?" he demands. "How angry it already is? It *knows* what I'm going to do, and it can't stop me."

I thrash against my restraints, screaming, but even through my rage, I sense what he's talking about. The death-roar snarling in the back of my mind, the panic of the swamp, its strange consciousness pushing into my mind. It's desperate. Whatever me and Maeve are to it, something about our deaths will weaken it. And Ruben will take it for his own. All of it.

Well, fuck that for the hideous joke it is.

"Where's Sheb?" I growl. Ruben shrugs.

"How should I know?" he says. "He'll be dead soon, and the power he kept from me will be mine. As it always should be."

I think he meant that to scare me, but it doesn't. Instead, my heart lifts. *Sheb's still alive.* Ruben hasn't felt Sheb's power transfer to him, which means my best friend is still alive.

Ruben scans the skies. "My murdered brother will have his revenge soon enough," he murmurs. "You wait."

I blink, say nothing. If Ruben thinks the Corvos is Jeelie's, I ain't going to correct him. I clutch Jeelie's death-talisman tighter in my fist. Maybe there's hope for us yet.

I hear footsteps from below. Lucius appears, clutching the arm of a girl a little taller than Kai. Her tightly curled black hair is bunched behind her ears. Bruises mar her black skin above her shirt collar and along her arms. Still, she fights like a darkeye fox in a trap.

"Get off me, Pa! You don't know what you're—"

Her eyes light up when she sees Einan. She cries his name. Lucius lets her go so she can run to him. I expect her to embrace him. Instead she thumps him over the head.

"You *idiot!*" she snaps, whacking him again. "Don't you listen to a word I say? Now look what you've done!"

A shrill cry comes from above. My mouth falls open as Bartok—bloody Bartok—lands on her shoulder, still carrying that Oak-forsaken shoe. He fluffs his feathers, glares at me with all the resentment in the world.

Oh.

Clever owl-squirrel.

I make a mental note to pay more attention to his tantrums in future.

The girl—who is clearly Zuma—takes her shoe from Bartok's mouth. "Thanks, Buddy," she says, nuzzling his fluffy belly. "I know you tried. My brother is a moron."

Ruben rolls his eyes. "Enough," he says. "Lucius, our guest no longer has need of our services. Please escort her and her brother to the shore."

Lucius' eyes widen. "Ruben, they're my children—"

Ruben rounds on him. "Do I look like I *care*, Lucius?" he snarls. "They're a liability. They will be left here until our task is done."

Lucius pales. I see his gaze flick from Ruben to his kids. I can't believe he's even weighing this up in his mind. They're his *children!*

Einan starts to cry. "Pa!" he sobs, running to his father. "Pa, don't let him—"

Lucius wrenches his arm from his son's grasp, turns away. Ruben's jaw sets. "Fine," he says. "If you won't do it, the others will."

Einan starcs at his father, realizing he'll get no help from him. He turns to Ruben. "Please," he begs. "You said if I did as you asked, you'd let us go—"

"I said I'd release your sister," Ruben drawls. "I never said where."

Locke laughs, but Cheran's face is bone pale.

"Brother," he starts. "They're just children—"

Ruben rounds on him. "Do you want to stay with them?"

Cheran closes his mouth, lowers his eyes.

Without ceremony, two of Ruben's men grab the children, hurling them onto the jetty. Lucius winces at the sound of their cries. I yell, bucking against my restraints, but Locke's boot connects hard with my gut. I double up. I hear Maeve yelling expletives until she's delivered a similar blow. Ruben calls orders. His men scurry across deck and someone sends the engine thrumming to life. We rumble away from the graveyard, from Einan and Zuma yelling. Bartok flies in wild circles above them, shrieking his head off.

"Bartok!" I yell, but he ignores me. Instead, he flutters onto Zuma's shoulder. I watch the three of them grow smaller on the jetty.

Ruben turns and fixes me with a feral grin that makes my insides turn to ice.

CHAPTER FORTY-TWO

BATTLE FOR THE SOUL OF THE SWAMP

RUBEN POINTS HIS HARPOON at me. It glows faintly, its light pulsing in time to the light in his warriors' talismans. He sneers.

"You'll be first," he says. "I'll enjoy watching you die."

I glare, hard as I can. I swear, before this is over, I'll kill this man.

Ruben sneers. "Locke!" he calls, "tell Lucius and Kane to speed her up! I will have this bloody swamp under my boot. *Now*."

I scan the deck. Cheran's nowhere to be seen, though I spot Lucius at the helm, and others of Ruben's men scurry about, chests puffed with self-importance. Lucius steers the boat. I know immediately where we're headed, can feel the death-roar buzzing in my brain. Into the Deep Swamp. Further than I've been before.

Ruben's heading for the heart.

"What're you gonna do?" Maeve demands, still doubled up where Cheran kicked her. I know she means it to sound fierce, but her voice shakes. Ruben prods her with the butt of his harpoon.

"Give you back to the swamp," he says. "Both you, and your monsters. If one or the other of you survives, it'll keep both of you locked to life." He grins, grabbing Maeve's face and squeezing. "But if I hold you both underwater together, neither can save the other."

Maeve struggles in Ruben's grip, but I hear her breath quicken. Her fear is a stake through my gut. My family. All I have. And this bastard wants to take them from me.

"Why not just stick a harpoon through our gut and be done with it, then?" Maeve demands.

Ruben laughs. "It's the swamp's grief I need," he says, "not just your death. You'll die in its waters. That way, it will break, no longer resist me. Once Jeelie destroys Sheb and you two are on the riverbed, I'll have what I've always deserved."

"And what's that?" I spit.

Ruben turns to me, his eyes so full of light he looks half mad. "Everything," he says.

I hold his gaze, rage simmering in my core, but Locke's harpoon through Wriggler's wing keeps it dampened.

Lin kicks out, catching Ruben in the ankle. He shouts.

"You little—" he growls. He grabs her by the collar, punching her in the jaw. Lin lets out a tiny yelp of pain. Her head lolls.

"Don't you dare!" I roar, thrashing against my restraints. Maeve howls, spitting curses as Ruben drags Lin towards the bow, ignoring me and Maeve. But I see Lin's eyelids flutter open. She catches my eye, winks at me.

"Locke!" Ruben yells. "Tie this little serpent to the gunwale. And if she breaks a few bones in the process, I won't be sorry."

"But I—" Locke starts.

"Now!" Ruben yells.

Locke grumbles but does as he's told. I feel the pressure on Wriggler's wings ease and, as Locke goes to secure Lin to the railings, I see the look in her eyes. Realize what she's about to do.

Clever girl.

Locke leans down. Lin smiles at him. He frowns.

"What the—"

And the whole deck is awash with a web of silver light. Lin's soul-tethers call down the remnants. They swarm the boat, flashing across the deck, their misty touch searing my skin. Ruben's men howl with terror, fling themselves to the deck. Lin headbutts Locke in the face.

"Ha!" Maeve yells.

Annie, Wriggler says, his voice faint in my mind. *Send me rage. Now.*

I don't question him, just gather all my strength, every ounce of hatred and fury. I feel my eyes glow bloody, an otherworldly wind stirring my black curls.

Wriggler, growing, grabs Locke's harpoon between his teeth and wrenches it from his wing, hurling it to the deck. I gasp as a flood of power surges through me. Wriggler roars, spitting lightning, lunges for the nearest of Ruben's warriors. He grabs the screaming man by one leg and sends him flying overboard. His wings unfurl, smashing the gunwale. The remnants howl and scatter.

Annie! Wriggler cries. *I'm coming. Tell Maeve to—*

The boat lurches sideways and I'm thrown across deck. The whole vessel creaks and groans and I hear a strange, chitinous click-squeal as something—something big—climbs aboard.

"What the—" Maeve gasps.

Ruben stands in the center of the deck, arms spread wide, harpoon aglow, as a gigantic creeperscorp scuttles over the gunwale. I freeze, staring at the hideous thing. Its armor-plated body is easily three times as long as mine. Its eight, dagger-like legs splinter the wood as it stamps across the boat. Three sets of mean, yellow eyes blink in the moonlight, and its wicked, stinger tail curls over its back.

It raises two powerful pincers. Swamp weed dangles from its joints.

Wriggler lunges for Ruben, but the creeperscorp charges, grabbing Wriggler's neck in one mighty pincer.

My throat tightens as my air is choked off. Holy hell! Is that vile thing at Ruben's command?

"Maeve!" I gasp, as both me and Wriggler thrash in the creeperscorp's grasp.

Maeve's eyes glow poisonous green. I hear Bear roar, feeding off her power. But just as he manages to break free, charging across the boat with that white fire burning across his fur, Ruben launches his harpoon. The barb strikes Bear in the chest. He falls. Maeve screams in pain. I hear Lin crying, fighting somewhere across deck.

Bear howls, trying to claw the harpoon from his chest, but it's stuck fast. The green light in Maeve's eyes sputters and dies.

"No!" I scream. "Let them go!"

A fist flies at my face, catching me on the temple. My head cracks against the hull and stars dance in my vision. Someone grabs my hair, wrenches me upright. My eyes meet Locke's. I see triumph and disdain in his sneer.

"Stop it," he says, shaking me. "You've *lost*, got it?"

I fight him, but he holds me fast. Wriggler thrashes against the creeperscorp, but now Cheran's charging across deck, harpoon raised. He meets my gaze.

"I'm sorry," he says, and thrusts the barb into Wriggler's side. There's a pulse of white light. I feel my bond with Wriggler loosen, the rage-thread between us snapping.

"No!" I cry. Locke punches me again.

Wriggler writhes in the creeperscorp's grip, but it won't let go. With Ruben's terrible magic blocking our bond, I can't give him the power he needs. The light in my eyes goes out. I fall against the deck, gasping for air. I feel the creeperscorp squeezing the life from me and Wriggler. We can't escape. Darkness creeps across my vision.

The creeperscorp shakes Wriggler until blood flies from my lightning-snake's nostrils. He falls limp. I feel the pain of his wounds ricochet through me. The creeperscorp drags him off the boat, holding him above the water. Ruben flicks a speck of dust from his coat.

"Right," he says. "Well that was a tiresome spectacle. Bring them to me."

Locke throws me down beside Maeve. Cheran drags Lin across deck. I scramble to position myself between Ruben and my family, hating how hungrily he stares at them. He knows he's won. Knows no-one will stop him doing whatever the hell he wants.

That's the trouble with these people.

But I ain't done fighting. I kick out, catching Locke in the knee. When he falls, I kick him again, this time right in the groin. His face reddens. He collapses in a heap. I lift my bound legs, ready to ram my heels into his head.

Ruben kicks my legs aside. He grabs my chin, forcing me to look at him. He stuffs a foul-smelling rag in my mouth, binds it in place with a rope. He drags a set of chains from beside the gunwale, wraps them round my ankles.

"You're a fool, girl," he tells me. "And you're more trouble than you're worth. This swamp is *mine*. Neither my soft brother, nor his pet bitch, will take it from me. Understand?"

I say nothing. Can't, can I? Even if I could, I would never agree with him. Never submit to someone like him. I hope he sees in my eyes how much I hate him. I hope he sees I'll kill him the moment I get a chance.

He does see. I can tell. Because he grins.

"Thought not," he says.

And hurls me overboard.

Chapter Forty-Three

FIGHT FOR YOUR LIFE, ANNIE

I HAVE JUST ENOUGH time to hear Maeve scream, sense Wriggler thrash in panic. Then I'm plunged into the water. My mouth's stuffed with cloth, wrists and ankles bound, chains weighing me down. My monster—the only thing that could save me—is held in the vice-like grip of Ruben's creeperscorp.

I sink like a bloody stone.

It takes a second for the panic to set in, but when it does, I fight with all I'm worth. The water drags me down. Above, I see the silhouette of the boat leaving. I hear Maeve's muffled screaming, imagine Lin fighting with all her might. If I could only throw my rage to Wriggler, unleash him, that creeperscorp wouldn't stand a chance.

But the thread that connects me to him remains choked. And what little rage I have is muted by fear.

The swamp drags me down. Its death-roar howls in my head. I feel the swamp reaching into my mind, pleading. It doesn't want me to die, but it can feel me drowning. My lungs scream as I fight. I feel Wriggler's voice in my head, faint and desperate.

Annie!

Then I'm alone, held in the death-cradle of the swamp's unbreakable clutches.

Something stirs in the water, I blink against a sudden brightness. The water turns milky, then Jeelie's remnant appears in front of me. He holds my face in his hands. When I look into his eyes, it's like I'm staring at the apparition of my best friend. His mouth moves, his voice floats to me through the inky water.

"Annie," he whispers. "Fight it! You've got to survive!"

He grips me under the arms, trying to pull me towards the surface, but some strange power keeps dragging me down. It's Ruben. I can feel his strength over the swamp here. The way the death-roar sizzles at the back of my throat. The swamp's fighting his influence, but he's powerful. Ruben wants me to drown, so the swamp can't let me go.

"Annie!" Jeelie says. I feel his misty arms wrapped around me, but he can't pull me against the swamp's intent. "Fight, dammit!"

I glare at him. What the hell does he think I'm doing? I kick out against the water, trying to right myself and push upwards. But my feet are bound, my arms tied behind my back. My lungs burn for air and my head feels fuzzy. Jeelie's straining with all his otherworldly might, but it's no use.

I'm going to die.

Oak, I hope they never find my body. I hope Maeve and Lin never have to see that. The thought of them weeping over me makes me thrash with renewed vigor, but my limbs feel heavy, my head full of fog.

Sasha's face bursts into my mind. His dark eyes, flecked with gold. I think of his lips on mine, how right it had felt. I'll never feel it again. All the things we never had time to say. To experience. To *be* to each other.

My kicks slowly fall still.

I'll never see Sheb again. Never wrinkle my nose at how awful he smells. Never roll my eyes at his terrible jokes while secretly trying not to laugh. Never sit with him by the fire, listening while he prattles on about his latest research, or his new theories about monsters, or what he's discovered about Lin's magic that day.

"Annie!" Jeelie howls.

But what's the point? I've stopped fighting. The swamp pulls at my mind as well as my body. My eyes drift closed. I stop fighting the urge to breath, take a great gulp. Water stings my lungs. My eyes flare wide with death panic. But the fog in my head is so thick now, I barely remember what I'm scared of. It's only death. It's not so bad.

"Dammit!" Jeelie cries.

He disappears. Maybe he's given up, too.

There's a rhythmic thud of something above. Steady and comforting. Like the beat of a drum.

Or giant wings.

My eyes fly open as a huge pair of taloned feet grip me by the shoulders. I shriek as the black claws pierce my flesh. But there's only water in my lungs now, so the scream comes out as a jet of fluid. My vision sears white. I'm torn upwards, out of the swamp's death-grip, into the air. For a moment, I peer down at my bound feet as they dangle above the swamp. Then blackness envelopes me.

· · · ● · ● · · ·

I bolt upright, arms flailing, clawing at my throat. Strong hands grip me, flip me onto all fours and give my back a firm wallop. I vomit a *lot* of water. It's a foul color, tastes even fouler, which makes me throw up some more. When I've finally spat the last of the bile from my throat and taken several huge, delicious lungfuls of air, I sit back.

I'm alive.

Shivering, weak, weeping with relief. But alive.

"Easy, dear Annie," someone says beside me. A hand rubs my back. "Take a moment. That was quite an ordeal."

I nod. It's true. It *was* an ordeal. It—

Dear Annie. He called me *dear Annie.*

My eyes fly open. Before I've even fully registered what I'm doing, I throw my arms around my best friend, sobbing into his shoulder. "Sheb," I choke. "You're okay. You're alive."

Sheb chuckles, hugs me back. When we pull away from each other, I'm almost afraid of what I'll see, of which Sheb will be staring at me. But the moment I meet his gaze, I know. That old sparkle is back. The mischief in his smile.

I laugh, hug him again. I let him go, wipe a hand across my forehead. I see my cut bonds lying in a heap to one side, along with the sodden cloth that was stuffed in my mouth and the chains Ruben weighed me down with. The night has lightened to a steely grey as dawn approaches. How long have I been unconscious?

"How did you find me?" I ask, gripping Sheb's hand.

Jeelie's remnant appears beside Sheb in a flash of light, puffed up and proud. "I called him," he says.

Sheb smiles and holds out his hand. The brother he murdered takes it. "He did," Sheb says. "And I'm grateful, brother."

They hold each other's gaze for a moment. I can't help the wave of sadness that rolls over me. What these two might've been to each other, had they not grown up the way they did ... had Deimos not been their father. Their hands drop, but Jeelie stays, floating above the ground while Sheb sheds his fur jacket and wraps it round my shoulders.

"Where've you *been?*" I ask him.

Sheb smiles softly, glances at something above me. "Talking with someone I've really missed," he says.

I feel a blast of hot air on my neck, the fetid stench of digesting meat. I freeze, but Sheb doesn't seem afraid, though I see Jeelie float back a few feet.

Slowly, I turn, stare at what's stood behind me. There's a pair of huge, bird-like feet. Talons gouging the wet earth. Powerful legs, with a thick, spiny tail flicking behind. A feathered torso. Huge, leathery wings, peppered with scars. And then I'm staring into the face of the Corvos. Its scarred beak, its dark, fathomless eyes.

But somehow, it doesn't seem so frightening as before. I feel its influence needling my head, but when I shrink back, it withdraws, like it doesn't want to scare me.

Sheb places a hand on my shoulder. "It's okay, Annie," he says. "She won't hurt you. She's ... well, it's complicated."

I can't take my eyes off the monster. I nod slowly. "I bet it is."

I wonder if the *she* he's talking about is the Corvos itself, or the person driving it. Something tells me it's both. The Corvos lowers her ragged head. I flinch away instinctively. She blinks, huffing putrid air in my face. I could be wrong, but I reckon I hurt her feelings.

Gritting my teeth, I reach a shaking hand towards her. This is the monster that it took both Wriggler *and* Bear to see off when she attacked. The monster that stole my best friend. But Sheb's alive. Looking better and more like Sheb than I've seen him in weeks.

So why *did* she attack us at the house? Was she after Sheb? Or did she just miss him? I remember her in my head. The grey, colorless landscape of the graveyard around me as she picked through my doubts.

I close my eyes as she lowers her head further, touches the tip of her huge, serrated beak to my palm. It's smooth, cool beneath my fingers. I let my hand linger for a moment before I snatch it away. Something about her still makes my skin crawl. I shudder. She cocks her head, appraising me.

"She's marvelous," Sheb says, stroking her feathery neck. "And I was right! Completely different to both Wriggler and Bear. I've had a brief chance to study her, and her powers are remarkable. Entirely based in the psychic plane! Can you imagine? I think Winged Furies might be a truly spectacular kind of monster, though of course, I'd need to study a few more specimens to draw any true conclusions—"

I smile as he prattles on, shoot Jeelie a warning glance when he rolls his eyes.

"I've missed you," I say.

Sheb smiles, grabs my hand. "I've missed you too," he says. "I'm sorry I was gone for so long. I had ... things to do. I thought perhaps I could persuade her to release the magic she bound in me, to let me fight Ruben, but she wouldn't. She's still so scared. So confused."

I nod, find I'm not surprised. "Luana," I say. "The Corvos is hers, ain't it?"

Sheb's smile falters. He looks to the misty figure of his dead brother. "Yes," he says. "She called it the moment I ... did what I did to Jeelie. She couldn't stand it. A son dead, another a killer. And she knew her husband was behind it, knew he'd choose the fiercest and most brutal of his sons as his Heir." He turns to me, sadness sparkling in his eyes. "Mama was a swamp maiden, chosen by the swamp as its defender. She felt responsible for what happened. It broke her. Just like it broke the swamp. And so the Corvos came to her. It was when Pa killed her that everything really fell apart.

The Corvos held her soul between life and death, but the swamp was so broken by what I'd done that it couldn't cope. It threw out other souls, too."

"Like mine," Jeelie confirms. "And the more the swamp broke, the stronger Ruben became."

"He knows he only needs my share of the de Callis power," Sheb says, "and he can invade the Deep Swamp, expand his territory, even challenge the other five families for their land."

"Why won't Luana give it back?" I whisper.

Sheb shakes his head. "She's afraid," he says. "And confused. She thinks she's protecting me. It's hard to get through to her. She won't even show herself."

I nod. While Jeelie's remnant has been following me round Marsh Wilds like a bad smell, I've never even seen a glimpse of Luana. Wherever she is, she's too frightened and confused to understand what she's doing.

"What now?" I ask. "Ruben's got Maeve and Lin. And Wriggler. Sasha's trying to find the swamp maidens but Alphonz is after him. Einan and Zuma are stuck in the graveyard. And I—"

Bile floods my throat as it occurs to me Ruben might have thrown the girls overboard too. Einan and Zuma are still trapped. I've no idea if Nora and the swamp maidens are okay, or if Sasha—

Sheb grips my arm. My gaze snaps to meet his.

"It'll be okay, Annie," he says. Trust him to know what I'm thinking. "Ruben hasn't hurt Maeve yet. He needs to take her right into the Deep Swamp, and he still thinks the Corvos belongs to Jeelie."

Beside us, Jeelie scoffs. "Fool."

I suppress a smile.

"Ruben will wait until he thinks I'm dead, and feels my power flood to him, to sacrifice Maeve. And the swamp will fight him with everything it has left." He smiles. That beloved, toothy grin that makes my heart swell with love and relief. "It likes you, Annie."

My eyebrows shoot up to my hairline. *"Why?"*

Sheb laughs. "Hell if I know," he says. "Maybe you remind it of all the good things a person can be."

I throw Sheb a withering glare. I find that hard to believe.

"Ruben has Wriggler," I say. I still feel the creeperscorp's pincers clamped around my lightning-snake's throat. It makes it hard to breathe. "I don't understand. Why didn't he just kill us both? What's he waiting for?"

Sheb strokes hair from my face. "Ruben might be a tyrant, but he's also scared. He's scared the swamp won't obey him, so he'll do everything he can to break it. At its heart. He's hoping you're stuck somewhere between life and death, and he'll take Wriggler, Maeve and Bear to the heart of the swamp, where death will hit it hardest. That's where he'll—"

He can't bring himself to say it, and I'm glad. I can't think about it. I stand, wincing from the pain in my limbs and throat.

"I need to stop him," I say. "I can't let him hurt them."

Sheb squeezes my arm. "Dear Annie," he says. "Always trying to be the hero. To fix everything."

I scowl at him. "Yeah," I drawl. "And?"

Sheb's grin widens. "Do you trust me?"

Now there's a question. Do I trust Sheb? Sheb, who once thought riding a howler horse across the snatching sands was a good idea. Sheb, who once tried to save a baby nosta bird and nearly lost us both to its song in the process.

Sheb who grounds me. Holds me within my sanity. Reminds me of my light.

I trust him. I probably shouldn't. But I do.

He winks. I roll my eyes. "We should get going," he says. "Ruben will wait, but once he realizes the truth about the Corvos, he'll act fast. And we won't let him take another life, will we?"

The smile falls from my face. "Never," I vow.

Sheb cups my chin. "Right then," he says. "Let's go get our girls."

"And my monster," I say.

Sheb nods. "And your boyfriend."

"He's not my—"

Oh, I give up.

Sheb chuckles, rummages in his belt and pulls out a throwing knife. It's the same as the ones I lost. The ones Sheb made for me. Except—

"I've been making a new set for you anyway," Sheb says. "But you know how long it takes to get the right materials in Nowhere. I'm sorry I can't give you all of them. This one will have to do." He looks up at the Corvos, pats her feathery side. "It's made from the shaft of her flight feather," he says. "Tough as iron and light as ... well, a feather."

I take the knife and scrub a hand over my eyes, hating how they burn. The weapon is astonishing. Deep, obsidian black with a shine like it's made of moonbeams. It's beautifully forged. Sheb's made the hilt and pommel from some kind of wood ...

"Black ash!" Jeelie breathes. "Brother, is that ...?"

Sheb nods. "I hope you don't mind," he says. "But I needed a wood with power."

Jeelie says nothing. When I glance at his face, he doesn't look angry. Rather, he seems moved. "Thank you, brother," he says. "And ... I'm sorry."

Sheb smiles. "I know," he says. "Me too."

I balance the knife in my hand, feeling how strong and weightless it is. It'll fly like the wind, land true. I grip it tightly.

"Thank you," I croak, then gather Sheb into a hug. "And ... I'm sorry, too."

Sheb blinks at me as I withdraw. "For what?"

"For not seeing you," I say. "For not understanding what you needed. I'm good at the fighting bit. You know that. But I can't ... I'm no good at feelings. When there's nothing to defend you from, I don't know what to do."

It's true. Watching him suffer ... that's been harder than any battle I've fought.

Sheb touches my shoulder. "Annie, you know you don't need to save me from everything."

I raise an eyebrow at him.

"Have you been talking to Maeve?"

Sheb laughs. "Clever girl, that one," he says. "She understands you." His smile broadens. "Look, Annie, sometimes I don't need you to save me, I just need you beside me. I need the strength I get from you to help me save myself. My feelings are complicated and you can't rescue me from them. No-one can. But I don't always need res-cuing you know. I just need my best friend at my side."

My eyes burn again. I blink furiously, nodding. "Reckon I can do that," I say. "I can always do that."

Sheb winks. "I know."

The Corvos rumbles gently. I turn as she lowers her body. I blink. Her unfathomable black eyes slide across to meet mine.

Sheb nudges my arm. "She wants you to climb on."

"*What?*" I say.

Sheb laughs. "How else did you think we were going to get across the swamp with no boat?"

I scowl. "Not riding a giant corpse-bird," I mut-ter. Still, I grab a fistful of the crow's feathers, scramble up, and settle between her wings. Her ridged back digs into my thighs.

"Not exactly the comfiest," I point out.

Sheb looks scandalized. "Don't say that! You'll hurt her feelings!"

I can't help grinning. He's back. My best friend, the way I love him most. He swings up behind me, like he's been riding death-crows his whole life. He wraps my waist in one hand and grips one of the bone crow's black spines in the other. Jeelie's remnant dissipates, but I feel him close by. I tuck his death-talisman in my pocket, knowing he'll be with us as we fly.

"Alright then," Sheb says gently. "Let's go."

CHAPTER FORTY-FOUR

THE HEART OF THE DEEP

THE SWAMP RACES BENEATH us. A journey that would take a day by boat takes a few hours on the back of the Corvos. Not that I see much of it. I refuse to open my eyes as soon as we leave the ground.

"This is awful!" I yell over the wind.

Sheb laughs. "This is wondrous!"

I ignore him. Too busy trying not to throw up.

The swamp pulls at me, the death-roar humming at the back of my skull. Below, the trees grows thicker. There won't be space for the Corvos to land if we keep going. On the few occasions I manage to open my eyes, something seems wrong. The leaves are blackening, the bark peeling. Tendrils of some strange, black substance run through the water. It smells like infection.

The Corvos dives. Bile rises in my throat as she stoops, landing on the nearby bank. I slide off her back, cast her a worried glance. She stamps her taloned feet, agitated. I feel her presence in my mind, but not her voice. Sheb, though, seems to hear her. He presses a palm to her side.

"Are you sure?" he asks. "Can you try?"

The Corvos snaps her beak at empty air. Sheb nods. "Okay," he says. "We go alone then."

I frown. "What's happening?"

Sheb turns away from the Corvos. "Mama is calling her back," he says. "She's afraid for me, doesn't want me near Ruben. She won't let the Corvos come with us."

"That doesn't make any sense," I grumble. "Surely it would be safer if we were *with* the giant death-bird?"

Sheb shrugs. "Love and logic don't always work well together," he points out. "And Mama ... isn't her whole self, remember? Being dead does funny things to you."

"Doesn't it just," Jeelie mutters, making me jump. I'd forgotten he was with us. He catches me scowling, winks.

"Don't fear, Annie," Sheb says. "You will have Wriggler and Maeve will have Bear."

I nod, and decide not to tell Sheb I ain't sure that makes much difference. Ruben can dampen our bond with our monsters. Sheb's power is still bound by Luana, and she seems in no hurry to let him go. Without Sheb's share of the de Callis magic, I ain't convinced we can overcome Ruben. The best we might hope for is to grab our girls and haul ass for the portal.

But I know Sheb. He won't leave Allise and the swamp maidens to Ruben's terrible mercy. He'll want to fight.

Which is what got us into this mess in the first place.

"Sheb," I say. He turns and I grab his shoulders, just ... look at him. That floppy hair, those earnest grey eyes. He's got his harpoon strapped across his back. Five years I've spent with him, never known how that simple weapon carries the weight of his family history. His inheritance.

His eyes soften when they meet mine. "Don't worry, dear Annie," he says. "My brothers are strong, but the swamp likes me better."

I cover my mouth to muffle my nervous laugh. I don't doubt it, but Ruben ain't going to give up easily.

We creep along the bank, careful to avoid the grabbing weeds that snake up from the murk. The tree branches hang low here. We duck to avoid them whipping in our faces. Though I know it's dawn, the dark under the trees is so complete I can barely see. The only light comes from the remnant mist that swirls between the branches, the ghostly glow of Ruben's talismans carved into the trees.

I realize I'm tugging on my bond with Wriggler, trying to find him. The pressure on my throat has eased, so Ruben's creeperscorp must have stopped trying to strangle him, but the thread that ties me to him still feels fuzzy. Ruben's magic is cutting him off from me. I clench my jaw, feel my eyes flash red.

Nobody gets between me and my monster.

I palm the throwing knife Sheb gave me, imagine throwing it at Ruben's face. Seems fitting to kill that bastard with the feather-knife of his mother's monster. He deserves it.

Jeelie hovers beside me, eyeing the knife. "What're you going to do with that?" he asks.

I roll my eyes. "What do you think?" I hiss.

Jeelie's mist flutters. "You won't stand a chance," he says. "Ruben's too powerful."

"Yeah?" I retort, and can't think of anything to add. We carry on in silence.

Ahead, I see a soft, green glow. Sheb raises a hand for us to halt. We duck behind a thick-trunked tree, peering out onto the darkened water. We're far enough away that it's hard to make out the flotilla of boats scooting over the inky water, but they're there. Five boats, with Ruben's huge one leading. I see Locke and Cheran wrestling with Maeve at the stern, Ruben stood at the helm. And—my lip curls into a snarl at the sight of him—there's Alphonz, in maned cat form, prowling from port to starboard. He hisses at Ruben's men when they get too close. Treacherous ass. If I had more knives in my belt, one would have his name on it.

The other boats are smaller, full of Ruben's men, their talismans pulsing light. Behind the boats swims the creeperscorp, holding my lightning snake in its pincers. Wriggler hangs limp in its grip, though I see his eyes rolling, feel him tug my mind.

Annie?

His voice is faint, but he knows I'm close.

Here, I think back, and hope he hears me. *Always here.*

There's still no sign of Sasha, or Bartok. And I haven't seen Einan, Zuma, or the hellgators. I hope they're safe. Nothing I can do for them now.

The river widens here, the waters mostly calm. There's a large island—maybe twenty meters across—squatting in the swamp's dark water. It's a little hill, covered in slick, damp moss, with a few spindly trees sprouting from its crest, each with Ruben's glowing crest carved into its trunk. The trees themselves are twisted, blackened as if burned. The grass across the island is withered, dying. Black tendrils of something poisonous ooze from the island into the water.

The death-roar pulses in my head.

"What is this place?" I whisper, though I reckon I already know.

"The heart of the Deep Swamp," Sheb says. "The wildest place in Riverfell. The place where death means something." He looks at me, ashen-faced. "Ruben intends to break the swamp here, by murdering you and Maeve."

My gut clenches.

Ruben's boat draws level with the island. He calls at Cheran to moor the boat.

"We need to get on that island," I say. I've no idea how, but Sheb doesn't argue.

Careful to keep foliage between us and Ruben, we scramble down the bank. I almost cry out when I see what waits for us, lounging half-in the water, then I remember the hellgators are on our side.

At least, I hope they are.

Sheb sees me balk, puts a hand on my back. "It's Nora," he says. "It's okay."

I scowl. None of this is okay, is it? And, now I'm closer, I see Nora ain't looking her finest. She's got a hefty slash down one side, leaking blood. Her snout is criss-crossed with dark cuts, one of her eyes half-closed. She hisses when we draw close.

"Imberg's hurt," she explains. *"Allise has gone to find Zuma, and Yarella is searching for the other swamp maidens. They're looking for a way to break Ruben's hold on us."* She pauses. *"I'm sorry, Sheb. Truly. If we'd known—"*

I scowl at her. "That the Corvos was Luana's, not Jeelie's?" I whisper. "Then what? You wouldn't have sacrificed Sheb. You think that makes it better?"

Nora snarls faintly, but her inky eyes look to Sheb. I wait for him to say he forgives her, that it's okay. But he doesn't. Instead, he unstraps his harpoon.

"One hellgator is better than none," he says. "Can you swim?"

Nora growls. *"Yes."*

I'm skeptical that Nora can carry both me and Sheb across the swamp, but when we climb aboard, she holds steady. I kneel on her broad back behind Sheb. We crouch as low as we can against her scaly spine, hoping the dark, and Nora's stealth, will keep us hidden.

I don't take my eyes off Ruben, the way he stands at the bow of his boat, chest puffed like a prancing bird while his brothers and men drag Maeve, Lin, and Bear onto the island. Arrogant bastard. Thinks he's untouchable. His power binds the swamp so tight I can feel it. The death-roar buzzes in my head, the swamp pulling at me. Desperate.

Don't let him take me! Don't let him win!

I shake my head, pushing it out. What does it think I'm *doing*?

I flip my knife into throwing position. If I can just get one clean shot ...

Sheb's hand touches my hip. "Not yet, Annie," he says. "Trust me."

I do. I trust him. But it's our family in that boat. When I look at Lin, slumped against the gunwale, her eyelids fluttering as she touches a hand to her bruised temple, I want to rip Ruben apart.

We slice through the water, keeping to the shadows, until we reach the other side of the island, hidden from Ruben's view by the trees and a slight incline. As soon as my feet touch the bank, the death-roar hammers through me. I clamp my mouth shut against a groan, drop to all fours until the nausea subsides.

"This place," I whisper. "Feels so sick."

Sheb helps me to my feet, but the death-roar still pulses against my skull. I steady myself.

"Be careful," Nora tells us. *"Death will fuel Ruben's power."*

"Not if it's him who dies," I mutter.

Nora eyes me. *"Not true, murk-girl,"* she says. *"The swamp is already damaged. Killing Ruben may not be enough to heal it. Spare as many lives as you can. I will try to reason with Luana."*

Sheb touches Nora's scaly side. "I don't intend to kill anyone tonight," he says.

I say nothing. I'm making no promises. If we can't fight Ruben with Sheb's power, killing him might be our only hope.

Nora swims away. I watch her disappear around the crest of the island, wonder if she knows where to find Luana. If there's any chance we'll escape this alive.

Sheb glances at me. "You ready?" he asks. I nod, but at the look on my face, Sheb's gaze takes on a worried shine.

"Remember, Annie, we only want him to *think* we're—"

"Nobody threatens my family," I growl, cutting Sheb off. "I'll do what I need to."

Sheb watches me.

"He's my brother, Annie," he says. "I might have no love for him, but I don't want him killed."

I clench my jaw. I guess we both have to hope Luana sees reason, releases Sheb's magic, before I become a murderer again.

Chapter Forty-Five

Brothers, Lovers, and Traitors

Me and Sheb crawl up the island's incline. Jeelie's nowhere to be seen, but when I curl my fingers around the piece of bark in my pocket, I feel he's close.

We reach the crest of the hill, hunker down, watching Ruben and his men through the trees. He thinks he's won. He thinks my body is at the bottom of the swamp, me a remnant, clinging to life only because he hasn't yet drowned my monster. And he's willing to murder Maeve and Bear because he's drunk on his own power.

I let the rage build in my core. Let its caustic waves break over my heart. I feel my eyes start to glow, duck my head so their light doesn't give us away.

I wait, listening to the death-roar—though it makes nausea roll in my gut. Watching as the boats empty onto the island and Ruben's men hurry to form a perimeter, as Alphonz stalks back and forth, tail lashing. Ruben ignores them all. He barks at Locke to stay on the bank with Bear, and drags Maeve up the incline.

"When I give the order," he calls. "You hold the cub's face in the murk until he stops struggling."

Maeve screams. Lin, still on the boat's deck, held fast by Cheran, struggles with all her might. Ruben grabs Maeve by the hair and wrenches her uphill, towards where me and Sheb wait in the shadows.

He's five meters from me.

Four.

Three.

I reach for my bond with Wriggler with every ounce of strength I have. I force my way through the magical tourniquet Ruben's using to squeeze the thread closed. It shatters with such force that shock waves sweep across the swamp, throwing the flotilla into disarray.

WRIGGLER! I scream down our link. *BREAK THEM!*

Wriggler's heady laughter echoes in my mind. His coils expand, his scales thickening. He grows and grows until he's too huge for the creeperscorp to hold. That crown of spiky scales sprouts from his head. His scales turn green. Lightning lances off him, sizzling into the water. He roars, so loud it makes the island quake. Birds erupt in panicked clouds from the trees.

Ruben drops Maeve, yells as one of the boats capsizes, tipping six men into the water. Locke and Cheran dive for their harpoons. Pistol shots crack against the air. A bullet narrowly misses my ear.

"The cub!" Ruben yells, drawing his pistol. "Kill the bloody cub!"

But Bear has broken free. Maeve's eyes are aglow. Ruben tears back down the island, thrusts his harpoon into the water and begins to mutter, conjuring things from beneath the murk. Wriggler snarls. In one, fluid movement, he dives onto the creeperscorp that held him prisoner. He's now so huge that it disappears into his maw in one go. He snaps his jaws closed. I hear the sickening crunch of its exoskeleton. A single claw, hanging from Wriggler's mouth, tenses for a moment, then falls still. Wriggler spits the broken corpse into the water, where it sinks. He turns his glowing, scarlet eyes on Ruben.

You ... he growls.

Sheb grabs my wrist. "Annie," he says, warning in his voice. "He's my brother."

I throw him off.

"That man," I growl. "That man threatened everything I love."

And my monster feels the full force of my rage. Wriggler knows what I want, and for once, I submit to the darkness inside me. Ruben is too dangerous to live.

Wriggler opens his mighty jaws and charges. Cheran and Locke jab their harpoons, trying to subdue him, but Wriggler snaps at them. Cheran falls on his backside. Locke crashes into the water.

Some of Alastor's men aim their pistols at Wriggler, fire. But my lightning-snake is so huge, the bullets bounce off him. He rears, laughing.

Lin, her wrists and ankles still bound, hurls herself over the gunwale. I yell out, but Maeve's several steps ahead of me. A dog-sized Bear dives into the water, dragging Lin to safety, to Maeve's side.

"Annie!" Sheb pleads, but I'm not listening. My eyes glow bloody red. I'm lost in my darkness. I'm aware of Sheb leaping to his feet, haring down the island, and wonder who he's going to help.

Ruben's men fight to reach him, sabers raised, like that'll make a difference against Wriggler.

Ruben's frantic muttering speeds up, his eyes widening as he realizes what Wriggler's about to do. He fights to pull more creatures up from the swamp. Creeperscorps or fanged eels, or whatever else lurks in the depths.

Wriggler tosses his head. With a flick of his tail, he throws the harpoon from Ruben's hands. It flies away, landing harmlessly on the island's muddy bank.

I stand now, eyes glowing, urging my lightning-snake on. Hands grab me but I shrug them off. Something misty stings my cheek but I bat it away. This is how it ends. I'm going to tear Ruben to shreds.

Wriggler bellows, massive teeth glinting in the glow of Ruben's talismans. My lightning-snake raises himself up, high above Ruben, glaring down at the puny little man, nothing more than an insect without his precious harpoon. Ruben's face blanches. His pistol drops from his hand. Wriggler crushes it.

Die, little pest ... my monster sneers.

And lunges.

I close my eyes, ready for that sickening shudder of Wriggler taking a life.

But it never comes. Pain blasts through my face and I stagger.

"What the—"

Wriggler shrieks, thrashing against the lithe, grey figure that's now attached to his head. I blink. Alphonz is still on the island, staring in confusion at the second maned-cat attacking Wriggler.

My anger spikes. How *dare* he?

Sasha swipes at Wriggler, raking a gash across his snout.

My rage flares. "What the hell are you *doing?*" I scream.

Sasha leaps aside as Wriggler throws out lightning. He bounds down Wriggler's back, drawing my lightning-snake's attention away from Ruben.

"Saving you from yourself!" he snarls. *"This isn't the way!"*

I gape at him. I can't believe this. He's supposed to be helping me. Not *saving* the man who threatens this entire Oak-forsaken *world!*

Wriggler howls and turns on Sasha. I gasp as he pulls my rage, drawing it from me like blood.

"Wriggler!" I yell. "Stop!"

But Wriggler's not listening. *He tried to stop us!* My lightning-snake snarls. *He's a traitor!*

I clench my jaw, trying to hold back the rage. But Wriggler pulls at it. I can't hold back. It surges from me in a vast flood, igniting every vein and nerve ending until I scream.

Sasha scurries down Wriggler's monstrous body, leaping aside as Wriggler lashes his tail. But Sasha's injured, ain't he? Blood drips from the wound on his side. Through the red haze of my fury, I see him tiring.

Wriggler ... I think frantically. *Please* ...

But Wriggler's lost. He can't feel my fear. My love. He's drunk on rage.

Sasha stumbles, scrabbling for purchase across Wriggler's scales. Wriggler laughs, rolling so Sasha is thrown into the water. The inky murk turns red with Sasha's blood.

In the confusion, the de Callis brothers gather themselves. The men from the capsized boat swim to shore. Ruben grabs his harpoon from the bank and turns, his face contorted with fury. He sets his sights on Maeve.

"Don't you *dare!*" Sheb snarls. He dives between Ruben and the girls, his own harpoon clashing with his brother's. There's a pulse of green light and Sheb is thrown backwards.

Ruben bares his teeth. "This is your chance, brother," he growls. "Pledge your power to me, or I will kill you."

Sheb's eyes flash. "Killing me breaks the laws of the swamp," he says. "You will shatter it beyond repair."

Ruben laughs. "Exactly," he says.

He swings his harpoon, aiming at Sheb's head. Sheb ducks, rolls, and leaps to his feet in front of me, blocking Ruben's jab at his throat.

I manage to crawl to Maeve's side. She rolls so I can cut her bonds, but my heart's thudding hideously, my vision blurring. My hands tremble. I can barely control the knife to free both her and Lin. Wriggler's huge, now. Crashing through the swamp, his wings snapping trees. Sasha swims for his life, diving to avoid Wriggler's clashing teeth.

Finally, I manage to slice through Maeve's ropes. I drop my knife, fall against her. "Help me!" I beg. I feel her arms around me, dimly aware of her voice as she tries to pull me back to myself. Lin's hands hold mine. I feel her pull at my soul-mist, but it's no use.

And I can't stop. Can't hold back.

All that fury. All that frustration. All the times Sasha's let me down, kept secrets, disappeared. All the times I thought we might finally be able to give in to this pull between us, only for him to ruin it. It pours out of me now, feeding Wriggler's power.

Do you have any idea how often she's cried over you? Wriggler roars, his jaws closing on empty water where Sasha's head was a moment before. *And all you do is hurt her, you useless, traitorous fool!*

I collapse in a heap of trembling limbs. Sheb battles furiously with Ruben, but he's losing. Ruben pushes him up the island, every clash of their harpoons throwing Sheb back in a burst of power. Ruben's men charge us from all sides. It's only Bear keeping them at bay. Alphonz watches Wriggler and Sasha battling, a cruel grin on his feline face. His amber eyes turn to me. He prowls up the island.

"Dammit, Annie!" Maeve roars. She grabs me, shakes me. "Please!"

Wriggler erupts from the water with Sasha in his jaws. I grab Maeve's arms.

"Don't let him!" I beg. "Maeve, don't let him!"

Maeve closes her eyes. When she opens them, the green glow is gone and I see nothing but defeat there.

"I won't," she says. "Hugging me close. "But hell, Annie, this ain't how it was meant to be."

Wriggler stretches his mighty maw, but before he can bite down a huge black shape, wreathed in white fire, leaps from the bank. Bear bellows as he sinks his teeth into Wriggler's hide. Wriggler shrieks, lets go of Sasha, who swims limply for shore. I watch him, still too weak to stand. He's going to make it. He's going to be okay—

Pain shoots across my scalp. A mighty fist grabs my hair, jerking my head back. I stare into Locke's snarling face. Maeve yells as Cheran wrenches her arms behind her back. Lucius has a knife to Lin's throat. More of Ruben's men rush to help him battle Sheb.

Blood pours down my best friend's face. He's thrown back by every blow of Ruben's harpoon, but he keeps getting up.

Wriggler thrashes in Bear's grip as Maeve's monster grapples to control mine.

The silver shape of a maned cat cuts through the murky water. Alphonz, swimming towards where Sasha lies, collapsed, on the shore.

And, of all the times for her to turn up, the necrotic vulture, I feel a stab in my mind.

Annie, says the Corvos, as I fall into her power. *Come to me.*

Chapter Forty-Six

FIND YOUR POWER

No. Not now. I can't ...

I struggle against the bone crow's power as her darkness takes me.

But it ain't darkness. I blink. I'm in the graveyard. Alone?

No, not alone. It's evening. Remnants drift on the cool breeze. The sun paints the sky vivid pinks and oranges. I'm barefoot, back in the cotton dress I was wearing when I first entered Nowhere.

The one I wore when I murdered my daddy.

Jeelie's remnant floats beside me, glancing nervously around.

I blink again and the Corvos is standing before me, her huge form casting a deep shadow. I peer at her.

"Now is *not* a good time—" I tell her.

She tosses her gnarled head. *Now is the perfect time, Annalise,* she says.

I charge at her, fists raised. Like last time, she's taken my knives. My bare feet pound the dirt, kicking up loose soil.

"Let me *go!*" I rage. "My friends—"

Need you to control yourself, the Corvos hisses. In an instant, I'm stood back where I started. I yell, trying to work out how she transported me. But I'm in her world, ain't I? This is her magic. She's trapping me here. I glare.

"Let. Me. Go."

She cocks her head, regarding me. *Or what?*

I bare my teeth. "I'll—"

But she makes a good point. I don't have my knives. Wriggler ain't here. And even if he was, he's part of the reason we're in this mess. He fed off my anger. Pulled so much that I lost him and needed Maeve to bring me back. I close my eyes at the thought. This ain't how it's supposed to be. Maeve shouldn't be the one calming me.

"Annie," Jeelie says quietly. "Do as she says. It's important."

I drop to my knees, hugging myself. "I messed up."

The Corvos rumbles, stepping closer. *So what? You're human.*

I frown at her as she thuds in a circle around me, her tail dragging behind her. She ruffles her wings, settling broken feathers.

"I can't afford to mess up," I say. "My family need me. They can't do this without me."

The Corvos laughs. *Can't they?*

That pulls me up short. Maybe she's right. So many times, Maeve has shown me how strong her bond with Bear is. Lin's tougher than anyone gives her credit for. Sheb was willing to sacrifice himself to save us, and Bartok always manages to show up when we need him.

It's me and Wriggler. We're the broken ones. We're the liability.

My lower lip trembles. "They *shouldn't* have to do this without me," I say.

It's been a while since I felt the weight of my own darkness, the horror of what I had to do to survive. Me and Wriggler have come so far. But now I think about it, is that why I've been holding Maeve back? Is that why I abandoned Sheb to his past?

Because I think I'm the only one who deserves the pain, the horror, of what has to be done? Because I'm scared of breaking them. Because I'm scared of losing them.

That's it, the Corvos hisses. *Keep going.*

And Sasha. What do I expect of him? I'm sick of him trying to save me, leaving when I need him to stay, messing up when I need him to get it right.

But I haven't stopped to think how much it hurts him when he sees me messing up, too. How, despite everything, he keeps coming back. Okay, he's a pain, drives me to distraction, but it ain't fair that he has to perfect and I get to let my world-ending monster loose every time I feel cross. He's hurt me, and that ain't okay.

But I hurt him too, and that ain't okay either.

I feel a breath on my forehead, open my eyes to find the bone crow's massive head inches from mine. Her nostrils flare.

Good, she says. *Now you understand. And that makes you perfect for what your friends need. For what Sheb needs.*

I frown. "What—?"

Wait, the Corvos says. *She's on her way.*

I almost ask who, but I already know. The air behind the Corvos shimmers with remnant mist, forming a flickering shape. The remnant stutters, fading and reforming, like she's not sure who she is anymore. Still, there's enough of her that I know her. Flaxen hair, braided over one shoulder, floats about her as if she's underwater. She wears vambraces, a leather breastplate over a simple dress. But her eyes are wide, darting, like she's unsure where she is.

At her throat is a pendant. A hellgator tooth. It glows white, but I see a darkness in it, where the de Callis crest is carved.

She floats towards me. I realize there's a little figure guiding her, his tiny hand somehow holding hers.

"It's okay, Grandmama," Kai says gently. "This is Annie. She'll help."

Luana's frightened eyes meet mine. A flicker of recognition crosses her face.

"I've seen you," she says. "You are with my Sheb."

I nod, then shake my head, then nod again. Holy Oak, I ain't sure how to do this.

"Hello Luana," I say. "Sheb told me about you."

Luana's face softens. "My darling Sheb," she says.

I spare a small smile for Kai. The kid looks embarrassed. "Nice work," I tell him. "How'd you find her?"

Kai rolls his eyes. "The owl-squirrel found me," he explains. "He yelled until I got in a boat and followed him to the graveyard. Einan and Zuma were there and they helped me, but it was me Grandmama wanted to come with her. So, I'm here." He frowns. "Wherever here is."

Yeah, I ain't sure how to explain that to him. Instead, I put a hand on his shoulder. "You did great," I say.

Kai looks pained. "I dunno," he says. "Pa's gonna be so angry—"

"Sometimes," I tell him, "our daddies get it wrong. You want to save Uncle Sheb, don't you?"

Kai brightens, nods. "Yeah," he says. "I do."

I turn to Luana. I've got no idea how to do this, but I need to make her release Sheb's power.

"Luana?" I say. She jumps at the sound of her name. Oak, she's like a frightened bird, fluttering and panicked. "It's okay," I tell her. I raise my hands, show her I ain't armed. I ain't gonna hurt her. She looks from my open palms to my face and back, like she doesn't trust me yet. "I know you love Sheb," I say. "Don't you?"

She grows more solid for a moment. "More than anything," she says. "More than my life."

Beside me, Jeelie squirms. For the first time, his mother notices he's there. Again, her form stutters. She disappears, reappears, seems faint. "I—" she starts. "No, I can't—"

She starts to vanish. "No!" I cry, grabbing for her. "Please!"

My hand goes through her, the ice of her remnant-mist stinging my skin.

But her grandson reaches for her and, by some magic I don't understand, grasps her hand. "Stay, Grandmama," he says. "Please. We need you."

Luana's form stutters again, but holds. She stares at Kai, eyes shining. "You're so like him," she says. "You have more of you uncle in you than your father."

Kai blushes, frowns at his feet, but keeps hold of his grandmother's hand.

"Mama?" Jeelie says, floating forward. "Mama, it's me."

Luana stares at Jeelie, face stricken with terror. "I know, my son," she says. "My Jeelie. I know you." She pauses. "I mourned for you," she tells him. "I know you never believed I would, but I did. I hated what you made Sheb do, but I mourned for you."

Jeelie nods. He takes his mother's other hand in his. "I know," he says. "I know that now."

"Your sons need you, Luana," I tell her. "All of them. Ruben will break the swamp if we let him. He'll take it for his own and everything will collapse. There will be war. You know that."

Luana looks at me sadly. "What can I do, girl?" she asks. "I'm dead. I have no power."

Irritation spikes in my core, but I shove it down. Now ain't the time for rage. I look into Luana's eyes, see she believes what she says. It's a helplessness she had in life as well as death. Despite being a swamp maiden, able to shift into a monstrous hellgator, Deimos convinced her she was nothing.

Like Ruben did with Nora. Like Locke did with Allise and Lucius did with Yarella.

Like my daddy did with Mum.

We're only as powerful as we believe we are. Even when we've got the power of a monster behind us. The power of all our rage and experience. Sometimes, that's when we feel most alone, ain't it? When we think the weight of everything is on our shoulders, but there's nothing we can do to fix what's broken.

That's right, Annie, the Corvos says. *So, tell her.*

With Jeelie and Kai holding Luana in her shape, I step towards her. We're close enough that I could cup her face in my hands. "You've always had power, Luana," I say. "Maybe not the kind you think. But after everything that happened, you still chose to protect Sheb, didn't you? You knew Deimos would kill you for it, but you did it anyway."

Luana searches my face, nods. "For Sheb," she says. "Always for him."

"And now he needs you again," I tell her. "He needs you to release his power. Let him go."

Luana's shape flickers. "No," she says. "No, I can't! You don't understand. Ruben will find him. He'll kill him—"

"Ruben has already found him," I say. "After everything, Sheb came back. He came back to rescue a child. He came back to fight his brothers, save the swamp. The swamp you love."

Luana shakes her head. "No," she says. "He's too gentle, my Sheb. This fight will break him. You don't understand how his father tricked him!

How he tricked them all! I can't. Don't ask this of me!"

Her shape starts to unspool. Kai cries out, but this time even his fingers won't hold her solid.

"Luana!" I cry.

"Ma!" Jeelie yells.

But she's leaving. Too traumatized to see she's dooming Sheb a second time. And there's nothing I can do. I can't stop it.

The Corvos flares her vast wings. *Hold, Luana! she says. You know the truth. It's hidden in you. In both of us. Remember now. Remember what really happened.*

Luana's mist pauses. She's almost entirely vanished, but her face is still visible in the roiling white fog. She blinks, frowns.

"I can't," she says. "I don't want—"

You must, the Corvos says. *I will help you. Come with me, now.*

She turns away, heading up the path. Kai and Jeelie hold Luana as she reforms, drifting after her monster. I follow last, foreboding unfurling in my gut. I've walked this path many times in the last few weeks. The path to the black ash.

I brought them all, the Corvos says as we enter the tree's vast clearing. Others are already here. *They need to see this. To understand.*

"No!" Luana cries, fighting as the faces of those gathered turn towards her.

They're all here. Ruben clutches his head, blinking. Beside him, his brothers get to their feet, looking around in confusion. Sheb's there, too, stood apart from his brothers. Despite a bruised temple and a split lip, he seems unharmed. He smiles when he sees me.

And there's another figure with them. A remnant, hovering by the trunk of the black ash. Unlike the others, with their silvery white light, this remnant is darkness. A mist so thick and black, it seems to drink the light. Lightning flickers in those furious clouds. Even in death, Deimos is towering and terrible, twice the size he was in life. Full of thunder. When Luana sees him, she screams, her figure starting to fade. Jeelie and Kai hold her fast.

"Please, Mama," Jeelie says. "I know you're scared. Do this for me."

I watch Luana fighting with herself, her form flickering like lightning, changing color from silver to grey to bright white. I remember what the Corvos said when I first met it.

Mothers are wounds others can use against you.

Is that all Luana believes she is? A scar in the hearts of her children? I think how my own mother left me, found me, left me again. When she disappeared the second time, it was without a word. No goodbye, no message. Nothing. Her silence is still a blade in my gut, twisting. I spent the last two years believing she ran away because she hated me. But maybe that's not true.

Maybe she felt like Luana feels. Maybe she thinks she's nothing to me but a wound.

Is that true? I don't know. Maybe. But I don't want it to be. Not anymore.

I move towards Luana. Reach for her.

"Luana," I say. "Your sons need you."

My voice cracks as I say it. I clamp my mouth shut before the tightness in my throat turns to tears. Luana looks at me curiously, but her form stabilizes. She gazes at Jeelie, her eyes coming into focus. She reaches a silvery hand to touch his cheek.

"My poor boy," she says. "You needed me, and I failed you. You might've been so different."

Jeelie leans into her hand. "We failed each other," he says. "I see that now. We were facing a devil neither of us knew how to slay. Let's make it right. Together. Show everyone the truth."

"The truth," Luana agrees. Her shape grows more defined. A ghostly crossbow appears on her back. She draws herself up straight, meets Deimos' cruel glare. "The truth in all its ugliness."

CHAPTER FORTY-SEVEN

A FATHER'S PROMISE

THE CORVOS HOWLS.

Now, she says. *Watch*.

Luana leaves her son and grandson, stands beside the remnant of her husband. "It didn't happen here," she says. "Not all of it. Show them the truth, my love."

Love? For a terrible moment, I think she's talking to Deimos, but the dead man simply snarls at her. It's the Corvos that answers.

Very well, it says. *You will play your part?*

Luana's form flickers, but holds. "I will," she says.

The Corvos opens her mighty wings. The scene around us fades. The black ash disappears and, now, we're in a house. A vast house, in Marsh

Wilds. We stand in a circle in a living room grander than I remember, decorated with vases and ornaments, and a huge portrait over the fireplace that wasn't there when I was last in this room. But I know where we are. I recognize the huge chandelier hanging above us.

Deimos' empty eyes stare at me from that painting, making my hackles stand on end. This is the de Callis family house. Which is impossible, because me and Wriggler tore it apart.

Only we're here. Now. Deimos stands by the fireplace, under his portrait. Luana takes her place beside him.

"Now," she says. "The truth."

Deimos sneers, lightning flashing in his mist. "The truth," he growls. "As if you could handle—"

It happens so quickly, it takes me a moment to realize what's happened. Deimos' head snaps back. His mist flickers, the lightning inside him falling dark. He staggers, blinking at his wife.

"You—"

Luana raises a silver-pale hand to strike her husband again. "You cannot hurt us anymore, Deimos," she tells him. "This is my world, ruled by my monster. You will show our sons the truth!"

The Corvos stands behind her, wings wide. Deimos looks from his wife to her monster, back again. His jaw sets. "Very well," he says. "The truth."

Deimos and Luana take positions by the fireplace. I realize, watching the faces of their sons, that they're about to play out a scene that happened years ago. This is a memory.

"Deimos, this is madness," Luana says. "You've been fighting the Deep Swamp for a decade. It only grows stronger. If you start this war, it will end in death for us all. Stop this. Listen to us. Learn to work with it. Give Sheb the Heirship."

I cast a sideways glance at my best friend. The corner of his mouth twitches, but otherwise, he doesn't react. His three living brothers, though, glare at him with utter hatred.

Deimos laughs. "The weakling?" he scoffs. "The boy can't bring himself to step on a worm. What use will he be?"

Luana shakes her head. "Your kind of strength is failing," she says. "Sheb's strength will preserve our way of life. His magic soothes the swamp."

Deimos sneers. "Then what good is he?"

His wife's eyes flash with anger. Deimos steps back.

"Don't forget that when you talk to me," Luana says, her voice harsh. "You are talking to the swamp."

Deimos growls. He reaches forward, touches the pendant at Luana's throat. Her hellgator tooth glows, and I see the de Callis crest, carved in its surface, flare. He grins. "The swamp is mine," he says.

"Not yet," Luana bites back, snatching her pendant away.

Deimos' smile disappears. "Fine," he says. "A contest, then. Your pathetic lastborn is helping the swamp-maiden escape tomorrow. Let's see whose strength wins out over this, shall we?"

Luana's eyes widen. "No, Deimos," she begs. "Please ..."

But Deimos is no longer listening. "Get out of my sight, woman," he says. "This is my decision."

Luana shrieks, but some invisible force drags her back. I realize, when this memory really took place, that Deimos must have had men with him. They took his wife away, never gave her the chance to save her sons. I hear her screams echo as her remnant vanishes, waiting for its time to reappear.

Deimos turns to Ruben, standing outside the memory, looking in. "Where is my firstborn?" he demands.

My mouth falls open when Ruben starts to tremble. "No ..." he breathes. "Not again."

Beside me, Kai wriggles. He watches his father, watches that fear. I see how it hurts him. I put a hand on the kid's shoulder, smile at him. Kai stills, but tears stand in his eyes.

Deimos beckons Ruben. "Come here, son."

Ruben's legs move without his permission. He stands before the memory of his father, shaking his head. He clenches his fists, juts his chin, though I see fear in his eyes. He's a boy again. Alone. Scared.

Deimos cups his son's chin. "You want the Heirship, don't you?"

Ruben hesitates, says. "Yes, father."

Deimos smiles. "Your ridiculous brother is trying to rescue Jeelie's bride. You will hunt her and her mother down. Bring them back."

Ruben swallows, throat bobbing. "But father," he says, and I imagine he said these exact words all those years ago. "You know what they are. If I harm them, the swamp will—"

"Swamp be damned!" Deimos spits. "Bring back Jeelie's bride, bind her power to us, and you will have the Heirship. That it my promise. Now go."

As if a spell is broken, Ruben stumbles back, clutching his head. He returns to his place in the circle, eyes cast down.

"Pa?" Kai murmurs, but Ruben doesn't look at him.

Deimos' cruel eyes scan the circle of spectators. "Don't hide from me, Jeelie," he says. "This time, you will not cower in the shadows."

Like Ruben, Jeelie resists, but the memory pulls him. He floats towards his father, face is twisted with hatred.

"You bastard," he whispers.

Deimos laughs. "You pathetic weed," he says. "You know your twin is stealing your bride. What were you planning to do?"

Jeelie shakes his head. "Nothing," he admits. I imagine when he spoke those words the first time, when he was alive, his cheeks colored with shame.

Deimos smirks. "Your share of magic is as powerful as your brothers'," he says, "Yet you squander it on bullying the younger boys, intimidating the girls. Put your power to use. Go get your bride. Bring her back."

Jeelie shakes his head. "Sheb loves her," he says. "He'll defend her with his life."

"Then take his life!" Deimos spits. "You are a de Callis! Kill your twin and claim your bride, and I will give you the Heirship. It's that simple."

Jeelie's eyes widen. He gasps with pain. The memory releases him and he dissipates. I grip Sheb's hand. I know what's coming next and I don't know how to protect him. I look at him. His eyes are huge, dark with fear.

"Annie …" he says.

I can't save him from this. There is no knife that can cut through his past. No monster can eat his demons. There's only one thing I can do, though fear gallops through me at the thought.

"I'm here," I tell him. "I'll stand with you. We'll face this together."

Sheb doesn't look at me, but I feel his fingers tighten around mine.

Deimos' eyes find his youngest born. Jeelie's junior by only a few minutes. Sheb. His mother's pride and his father's disgust. Deimos lifts a hand. His fingers beckon.

Sheb's legs move. I hear a strangled whimper at the back of his throat, know he's got no choice in this. I grip his hand, step forward with him. I'll live this beside him. Face the nightmare of his father with him. He doesn't let go.

Deimos' cruel eyes appraise his youngest son.

"What is it you want from me?" he asks, like he doesn't really care.

Sheb trembles. "I want you to let Allise go," he says quietly.

Deimos laughs. "Let her go? She's a swamp creature! You understand what we're doing here, don't you? Those women have dampened our power for too long. I'll not let her go."

"You're making a mistake," Sheb says. "This isn't the way to get what you want."

Deimos' smile becomes a snarl of contempt. "You're a fool, Sheb," he says. "But okay. Have it your way. Help the girl escape. Defy me. But you know your brothers will stop you. And then, Sheb, then we'll see who has the true strength. If you survive your brothers, maybe I'll make you Heir."

"I don't want to be Heir," Sheb says, his voice stronger this time.

Deimos waves a dismissive hand. "You all want to be Heir," he says, as if his saying it makes it true. "Squabbling like rats over a carcass. Well, that's fine. But I'll pick the strongest. You have a choice. Prove your strength to me in defending Allise, or you will die trying. Do I make myself clear?"

Sheb lifts his chin. "I know what you're doing," he says. "I know you have spoken to my brothers. I know you want us to battle, and once your one surviving son stands amongst the broken bodies of his brothers, you will name him Heir. I know this, Father. I've always known it would come to this."

Every other face in the room turns to face him.

"You *what?*" Ruben demands.

"He knew?" Locke squeals. "How could he know? None of us knew—"

Jeelie says nothing. Cheran shuffles his feet uncomfortably. I cast them a sideways glance, realize the truth. They all bloody knew, didn't they? They knew how vicious their father was, that only one of them would survive his cruelty.

They were just so desperate to please him, they didn't want to admit it. Even to themselves.

Deimos sneers. "Clever boy," he drawls. "So, what will you do? Leave your swamp-girl to the mercy of your brothers?"

Sheb turns his back on his father. "I will do what's right," he says. "That's all."

Deimos flicks a wrist in dismissal. Sheb lets out a shaky breath as the memory releases him, shuffles to his place in the circle. Luana's remnant reappears by the fireplace. She's crouched at Deimos' feet. Her shoulders shake as she sobs. She clutches his ankle.

"Please," she begs. "Please don't do this."

Deimos wrenches his foot away. "Pathetic wretch," he says. "It's done. The swamp will be mine. I will have my Heir."

Sheb stiffens. I feel the pulse of Jeelie's anger as he drifts around us, unable to find his form. Ruben's eyebrows lift. I see Cheran look at his oldest brother with shock and hurt, Locke with barely concealed contempt. They weren't even discussed in Deimos' plans. His two invisible sons.

Luana's remnant stands, all appearance of grief and helplessness gone. She glares at her husband.

"You sicken me," she tells him. "Now leave."

Deimos opens his mouth to retort, but the Corvos roars. The house shakes. Deimos vanishes in a cloud of black smoke.

There's a moment's silence, then the house around us disappears. We are back under the black ash. I keep hold of Sheb's hand as his mother's remnant turns to him, takes his face in her hands.

"You knew," she says. "And you chose to save Allise. You knew you might die, might have to kill, but you went anyway."

Sheb lets out a small sob. "I knew," he admits. "And it has broken me every day since, what I did to my brother. But I remade myself, Mama. I'm stronger, now."

Luana smiles. Tears shine in her eyes. "A strength your father never understood," she says. "I should've trusted you, my son. I should've known you had the courage to face this."

She grasps the tooth at her throat and pulls. The ghostly cord holding it to her neck snaps. Tenderly, Luana wraps her pale arms around Sheb. "Fight him," she whispers. "Beat him."

Chapter Forty-Eight

KAI'S CHOICE

I BOLT UPRIGHT IN Maeve's arms, gasping.

"Easy, Annie," Maeve says. There's relief in her voice. "You're okay."

I'm back on the island at the heart of the swamp, surrounded by Ruben's men.

Lin's on her knees in the dirt. Lucius holds her hands behind her back, saber drawn. Others have their weapons aimed at me and Maeve, waiting for orders. One of them goes to grab Maeve's arm but she kicks him away.

"Can't you see I got my hands full?" she snarls.

The soldier smirks, says nothing. Where can me and Maeve go, anyway? We're surrounded.

Wriggler's fallen limp in Bear's grip. I see him shrinking.

Annie, he says, scales still spitting sparks. *Annie, I'm sorry.*

I hold my head while a wave of dizziness crashes through me. *Later,* I say. *We've still got a battle to win.*

Though, by the looks of it, we might already have lost.

Ruben, Sheb, and their brothers gather their wits. The Corvos has released them, too. Ruben comes round quickest, snatching his harpoon as he leaps to his feet. He roars, aims a blow at Sheb's head, but my friend is ready for him. Sheb's harpoon blocks Ruben's stab. There's another blast of magic. Sheb is thrown back.

Ice closes my throat. No. That shouldn't be! Luana said she'd give Sheb back his power. How could she—

Movement on the far bank catches my eye. I remember Sasha and Alphonz. Sasha still lies, prone, in the dirt, though I see his eyes flicker open. Alphonz drags himself out of the water, snarling as he advances. Holy Oak, this is going so horribly wrong!

"Sasha!" I scream.

He glances up, amber eyes widening. He sees Alphonz crouch, spring, claws outstretched ...

And then a monstrous shape crashes sidelong into Alphonz, hurling him into a nearby tree. The massive creature throws back its reptilian head and roars. I hear its voice echo across the water.

"Get them!"

My mouth falls open. "Imberg?"

But it isn't just her. Yarella and Allise, both in hellgator form, erupt from the inky murk, launching themselves onto the island. Ruben's men scatter, leaving me, Maeve, and Lin unguarded. Still, the Marsh Wilds maidens can't attack. Their power is bound to Ruben, after all. They snarl and snap, but the de Callis magic prevents them from doing any real damage.

It doesn't matter, though.

Other hellgators appear. Petya and her warriors, I reckon. They splinter the boats, cutting off Ruben's escape. They scramble onto the island, snarling as Lucius and the other warriors cower. Cheran and Locke wield their harpoons, but the hellgators are vicious. One grabs Locke by the leg, hurls him, shrieking, into the water. Two more corner Cheran at the edge of the island.

"Look!" Maeve cries.

But I've already seen. The hellgator that is Nora drifts quietly to the island shore. Unlike the others, she doesn't come leaping into battle. On her back, she carries precious cargo. Einan and Zuma. And Kai. Bartok is with them. That bloody owl-squirrel, perched primly on Zuma's shoulder. His tawny's eyes meet mine. He lets out a smug hoot. My lips quirk into a smile.

The children clamber off Nora's back. Einan and Zuma rush through the rampaging hellgators until they reach me and the girls.

"You okay?" Einan asks, helping me to my feet.

I nod, casting a glance at Zuma as she bobs on her toes beside me.

"Mama wouldn't let me fight," she says. I realize her pupils are huge, that tell-tale blackness filling her eyes. I don't know if she yet has the swamp maidens' power to skin-switch. Something tells me it's not fully formed. But her courage is as vibrant as ever.

"Too right," I say, grabbing her hand before she can do something reckless. "Where's—?"

But Kai doesn't come to join his friends. As his mother prowls beside him, he stands frozen, watching his uncle and father.

Sheb and Ruben haven't stopped fighting, despite the chaos raging around them. Ruben roars as he jabs at Sheb, pushing him up the island towards us.

"You think you can outfight me?" he bellows. "You're pathetic! I'll kill you!"

Sheb counters desperately, his harpoon meeting Ruben's with a clash of metal.

"You don't need to do this, brother," he shouts. "Please! Listen!"

"Like I'll ever listen to you!" Ruben snarls. "Weak! Useless! You always were!"

Sheb's gaze hardens. "I'm not afraid of you, Ruben," he says. "But I know you're afraid of me. I see you, brother. I see your fear. I see your pain."

"Shut up!" Ruben screams. "Shut up! Shut *up!*"

He swings his harpoon at Sheb's head. Sheb ducks, raising his own harpoon to parry. But with every blow, Ruben's power blasts around him. The swamp shudders. Sheb is thrown back another few feet.

I draw my knife. "We have to help!" I cry.

But Lin grabs me, pointing at Kai. The kid's clutching something in each fist. His breath quickens and, though there are tears in his eyes, determination shines in his face. I realize what's happening all at once.

"Luana gave him the ring," I say. "And Jeelie's finger bone."

Kai looks from Sheb to Ruben and back again, watching as they battle. I feel the swamp tremble with every blow of Ruben's power. The murk around the island bubbles, creeperscorps ooze from the depths. The hellgators turn to battle them, but Ruben's power gives the creatures terrible strength.

My fingers tighten around my knife. "There's no time!" I say. "We need to help!"

Lin signs at me, smiling. I catch the signs for *possible,* and *think* or *consider,* and look at Maeve for a translation.

"She says we can help," Maeve explains. "Just not in the way you think. Go to Kai."

I blink at her. *"Me?"* I squeak. "Maeve, I'm no good at that stuff. I—" I bite my lip.

It's okay, Annie, Wriggler says. He slithers beside me, now dog-sized. *You can say it. It's time.*

I take a deep breath. "You're better at this than me, Maeve. I should've told you that earlier. You're learning so fast, sometimes I feel like I can't keep up. I don't reckon I can do this." I grab her hand, squeeze it. "But I reckon you can."

Maeve winks, squeezes my hand back. "Thanks, Annie," she says. "But actually, that's howler horse-shit."

I open my mouth, then close it again. *What?*

"Kai needs someone who gets him," Maeve says. "Who knows what it's like to try and please a father who he'll never be good enough for. It ain't your rage you need now, Annie. It's your pain. And that's okay. I know it scares you. But we're here. Sheb needs you."

Einan and Zuma stare between us, nonplussed. Bartok chirps, flutters from Zuma's shoulder to mine. I'm pleased to see he's no longer got that bloody shoe clamped in his beak. It's back on Zuma's foot, where it belongs.

I grip my knife tighter. "I—"

Another blast from Ruben's harpoon rocks the island. We grab hold of each other to stay upright. Ruben has nearly pushed Sheb to the crest of the island. Sweat and blood pour down my friend's face. His chest heaves, eyes glassy with fear. He's tiring.

"If we're gonna do this," I growl. "It has to be now. Stay with the kids."

"You got it," Maeve says, her eyes glowing green as Bear lumbers towards us. "Go."

I race towards Kai. His mother still prowls beside him, snaps at us when we approach.

"Hey!" I say, leaping back to avoid her massive jaws. Nora growls but lets me pass. I drop to my knees beside Kai.

"Kai," I say, breathless. "C'mon, kid, we have to—"

But he shakes his head. Tears fall freely down his face. He's panicking. "He'll hate me," Kai says. "He'll hate me forever if I do this."

I watch him, realize I know the turmoil raging inside him. His father is his hero and his nightmare. Ruben is everything he's terrified of, but he's desperate for his father to love him.

Hell, I know that feeling. I've known it all my life. I put my knife away, gently put my hand on the small of Kai's back. Wriggler slithers beside me, shrunken down so as not to scare the kid. I don't know if I can do this. It's always Sheb who knows the right thing to say.

It doesn't have to be perfect, Annie, Wriggler tells me. *It just has to be true.*

Right. I can do that.

"Kai, I get it," I say. "My daddy was like that, too. He was so ... vicious, sometimes. Like an animal. But I guess I just wanted him to love me, to look at me and be proud."

Kai turns his tear-stained face towards me. "Really?"

"Yeah," I say. Another blow from Ruben's harpoon rocks the island. I shudder. "He was a bully, my dad. In the end, I had to betray him. I had to do it to survive."

Kai's eyes widen. I see his fists uncurl. Luana's ring glints in one palm. I see Jeelie's fingerbone in the other. Beside it is another hellgator tooth, carved with Ruben's crest. Luana's tooth.

"How did you do it?" Kai whispers.

I look at Wriggler. *Maybe keep that vague,* my lightning-snake says. It's a fair point. Perhaps best not to talk about murder when you're trying to convince a kid to do the right thing.

"I had to find my courage," I say. "I realized that Daddy was turning me into him. I didn't want to live like that. I wanted to be good. I dunno if I've managed that yet, Kai. Truth is, my daddy's shadow still hangs over me some days, but I'm trying. And I'm trying because I broke free of him."

Kai's breathing slows.

"You can break free of your daddy, too," I tell him. "You can save the swamp. Give it back the thing Luana took from it. Free the maidens. Unbind Sheb's power."

Kai wipes away his tears. "Uncle Sheb is kind to me," he says. "He teaches me things. He makes me feel ... important."

"You are important!" I tell him. "That's why Luana gave these things to you. Because she trusts you."

Kai nods. "To do the right thing," he says. "So that's what I gotta do."

He turns and charges down the island, dodging hellgators, creeperscorps, and warriors. He stumbles as the island shudders, picks himself up, keeps running. I hurtle after him, Wriggler at my side, stabbing at a creeperscorp when it gets too close.

"Annie!" Maeve yells.

I glance over my shoulder in time to see that Sheb has fallen, his weapon thrown from his grip. Ruben, laughing, raises his own harpoon, ready to strike.

"*Sheb!*" I yell. My rage kicks. Wriggler expands beside me.

But Kai has already reached the bank. He skids to a halt, inches from the lapping water and, without hesitation, he hurls the ring and fingerbone as far into the swamp as he can. I watch them arc through the air, so small they're swallowed by the dark.

They land with barely a sound. I don't even see the splash.

Then, he throws Luana's tooth onto the ground. With a cry, he brings his heel down on it. Hard. It shatters. A shockwave shoots outwards, throwing me off my feet. Around me, the hellgators roar. I catch sight of Nora, her eyes swirling with energy as her power is released. She grows to twice her usual size, rearing onto her hind legs.

Kai clenches his fists, glares out onto the water. "Now, let Uncle Sheb go!" he yells.

There's a moment when the whole world holds its breath.

Then the island rocks so violently that I'm thrown off my feet. Warriors cry out as they're hurled sideways, firing shots as they fall. Maeve and Lin grab the kids, shielding them as the island bucks. The Marsh Wilds maidens, now huge in hellgator form, snarl as they charge into battle, finally released. Ruben's creeperscorps pause, mid-sting or jab or bite, like they've suddenly woken up. As one, they turn and march up the island, towards their former master.

Then I see him. My Sheb. He's standing, now, his harpoon back in his hand. And he's awash with light. Energy swirls around him in threads of green and silver. Remnants float from the trees, drawn to his glow.

Ruben throws his hands in front of his face to shield himself. "What the—?" his lip curls. He aims his harpoon at Sheb's heart. "You treacherous—"

But he doesn't get to finish. Instead, he's buried under a heap of creeperscorps. Their chitinous clicks drown out the dying sounds of battle. Ruben howls, lost beneath their fury.

Sheb turns to me. I feel my ribs expand, like there's so much love inside them, they can't hold it in. His glow is so bright, I can barely see him through the film of my tears.

My beautiful, brilliant, bright best friend. More powerful than I've ever seen him.

More himself than he's ever been.

Chapter Forty-Nine

THIS WILL ALL CHANGE

SHEB WAVES HIS HAND, light curling from his fingertips. The creeperscorps fall back. Beneath them, Ruben is curled up, shaking. His harpoon has fallen away and he's awash with blood. Cuts criss-cross his arms and shoulders. Still, he's alive.

Because Sheb is Sheb, and mercy is what he does.

My throat tightens, cheeks heating with shame. I wouldn't have shown the same mercy. I would've killed Ruben and it would have hurt Sheb. Deeply. My gaze drifts towards the bank where I left Sasha. He's with Imberg, struggling to stand. After all that, he was right to stop Wriggler devouring Ruben. And I almost ... Wriggler could've ...

I clamp down on that thought before tears sting my eyes.

The hellgators disarm Ruben's men. At the sight of his older brother cowering, and his youngest brother bright with a blinding glow, Cheran drops his harpoon, throws up his hands. Locke, who is a fool, keeps trying to fight, but a hellgator—I suspect it's Allise—wallops him with her massive tail. He goes flying into the water with an almighty splash. After that, the rest of Ruben's men surrender. Sensible.

"It's done," Sheb says. "It's finished."

Beside me, Kai heaves a mighty sob, collapses into me. On his shoulder, Bartok croons gently. I blink at the boy now, glance at Wriggler.

What do I do?

Wriggler flicks his tongue. *Maybe give the kid a hug?*

Right. Tentatively, I wrap my arms around Kai. "It's okay," I say. "You were great. You did so great."

Wriggler's pride sings through my brain. *Good work, Annie,* he says. *Knew you could do it.*

I smile, but my gaze snags on the hellgator now snaking through the water. Imberg hauls herself ashore. With a growl of pain, she shifts to human form. She rings water from her silver braid, hobbles to me.

"Where's Sasha?" I ask, scanning the far shore.

Imberg shrugs. "He limped off," she says. "I looked for the other skin-switcher, but I couldn't find him. As far as I know, they're both alive."

I nod my thanks, though my belly squeezes with unease. I'll have to trust Sasha for now. I guide Kai up the island towards Maeve and Lin. The girls are shaken, but okay. Bear prowls protectively around them. Einan and Zuma are still with them, staring wide-eyed at the scene.

Zuma nods with satisfaction.

"That's better," she says. "That's the way it should be."

Einan reaches for Kai's shoulder, but the kid flinches away. Einan's face falls but Maeve puts an arm round him.

"It's okay," she whispers. "He's just ... had to do a really hard thing."

Maeve's right. I glance at Kai. I know what kind of awfulness he's going through. How that shame and terror shreds through him like a hurricane. I crouch beside him.

"You know," I say softly. "It gets easier. One day, you'll realize how brave you've been today."

I hear his breath hitch. "I will?"

I nod, staring at the bizarre scene in front of me. Sheb reaches down to grasp Ruben's hand, pull him to his feet. Ruben flinches away, but a creeperscorp scuttles behind him, grips him in its massive pincers. Ruben roars but can do nothing.

"It hurts," I say. "I get it. But you know, our daddies ain't always right. Sometimes they make mistakes."

Kai frowns. "Men don't make mistakes," he says.

I chuckle. "Oh, they do. Men and women, boys and girls and everyone else. We all make mistakes, Kai. That's being human."

Behind me, Wriggler rumbles approval. *Keep talking,* he says.

"I know it feels like you've broken every rule your daddy made for you," I say. "Like you've betrayed everything he hoped you'd be. But that ain't a bad thing, Kai."

Finally, he looks at me. "It's not?"

I shake my head, smiling. "No," I say. "Listen."

We both do, straining our ears. The only sounds are the swamp's birds stirring in the trees, the gentle susurrus of water lapping the banks, a morning breeze stirring the canopy. I notice, too, that the blackness spreading across the island, those tendrils of dark reaching into the water, are slowly receding. Kai frowns.

"I don't hear anything," he says.

My smile widens. "Exactly," I say. "Remember the death-roar? That fear that hung over your town? It's gone now. The swamp is healing. Thanks to you."

Kai's eyebrows lift. "Really?"

I nod. "Really."

I don't know what else to say, so I just stand beside the kid, try to show him that I'm here. That I know it's hard, but I get it. Like I should've done for Sheb all those times. For all of them, really. My little family. I'm a coward.

Wriggler nudges my shoulder. *Mistakes are human, Annie,* he tells me. I half-scowl, half-smile at the way he echoes my own words back at me.

"We should get over there," I say. "I ain't having Sheb make any more terrible decisions alone."

I become aware of Zuma and Einan squabbling.

"No, I'll do it later!" Einan protests. Zuma kicks him in the shin. "Ow!"

"I'll give you worse if you don't do it right now!" she says. "You owe him!"

I frown. "Owe who what?" I ask.

Maeve barely suppresses a smile. "Sheb," she explains. "Zuma wants Einan to apologize."

Einan looks at me, pleadingly. I sigh. I know Einan only did what he did to protect his sister. I know his dad and Ruben have filled his brain with nonsense about the swamp and its maidens.

But Zuma has a point.

"You know what?" I say. "I think that's a great idea. I owe Sheb an apology, too. Let's go together."

Everyone stares at me. Maeve's mouth falls open. I glare at her. "What?"

Mave holds up her hands. "Nothing!" she says. "Nothing at all!"

I take Einan's hand and we trek up to the island's crest.

Einan creeps towards Sheb, eyes lowered. "I'm sorry," he mutters to his toes. Zuma nudges him.

"Say it properly," she hisses.

Einan lifts his head and, with great effort, meets Sheb's eye. "I'm sorry," he says again. "I thought my sister—"

Sheb claps his hand on the boy's shoulder. That strange glow still hangs around him. A swirling vortex of light. And oh, this close, I can *feel* his power. It pulses off him in waves. I can smell it. The crackle-whisper-chime of deep, ancient magic flowing through him. The swamp leans into him. The creeperscorps scuttle closer, desperate to be in his light. The trees lean down to caress him. I hear the swamp chant his name.

Sheb. My Sheb. You're back. You're here.

I don't know why it makes me feel so sad, but it does.

Sheb smiles at Einan. "I forgive you," he says. Einan's mouth twitches in a smile.

Things are happening, Wriggler says, drawing my attention to the water. Some of the hellgators have left off prowling round the boats and now head up the island, shifting back into women as they approach. I wince at the sound of their skeletons cracking and popping. Now, a group of women, bristling with weaponry, stands in front of me. My mouth falls open. There must be dozens. A few pause to deal with Ruben's brothers and warriors, corralling them into a circle, securing their hands behind their backs.

I notice Yarella taking great pleasure in securing a rope around her husband's wrists.

The rest of the swamp maidens trudge up the island, stand in front of us. Their weapons are drawn, but lowered. They gaze at Sheb with something like awe. A powerful blond woman steps forward. I recognize her. It's Petya. She inclines her head to Sheb.

"I'm sorry," she says. "Had I known, I would have done things differently."

Sheb chuckles sadly. "Yeah," he says. "People keep saying that."

Imberg folds her arms, smirking.

"Good," she says, as she limps towards me. She drops a hand onto my shoulder. "This is good." I think this might be the first time I've seen her really smile. It changes her whole face.

Petya draws her saber, aims it at Ruben's throat.

"He broke our laws," she says. "He endangered us all and almost damaged the swamp forever. There is only one thing to do with him."

Ruben lifts his head, snarling. "I make the laws!" he growls. He bares his teeth, though his eyes are wide, shining with fear.

"Be still!" Petya booms. "You have broken every oath we swore to the swamp when we settled here! You and your brothers ruptured the swamp's magic with death and cruelty. You drove your swamp-maiden mother to grief-stricken insanity! You allowed murder and trickery. You tried to grab power like it was yours to take. You have broken *every* law of the swamp. And it is angry."

A murmur of agreement ripples around the other swamp-maidens. The hellgators still on the water rumble with agreement.

"It's decided, then," Imberg says. "Make it quick."

Petya draws her saber back, ready to strike. Kai's eyes widen. "No!"

But I don't bother shielding the kid's view. I know what will happen. Sure enough, Sheb steps between his brother and Petya's raised saber.

"No," he says.

"*No?*" Imberg squawks. "Sheb! He broke our laws! He tricked you into returning and then plotted to murder you! He was going to drown your friends! He—"

"I know all that," Sheb says. "I'm not saying we should do nothing. I'm saying there has been enough death. The swamp has been clogged with death for far too long."

He gestures behind him. Around the island, remnants have formed, their mist swirling eerily. They hang in the air. Silent. Watching. I spot Jeelie amongst them. He gives me a small smile.

The swamp maidens fall still, staring. A few of the younger women wipe their eyes or turn away. I wonder how many of these ghostly shapes are relatives of the people gathered here. How horrifying it must be to know they're trapped in this half-death.

"The swamp needs balance," Sheb says. "And we start with showing mercy. Working together."

Imberg raises an eyebrow. "So ... what, then?" she asks.

Sheb's gaze scans the gathered swamp maidens, then falls on me, Maeve and Lin. He grins, that same, cheeky smile I love. He holds out his hand, and I take it.

"That's not a decision I should make alone," he says. "It's for me and my family to decide."

Imberg huffs, but Petya bristles.

"This is not their world, de Callis," she says. "I don't think—"

I've had enough of what Petya *thinks*. "This world nearly destroyed my family," I snap. "I reckon we've got as much of a say as anyone!"

The maidens snarl. "This is not your fight, little murk-touched," Petya says.

Wriggler rears, hissing. *Little! Annie, I'll—*

No, I say, before he can suggest it. I glare at Petya, though. Murk-touched, my ass.

"I *did* fight," I say. "We all did. Me and my family. For you. For this town. For Einan and Zuma and Nora and Kai. For the swamp. Ruben tried to use me and Maeve to strengthen his power but he failed. Because we fought."

There's a confused murmur among the maidens. Nora appears through the crowd, gently touches Petya's arm. "It's true," she says. "And they *are* murk-touched, Petya. They are the bridge. Perhaps it's right they choose."

Petya sighs. "Fine," she says. "The swamp speaks in riddles at times. Let the murk-touched decide what happens to Ruben. His fate is yours."

They look at me earnestly. I clench my fists. Great. This was the last thing I had in mind. But Wriggler's gentle nudge in my brain reminds me it ain't just my decision. I look to my family. To Sheb.

"What do you want?" I ask him. "What do you need?"

Sheb's smile falters. His grip on my hand tightens. "Forgiveness," he says. "Balance. I need ..." he sighs. "I need someone to help me. Tell me what to do, Annie?"

I glance at Maeve. She takes a deep breath, grips Lin's hand. "No more death," she says. Lin signs enthusiastic agreement. I think this might be the first time we have ever been wholly *together* on something. I smile.

"Okay," I say. I turn back to Petya. "I think—" I pause. "*We* think ... Ruben shouldn't be Heir anymore. Is it possible to remove his power without killing him?"

Imberg raises an eyebrow at us. "The magic will want somewhere to go," she says. "And you know what that means, Sheb? The swamp wants you. It always wanted you."

My breath catches. I squeeze Sheb's hand without thinking. Does this mean—?

The idea of leaving Sheb here, of heading back to Nowhere without him, makes my heart tighten.

I want to clutch his shoulders. Shake him. Remind him we love him. We need him. He has to stay with us.

But Wriggler tugs at my mind. *Not your choice to make, Annie.*

He's right. I hate that he's right. So, I drop Sheb's hand, hold my breath, and I wait. And Sheb, my dear, darling Sheb, looks utterly forlorn.

"I—" he stutters. "I don't know if—"

More commotion among the swamp maidens. Allise forces her way through the crowd.

"Sheb!" she gasps. She falls against him. "My Sheb!" she wraps her arms round him, sobbing into his shoulder. Sheb blinks down at her. Then, slowly, he folds her into an embrace, lays his cheek against her head.

No-one moves. No-one says anything. Grief and fear make a tourniquet around my throat. I can hardly breathe. My hands tremble, but I don't resist when Maeve laces her fingers through mine. I know she's just as scared. Know Lin is, too. We could lose Sheb today, and none of us have a right to fight it.

Finally, Sheb pulls back from Allise, brushes tears from her face. "I'm sorry," he tells her. "I'm sorry I failed you that day. I'm sorry I ran rather than fight them. I'm—there's so much I'm sorry for."

Allise nods, hands rubbing her swollen belly, where a child—a daughter, perhaps? Maybe another swamp maiden—waits to be born. "I know you are," she says. "And I am, too. I'm sorry you went through that. I'm sorry for what hurt you, and who you hurt. But Sheb—" She grips his hands tightly. "You can't do this. You mustn't stay."

My eyebrows shoot up. A murmur ripples through the swamp maidens. Sheb blinks.

"What?"

"You mustn't stay," Allise says, tears pouring down her face. "I love you, Sheb. I've always loved you, you know that. But this world turned its back on you, and it's not yours to fix. You have your family now." She turns to me, smiling. "People who love you. Who understand you. A place to call home. You can't give that up. Not for us. Not for this."

Sheb cups her face in his hands. "Will you be okay?"

She lets out a small sob, but nods. "Of course I will," she says. "We all will, now. But it can't be you, Sheb. You can't take on the Heirship. We can't ask that of you."

Sheb kisses her forehead. "I know," he says. "I am not de Callis anymore. I haven't been for a long time. I never wanted the Heirship. And you ..." he draws back from her, smiling again. "This was always your home. This place. This swamp. This magic."

"Yes," Allise says. She pulls away from him but keeps hold of his hand. I realize I'm crying. Wriggler winds himself round my ankle and Bartok hops from Kai's shoulder to mine, beaking tears off my cheeks. Maeve's still holding my hand.

Petya, though, is all business.

"Well, that's all very well," she says. "But this territory needs an Heir. It's your blood, is it not? Would you trust it to either of your foolish brothers?" She gestures to where Locke and Cheran kneel among the rest of Ruben's men, guarded by menacing swamp maidens with their sabers drawn.

"No," Sheb says. "But there is a de Callis who's learned mercy. Who broke his heart to do the right thing." He smiles at Kai, kneels beside him. "Kai?" he says.

The kid wriggles, twisting his hands together. He glances from his mother to his father and, finally, his gaze lands on his uncle. "Yeah?"

"I know this is a lot to ask of you," Sheb says. "You are so young, and I'm sorry that it's come to this. But you've shown how merciful you can be. You've shown you'll choose gentleness over force. I think you'd make a great Heir. Will you do it?"

Kai hesitates, chewing his lip. I see his gaze flick to his father. Ruben has fallen still, staring at his son in shock. Finally, Kai's jaw sets. He nods.

"I will," he says. "I want to. I want to make things better."

Sheb hugs him. "Thank you," he says. Kai leans his head on Sheb's shoulder.

But Imberg's clearly not done arguing. "He's far too young!" she says. "We can't allow this."

Sheb shrugs. "Let it lie dormant in his blood, then. Safe. And you take charge of his training. The swamp-maidens of Marsh Wilds. Let him learn how to manage the swamp with gentleness and compassion. When he's ready, the swamp can release his power."

Another murmur sweeps the gathered swamp-maidens.

"Is that even possible?" Allise whispers. I see Imberg shrug.

"Whatever the swamp wills," she says.

After a while, the maidens fall silent. Petya speaks again. "Fine," she says. "Mercy it is. Though we still need to decide what to do with him if he is to live."

Kai lets out a whimper but seems to know better than to fight this.

Petya looks to Sheb. "A single cut will do it," she says, holding Ruben's harpoon out to him. "With his own blade. Tell the swamp what you want." She smiles. "It always seems to listen to you. The magic will leave him and can then be placed in the son."

Sheb hesitates, then takes the harpoon. Ruben struggles in the creeperscorp's grip as Sheb lifts the weapon, aims the barbed tip at the back of his brother's neck. I see Ruben's teeth clench as the skin splits. A thin trickle of blood draws a red line under his shirt. There's a sudden rush of wind. For a moment, I'm afraid the death-roar has returned, but I realize the wind is focused around Ruben, pulling his clothes, dragging his hair. His back arches. He howls in pain as a great surge of light pours from his mouth, nose, eyes, ears. The light is silver and green, like Sheb's. But unlike Sheb's, I see darkness running through it. Veins of red and black, like an infection. The light grows so bright that even the remnants shrink back. Ruben's magic leaves him.

Nora beckons for her son to come to her, holding him by the shoulders as Sheb clasps his hands. My dear friend glows so brightly I can barely see him. He's a beacon of silver and green light, humming with the power of the swamp.

"Are you ready for this?" He asks Kai.

The kid blinks against the brightness. "I don't know," he whimpers.

Sheb smiles. "That's okay," he says. "It's okay not to be ready. It's okay to be scared."

Kai thinks for a moment, then nods. "I want to try," he says. "For you, Uncle Sheb. For the swamp."

Sheb folds the kid into a gentle hug. "And for you," he says. "To make the world better for you."

Kai sighs in Sheb's embrace. Ruben's magic rushes out of him and, directed by Sheb, siphons into his son. The wind tears around Ruben and Kai, so fierce, I shield my eyes.

And then it's gone. I blink, lower my arm. Ruben is on all fours, heaving his guts into the damp grass. Kai stands, blinking and confused. The blackness on the island is receding. The remnants are gone. Not even their mist lingers in the tree branches. With the swamp healing, perhaps they've finally found a way to die properly. I feel a pang of regret at not saying goodbye to Jeelie, but the poor kid lived with such fear and hatred, I reckon he deserves a peaceful death.

Nora turns to her husband. She looks him up and down with disgust. "What about him?" she demands. "He might not be Heir, and we will let him live. But there's still the question of what to do with him. And them." She jabs a finger at Locke and Cheran, who've both fallen still in their captives' grip.

Sheb grins. I see a sparkle in his eye. "I believe," he says, "there is a place, deep in the swamp, that the hellgators call home. A haven for the swamp's women warriors, where they learn to fight, and to listen to the swamp."

Imberg and Petya both raise an eyebrow.

"Maidens' Creek," Petya says. "What of it?"

"I think," Sheb says, "it would be a good place for my brothers to learn to be better. They can work for you. Tend the swamp, stoke your fires, cook your meals. They will learn humility. Patience. And perhaps, once they have learned, they might be allowed to return, should the new de Callis Heir allow it."

He turns to his brothers, and I sneak a glance to gauge their reaction. Cheran looks relieved. Locke's blanched so white, I think he might faint. Ruben, though? For the first time, he just seems ... lost.

The swamp maidens retreat, huddling together. There are urgent whispers, gestures. Then Petya returns to us, her face grave.

"Fine," she says. "It's agreed. We will take them with us."

Ruben makes a strangled noise of protest, which is quickly smothered by the maiden holding him. The other women shift, slithering into the water. Ruben, Locke and Cheran are bundled onto their backs, their wrists and ankles secured. Locke kicks out, trying to escape, but Cheran just kneels carefully on a hellgator's back. I see him lean down and whisper something to her. I think it might be, *thank you.*

In moments, they've vanished, leaving Marsh Wilds to deal with the fallout of its own battle. I let out a sigh. It's time to go home.

Nearly.

CHAPTER FIFTY

ARE WE READY FOR THIS?

I CLAMBER OFF WRIGGLER's back, careful not to damage the wildflowers I'm clutching. I wait on the crumbling jetty while Wriggler shrinks to dog-sized. He slithers up beside me.

You ready for this?

I shake my head. "Nope. But let's do it anyway."

Together, we head up the path to the graveyard. It's the only place I haven't searched yet, so Sasha must be here somewhere. If Alphonz hasn't got to him first. Two days ago, I came here with Sheb, Nora, and Kai to rebury Jeelie's stolen finger bone. By some miracle, Nora found it floating on the tide by the heart of the swamp. It seemed only right to return it to its owner. I expected some sort of spectacle. A surge of remnants, an echoing cry from Jeelie's grave, but there was nothing. The remnants are gone and no-one's seen the Corvos since the battle. I guess, now that Luana is truly dead, the Corvos died, too. For some reason, the thought makes me grab Wriggler, hugging him tight. He splutters in protest.

Boundaries!

I laugh, let him go.

With Ruben and his brothers spirited away to Maidens' Creek, Imberg and Nora have taken over the running of the town. It hasn't gone down well with everyone. Still, they're trying. I've seen Yarella talking with the townsfolk, building friendships. Allise has started teaching at the school. They're trying to do better than Ruben did. Petya appeared a few times in the last week, too. She arrived at dusk, disappearing into Nora's house, not emerging until after midnight. I suppose she's helping with Kai's training, and updating the Marsh Wilds maidens on how the de Callis brothers are getting on. I've not seen Kai since that night, either, though I know Sheb's been visiting him.

Zuma's in and out of that house, too. Lucius protests, but what can he do? He's under arrest, ain't he? He hates what his daughter is to become, that's plain to see. But he can't fight it now Ruben's been stripped of his power.

The swamp's healing. I feel it as me and Wriggler pick our way between the headstones. The graveyard is silent, more a place for the living than the dead. As it should be. For the first time since arriving in Marsh Wilds, I've seen other people here. There are fresh flowers, new candles by the graves. With the remnants gone, the death-roar silent, people can visit here again.

I pause by Luana's crumbling grave, kneel, and place the wildflowers before her headstone.

"I'm sorry," I say. "And thank you."

There's no reply. Of course there ain't. The swamp is healed. It's taken back its dead. Luana is gone. Still, I rest my palm against her headstone, hoping she feels my goodbye. There's a rush in my ears, a tingle through my fingers. I brace, expecting an onslaught of the memories I felt when I last touched this grave, but I don't need to worry. No terrible visions blast through me. There's just a rush of love. Gratitude. Peace.

I take my hand away.

Annie! Wriggler says. *Look what I found!*

I turn to find he's got a huge black feather held carefully in his jaws. It's as long as my forearm. He drops it into my hands. I smile, unsheathing the knife Sheb gave me and holding it beside the feather. That beautiful black shine. The lightness.

I tuck both my knife and the feather into my belt and imagine the Corvos taking to the skies for the last time.

"She's resting," I murmur, scooping Wriggler up. "She deserves it."

We head off the trail, towards the black ash. I keep a hand on the hilt of my throwing knife, eyes darting at every shadow. As far as I know, Alphonz is out here somewhere. I need to be ready for a fight.

The black ash looms above us, its sprawling boughs blotting out the grey sky. I blink against the gloom.

"Sasha?" I whisper. Wriggler sets my eyes aglow. I use the scarlet light to search the roots and undergrowth. "Sasha, are you here?"

There's nothing. He's nowhere.

I flop onto the ground, drop my head into my hands. Wriggler extends a wing around my shoulders.

Maybe he went through the portal? He suggests.

I throw him a filthy look. "Maybe *you* scared him off!" I close my eyes against the memory of Wriggler charging after him, fueled by my anger, how I was unable to rein him back. "You should never have attacked him like that."

Wriggler sticks his nose in the air. *I was only acting on your feelings,* he points out. *He's done nothing but lie and hurt you since you met. It's not like—*

"That's not true!" I blurt. "Look, I know he's made a lot of bad decisions, but he's trying, okay? Anyway, it ain't like I'm blameless. I hurt him, too. I'm so angry all the time. I'm always demanding more from him than I'm willing to give myself. How's that fair?"

It's not, Wriggler concedes. *None of this is.*

My throat tightens against a sob. "I'm not ready for this, am I?" I say, as the tears finally come. "Me and Sasha ... it can't work, can it? Not the way we are right now."

Wriggler doesn't answer, which is answer enough in itself.

A rustle of undergrowth makes my head snap up. I'm on my feet, throwing knife in hand. A pair of amber eyes glows from the darkness. Alphonz? I raise my throwing knife. The head of a maned cat emerges, snarling.

"Don't you dare throw that at me," the cat says in Sasha's voice.

I drop the knife, run to him, falling to my knees as I throw my arms around his neck and hug him tight. I kiss his matted pelt.

"I'm sorry," I sob. "I'm so sorry."

Sasha hisses as he shifts to human form. He kneels in front of me, his gentle face crisscrossed with cuts, a bruise half-closing one eye. I notice his torso's been bandaged, as has his wrist. It looks like Sheb's work. I frown.

"Don't be angry with him," Sasha says. "He wanted to tell you where I was. I … asked him not to."

My eyebrows shoot up. "Why?"

Sasha chuckles. "Because last time I saw you, your lightning-snake tried to kill me," he offers.

I open my mouth, close it again. Fair point.

He cups my face, and I let him, though I can hardly bear to look at him. It's over, ain't it? This thing that never started in the first place.

"I've hurt you," Sasha says. "I'm sorry."

My eyes snap up to meet his. "It's no excuse for Wriggler trying to kill you."

Sasha barks a laugh. "No. It's not. But we were both under a lot of stress at the time." He strokes a curl of hair from my face. I close my eyes as his fingers draw traces down my jawbone. I lean into his touch, wondering if the killer blow will come shortly, punch the air from my lungs.

I can't do this, Annie.

I can't love you like you need.

Better we stop now before one of us gets hurt.

But instead, what I feel is his lips against mine. The lightest brush of his touch sending lightning through my veins. I tilt my head back, wanting more, but he's gentle. Tentative. He leans back.

"Alphonz is still after me," he says.

I sigh. Bloody Alphonz.

Want me to eat him? Wriggler asks hopefully.

No, I say quickly, then slam our bond closed before I change my mind.

Sasha frowns at something in the distance, looks back at me. "Annie, I ..." he starts, then bites his lip. "I need you to know that I care for you a great deal. That not being with you makes me ache more deeply than I've ever felt. That parting from you weeks ago was the hardest decision I ever made, but—"

"But it was the right one," I whisper. "For us both. For now."

"Perhaps," Sasha says. "Or perhaps I should have done things differently. Perhaps I took a coward's way out, abandoning a woman who has faced a lifetime of abandonment. It's no wonder you were angry."

I feel my lips quirk. "I promise I won't try to kill you again," I say, shoot Wriggler a warning glance.

What? My lightning-snake says, all wide-eyed innocence. *I haven't promised anything!*

I meet Sasha's gaze, feel my eyes burn with disappointment. I scrub the tears away before they can form. Sasha cups my face again, lifts it. His dark eyes hold my ash-grey gaze.

"I'm here," Sasha says. "And I feel you wherever you are. In whatever world. All you need do is call, and I will charge through the portal and be at your side. I will not hold back from you. I will not fight for you, but I will fight *with* you. Always."

I nod, letting the tears come again. They draw hot tracks down my face. "But you can't come with us now," I say. Sasha wraps his arms around me. He winces as I brush his bandages, but doesn't let go.

"Not this time," he says. "Not with Alphonz on my tail."

I scowl into Sasha's shoulder. "I can take Alphonz," I growl.

Sasha chuckles. "I know you can," he says. "But it's my fight. Let me end it my way. Just know I'll always come back to you."

I let him hold me, breathing in that strange scent of his that makes me think of dark forests and full moons. He presses his lips to my hair, kissing the top of my head.

"Annie ..." he says.

The sound of my name in his voice makes me crumple. I cling to him, hating how this cleaves me in two. Hating that we're saying goodbye. *Again.*

Then I let go of him. He lets go of me. With a yelp and a crack of bones, he's a maned cat again, his bandages hidden by the change. His tail switches, impatient to be off, but he fixes me one more time with that amber gaze, nuzzles my face. I let my fingers sink into his fur. Then he turns and is gone.

I kneel under the black ash for a long time. Hating Alphonz. Hating this stupid world. Hating that I've let my best friend down, let Maeve down. And Lin. And Sasha. I shoot Wriggler a filthy look, mainly because he's me, so it feels like directing my anger the right way.

"This is all your fault," I snap.

For once, Wriggler doesn't reply. He extends one wing over my shoulders, waiting until I no longer want to scream.

We should find the others, he says at last. *And go home.*

I wipe my nose with the back of my hand. He's right.

I gaze into the darkness where Sasha disappeared. Hoping. Despairing.

CHAPTER FIFTY-ONE

I SEE YOU, FINALLY

I FIND SHEB STOOD on a bridge, watching as a team of Ruben's old warriors dredges pieces of the house I destroyed from the swamp. Some of the Marsh Wilds maidens are watching in human form, though I see Nora's eyes darken to deep black when Lucius tries to start an argument with Yarella. He quietens down quickly.

Sheb startles when I touch his back, then smiles, realizing it's me. He puts an arm round my shoulders.

"What're they doing?" I ask.

Sheb's smile falters. "There was a lot of pain in that house," he says. "We can't leave it underwater. It needs to be pulled up—as much as possible—and destroyed properly. It's time the swamp, and Marsh Wilds, was given space to heal."

I nod. I'm only half listening. My mind is still back at the graveyard. With Sasha. Sheb, typical Sheb, senses something's off. He casts me a sideways glance.

"Did you find him?" he asks.

I nod, then bury my face in his shoulder when I feel my lower lip trembling. Sensing my distress, Wriggler slithers from my jacket to the floor, expanding to dog-sized. He says nothing, though. Just lets Sheb hug me.

"I really messed up," I say, hating how my voice wavers. "All of it."

Sheb holds me, hushes me. It feels good to be like this with him. My dearest friend, who understands me, even when I don't understand myself.

"It's okay, Annie," he says. "It's been hard. For all of us."

I pull back and look at him. Really look at him, for the first time in weeks. He's got his old smile back, the sparkle in his eyes I love so much. His hair flops into his face and he pushes it aside. He has all his notebooks, vials, and samples strapped to his belt again, his harpoon on his back. He should look just like the old Sheb.

But he doesn't.

The harpoon still glows faintly, pulsing a strange green light. Sheb himself seems to glow, too. A gentle light emanates from him, and whenever he moves, I feel the swamp respond. Its birds flock to him. Creeperscorps gather quietly in the waters below. The trees lean over the bridge, trying to reach him.

He's properly himself now, Wriggler says. *The way he's supposed to be.*

I nod. But it's not just that. There are fresh lines on his face, a set to his mouth that wasn't there before. My friend has had to relive his demons, and I let him do that mostly on his own.

"Sheb—" I start, but Sheb holds up a hand.

"Walk with me, Annie," he says. So, I do. We head over the bridge, down a wooden walkway—dodging a couple of kids chasing each other over the water—and wander along beside some of the older-looking houses. Wriggler shrinks, slithers behind us, keeping to the shadows. The townsfolk flock to Sheb as he passes. Just like the swamp, they can't help but be near him. They take off their caps, bowing their heads, reaching to brush his hands. They want to offer him things, like he's some kind of god. A being from the swamp they want to appease.

One girl, no older than six, stumbles up to him, eyes shining with awe. She presses an old fishhook into his hand, then scuttles away to hide behind her mother. Sheb winks at her. He smiles at them all, greets them, but there's a distance to him. He's not the Heir, after all. He's leaving, soon.

Still, pledging his allegiance to Kai doesn't seem to have drained his power. It makes me think of Everyn Vane de Callis. I look at Sheb in a whole new way.

Gradually, we move away from the busiest part of town, wandering the walkways until we find somewhere quiet to lean against the railings, gaze out over the swamp. Weak sunlight pushes through a thick layer of cloud, and dances on the water, attracting flies. It's quiet out here, and I have time to think about the death-roar, how good it feels that it's finally gone. Neither of us speaks for a while. Then we both talk at once.

"I should say—" I start.

"Annie—" Sheb says.

We both fall silent, faces flushing with heat. Wriggler does his weird equivalent of a serpentine eyeroll.

Humans, he drawls, then oozes into the water to hunt fish. Good. This will be easier without him around.

Sheb smiles. "You first," he says.

I take a breath. Now it comes to it, I ain't sure what to say. But I remember Kai back in the heart of the swamp, what Wriggler said. It doesn't have to be perfect. It just has to be true.

"I'm sorry," I say. Best start with that. "I haven't been there for you, and I should'a been. It's just ... hard ... to watch you suffer, y'know? And I couldn't fight it for you. I dunno what to do when I can't yell at something or set Wriggler on it. It's ... well, I'm sorry."

Sheb watches me while I stumble over what I'm trying to say, nodding gently.

"I know, Annie," he says. "I'm sorry, as well. I think ... it's hard for me, too. When you look at me, I see everything you wish I was. This perfect man who always says and does the right thing, always knows the answer."

I blink. "But you *do* always know the answer!"

Sheb chuckles. "See?" he says. "But it's not true, Annie. I'm hurt. I've got pain in my past, too. And I just ... I couldn't bear you seeing me the way I used to be. The anger. The darkness. I needed to keep seeing myself through your eyes, to believe I could be better."

I stare at him. I don't know what to say. Does he really feel like that? That I'd love him less now I know the truth? I frown. Maybe I do expect too much from him. Maybe I need him to be perfect so I can believe in how he sees *me*. And that ain't fair for either of us. We can't be each other's life-rope if we're both drowning. I touch his arm.

"Sheb," I say. "You're my best friend. The only friend I ever had, till Maeve and Lin came along.

I'm sorry. You needed me to see your pain and I didn't."

Sheb shrugs. "I didn't tell you," he says. "I kept all those secrets, for all that time."

My throat tightens. "It was easier, that way," I admit. "Because then, I didn't have to tell you my own truth." I pause. "Didn't do neither of us any good in the end, did it?"

Sheb laughs. "No."

"I should've asked you. I should've listened."

"I should have told you," Sheb says. "I'm sorry, Annie. For all of it."

"Okay," I say, watching Wriggler slither back onto the walkway with an ugly fish in his jaws. "So, we need it to be different from now, don't we? We make a promise. No more secrets. And we look at each other with our eyes wide open. We ain't perfect."

Sheb smiles. "Not perfect," he agrees. "Just people." His smile falters a little. "But Annie," he says. "We're honest with each other when we can be. These things are hard to talk about, aren't they?"

They are, and if I'm honest, I ain't ready to talk about my own past yet. Not with anyone. But this promise feels important. I grab Sheb's hand.

"Eyes wide open," I say.

Sheb squeezes my fingers. "Eyes wide open," he agrees. He throws an arm round my shoulders, and we talk as we head back towards the ruins of the old house. We talk about daft things. About Lin's cooking. How well Maeve's doing with Bear. How ugly the fish is that Wriggler's chomping on.

It doesn't even taste good, Wriggler admits, spitting it into the water.

I laugh. Sheb laughs too. There's still an ache in my chest. Old wounds take a while to heal, and I reckon we picked up more than our fair share in this world. All of us. But with Sheb by my side, it feels like I'll be okay.

We'll all be okay.

I hope.

Chapter Fifty-Two
LESSONS

I FLEX MY SHOULDERS, as the air around me ripples with energy. Maeve stands before me. We're in our clearing, back in Nowhere, beside the rainbow river. The place where we practice with our monsters.

Only this time, it's different.

"Okay," I say, my throat feeling weirdly tight. I reach through the bond to Wriggler. "I think I'm ready."

Maeve folds her arms. "Good," she says. Behind her, Bear paws the ground. He's the size of a horse, horns catching the low-hanging branches. White fire crackles on his paws, but he stands silent, watching. Maeve's got him under perfect control.

"Now," Maeve says. "Send a rush of energy. Really fast. Then, just when it feels too much, snap the bond closed."

Behind me, Wriggler spreads his wings, crackling with power. He's bigger than Bear, feels how I'm flooding him with our shared energy. He wants more.

"You sure about this?" I yell over the sizzle of Wriggler's lightning.

Maeve quirks half a smile. "Nope," she says. "But this is how I learned to do it. Just let go. Trust me. Bear and I've got your back."

I grumble under my breath, then stop myself. Maeve's proven her control over the last few weeks, when I've proved anything but my own. She deserves my trust.

On the other side of the river, Sheb stands with Lin, Bartok on his shoulder, watching anxiously. It's the first time I've allowed them to see our training sessions. Sheb's already scribbling frantically in a notebook, about six others strewn across the ground at his feet.

"You'll have to be quick, Annie!" he calls, still writing. "My observations suggest Serpentines are more sensitive to their humans' anger than Hot Bloods. So be ready to jump on it!"

I roll my eyes, can't help the grin that comes to my face. Sheb and his monster categories. He's been regaling us with his theories, recently, about the Winged Furies, like the Corvos. How they're linked to pain and regret, more than anger. How their powers are of the mind, unlike Wriggler's storm power and Bear's elemental power. Based on the papers constantly scattered across the floor of our cave home, he's writing a whole bloody book about it.

"To be prepared," he keeps saying. "For the next one."

The *next* one? I'll be damned if I'm letting my family through that bloody portal again! But of course, Maeve and Lin's eyes go shiny at the thought of another adventure. We agreed we'd make these decisions together.

So apparently, there will be a next one. Even if I think it's a terrible idea.

I let out a breath.

"Okay," I say, even though it ain't. "I'm ready." Even though I'm not.

We've been trying this for days, ever since we returned from Riverfell. Every time, I flood Wriggler with too much power and lose all control. Luckily, Maeve and Bear have proved more than capable of wrestling him into submission until I can clamp the bond closed. But it's exhausting. And a bit humiliating. Still. Maeve's a good teacher. I hate admitting it, but to be honest, she's better than me. Patient. Positive. Encouraging. I'm learning a thing or two from her, and not just about controlling my monster.

Maeve nods. Bear lumbers to her side, ready to leap if he needs to.

Tell that oversized fuzzball to stand down, Wriggler hisses. *We've got it this time, Annie!*

I scowl. *Only if you don't ruin it,* I point out.

Wriggler affects hurt. *I never ruin anything!*

I refrain from mentioning Sasha's name, though it lingers at the back of my throat. Sometimes, I wake in the dark, reckon I see a pair of amber eyes watching me. At first, I smile, thinking it's Sasha. Then I bolt upright, knife in hand, remember it could be Alphonz. It's never either of them. It's a trick of the light; a still smoldering candle, or dawn creeping through the gaps in the door. And I'm both relieved and disappointed.

Concentrate! Wriggler says. I snap back to attention. He's pulling our bond, trying to wrench open my mental tourniquet. He can feel my power as I draw on every ounce of rage. Slowly, I let him loose. Let the threads of our connection spill open so my anger surges to him. I think of every awful thing I've endured. My scar twinges. Wriggler lifts his head and roars, pulling power from me. He grows huge. Monstrous. That crown of horns bursts from the back of his head. Lightning shoots off him. His massive wings clip the tops of the trees. He's becoming my nightmare. The monster I fought all those years ago. The Oraqua. Pushing past the boundaries of my control. And then, just as I think I can't hold it any longer ...

"*Now,* Annie!" Maeve yells. I fight with every ounce of myself. Mentally, I grab the threads and squeeze, suffocating the bond. I shut down my anger, shoving it behind a wall, the way Maeve's taught me. A wall of love. I imagine it emblazoned with a mural of my family's faces. Sheb's infectious grin. Maeve's determination. Lin's twinkling eyes. Even Bartok's tawny glare. And it's amazing. Maeve's right. Every time I think of them, of what they mean to me and what I mean to them, the anger falls away. It doesn't disappear. I don't think it ever will. It just becomes less important.

There's a sudden jolt of energy behind my solar plexus. I grunt as I stumble forward, landing on all fours. I blink at the leaf litter, suddenly realizing I can't hear Wriggler's lightning strikes. There's no sound of Bear and Wriggler locked in battle. The rest of my little family are applauding.

I glance up. Maeve punches the air.

"*Yes!*" she cries. "I knew you could do it!"

She rushes to me, gathers me in a huge, suffocating hug. Lin and Sheb splash across the river to join in as Bartok takes to the skies, trilling his congratulations. I'm scooped up by my family, my feet leaving the ground. They gather to kiss my head, hug me, tell me I'm brilliant. I'm grinning furiously. Can't help it. I see Wriggler curled up on the riverbank, a harmless little black snake, his vestigial wings pressed to his sides.

Well, he drawls. *It's a lot more boring when you can control it like that.*

I laugh. *At least Sasha's safe from you, now.*

Wriggler sticks his nose in the air. *He's safe as long as he stops being a pain in your ass.*

I don't reply. It doesn't matter what Wriggler thinks. Maeve's taught me something I never thought I'd master. I meet her eye and she winks. I grin back. Sheb touches my cheek.

"Dear Annie," he says. I can't help the tears that burn my eyes. "You brilliant, brilliant woman."

I let my forehead rest against his, close my eyes. It's so good to have him back. The Sheb I know and love. All sparkles and hare-brained plans and boundless enthusiasm.

Maeve steps back from us, rubbing her hands together. "This is brilliant!" she says. "A couple of weeks, and we'll be ready for our next rescue!"

I raise an eyebrow at her. "Four weeks," I remind her. "We agreed."

Maeve tempers her enthusiasm. "Yeah. Four," she says, grinning. "That's what I meant."

The others might be ready to leap through the portal at a moment's notice, but I need rest. And really, Sheb does, too. He's been through a lot, and though he'd never want to disappoint the girls, I see in his face that he's tired. There's sadness behind his eyes sometimes. I know he's thinking of Riverfell. Of Marsh Wilds. Of his nephew, now the dormant de Callis Heir. Of Allise, separated from Locke, but still carrying his daughter. Of the many battles they'll face to keep the swamp safe. It's not his fight anymore. He knows that. But it doesn't stop the ache I know has settled in his heart.

"C'mon," I say, grabbing Sheb's hand, throwing an arm round Lin's shoulder. "Maeve might be a great teacher, but her mushroom soup could do with work."

Sheb and Lin laugh. Maeve looks affronted. "Sheb said my cooking's getting loads better!"

I raise an eyebrow. "Sheb's too nice for his own good."

Maeve's mouth falls open. I snort a giggle. The four of us fall to good-natured bickering all the way home. The light's fading. I hear the first cry of the howler horses in the distance. Time to tuck ourselves inside.

As we reach our Soother Tree, I cast a glance up the hill towards the portal tree. I can't see it from here. But is it my imagination, or is its golden glow brighter than normal? I frown, shake that thought away.

Four weeks. We promised. Whoever comes through that portal before then will just have to wait.

CHAPTER FIFTY-THREE

DAUGHTER, MY DAUGHTER

I SNAP AWAKE, SWEAT beading on my forehead. The dregs of some frantic dream slip away before I can grab hold of the memory. I push myself upright, wondering what woke me. On my pillow, Wriggler stirs.

Bad dream? He asks.

I shrug. *Don't remember.*

I scrub my face, rubbing sleep from my eyes. Something disturbed me, I know that much. But the others are sleeping soundly. Bartok's on his perch, head under his wing. Maeve's snoring slightly, which makes me smile. She insists she doesn't snore, but she *does.*

I push the blankets back, get to my feet. Padding across the earthy floor, I grope for a candle. I manage to strike a light, shielding it so it doesn't wake the others. Lin lets out a soft moan, turns over. Wriggler slithers to my side.

Probably a cherish screamer, he says. *They're jumpy this time of year.*

I don't reply. Too busy listening. Outside, the world seems unnaturally quiet. There's no snarl of howler horses. No shuffle of snufflehigs or muttering of grumbleshrooms. All the sounds I'm used to have fallen still. Like Nowhere is holding its breath.

I frown, grab my knife belt. Sheb, true to his word, has given me two more knives to go with the one he gifted me in Riverfell, both made from the bone crow's feathers. They're beautifully balanced, fit snugly in my palm like an extension of my hand. I buckle the belt round my waist, then ease the door out of its frame. I flip a knife into my hand, pad into the night. The Soother Tree worries as soon as I'm outside. Its vines snake down, trying to persuade me back into the cave. I bat it away, creep round its trunk so I can stare up the hill, towards where the portal tree stands.

A jolt rushes through me when I see the golden glow against the sky. It's brighter than normal, like something or someone is threatening to come through. The air tightens. A strange breeze stirs my curls. I grip my knife tighter.

Something's not right, Wriggler says, like I ain't already worked that out. I clench my jaw. Whoever the hell is coming through that portal, they need to know we ain't going anywhere until we've recovered. Monster or not. Evil tyrants, shifter priests, brothers with magic powers be damned. We need to rest. And that's …

"Annie …"

The voice drifts on the air like the sound of bells. Bright, frightened, desperate. I freeze. My throat tightens. Wriggler flares as he senses my panic.

"No," I say. Because it can't be. It *can't* be.

"Annie …" the voice says again. I close my eyes. My hands tremble. I recognize that voice, though I don't want to. I've hoped I'll never hear it again. I've feared she might never come back. It can't be.

It is though, Wriggler says. I want to kick him for being so bloody *right* all the time.

Because he *is* right.

"Annie ..." says the voice of my twice-disappeared mother, clear and frightened. The glow of the portal fluctuates in time to her words. *"Annie, help us ..."*

I can't move. That voice sends lightning through my veins. She's here. She's calling me. After all this time. Bloody mothers! What is it with them? Turning up when you least want them. When you need them most!

Wriggler glances at me. *Four weeks?* he says, though he and I both know what this means.

"Hmm," I say.

Then I march back to wake the others.

DO YOU WANT TO READ MORE?

Did you fall in love with Annie and Sheb? Do you want to keep up with my new releases, get early bird deals and discounts, and receive a gift ebook? Sign up to my newsletter to get all this and more! Sign up by scanning the QR code below.

Or visit:

https://subscribepage.io/rlfreaderclub_tnc

COULD YOU HELP OTHER READERS?

Did you love reading Annie's story? Did you root for her and Sheb as they solved the monstrous mystery? Did you fall in love with Bartok, Wriggler and the cracklemice?

You can help other readers to discover this series by leaving a review. Just a few sentences and a rating can make a huge difference to future readers.

Thank you!

ALSO BY REBECCA L. FEARNLEY

The *Silent Skies* Series **(Complete)**
The Last Beekeeper
The Hive Child
War Song of the Wild

The Nowhere Chronicles Series **(In Progress)**
Doorway to Nowhere (Novella)
The Darkling Thief (Short Story)
The Howling Mare (Short Story)
A Song of Forgetting (Short Story)
The Shadow and the Scream
Flight of the Bone Crow
A Fearsome, Lonely Heart
Under a Tortured Mountain

The Girl in the Nightmare Tree
A Soul for a Secret
The Rage-Scaled Serpent

THANKS TO ...

Writing can sometimes be a lonely business, which is why it's important for writers to surround themselves with allies, champions and people who will be gentle but honest with us when the worlds in our heads sometimes spill over into the real one. There are many people who have helped me through the process of writing this book, and helped me see the power of Annie's story.

Firstly, a huge thank you to my best friend, Tess, whose brilliant knowledge of psychology, emotional intelligence, and faith in my writing, have kept me going through many doubts, and helped me realize that Annie's story could help a lot of people feel less alone. Thank you to my family, who have shown nothing but pride and faith in me, even when things felt like they were too much. A particular thank you to my sister, Lizzee, who has reassured me more times than I care to count that I can write, my stories are worth telling, and I should keep going.

Thanks to my wonderful writing friends, Katie, Lou, and Daisy, who read this book in its earliest form, and whose gentle honesty has helped Annie's story grow.

Thanks to Sue and Charlotte, two brilliant school librarians and absolute forces of nature, who continue to champion me and my work. I am eternally grateful for your support.

Thank you to my brilliant, patient, ever-supportive partner, David, who has celebrated with me, comforted during periods of fear and doubt, and reminded me that what I'm doing isn't easy, and encouraged me to have pride in my achievements.

And lastly, but by no means least, thank you to you, my readers. You bring this story alive with your minds. Annie lives on through you and, for that, I am forever grateful.

ABOUT REBECCA L. FEARNLEY

ABOUT REBECCA L. FEARNLEY

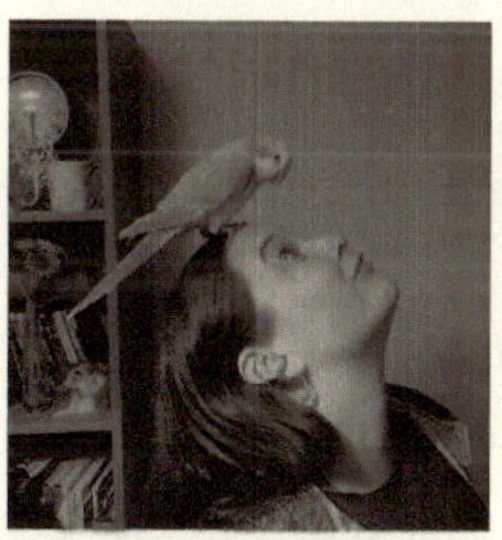

Rebecca has been obsessed with two things since she learned to walk and talk: stories and animals. Luckily, the two seem to be very compatible. In addition to writing, Rebecca is also a teacher and, in 2018, decided that she wanted to write quality books for the young people she works with. Her books tend towards themes of respect for the environment, compassion to our fellow humans and creating a more thoughtful world, all with magic, mystery and mayhem thrown in!

She lives in Reading with her unusual little family, which includes herself and her partner, a friendly little mini-lop rabbit (called Cleo) and a gregarious and feisty quaker parrot (called Maya).